Chapter 1

Whalers returning from the Arctic seas in the summer of 1803 reported an *aurora borealis* of an intensity never observed before. Professor Wollaston had described the phenomenon of polar refraction to the satisfaction of the scientific community some years before. Of course, that fact did not diminish the awe of the folk who dwelt along the Baltic seaboard. All those who lived in Lotingen, myself included, not eight miles from the coast, stared up at the night sky. We could not fail to be stupefied by what we saw. The massive clouds were painted as darkly crimson as fresh blood, the Northern Lights flashed like a lady's fan of mother-of-pearl held up to the mid-day sun. Little Lotte Havaars, the nursemaid who had been with us since the day that Immanuel was born, told us that the neighbours in her village had noted unnatural behaviour in their animals, and autumn brought news of hideous plants and monstrous births which seemed to defy the laws of Nature. Two-headed piglets, calves with six legs, a turnip as large as a wheelbarrow. The coming winter, Lotte muttered darkly, would be like no other in the history of Man.

My wife's dark eyes glittered with amusement as Lotte prattled on. Helena glanced at me, inviting me to share her mirth, and I was forced to return her smile, though it went against my nature, for I was born and bred in the country. My heart seemed to knot itself in a tight ball, I felt a heavy sense of oppression, suffocation almost, the sort of unsettling sensation that a distant thunder-headed cloud provokes on a broiling summer's day. And when it came, it *was* a terrible winter. Lotte's intuition had been proved correct. Lashing rain by day, biting frost by night. And then, snow. More snow than I had ever seen before.

Indeed, the first day of February, 1804, was the coldest in living memory. That morning, I was busy in my office at the Court House in Lotingen, writing out the sentence of a wrangle which had required the better part of a week to decide. Herman Bertholt had taken it upon himself to improve the landscape. He had lopped two branches off a valuable apple tree belonging to his neighbour, Farmer Dürchtner. That tree spoiled the view from his kitchen window, the offender argued. The rights and wrongs of the case had divided the town, of course, it was a matter of vital importance. If a precedent were allowed, we could expect an epidemic to follow. I was in the very act of writing up my conclusion – *I therefore sentence Herman Bertholt to pay thirteen thalers, and pass six hours in the village stocks* – when a knock sounded at the door and my secretary entered.

'There's a man outside,' Knutzen slurred.

I glanced with distaste at my aged secretary. His grubby shirt was still unchanged, the collar stained a grimy brown, his heavy boots unpolished. He had been working in his duck-run again. I had lost that battle and had long grown tired of complaining. Gudjøn Knutzen was one of a handful of men in the village who were able to write their own names. On that strength alone, he had escaped the destiny of his father, and all the male ancestors of his family. But the Royal purse was empty. The King had chosen armed neutrality, while the other great states of Europe took their chances against the French. Civic expenses had been cut to pay for military necessities as a consequence. Soldiers had to be re-equipped, generals better paid, horses pampered and fed, fit and ready for the war which everyone knew was bound to come. Heavy cannon had been purchased from Bessarabia. All this brought hardship, even misery to Prussia. The lower ranks of the judicial administration, myself included, had been hard hit by the latest economies. But Knutzen had been thrust back into the Dark Ages. His wages had been halved. Consequently, he worked as little as possible, and spent as much time as he could filch from me with his ducks. He had become a peasant again. Like every man in Europe, he was paying for the French Revolution and for the fright that Napoleon was spreading throughout the continent of Europe.

Helena had promised to give him one of my cast-off shirts next time the pedlar came to town. I glanced out of the window, reflecting that the pedlar's wagon would not be coming through for quite some time. Snow had begun to fall again, the flakes as large as laurel leaves. It had fallen all day the day before, and had been threatening all the morning. What – I wondered idly – could drive a man abroad on such a day? My curiosity was piqued, I admit. Even so, I decided, the minute the visitor has finished his business, I shall close the office and take myself home for the rest of the day.

'Show him in,' I said.

Knutzen wiped his nose on his sleeve. Whenever he happened to take his one-and-only jacket off, which was rarely, I was inclined to believe that it stood up of its own accord.

'Aye,' he said, withdrawing slowly from the room.

He left the door wide open, and I could hear him mumbling out in the hall.

Some moments later, a heavily built man in dark travelling clothes and high riding-boots clumped determinedly into the room, leaving a trail of scattered drips and melting slush in his wake. The ghostly pallor of his face, and the unhealthy tremor which shook his body as he stood before me, led me to believe that he had mistaken his destination. He seemed to require the care of a physician, rather than the services of a magistrate.

'What can I do for you, sir?' I asked, waving him to the visitor's chair, sitting myself down again behind my desk.

The stranger pulled his copious black cloak more tightly around his shivering frame and loudly cleared his throat. 'You are Magistrate Stiffeniis, are you not?' he said gruffly.

'Indeed, I am,' I nodded. 'But where are you from, sir? You are not from Lotingen.'

The visitor's large, grey eyes flashed defiantly.

'Weren't you expecting me?' he asked with evident surprise.

I shook my head. 'Given the sudden turn in the weather,' I said, glancing out of the broad bay-window at the snow, which fell even thicker than before, 'I was expecting nobody this morning. What can I do for you, sir?'

He was silent for a moment. 'Didn't the Königsberg coach arrive?' he asked suddenly.

'I have no idea,' I replied, wondering what this was leading up to.

'You received no news from Procurator Rhunken?' he insisted.

'I received no post at all this morning,' I replied. 'Nor do I know Herr Procurator Rhunken. Except by reputation.'

'No post?' the stranger muttered, slapping the palm of his right hand down hard on his knee. 'Well, that throws a stick in the wheel!'

'Does it?' I asked, perplexed.

He did not reply, but opened his leather shoulder-bag and started to rummage around inside it. Any hope I had that he might produce something to explain his presence in my office was dashed as he pulled out a large white linen handkerchief and loudly blew his nose.

'Am I to presume that *you* are Procurator Rhunken?' I probed.

'Oh no, sir!' he spluttered behind the white square. 'With all respect, he's the very last person I'd wish to be at this moment. My name is Amadeus Koch, Sergeant-of-Police in the city of Königsberg. I work as the administrative clerk in Procurator Rhunken's office.' He pressed the linen cloth to his mouth to stifle a cough. 'In the absence of the post, sir, the best thing I can do is to tell you why I have come.'

'Please *do*, Herr Sergeant Koch,' I encouraged, hoping to make some sense of this puzzling interview.

A weak smile appeared on the man's white lips. 'I won't waste any more precious time, sir. In my own defence, and given the present state of my health, I will only say that the journey from Königsberg has done little to assist my powers of reasoning. To be brief, I have instructions to take you back with me.'

I stared at him. 'To Königsberg?'

'I only pray the snow will not prevent us . . .'

'Instructions, Herr Koch? Tell me exactly what brings you here!'

Sergeant Koch began to search about in his bag again. At length, he pulled out a large white envelope. 'The official communiqué regarding your appointment was sent yesterday by the post. For reasons unknown, it has not arrived. But your commission was entrusted to me. This is for you, sir.'

I tore the packet from his outstretched hand, read my name on the cover, then turned it over. A large red Hohenzollern seal closed the flap, and I hesitated an instant before daring to break it and examine the contents.

Most honourable Procurator Stiffeniis,

Your talents have been brought to Our attention by a gentleman of eminence, who believes that you alone are capable of resolving a situation which holds Our beloved Königsberg in a grip of terror. All Our faith and consideration are due to the notable personage who suggested your name, and that same faith and consideration now resides in you. We have no reason to doubt that you will accept this Royal Commission, and act accordingly with all haste. The fate of the city lies in your hands.

The note was signed with a flourish by King Frederick Wilhelm III.

'There have been murders in Königsberg, Procurator Stiffeniis,' Sergeant Koch pressed on, his voice hushed as if fearing that we might be overheard. 'This morning I was ordered to inform you of the matter.'

Confusion clouded my mind.

'I am at a loss, Herr Koch,' I murmured, staring hard at the paper in my hand, reading one particular phrase over and over again. What were the 'talents' that I was supposed to possess? And who was the 'eminent gentleman' who had brought them to the attention of His Majesty, the King? 'Are you certain that someone hasn't made a mistake?'

'There's no mistake,' the sergeant replied, pointing to the envelope with a smile. 'This *is* Prussia, sir. That envelope's got your name on it.'

'Isn't Procurator Rhunken investigating the case?' I asked. 'He is the senior magistrate on the Königsberg circuit.'

'Herr Rhunken has suffered a stroke,' Sergeant Koch explained.

'He has lost the use of his lower limbs. It would appear that you have been chosen to carry on his work, sir.'

I considered this proposition for a moment. 'But *why*, Sergeant Koch? I have never met Herr Rhunken. Why should he recommend me in such glowing terms to King Frederick Wilhelm?'

'I cannot help you on that point, sir,' he said. 'All will be made clear in Königsberg, no doubt.'

I had no alternative but to accept this assurance. 'You mentioned murders, Sergeant. How many are we talking about?'

'Four, sir.'

I caught my breath.

I had never had to deal with a serious crime in my career as an arbiter of the law, and had always considered the fact a matter of good fortune. The sentence I had been writing not ten minutes before was the most important to come my way in the three years that I had been employed in Lotingen.

'The first victim was found a year ago,' Koch ploughed on, 'though the police made no progress on the case and they forgot about it quick enough. But three months ago, another corpse was found, and a third person died last month. Just yesterday another body came to light. The evidence would seem to suggest that they all died by the same . . .'

A knock at the door froze the words on Koch's lips.

Knutzen came shuffling in again and dropped a letter on my desk. 'This has just been delivered, Herr Procurator. The post-coach lost a wheel on the outskirts of Rykiel and was four hours late getting in.'

'I took the coast road, fortunately,' Koch murmured as Knutzen left us alone once more. He gestured to the unopened letter in my hand. 'You'll find confirmation there of what I've just told you, sir.'

I opened the envelope, and found an order signed by Procurator Rhunken in a spidery, uncertain hand, which seemed to confirm what Sergeant Koch had said about the magistrate's poor health. It provided formal notification of the fact that the murder case had been handed over to me, but added nothing more. I set the letter down, swept by waves of conflicting emotion. Obviously, I was gratified that my professional talents had been recognised. And by Procurator Rhunken, whose name was foremost among magistrates in Prussia by reason of his rigour and his determination. What surprised me more, however, was the fact that he had even heard my name. And that he had passed it on to the King. What had I done to attract their notice? Why should such powerful people place their trust in me? I was not so vain as to imagine that nowhere in the whole of Prussia was there any man better suited to the task. Except, of course, for the unresolved question of my mysterious 'talents'. The concluding words of Herr Rhunken's communiqué did nothing to set my doubts at rest:

> *. . . there are particular aspects of this case which should not be committed to paper. You will be informed of them in due course.*

'Are you ready, sir?' asked Sergeant Koch, gathering his shoulder-bag and standing up. 'I am yours to serve in any way which will expedite our departure.'

I remained seated in mute protest against this driving sense of urgency. The contents of another letter that I had received from Königsberg seven years before echoed in my mind like a taunt. On that occasion, I had been compelled to make a promise which the simple act of accompanying Sergeant Koch to the city would force me to break.

'How long will I be required to stay?' I asked him, as if it were, above all, a practical question.

'Until the case is solved, Herr Stiffeniis,' he answered flatly.

I sat back in my chair, wondering what to do for the best. If it were a matter of passing a few short days in the city, closing a case which Procurator Rhunken had been preventing from completing by ill health, no harm would come of it. If I proved unequal to the task, I would simply be ordered to return to the oblivion from which I had come. But then, I thought with a spurt of mounting ambition, what would be the limits to my future career if I were to succeed?

'I must take leave of my wife,' I said, jumping to my feet, the choice made.

Sergeant Koch pulled his cloak more tightly around him. 'There's not much time if we're to reach Königsberg before nightfall, sir,' he said.

'I need but a few minutes to wish my wife farewell and kiss my little ones,' I protested on the strength of my new authority. 'Neither Procurator Rhunken nor the King would deny me that small luxury, I think!'

Out in the street, a large coach bearing the Imperial coat-of-arms stood waiting in the snow. As I climbed aboard, I could not avoid reflecting on the incongruity of my situation. There I was in a state coach, holding a letter signed by the King imploring me to solve a case that not one of the great magistrates in his service had been able to resolve. It should have been the crowning moment in my short career, the day the dark clouds parted and the sun shone brightly on one of her own, my abilities not only recognised, but usefully employed for the good of the nation. But then the words of that old letter came echoing back once again:

Do not return. Your presence has done more than enough damage. For his sake show yourself no more in Magisterstrasse!

The coachman cracked his whip, and the vehicle leapt forward. I took it as a sign of destiny. I should leave the past behind, and look towards a brighter and more prosperous future. What more could I possibly want? It was, when all was said and done, a glorious opportunity for professional advancement.

Helena must have been sitting at the window as the splendid vehicle pulled up outside the small, draughty house on the edge of the town which was tied to the prebend of Lotingen. As I climbed down, she ran out to meet me with neither hat nor coat, ignoring the biting north wind and the driving snow. She stopped before me, looking uncertainly up into my face.

'What has happened, Hanno?' she gasped, stepping close and slipping her arm through mine.

She listened as I told her all that had come to pass, slowly drawing away from me, clasping her hands protectively across her breasts. It was a gesture that I knew only too well when she was disturbed or upset by something I had said or done.

'I thought that you had chosen Lotingen precisely to avoid such things, Hanno,' she murmured. 'I truly believed that here you had found what you were seeking.'

'I did, my dear,' I told her instantly. 'I mean, of course, I have.'

'I do not understand you, then,' she replied. She hesitated for a moment, then went on: 'If you are doing this for your father's sake, nothing can change what happened, Hanno. Nothing will ever change *him*.'

'I hoped you would be proud to see me getting on,' I said, perhaps a trifle more harshly than I intended. 'What ails you, wife? I have no choice. I must go when the King commands it.'

She looked down at the ground for some moments.

'But *murder*, Hanno?' she challenged suddenly, glancing up. 'You have never dealt with such a heinous crime before.'

She spoke with fierce passion. I had never seen her in such a nervous state before. She threw herself upon my chest at last to hide the evidence of her weeping, and I glanced quickly in the direction of Sergeant Koch. He was standing stiffly by the carriage door, his expression blank and unchanging, as if he had heard nothing of what my wife had just said. I felt a flash of resentment for the embarrassment she had caused me.

'Wait there, will you, Sergeant?' I called back. 'I'll not be long.'

Koch bobbed his head, a tight-lipped smile traced faintly on his thin lips.

I led Helena quickly into the hall. Her manner was restrained and watchful. I cannot say what reaction I had expected from her. Pride, perhaps? Joy at my rapid promotion? She had shown no sign of either.

'The King has called me to Him,' I argued. 'A senior magistrate in Königsberg has given His Majesty my name. What would you have me do?'

Helena looked at me, puzzlement traced upon her face, as if she failed to understand what I had just told her. 'I . . . I do not know. How long will you be gone?' she asked at last.

'I cannot tell,' I said. 'Not very long, I hope.'

'Run upstairs, Lotte. Fetch your master's things,' Helena cried suddenly, turning to the maid. 'His carriage is waiting at the door. Be quick! He'll be gone some days.'

As we stood in the hall alone, I knew not what to say. Helena and I had been wed four years, and had never spent a single night apart. A special bond of shared suffering tied us, one to the other.

'I am not going off to fight the French!' I declared with a nervous laugh, reaching out and drawing my darling close, kissing her gently on the forehead, cheek and lips, until the return of Lotte interrupted those brief, welcome moments of intimacy.

'I'll write every day, my love, and tell you of my doings. The minute we arrive, you'll have word of me,' I said with all the bluff sanguinity that I could muster to brighten the melancholy of parting. 'Kiss Manni and Süsi for me.'

As I took the travelling-bag from Lotte, Helena threw herself upon me once again and let forth her emotions with a force and intensity I had never known in her before that moment. I thought it was on account of the children: Immanuel was not yet one, Süsanne barely two.

'Forgive me, I am so troubled, Hanno,' she cooed, her soft voice almost lost in the deep folds of my woollen cloak. 'What do they want from *you*?'

Unable to reply, unwilling to speculate, I drew back from her embrace, straightened my mantle, threw my bag over my shoulder and walked quickly down the path towards the waiting coach and Sergeant Koch, my head bent low against the blizzard. I skipped aboard the coach with a light foot and a heavy heart.

As the vehicle slowly pulled away, the wheels crunching on the thick carpet of snow, I looked behind, watching until the dear, slender figure in the white dress was entirely swallowed up by the snowstorm.

The question that had perplexed Helena now returned to vex and puzzle me. Why *had* the King chosen me?

Chapter 2

The coach jolted onwards for more than an hour, and barely a word was said. Sergeant Koch sat in his corner, I sat in mine, both as melancholy as the world through which we journeyed. I stared out at the passing countryside. Bleak villages and isolated farms dotted the landscape here and there, marking out the hill-tops and the highway. Peasants toiled in the fields, up to their knees in the snow, to save their stranded cows and sheep. The world was all a massive grey blur, the distant hills blending into the horizon with no precise point at which the earth ended and the heavens began.

We had just passed through a little village called Endernffords when our coach was forced to stop on the ramp approaching a swing-bridge over a narrow river. Screams of suffering rent the peace. Such wild, blood-curdling howls, at first I thought that they were human. I leapt up from my seat, pulled hard on the sash, dropped the window, and leaned out of the carriage to see what was going on.

'A farmer's cart has skidded on the ice,' I reported over my shoulder to Koch. The horse had slipped its traces, and it lay on its back in the middle of the road, one of its fore-legs dangling broken in the air. A man stood over the animal, howling drunken curses and lashing out viciously at the fallen beast with his whip. My first impulse was to get down, though whether to help the doomed horse, or to berate the senseless cruelty of the driver, I cannot say. What followed happened so quickly and in a manner so well-ordered, I was convinced that such things were a common occurrence at that isolated crossing, and I remained where I was.

Every man present at the scene – there were four of them sitting on the wooden beam of the bridge – seemed to know exactly what was going on. Three of these idlers rushed out suddenly, one brandishing a long curved knife, the other two with raised axes in their fists. The knife-blade flashed, then sliced through the horse's straining neck. The keening wail of the beast's distress died in a whistle of spouting blood and froth which turned the snow beneath the murderer's feet into a gory, reddish mash. The driver froze, the whip raised high above his head, then, in a flash, without a word, he dropped his whip, turned, and ran away, slithering and lurching across the bridge to safety. In silence, the butchers fell upon the carcass with their axes. It was the work of a minute. Steam rose all about them in a swirling cloud as they furiously hacked and chopped the fallen animal into a dozen pieces, then quickly loaded the meat up onto the cart. The fourth man hurried forward, helping the brigands load the cart, then push it out of the way, signalling to our coach to pass across the swing-bridge.

My legs gave way and I sat down. But I jumped up quickly again to close the window. As we passed by the cart with its disgusting load of offal, flesh and guts, the stench of fresh blood filled our coach in a warm, engulfing haze. It was sweet, nauseating, corrosive, painful to my sensibility.

'Hard times breed hard men,' said Sergeant Koch quietly. 'What are we to do about that, sir?'

I closed my eyes and leaned back against the leather bench.

'They're probably starving,' I murmured. 'Hunger has driven many a good man to shame.'

'Let's hope they're ready to butcher Frenchmen with the same enthusiasm,' Koch said dryly. 'If Bonaparte turns up in Prussia, there won't be anything left to eat, let alone horses. Then we'll see what sort of men they really are.'

'Pray God, we are never put to the test!' I replied, more sharply than I meant.

Another hour passed with very little said on either side.

'Whoever saw such a sky!' exclaimed Koch suddenly, shaking me from my lethargy. 'It looks as if the whole lot's going to come crashing down about our ears, sir. Foul weather's fit punishment for our sins, the proverb says.'

There was something almost comical about the seriousness of the man. The lurching of the coach had shifted his tricorn hat on his head, stark black strands of hair peeping out from beneath the stiff white curls of his periwig like shy maidens. I gave a nod and smiled, making the decision to pass the remainder of the journey in a more sociable manner. And yet, I hardly knew how. From a professional point of view, Koch was my inferior, little better than a servant.

'This would be a good moment for you to examine these papers, Herr Stiffeniis,' Sergeant Koch announced, reaching for his bag before I had the opportunity to speak.

The good humour I had decided on dissolved in an instant.

'Do you mean to tell me that you have kept something from my sight, Herr Koch?'

'I'm only doing as I was instructed, sir,' he said as he pulled a sheaf of papers from his leather bag.' I was told to hand these documents to you once we'd reached the Königsberg highway.'

As if in response to his words, the coach swung left at the Elbing crossroads.

So, *that's* your game, I thought. I have been flattered into accepting an unpleasant commission and now that it's too late to pull out, I'm to be told all the nasty details that would have convinced me to refuse it.

'The authorities must guarantee the peace,' Koch continued blithely. 'All those involved in the investigation have been sworn to secrecy.'

'Does that include you?' I asked sharply. 'You must have given your wife some reason for leaving her alone so early this morning.'

I felt mounting anger at the thought of this graceless messenger concealing information from me. 'You hold back facts, Koch, unveiling them whenever the need arises, or it suits your mood.'

The suspicion was growing on me that Sergeant Koch was not simply taking me anywhere; he was observing me, judging me, mentally preparing critical notes to be written up for the eyes of his superiors. That was the normal procedure in the Prussian civil service. To spy on others was the surest way to step up a rung on the uncertain bureaucratic ladder.

'I have nothing to hide from you, sir,' Sergeant Koch replied through clenched teeth, his handkerchief out again. 'I am a clerk. I have played no active part in the investigation. This morning, like any other, I took myself to work at five-thirty and I was instructed to do what I have done. I had no need to tell my wife, or anyone else, of my doings. I live alone.'

Koch and I had got off to a bad start.

'You claim to know so little of this affair, Herr Koch. I find it odd that you should be charged to illuminate a person who knows absolutely nothing. A case of the blind leading the blind, is it?'

'Those documents should answer your questions, sir. Obviously, I was told not to let you see them until you had accepted the task.'

'Do you mean to say that I could have refused?' I said, and snatched the papers from his hand.

He looked out of the window, but he did not reply.

With a bad grace I turned my attention to the documents. The first murder had been committed more than a year before. Jan Konnen, a middle-aged blacksmith, had been found dead in Merrestrasse on the morning of 3 January 1803. Police enquiries revealed that he had spent the previous evening at a dockside tavern not far from the spot where his corpse was found. The innkeeper did not recall ever having seen Herr Konnen before and denied that he had seen him gaming in the company of foreign sailors. He believed that the man was a foreigner, he said. A Lithuanian sailing ship had docked that day and the tavern had been particularly crowded until the early hours of the morning. Konnen had left the tavern shortly after ten o'clock that evening, but no one had noticed him outside. It was very cold that night and the streets were empty of casual passers-by. His corpse had been found at dawn by a midwife on her way to assist at a birth. Hurrying through the fog, which was exceptionally thick that morning, she had almost fallen over Konnen, who was kneeling up against a wall. The midwife thought that he was ill, but on drawing closer she saw that he was dead. The report had been signed by two officers of His Royal Majesty's night-watch, Anton Lublinsky and Rudolph Kopka. Penned in passable German, it was dated six months after the murder. I glanced up, noting that heavy sleet had now begun to lash the windows of the coach, determined to ask Koch for an explanation. He was a bureaucrat, he was from Königsberg: he must know what the standard procedure was in such matters. But Koch's head had fallen forward on his chest, his face half-hidden in the folds of his cloak, and he let out a rattling snore. For a moment, I toyed with the idea of waking him up. Instead, I turned to the second fascicle.

First, I glanced at the date written at the foot of the fourth page. This report had also been compiled recently, on 23 January 1804, to be exact, a week before, and almost four months after the murder, which did not say much for the efficiency of the local authorities. Had the second killing prompted them to review the first? It seemed a most irregular way of going about things. The name of the second victim was Paula-Anne Brunner. And there went my first hypothesis! I had formed the notion that there must be something banal at the heart of the matter, something so simple that it had been overlooked. After all, there was nothing startling about gambling debts and violent litigation in a low tavern between men who diced and drank more than was good for them. But Prussian women, as a rule, don't drink in public or play at dice. Especially in Königsberg, which is renowned for its moral Pietism.

'On 22 September 1803,' I read, 'the corpse of Paula-Anne Brunner (née Schobart) was found in the public gardens in Neumannstrasse.'

An Austrian cavalry officer, Herr Colonel Viktor Rodiansky, a registered mercenary in the Prussian army, was strolling there while awaiting a lady whom he refuses to name. He arrived in the public gardens at four o'clock when he knew that a large part of the citizenry would be attending the funeral ceremony of the late-departed and much-lamented Superintendent Brunswig in the Cathedral. Colonel Rodiansky reports that the evening was neither excessively cold nor wet, but there was a sea mist

which reduced visibility to a maximum of six or seven yards.
The inclement weather exactly suited his purposes, he said.
Strolling up and down, smoking a cigar as the appointed hour
approached, Colonel Rodiansky spotted a woman kneeling beside
a wooden bench, and was not a little put out by her unwelcome
presence in that place. At that moment, the lady for whom he
had been waiting arrived, and Colonel Rodiansky's attention
was distracted from the kneeling woman. He thought little of
the fact that she was kneeling in a public park, attributing her
position to the fact that she was praying for the soul of Superin-
tendent Brunswig, like many another of her townswomen,
though, for some reason, prevented from adding her voice to
the others in the Cathedral.

Colonel Rodiansky's lady friend was more perturbed at
finding a third party present at the meeting, and looked often
in the direction of the kneeling woman, hoping that she would
finish her prayer and remove her person from the park. At last,
wondering if the woman had been taken ill or had had a mishap,
the pair drew close. They realised that the praying woman was
actually a kneeling corpse, and the police were called by
Colonel Rodiansky, who had first taken measures to protect
the anonymity of his mistress by sending her home.

The report was signed by the same two officers who had written up
the report of the first murder, Lublinsky and Kopka.

I sat back against the leather seat. The second account was rich
in detail, almost literary, but as with the first, there were missing
elements far too obvious to escape my attention. No mention was
made of how the victim had been killed. Nor of the weapon that
had been used.

I turned again to Koch. He was still asleep, his head jolting
uncomfortably up and down with the unpredictable lurching of the
carriage on the muddy, potholed road. His hat had fallen onto his
knees and his wig had now slipped down over his right ear. I closed
my own eyes and let myself be rocked by the motion of the vehicle,
trying to get the picture clear in my mind. How had these people

died? What purpose had been served by killing them? And why had two officers with considerable investigative experience (as I presumed from the fact that Lublinsky and Kopka had been present on both occasions) failed to confront these vital questions?

A deafening crash of thunder followed by a blinding flash of lightning put an end to my meditations, and to Koch's dozing. He sat up as if he'd been struck by a bullet, his first impulse to reach for his wig with one hand, his second to make the sign of the cross with the other.

'Good God, sir!' he grumbled loudly. 'Nature was created to plague the affairs of men.'

'It is only water vapour, Sergeant,' I smiled. 'Electrical discharges in the heavens. That is all. An eminent fellow citizen of yours once wrote a pamphlet on the subject. Nothing exists, he said, which the laws of Science cannot explain.'

Koch turned to me, his grey eyes flashing with unmistakable indulgence. 'Do you believe that, Herr Stiffeniis?'

'Indeed, I do,' I replied.

'I envy you your certainty,' he murmured, bending to pick his hat up from the carriage floor where it had fallen. He brushed the brown velvet, and set it on the crown of his head with care. 'No mysteries exist for you, then, sir?'

I could not ignore the vein of incredulity with which he expressed his doubts.

'I have always tried to follow the pathways of rationality to their logical conclusions, Herr Koch,' I answered.

'You do not admit the possibility of the Unknown, the Unthinkable?' He had a trick of sounding capital letters where there ought to have been none. 'May I ask what you do, sir, when you find yourself face to face with the Inexplicable?'

'I do not mean to suggest that human reason can explain and justify every human action,' I said with barely contained annoyance. 'There are limits to our understanding. What is unknown, as you call it, remains so for the simple reason that no one has chosen to explain it for the moment. I would call this qualified ignorance, not a defeat for Enlightened Science.'

Lightning flashed again and his pale flesh turned silvery blue against the rushing backdrop of dark trees and fleeting drops of rain, framed by the window pane.

'I hope the honour falls to me of taking you home when this affair has been successfully resolved,' he said, leaning close. 'I pray sincerely that I am wrong and you are right, Herr Stiffeniis. If not, God spare us all!'

'You seem to doubt my capacity to plumb these murders,' I returned with acid irritation.

'I would not dare so far, Herr Procurator. Indeed, I think I begin to understand why so much hope has been placed in you,' he said, and looked away.

I rubbed my nose, and took the plunge. 'My concerns are practical ones, Sergeant Koch. No mention is made in these reports of the cause of death. What am I supposed to do? Divine the nature of the weapon with which the victims were killed? The passage from life to death is not merely a religious question. It is a hard and fast fact, and there are very few facts here,' I said, holding up the papers in my hand and shaking them. 'I don't know how you go about your business in Königsberg, but we in Lotingen believe that if an egg has disappeared, someone has stolen it.'

Sergeant Koch ignored this barb.

'I've no idea what you may have read in those reports,' he said.

'Have you seen the bodies, Koch? Do you know how they died?'

'No, sir.'

'So, even you, a trusted employee of the police, have no idea how these people were killed? Doesn't the population talk of such things? Were the victims stabbed, strangled, beaten to death?'

'You mean to say no mention is made of the weapon used?' He looked genuinely surprised. 'I can understand the need for discretion, but the fact that even you have not been let in on the secret's hard to credit, sir. The town's full of rumours, as you can imagine.'

'What sort of rumours, Koch?'

'I hardly dare speak of such things to a rational thinker like yourself, sir,' Koch replied with an archness which seemed affected.

'Do not humour me!'

'I did not mean to offend, sir.' The sergeant took off his hat and looked penitent. 'The folk in Königsberg say that the Devil did it. Word's out that death came quick and mighty cruel.'

'What else?'

'This is wagging tongues and nothing more,' he said with sudden seriousness. 'What good will gossip do you, sir?'

'Wag your tongue, Sergeant Koch. Let me be the judge.'

He sat back against the seat and considered for a moment before he spoke.

'They say the woman who found the body of Jan Konnen saw the weapon.'

'She did?'

'They *say* she did,' Koch corrected me.

'What do they say she saw? What was this weapon that the Devil used?'

Herr Sergeant Koch looked at me and an embarrassed smile graced his lips.

'His claws, sir.'

'Claws, Koch. And what is *that* supposed to mean?'

Again, he seemed reluctant to speak his mind. 'I think you'd better talk to Procurator Rhunken, sir. I'm hardly qualified to say.'

'I want to know what *you* think, Herr Koch. I will ask Procurator Rhunken for his opinion of the matter when the opportunity presents itself.'

'I can only tell you what I've heard, Herr Stiffeniis.' Koch shifted uneasily in his seat and replaced his hat. 'These murders have been committed in a strange fashion. Everything points to it. All the facts . . .'

'Which *facts*, Koch?' I interrupted. 'I have not lighted upon one, single *fact* in all that I have read!'

He regarded me coolly for a moment.

'That's just the point, Herr Stiffeniis. Is it not? It's mystery which opens the gate to wild speculation. The word going the rounds didn't say that Konnen was stabbed, throttled, or beaten to death. Just that he was murdered by the Devil. And that the Devil used his claws to do the deed.'

'Claws, indeed! I say again, this is superstitious nonsense!'

'But if the authorities won't even tell *you* what caused the deaths, sir,' he hissed, pointing at the sheaf of official papers I held in my hands, 'it only leaves two alternatives. *They* don't know, or they don't want *us* to know! In either case, it leaves the door wide open to superstitious nonsense, as you call it.'

Koch fell back against the seat, his eyes clenched shut, clearly disturbed by what he had told me. I returned to my reading, making more pretence of work than progress, disconcerted by the sergeant's suggestion that the authorities were less than willing to reveal precise details of the murders even to myself, the magistrate appointed to direct the investigations. I was almost as much in the dark as I had been the day before when I knew nothing of the case.

I decided to skip the third report for the moment and look at the evidence that might have surfaced the previous day, hoping that the local police had established some method in their working and that the latest affair would be more illuminating than the first two.

On the 31st January, in the year of Our Lord, 1804, the body of Jeronimus Tifferch, notary, was found before dawn by Hilde Gnute, wife of Farmer Abel Gnute. The witness reports that it was a cold morning, snow having fallen most of the night, her eyes were watering and she could not see very well. As she walked along Jungmannenstrasse in the direction of the grocery shop belonging to Herr Bendt Frodke, to whom she intended selling eggs, she came upon the body of Herr Tifferch kneeling up against a wall. He had been murdered by a person, or persons, unknown.

The account was so short as to be ludicrous. The name affixed to the report was that of Anton Lublinsky alone. Could the officer find no more to say about how or why the man had been butchered? I rested my forehead against the cold window-glass and closed my eyes, which burned and ached from reading in the failing light. When I opened them again, we had entered a wood. Still, the rain poured down. A group of peasants had taken shelter beneath the trees waiting for the storm to end. The coach splattered them with mud as we passed. Silently, I prayed to the Lord our God, asking Him to protect both those poor people and myself. I realised that I would need to humble myself, I would need to pay the most careful attention and listen with a new ear to what the people in Königsberg might say. I would have to try to comprehend what they were truly thinking and interpret their beliefs, no matter how extravagant or superstitious their thoughts might strike me as being. I bent close to the window again, using the little light that remained to read a note which had been pinned to the report: *'Asked if she had seen any persons near the place of the murder, Hilde Gnute replied that only the Devil could do such a deed.'*

There it was, written in black on white, the possible identity of the murderer. Satan himself. That was to be my starting point. I could only wonder where such a beginning might lead. Was it simply a matter of faith? Perhaps, after all, the name of the murderer *was* truly known, and all that was lacking was my own willingness to suspend disbelief.

I cannot say how long I sat staring out of the window at the bleak landscape. The rain had ceased and snow began to fall heavily again. Slowly, the fields transformed themselves before my eyes from turgid grey to sparkling white, the moon a pale, shallow disc on the black horizon, and wolves began to howl in a chorus somewhere in the woods. I cannot recall what thoughts crossed my mind, but I must have fallen asleep at some point. Whether in pleasant dreams or foulest nightmares, the journey passed.

Suddenly, I felt a light tap on my shoulder.

'Our destination, sir,' Sergeant Koch announced. 'Königsberg.'

Chapter 3

The sky above our heads was an immense, dark sheet, furled, rippled and corrugated by the driving wind. Shards and shooting splinters of the Northern Lights shimmered low along a silver-edged horizon that I knew to be the Baltic Sea. The snow had ceased to fall. It lay on the ground in a sparkling carpet as we approached the city.

'The weather seems to be easing,' I began to say, as the coach drew up before a massive Gothic arch which marked the western entrance to Königsberg.

Sergeant Koch made no reply as a troop of heavily armed soldiers came running out of the gate and quickly surrounded the vehicle. Opening the window, he leaned out to face them. 'I am an employee of the Court. This gentleman is the new Procurator of Königsberg,' he stated boldly to the guards, inviting me to show my face at the window.

The soldiers looked at us, then at each other, their muskets at the ready, while one man ran back in through the gate. Not a word was said until he returned a few moments later in the company of an officer.

'Which one of you's supposed to be the magistrate?' he asked sharply.

The dark blue of his cape, his leather kepi and tall purple plume, the impressive array of silver decorations criss-crossing his uniform jacket lent little dignity to the man as he scrutinised my face. His eyes were bagged and bovine, his waxed moustache sagged heavily, his expression a disconcerting compound of mocking incredulity and alert tension. His podgy right hand, formed by Nature for the purpose of turning heavy clods in some secluded village out in the wilds of Bory Tucholskjie, pointed a percussion pistol in my face. Clearly, he would not hesitate to unload it.

'I am Procurator Hanno Stiffeniis,' I said, holding up my bag for him to see. 'I have a letter here which is signed by the King himself . . .'

'You are obstructing the Procurator in his duties,' Koch said suddenly, an unexpected authoritative tone in his voice.

'I'm sorry, sir, but I must see your *laissez-passer*,' the officer insisted. 'I have got my own instructions to follow. General Katowice's order-of-the-day. No one is to enter Königsberg by land without authority. Haven't you heard? There was a murder . . .'

'That is why I am here!' I snapped, handing him the commission which Sergeant Koch had delivered to me that morning.

The officer read it over, looked at me again, then handed the document back.

'Don't lose that paper, sir,' he warned, waving the guards back. He saluted, then called to the driver to proceed.

'What was that all about, Sergeant?' I asked as the coach rumbled over the cobblestones in the direction of the centre of the town. It was not yet four o' the clock, but all the shops were closed and shuttered, the streets empty, except for squads of soldiers marching through the town or standing guard with bayonets fixed at almost every corner. 'Has martial law been declared?'

'I've no idea, sir,' Koch replied. Indeed, he said nothing more for quite some time, until the vehicle came to a stop in a tree-lined square before a large, green, barn-like building.

'Ostmarktplatz,' he announced, skipping down from the carriage with surprising agility and pulling out the folding step for me. 'Herr Rhunken is expecting you, sir.'

I ought to have guessed that Herr Procurator Rhunken would wish to speak to me immediately. But why had Sergeant Koch not told me beforehand? I took a deep breath, and did my best to smooth my ruffled plumage, telling myself that all would soon be revealed. After all, Rhunken was the person best placed to instruct me in my duties. I hoped to obtain from him by word of mouth the essential facts which were missing in the documents I had been reading during the journey.

'You said that he was in no fit state to speak, Koch.'

The sergeant did not reply, but busied himself giving orders to the driver, whose oilskin and leather gauntlets glistened with crystals of hoar-frost in the gathering gloom. I had to repeat myself twice before I could manage to catch Koch's attention.

'Procurator Rhunken has suffered an apoplexy of the brain, has he not?'

'Indeed, he has, sir,' Koch replied. 'Herr Rhunken was an excellent magistrate to work for.'

I chose to ignore the implications of this compliment. 'Has he been ill for long?'

'Always in the best of health 'til yesterday, sir. Herr Rhunken collapsed in his office, and the physician diagnosed an apoplexy as the cause.'

Koch pointed beyond the ugly green building to a pretty pink villa with a tiny snow-covered garden set back from the road. 'That's his house, sir. It stands opposite the Fortress on the other side of the square, as you can see. The Court House is in there. Work was everything to him.'

My eyes followed the direction indicated by Koch's stubby forefinger, as it swept the vast, snow-strewn space and ran the length of an enormous building in soaring grey stone. Battlements, keep and watchtowers in bewildering display. A massive central doorway with a steel portcullis bore a marked resemblance to the rat-traps used throughout Prussia. Narrow pill-boxes on either side of the doorway were occupied by sentries wearing grey winter capes and black fur busbies. They stared fixedly ahead, long muskets frozen to their broad shoulders.

'I suppose I'll be spending much of my time over there,' I said warily. The building was an architectural horror. At the same time, I recollected, it represented the limitless power and authority that I would be free to wield in my new position.

'I'll take you over at the appointed hour, sir,' Koch said shortly, striding away along the pathway towards the villa, slipping and almost falling in the knee-deep snow in his haste. As I reached the door, the sergeant gave three short raps on a large brass knocker to announce our arrival. The door did not open for quite some time, and not before Koch had been obliged to knock again.

'Herr Stiffeniis to see His Excellency,' Koch announced to the pale young chambermaid who opened the door.

The serving-girl raised her watery blue eyes to mine for just an instant, then quickly looked down again. 'Doctor Plucker is with my master,' she murmured.

'How is Herr Rhunken today?' Sergeant Koch enquired, a note of genuine concern in his voice.

The girl shook her head. 'He's in a sorry state, Herr Koch. He was always such a fine, proud, handsome man . . .'

'Take Herr Stiffeniis through. I'll wait with the driver,' Koch said to me, rudely cutting in on the girl, whose words dissolved in sobs.

Closing the door, the maid looked uncertainly at me, as if she knew not what to do with me.

'Your master is expecting me,' I said, too sharply perhaps, taking my cue from Koch.

'This way, sir,' the girl mumbled timidly into her handkerchief, before leading me through a series of small connecting rooms, the walls of which were lined with glass-fronted bookcases full of leather-bound volumes. All the tables were piled high with books and papers, sofas and armchairs forced to do the camel's work of accommodating on their backs what would not fit on the crowded shelves. Procurator Rhunken seemed to have transformed his house into a private library. With the exception of the maid, there was no other indication of a female presence, no suggestion of the tempering influence of a mother, wife or daughter.

The girl stopped short before a door which stood ajar. A low voice could be heard murmuring inside, and suddenly a drawn-out whimper shook the air. I laid my hand on the wench's arm before she could knock.

'Can the Procurator speak?' I asked.

'Doctor purged him twice this morning. He's going to do it again . . .' She stopped to wipe her nose and dab her eyes. 'Sent me down the port this morning, he did, sir. To fetch those . . . creatures.' Her shoulders shook with fear or revulsion, or just possibly with the cold. The temperature inside the house was lower than the air in the street.

'A ship came in last night. The sailors laughed and told me to carry the bucket with care. If I touched one, it would suck my life out, they said.' She looked up at me with fear in her eyes. 'I did not know such creatures existed, sir. I did it for my master,' she whispered, sniffling into her handkerchief again.

I had no idea what she was muttering about. The sailors? The creatures, whatever they might be?

'If he has truly seen the Devil,' she added, 'all the physicking in the world won't save him.'

I did not shift myself to reassure her, reflecting only that the Devil's name enjoyed great popularity in Königsberg. Just then, the door was thrown open and a tall, gaunt man stepped out into the dimly lit passage. He was wigless, his head recently shaved. A tight, dark suit made him seem even taller and thinner than he really was. He saw the maid and his face lit up with some private satisfaction. But then he saw me, and his manner changed.

'Who are you, sir?' he barked in an uncouth manner. Without waiting for my reply, he turned on the girl and hissed, 'His Excellency is in no condition to receive visitors. I told you that before!'

'I am the new Procurator,' I announced. 'I have business with your patient, sir. Urgent business, which cannot wait.'

The doctor drew himself up like a hooded serpent preparing to strike. His eyes gleamed like points of light in the dim corridor.

'So, *you* are the person who is the cause of this distress!' he snapped in a blunt and accusing fashion. 'Herr Rhunken has been in a state of nervous anxiety all the day regarding you. I confess my surprise,' he continued, staring rudely at me. 'I was expecting someone altogether . . . *different*. An older man, let's say. A more . . . experienced magistrate.'

'I will not keep him long,' I said.

'I should think *not*!' he replied. 'I have work to do.'

If the doctor was rude, I put it down to strain. I was on edge myself as I followed him into the sick-room. Procurator Rhunken was not confined to bed, as I had expected, but lay on a leather chaise longue close to the far wall, his legs naked and raised on pillows towards an open window. This ice-cold chamber was more cluttered than the rest of the house put together. Three thin candle-tapers wedged together in a single candle-holder lit up books and papers scattered everywhere, great piles of them tottering like drunkards against the walls on either side of a four-poster bed which stood in the darkest corner.

If Doctor Plucker had been expecting someone older, His Excellency, Herr Procurator Wolfgang Rhunken, was far younger than I had anticipated. He could hardly have been forty-five years of age. I recalled the chambermaid's description of him as fine and handsome, but I could find no evidence of those attributes. He was propped up in a sitting position, large cushions at his back, a dark woollen shawl draped around his shoulders, his careworn face hollow with suffering, his naked legs raised to the freezing night air. Drawing nearer, I observed the sickly colour of his face, his mouth drawn tightly into a thin black slit, eyes half-closed like a man looking into the next world. Large beads of sweat stood out on his pale brow like condensation on a warm glass, his hair drenched, despite the glacial cold. He turned like a blind man as my boots clattered on the stone pavement.

I looked uncertainly at the doctor.

'Closer, sir. Go closer,' he urged. 'Let's get it over with, and quickly!'

As I approached the patient, I heard the doctor out in the passage, calling to the maid. 'Bring a stool for the *new* Procurator! And bring in that bucket!'

Rhunken's feverish eyes flashed open at the rude note of irony in the doctor's voice. He glared at me, though he did not speak. The stool arrived and was placed beside the couch. I hesitated for an instant as the sick man raised his quivering right hand with what seemed to be a superhuman effort, then let it fall with a heavy thump on the stool.

I took a deep breath and sat down, as the maid placed a large oak bucket covered with a linen cloth on the floor beside her ailing master. The sharp odour which I had at first taken to be the musty smell of a little-used room intensified. A heady compound of sweat, faeces and urine dosed with camphor and other medicines, it was the ethereal vapour of the magistrate's volatilising decay.

'I hope you'll soon recover your health, sir,' I began, uncertain what else to say, my voice lower than I might have wished.

Procurator Rhunken's mouth fell open, his lower lip trembled, the left side of his face twitched frantically. He struggled against the rebellious muscles, grasped my arm and pulled me close to that vile stench. Then, gasping desperately for air, he fell back against the cushions without having managed to say a word. For one moment, I thought that he was going to expire before my eyes. A violent tremor shook his body as he attempted to raise his head again.

'Do not exhaust yourself, sir!' Doctor Plucker exhorted. 'This gentleman has excellent young ears and patience aplenty. Now, stay still, sir, while I apply the remedy,' the doctor muttered. 'A ship came in last night from Rio del Plata. I had to fight for these with Surgeon Franzich from the Fortress infirmary. You'd baulk, Herr Rhunken, if you knew how much they cost. *Haementaria ghilianii*,' he announced, whipping the cloth cover from the bucket and raising it to his nose. 'Hmmm! The primal stench of the Amazon forests! You can almost see the dark, musky swamps where it creeps and crawls. These will do you the world of good, sir. They're a hundred times more effective than the hiruda worms that Monsieur Broussais brought back from Egypt. Military authorities throughout Europe are stocking up before the outbreak of war.'

I watched in awe as the physician extracted a massive black worm from his bucket with a pair of callipers. The creature squirmed and wriggled, trying to wrap itself around the doctor's arm. The instant it touched his patient's naked flesh, all the fight went out of it. Doctor Plucker stretched the massive leech out along Herr Rhunken's calf from the knee to the ankle, and left it there to feed.

'If I can help in any way,' I offered weakly, my gaze horridly attracted by the massive Amazonian slug. It was thirty centimetres long, at the very least. As it began to siphon off the invalid's blood, it seemed to surge and swell. 'I am . . .'

A yellow hand shot out from beneath Rhunken's shawl and came to rest before my face with such rapidity that the words froze on my tongue. 'You have come, then,' Rhunken gasped. 'From Berlin, I suppose?'

'Berlin, sir?' I repeated, uncertain what he meant. I darted a glance at the physician, but found no comfort there. He was busily engaged, laying out another giant leech upon the sick man's other leg. 'I have come this day from Lotingen, Your Excellency.'

Herr Rhunken frowned. A chasm seemed to split his brow.

'*Where?*'

'Lotingen. On the western circuit,' I said. 'I am the presiding magistrate there.'

'*Lotingen?*' Rhunken cried, the distress on his face painful to see. 'What are you doing here?'

The last thing I expected was to be quizzed about my identity by the man who had recommended me.

'I was ordered by His Majesty to relieve you of the case. I have your own note here in my pocket!'

Rhunken shook his head, disbelief writ large on his face.

'Surely you nominated me?' I pressed.

Procurator Rhunken turned his face to the wall as Plucker applied two more famished bloodsuckers to his naked thighs.

'I nominated no man,' the patient muttered angrily. 'This is *his* doing! That serpent does it to torture me!'

I chose to ignore his raving. Herr Rhunken was ill, after all. I could understand his situation. When a man is ill, he knows not who to blame, and so blames every man whose health is better than his own.

'I expected a special emissary,' he went on. 'From Berlin. From the secret police. Not you . . .'

'He's never heard of you,' Doctor Plucker hissed angrily in my ear, as he draped a smaller black worm across his patient's sweating brow, and another on his right temple. 'Any fool can see that. You are inflaming his brain, sir! You'll kill him! He was removed from the case. Sacked! Forced to cede. To an expert, he believed. Have you no grain of pity, sir?'

Suddenly, the magistrate gasped for air. Phlegm bubbled in his throat, and he coughed violently, spitting into a bowl which the doctor held up for him. 'Do not exert yourself, sir,' the physician implored. Looking over his shoulder at me, his expression tense, he cried, 'I beg you, sir!'

'I am not to blame if he is sick,' I replied stubbornly, then stopped short, uncertain how to continue. I had no wish to worsen his condition. 'I have been empowered to act by the King. Herr Rhunken knows more about these murders than any other living soul. I need his help.'

Doctor Plucker turned on me with anger.

'Herr Rhunken needs *rest*. You have robbed him of peace enough, I think, for one day. Leave him be!'

If the physician was determined to end the interview, the patient seemed intent on prolonging it. His hand clenched at my sleeve, dragging me down, and I was forced to my knees on the floor at his side. The leech at his temple throbbed and buckled, gorged with blood, sliding onto his cheek until the doctor picked it off with haste.

'Go to the Court House,' the magistrate said weakly. 'See if you . . . can do what I have failed to do.'

He fell back against the cushion, eyes closed, panting desperately for air.

'This will be the end of him,' Doctor Plucker protested, pushing me away from the stool without ceremony and sitting down himself, his hand on the pulse of his patient.

I stood back, my brain in a whirl, and watched the doctor administer to him.

'But you must know what weapon killed them!' I shouted, confusion giving place to frustration, as Procurator Rhunken closed his eyes and seemed to fall into a dead faint, those worms on his face and temples wriggling and twisting like the portrait of the Medusa I had seen in Rome at the Villa Borghese.

'Can't you see the state he's in?' Doctor Plucker shouted, taking hold of my arm, pushing and pulling me to the door. 'I must order you to quit this room!'

Throwing open the door with great energy, the doctor surprised me by his strength as he thrust me out into the corridor, where the maid was waiting.

'Show Herr Stiffeniis out!' he thundered.

I must have looked like a lost child, for the girl began to coax me gently along the corridor in the direction of the front door.

'Come along now, sir,' she said, retracing our path through the book-lined rooms and darkened corridors. 'Just follow me.'

As the front door closed behind me, I stood stock-still in the cold light of the low moon. Beyond the garden fence, Sergeant Koch was waiting. He turned at the sound of the door closing and began to advance towards me, his face mottled like veined marble in a church. The temperature had dropped while I had been inside, and fresh-fallen snow had settled on the crown of his hat.

'Is everything in order, Herr Stiffeniis?'

I ignored his solicitude. 'Who instructed you to come to Lotingen today, Sergeant Koch?' I was quivering with humiliation and with rage.

'Procurator Rhunken, sir,' he replied without a moment's hesitation.

'He had no idea who I was,' I said with a coolness which surprised me.

Koch opened his mouth to speak, then closed it again. Finally, he said, 'I *presumed* it was Herr Rhunken. I was handed a despatch by a messenger.'

'Who signed this despatch?'

'It was not signed, sir. I am an employee of the Procurator. The messenger said that the note had come from upstairs. Herr Rhunken does not need to sign his orders to me,' he said. 'That order told me what to do, and where to go. The same messenger handed me that letter with the Royal seal and those documents I was to consign to you while travelling to Königsberg. If I've done any wrong, I am most heartily sorry for it, sir.'

'You did not see Herr Rhunken at all?'

Koch shook his head. 'No, sir, I did not.'

'I must go at once to the Court House,' I said, turning on my heel, setting off in the direction of the massive Fortress on the far side of the square. I had gone some way before I realised that Koch had made no move to follow me.

'The Court House, sir?' he called after me. 'Don't you want to see your lodgings first?'

I turned on him. There was something ludicrous in what he had suggested. 'Do you think I am here on holiday? I have come to Königsberg to investigate murders, Sergeant!'

Koch took a step forward and removed his hat. 'The moon is not yet high enough, sir,' he said. For a moment I thought I had misheard him, but then he went on: 'We have time enough to . . .'

'Has the cold afflicted your brain, Koch?' I interrupted. 'What in the name of heaven has the *moon* to do with it?'

'I was instructed to take you to the Fortress after the moon had reached its peak, sir. Not a minute before.'

I strode back through the snow, resisting the urge to grab him by the throat.

'Is this the way that time is generally measured in Königsberg, Koch? By the phases of the moon? Or is this just one more instance of your superstitious nonsense?'

'There's to be a meeting over there, sir. When the moon is at its height. That's all I know,' Koch stated flatly.

'You made no mention of this before, Sergeant,' I observed. 'It is not the first time that you have tricked me.'

Koch looked at me with measured coolness. 'Mine is not to question why, sir. A person has been appointed to help you, that's all that I have been told,' he said.

'People have names, Koch,' I replied.

Snow began to fall again in drifting, wispy flakes, and Koch glanced up at the sky before deigning to answer. 'The person's name is Doctor Vigilantius.'

I opened my mouth to protest, but words would not come. Snowdrops settled cold on my lips and melted on my tongue.

'A *necromancer*?' I managed at last. 'What is *he* doing here?'

'I have heard,' Koch replied hesitantly, 'that the doctor will be conducting experiments of a scientific nature, sir.'

'Which *science* are you talking of, Koch?'

Sarcasm appeared to be lost on my stolid companion.

'I've been told that he is an expert regarding the flux of electrical currents in the brain,' he replied.

'Exactly, Koch. What is Vigilantius doing *here*?'

'I have just told you, sir. Experiments.'

'Let us try another tack, Sergeant Koch,' I persisted. 'Who called Augustus Vigilantius here to Königsberg?'

Koch stood to attention. 'I really am most terribly sorry, Herr Procurator Stiffeniis,' he apologised. 'I cannot answer that question.'

'Cannot, or will not? That seems to be your personal motto,' I muttered through clenched teeth, though Koch did not move a muscle or make any attempt to explain himself.

'You've time to spare before the appointed hour,' he said instead. 'I'm to take you to your lodging first, sir. The coach is waiting.'

I pointed to the Fortress on the far side of the square. 'Am I not staying over there?'

'Oh no, sir,' he returned quickly. 'I have been instructed to take you to another place.'

Suddenly, I felt drained of energy, as if I had just been leeched myself. Was there any point in arguing or complaining further with this intransigent man? I followed him to the coach as meekly as a ceremonial lamb being led to the slaughter.

Chapter 4

The coach pulled away slowly. The fresh snow on the cobbles made the horses nervous, the driver hesitant. The rattling wheels echoed off the towering walls of the dark stone buildings lining the narrow streets through which we drove, but I paid no heed to my surroundings. My thoughts were taken up with Procurator Rhunken. He had not been expecting me. He had no idea who I was, nor why I had come. In which case, why had I been sent to see *him*? If he had not given my name to the King, *who* had? Rhunken had admitted himself that he was expecting a magistrate from Berlin. The Imperial capital was home to the Secret Police. Was that who he had been waiting for, a Procurator from the Secret Police, a specialist in politics and murder? These new uncertainties, together with the host of unanswered questions lurking in the sparse official documents that I had been permitted to read on my way to the city, threw me into something approaching despair. And to make my situation even worse, I was bereft of reliable assistance. Herr Sergeant Koch was a minor official, an uninformed messenger following orders, as rigorous as he was unhelpful.

The raucous screeching of seagulls broke in on my thoughts. My nose began to twitch with the stink of stale fish and the nauseous tang of seaweed as I raised the blind and looked out of the coach. The listless grey sea stretched northwards beyond a narrow sand bar to infinity. The tide was out, and a small fleet of fishing-smacks lay awkwardly on their keels, the masts and rigging a forest of icicles. The shallow beach was a sheet of solid ice, except for a narrow channel of fast-flowing water in the centre of the estuary. A black stone pier projected out like an arm into the stream. Tall three-masters lining the sea wall were moored in line like dead whales waiting to be hauled on shore. Navvies carrying sacks and bales went running up and down the gangplanks, while ancient derricks creaked and groaned under the weight of the cargoes being loaded and discharged. Apart from the ubiquitous presence of the soldiers on the streets, this was the first sign of life that I had witnessed since arriving in Königsberg. The city was renowned for the industry of its inhabitants, the canny tight-fistedness of its merchants. It was, after all, the most extensive port on the Baltic coast. Hamburg and Danzig were rivals to some extent, but neither place could boast a tonnage equal to that of Königsberg. In a normal day, Koch reported, a dozen ships from the farthest reaches of the earth hove to along that pier, while another dozen weighed their anchors and plotted their route in the opposite direction. The labourers came and went, each one following an identical path to the dockside warehouses, hard on his neighbour's heel, then running back to the vessels, like ants carrying a grain of seed to their communal store. One of those ships, I thought, had journeyed all the way from the tropical jungles of South America with its cargo of leeches for the army.

'Where are you taking me, Herr Koch?' I asked.

'To your inn, sir. It's down on the quayside. It's out of the way, I admit, but the coach will always be . . .'

'An inn?' I snapped. 'Like a travelling salesman?'

Was this a further attempt to humiliate me? I had suffered knocks enough that day. First, Rhunken had denied all knowledge of who I was. Then, a meeting by moonlight had been arranged for me with a notorious alchemist, and now I was to be lodged in a low tavern in the company of smugglers and pirates, far from the Fortress and the Court where I ought to have been by rights.

'I am not in Königsberg for my pleasure, Sergeant,' I reminded him.

'My instructions were to bring you here, sir,' Koch answered bluntly.

Even at that early stage, I began to feel that a precise scheme had been laid out for me. My introduction to Königsberg had all the appearance of an elaborate courtly dance. I was being led deliberately from step to step by Koch, my taciturn dancing-master. But who had called the tune? And for what purpose?

'I only hope this place is comfortable,' I muttered to myself as the coach skidded to a stop in front of an ancient red-brick building with a ribbed, uneven roof. A weather-vane of a seagoing ship with her sails puffed by the wind spun furiously above the central chimney. In the gloom, the frosted glass of the bow window flickered with a lively amber glow, which suggested that a large fire was blazing inside. It was the first heartening thing I had seen that day. A wooden sign above the door was so plastered with driven snow that it was impossible to read the name of the inn.

'The Baltic Whaler, Herr Procurator,' Koch confided. 'The food here is excellent. Far better than the Fortress barracks, I believe.'

I ignored this attempt to smooth my temper, the icy cold penetrating my bones as we made for the entrance. Inside, a wave of muggy heat hit me in the face, and I glanced around the room while Sergeant Koch went to speak to a man who was busy stoking the fire. The fireplace itself was so wide as to take up almost the entire wall at the far end of the room. Tables had been laid for dinner. Fresh white linen tablecloths and gleaming silver made a favourable impression. The place seemed clean and inviting enough.

Sergeant Koch returned in the company of a tall, thickset man with an untidy mass of curly grey locks cascading over his forehead, and a brass ring in each ear, who nodded in welcome, then ducked behind the bar-counter. A waxed ponytail tied up with a bright red ribbon added to the impression that he had once been a whaling man. He returned with a large bunch of keys, smiling at me in a manner that was respectful without being obsequious.

'I am Ulrich Totz, owner of the inn. We've been expecting you all day, sir,' he said in a deep, strong voice which made him sound younger than his grey hair suggested. 'I've sent the groom upstairs to fuel the fire in your room. Now, let me get your bags from the coach.'

I thanked him and glanced around the room again, while Koch stood warming his hands before the blazing fire. There were few other people present at that early hour of the evening. Near to the fireplace, a knot of customers sat on high-backed wooden settles and regarded Koch and myself with undisguised curiosity. Having satisfied themselves that we were nothing more or less than two travelling gentlemen seeking refuge from the snowstorm, they turned back to their beer and pipes and resumed their conversations. Three of the drinkers wore Prussian naval uniforms, while another sported the garb of a Russian hussar with a short green cape and festoons of gold braid stitched like skeletal ribs across the breast of his uniform. The man seated nearest to the fireplace was dark-skinned, and stroked a huge handlebar moustache, a bright red fez sitting lopsidedly on his small head. I guessed him to be a Moroccan or a Turk, most probably a naval officer from a merchant ship. Mediterranean novelties had been arriving in Europe, and even Prussia, for some years now. Indeed, it was widely agreed that if the Egyptians had had the good sense to keep their exotic secrets to themselves, Bonaparte would have left them in peace. But the Emperor loved the fruits of the date-palm tree to distraction, and so he . . .

Before I had the opportunity to notice more, the innkeeper entered with my luggage. 'Yours is the second room on the left, first floor. Come up whenever you are ready, sir.'

I joined Koch in front of the fire and warmed my hands.

'This is a welcome sight,' I conceded.

Koch murmured agreement, without lifting his eyes from the crackling logs; we remained standing there together in silence for some time, as if bewitched by the dancing flames.

'We have an hour or so before your appointment with Doctor Vigilantius, Herr Procurator,' he reminded me.

'Ah yes, the moon!' I joked. 'You'll keep me company, I hope?'

Koch turned to me, a show of surprise on his face. 'Sir?'

'Do you have any other plans tonight?'

'Oh no, Herr Procurator,' he enthused. 'My orders were to make myself useful in any way you might think fit. I wasn't sure . . .'

'That's settled, then,' I said with decision. The thought of entering the bleak fortress in Ostmarktplatz and having to do so alone was daunting. Up to that point, my relationship with Sergeant Koch had been neither cordial nor easy, but he was the only person in the city to whom I could turn for aid.

'As I have had good reason to note today, Koch, you are both efficient and discreet,' I said, pausing for a moment. 'Discreet' was the most tactful word I could find to describe behaviour which had touched a raw nerve more than once. 'I was wondering . . . that is, I'd be grateful to benefit from your knowledge of the city. Will you assist me during my stay in Königsberg?'

'Procurator Rhunken has no need of me at the moment,' Koch considered, his eyes fixed upon the fire. 'If I can be of use to you, sir.'

Beneath the detached, austere attitude of Koch I thought I read a hint of willingness to help me in my task.

'I am Herr Rhunken's successor,' I said with relief, making a bluff attempt at humour, 'so I suppose I inherit you. Now, if you'll excuse me, I must write a letter. Can it be delivered this evening?'

'I'll take it myself, sir,' Koch replied promptly.

'Thank you, Sergeant. Order two large glasses of hot toddy, will you? I won't be long.'

Upstairs, I found my room without any difficulty. The door was ajar, so I walked straight in. Herr Totz, the innkeeper, was standing next to a boy who was down on his knees working a wooden bellows which caused the fire to roar. Their backs were turned to the door, so neither of them was immediately aware that I had entered the room. I laid my hat on the bed, conscious of the delicious warmth and general neatness of the apartment, noting the low, sagging ceiling with dark, tarred oak beams, the whitewashed plaster, and a carpet that was only slightly worn at the centre. A small desk was placed beneath the window, an oil lamp glowed brightly, while along the opposite wall a large trunk and a matching dresser of walnut stood on either side of a bed hung with curtains which appeared to be fresh and clean. A large blue Dresden ewer and washbowl on the dresser completed the furnishings.

Content with what I had seen, I glanced back in the direction of the innkeeper and his boy to announce my presence. But something in the *tableau vivant* stopped me. The red-faced boy was still crouching down before the fire, the tall innkeeper hovering over him, hands on his hips. I could see only Totz's profile, but there was no mistaking the menacing expression on his face. With the roaring of the bellows, the swoosh of flames and the crackling of wood, I could make little sense of what they were saying. Totz was speaking earnestly to the boy, the veins standing out boldly on his neck as if he suppressed a desire to shout.

'Play with flames, Morik, you'll burn your fingers!' he sneered.

'He certainly does know how to start a fire, Herr Totz,' I said out loud, taking off my travelling-cloak, and dropping it on the bed. When I turned back to the fireplace once more, I was astonished by the sudden transformation of the scene, the expressions frozen on their faces. Fear was written on the boy's pinched features like a cornered fox as the hounds close in for the kill, despite his attempt at a welcoming smile. Ulrich Totz, who had been so angry only a moment ago, was now all accommodating smiles and seasoned humility. His left hand rested with a heavy, proprietorial air on the skinny shoulder of his young charge. For all the world, innkeeper Totz looked like a village beagle who had just taken the lad up for thieving.

'Here's your room, sir,' the landlord said with a conspiratorial wink in my direction. 'Whatever you need, my wife'll be back from her sister's this evening. I'm downstairs in the tavern as a rule. This here's Morik, my nephew.'

The hand on the boy's shoulder gave a quick, hard nip, and the hollow smile on the boy's face was shattered by a grimace of pain.

'That fire is to my liking, Morik,' I said, measuring my enthusiasm to avoid increasing the animosity of the master in the boy's regard.

The innkeeper smiled again broadly, though I had the impression that his good humour cost him a great deal of effort when I told him to go, but ordered the boy to remain behind to unpack my bag. The mere fact that the master had been dismissed from the room seemed to put the young servant at his ease. He was a sprightly little lad, bright of eye, his round face as rough and shiny as a golden russet apple, no more than twelve years old. He fell on my valise like a quick little monkey, pulling out the contents, laying out my shirts, stockings and linen on the bed, positioning my combs and hairbrushes with excessive care beside the washbasin, opening and closing drawers. He seemed to take some pleasure in feeling the cut and the quality and the weight of everything he touched. In a word, he was slow.

'That will do, Morik!' I stopped him, my patience running short. 'Just pour some warm water into that bowl, will you? I need to wash before going out again. A gentleman is waiting for me downstairs.'

'The policeman, sir?' Morik asked quickly. 'Is the inn being watched?'

'All of Königsberg is under strict surveillance,' I replied vaguely, smiling at this impetuous show of childish curiosity. Then, I sat myself down at the table near the window, laid out my writing *necessaire* and began to pen a letter that I had never believed I should need to write.

Herr Jachmann,

Circumstances beyond my personal control bring me once more to Königsberg. I have been assigned a Royal Commission of extreme gravity and exceptional importance which I wish to explain to you in person at your earliest convenience. I will call on you at 12 a.m. tomorrow. I hasten to repeat my word as a gentleman that I will avoid any form of contact with Magister-strasse until I have spoken to you. RSVP. Obsequiously,

Hanno Stiffeniis, Magistrate.

'Shall I run to the post for you, sir?'

I turned around with a start. The boy was looking over my shoulder. I had been so involved in what I was doing, I had forgotten that he was still in the room.

'The post? At this time of night? Aren't you afraid to go out after dark?' I asked.

'Oh no, sir!' the boy replied with vigour. 'I'll do anything your Excellency may ask of me.'

'You're a brave little fellow,' I said, pulling a coin from my waist-coat pocket, 'but a foolish one. There's murder on the streets of Königsberg at night. You'll be safer indoors.'

He cast a furtive glance towards the door, then picked the coin from my hand like a thieving magpie. 'I wouldn't be so sure of that, sir,' he whispered. 'There's more danger in this here tavern than on the streets. The water's ready for you.'

I hardly gave a thought to what the boy had said, dismissing it as infantile braggadocio, as I slipped off my jacket and waistcoat, rolling up my shirtsleeves with a smile.

'Don't you believe me, sir?' he said, stepping closer.

'Why should I *not* believe you, Morik?' I replied, paying little attention to the conversation, my mind on the evening that lay ahead.

'There are strange things going on in this house, sir,' he whispered in an even lower voice than before. 'That's why you're here, is it not?'

'Of course,' I joked, splashing my face with warm water. 'What sort of things are you talking about?'

'A man who was murdered passed his last night here. Jan Konnen . . .'

A sharp knock at the door interrupted him.

Without waiting to be called, Herr Totz walked in, as I was drying my face.

'If you've finished with the lad, sir,' the innkeeper said with an air of tight-lipped anger, 'I need him down in the kitchen. Now!'

Before I could say a word, the boy had skipped around his master, and ducked artfully out of the door.

'That lad!' Totz said with a roll of his eyes and a shake of his head. 'He's a lying little scamp. An' workshy with it. With your permission, sir?'

'He was telling me that Jan Konnen was in your inn the night he was murdered, Totz,' I said. 'Is it true?'

Ulrich Totz did not respond immediately. Then, a thin smile appeared, and the reply flowed like warm milk and melted honey. 'That's right, sir,' he said. 'I have already told the police everything

I know. Under oath. Konnen was here one minute, gone the next. I cannot tell you more than that, sir. May I be excused now? We're very busy downstairs at the moment.'

I nodded, and out he went, closing the door quietly behind him. Had I been drawn into some sort of bizarre labyrinth, or was it mere coincidence that I had been roomed in the inn where the first victim of the murderer had spent his last hours? I decided to search out Ulrich Totz's statement to the police at the first opportunity. Clearly, there was more documentation regarding the murders than the scant evidence that I had been shown by Koch in the coach.

Down in the saloon Sergeant Koch was seated before the fire, two tall glasses of rum toddy set out on a small table beside him. The inn was busier than before, all animated – two women in loose, red skirts and low-cut blouses were the centre of attention – except for the Russian officer in his extravagant uniform who had fallen sound asleep at his table, his head propped up against the wall, a glass of grog upturned and dripping onto the floor.

'Koch,' I said, tapping him on the shoulder.

The sergeant jumped to his feet and slammed his hat on his head, as if I had caught him in a desperate state of undress. 'The coach is . . .'

'Jan Konnen was murdered here,' I interrupted. 'Did you know that?'

Koch paused long enough for me to wonder whether he was pre-varicating once again. 'I had no idea, sir. None at all,' he answered.

'Is that so?' I queried. 'That is strange. All the town must know.'

Koch took a deep breath before he answered. 'As I told you, sir, the details have been kept a very close secret. I knew, of course, that the man had been killed somewhere near the sea, but *not* in this very inn.'

'*Outside* the inn,' I corrected him mechanically. 'You may not know it, but whoever decided to lodge me here most certainly did, Sergeant.'

We stood there for a few moments, face to face in silence, while I felt the cold frost of misunderstanding fall between us once again. I held up the envelope I had been holding. 'This is the letter I mentioned before,' I said. 'It is meant for a gentleman in town. His name is Reinhold Jachmann.'

If Koch had ever heard the name, he gave no sign of it.

'I'll deliver it after we've been to the Fortress, sir,' he said with a dutiful nod. 'I'll take it there on my way home.'

This generous proposal cast a new light on Koch. I had done little all day, I suddenly realised, but blame him for mounting a conspiracy that I was quite unable to explain to myself. What I had taken to be interference and heavy-handed manipulation on his part might prove to be nothing more than excessive zeal in the execution of a tiresome duty.

'First thing tomorrow morning will do, Koch,' I said, relenting a trifle. 'Herr Jachmann's house is in Klopstrasse.'

'Do you require anything else, sir?' he asked.

'Transport, Koch. The moon should be in its mansion by now, don't you think?' I added in an attempt to be more jovial.

A barely perceptible shadow of a smile traced itself out on the sergeant's lips as we walked towards the door. 'Indeed, sir. I think it should.'

Outside on the quay, snow lay on the rough cobblestones in swirling piles and massive drifts, though it fell no longer. The wind gusted more fiercely than ever, a biting, hissing whistle of a gale whipping off the sea, which made the teeth chatter and the spirit rebel.

'God preserve us!' Koch muttered as he followed me into the coach.

As he shouted to the driver to pull away, I remembered the hot rum toddies we had left untouched on the table in the inn. That night we would both regret the omission.

Chapter 5

Darkness had fallen in Ostmarktplatz. There was not a living soul abroad. Even the sentry-boxes outside the Fortress and the Court House stood empty, the gendarmes having been recalled inside for the night. On either side of the main entrance, flickering firebrands cast weak pools of light and etched deep shadows into the sombre stone facade. As Koch and I stepped down from the coach and approached the gate, the massive building loomed high above us. In the pale light of the rising moon, its towering pinnacles, central keep and watchtowers cast an ominous gloom over the glistening carpet of snow.

Sergeant Koch raised a large iron ring and let it drop against a small lych-gate set into the gigantic defensive wooden door. A heavy bolt was drawn noisily, a Judas-window slid back, and a pair of needle-point eyes scrutinised us from within.

'Procurator Stiffeniis to see Doctor Vigilantius,' Koch announced.

The peephole closed with a metal clang, the door was thrown open, and we stepped into a small inner courtyard.

'Wait here,' the guard announced, and we were left to dally in the cold for some minutes. In the centre of the courtyard, two tall soldiers in shirtsleeves were labouring with spades beside a long wooden box. With such an abundance of fresh snow covering the city, I asked myself, what was the point of storing it in boxes?

'General Katowice!' Koch hissed suddenly, and I turned to see a cluster of officers in blue serge striding purposefully in our direction. 'He's the commander of the garrison,' Koch added in a whisper.

With some trepidation I braced myself to meet the general, and found myself confronted by a person of less than average height and wider than average girth. He also had abominably black teeth, and a huge white moustache which swept over his upper lip and red cheeks. Crossing his short arms over his massive chest, he formed his wrinkled forehead into a frown, then flashed his head to the left in a singular gesture which brought a long white braid of hair whipping through the air to rest along his arm like a snake on a branch. High-ranking officers have never ceased to wear their hair in the style made fashionable by Frederick the Great.

'Stiffeniis?' the general barked, offering his tubby hand.

I had to smile with relief. Here, it seemed, I *was* expected.

'I will not waste your time, except to say I am glad you've come,' he began, his beefy hand playing with the hilt of his sword. 'The city is in turmoil, as you know. These murders! The King wants to tidy the matter up without delay. It is clear to *me* what's going on.' He leaned too close for comfort, reeking of garlic and other nameless half-digested things. 'Jacobins!' he said. 'There, that's your answer.'

'Spies, sir?' I asked.

General Katowice placed his hand on my arm. 'Exactly! I want to know where they are hiding!' he said with some agitation, the white tress now dangling wildly on his chest. He looked more like a barbarian chieftain than a Prussian general. 'Never trust a Frenchman! They're cunning devils led by Satan himself! Napoleon would give his left arm and leg to seize the fortress of Königsberg. I have my forces strategically placed in and out of the city. They'll strike without mercy. A word from you, a word from me. That's all it takes.'

He placed his right hand on my left shoulder, looked straight into my eyes, then tightened his hold. 'If you find anything that *looks* French, *smells* French, I want to know of it. Rhunken suspected a foreign plot against the nation, but proof was lacking. Which tied my hands, of course. If you can track them down with more solid arguments, I'll persuade the King to take the initiative. We will strike before they do. All may depend on you. Any questions?'

The first that came to mind was more than sufficient to start a flood. *What was I doing there?* But I did not ask it. Nor did General Katowice wait.

'None? Good man! Now, they're expecting you, I believe.'

The general and his staff marched off to the left, while a corporal stepped up before us from the right and saluted. 'Follow me, gentlemen,' he said, spinning on his heel and marching away.

Was that the motive for the murders, a Jacobin plot to undermine the peace in Königsberg and in Prussia? I followed in a daze. We thundered along a dark corridor, through a large empty hall which echoed to the noise of our steps, passing beneath a low arch which led into a maze of gloomy corridors until we reached a narrow door cut into a damp grey wall.

'This way,' the corporal said, as he took a flaming torch from a ring on the wall and skipped lightly down a stairwell which spiralled into the bowels of the earth. The smell of mildew was sickening. Our guide's torch fought a guttering battle with the pitch darkness.

'Aren't the offices above ground?' I asked Koch.

'So they are,' he replied.

'Why are we going underground, then?'

'I've no idea, sir.'

We might have been descending into a crypt.

'This is a strange place for a meeting,' I said, my anxiety mounting. 'Where are you taking us, Corporal?'

The corporal stopped, glanced at Koch, then at me, his brutish face topped by a battered tricorn hat and framed by a tattered wig which had not seen powder in a month. 'To see the doctor, sir,' he replied brusquely.

Just then, a heavy clumping and clattering of steel-tipped boots sounded loudly on the staircase above us. Our guide raised his torch, lighting up the two soldiers I had noticed working in the courtyard above. They came hurtling down the stairs, manhandling a large box between them. The weight of it seemed to drag them downstairs faster than they wished to go, and we had to push ourselves up hard against the wall to escape being crushed.

'Has he come yet?' our guide called after them.

As the labourers stumbled past, I saw how very tall they were. Frederick the Great had set the fashion, visiting every corner of the continent in the search for new pieces to add to his collection of giant soldiers. Now, they flocked to Prussia. Those two were excellent specimens. Even so, they groaned beneath the weight.

'Dunno,' the soldier at the front cried back over his shoulder. 'Get a move on, Walter!'

'Are they being punished?' I asked the corporal as the darkness gobbled them up.

'They're just obeying orders, sir,' he replied, and cantered on down the stairway.

At the bottom of the shaft, a square skylight shone above our heads. The corporal looked up, an expression of bemused terror on his face. The full moon was perfectly framed by the window high above.

'Strike me blind!' he cursed. 'Right on bloody time!'

'What *are* you talking about?' I asked.

The corporal looked at me, his expression tense. 'That doctor's very keen on details, sir,' he murmured. 'He said the moon would appear from the clouds, and there it is!' The fear written on his face was childishly comical. 'Better not keep him waiting, sir,' he said, proceeding quickly on his way towards a door at the far end of the corridor, which opened into a large, empty store-room. It was cold in there, extremely cold. The other two soldiers were hard at work shovelling snow from the box onto a black tarpaulin cover.

'Well, Koch . . .' I began to say, vapour forming an ectoplasm in front of my face as I spoke.

'You are just in time, sir,' a haughty voice accused at my back.

I turned and gaped. I seemed to have been addressed by one of the age-encrusted ancestral portraits hanging from the walls of my father's country house. It was the style of his wig that impressed me. Grey curls cascaded from the crown of his head in undulating waves on either side of a long, gaunt face. Large, snow-white hands held a huge cloak of shimmering black velveteen clasped tightly to his body.

'My name is Vigilantius,' he announced rather stiffly. 'Doctor Vigilantius.'

He did not offer his hand or make any sign of welcome, but swept past me, his black cloak billowing and rippling out as he drew close to the waiting soldiers. There was only a hand-span of difference in height between him and the lesser of the two giants.

'I hope you have followed my instructions to the letter.'

It was not a question, though one of the men stood forward. Wiping his forehead on his sleeve, he said: 'All as you ordered, sir.'

'Let us begin in that case,' he said, his attention directed at the labourers, who were sweating despite the cold.

'Begin *what*?' I demanded in a loud voice, stepping forward to assert my authority before Koch and the soldiers.

Vigilantius arched his bushy eyebrow and stared back defiantly at me, but he did not answer my question.

'What are we doing in this dungeon?' I insisted.

'I am here to enter the Spirit World,' he said quite plainly, as if the place truly existed and might be found by any sharp-eyed person on the *mappamondo*. Before I could speak, he turned on Koch as if he meant to eat him.

'Who are you, sir?' he said, like a lizard snapping up flies.

'Sergeant Koch is my assistant,' I shot back.

The doctor made a face, but no objection. 'He'll remain, then. These two men are needed for the first part of the operation. Corporal,' he said, throwing out his forefinger like a dart, 'be gone!'

Our guide hurried out of the room without a backward glance.

'Bring our guest over here,' Vigilantius ordered sharply.

Instinctively, I took a step backwards, thinking that they meant to lay hands on me. From the other side of the room, with a tortured shriek like a hunting horn in the hands of a novice, the labourers began to push the snow-covered tarpaulin towards where we were standing.

A wave of anger swept over me. Was he trying to make a fool of me? Did my authority mean nothing to this vulgar showman? I had been designated by the King to take charge of the case. If anything were to be done, *I* would decide.

'Stop where you are!' I shouted, advancing on the soldiers.

'Are you not . . . curious to know what lies beneath this cover, Herr Procurator?' Vigilantius asked, a mincing smile on his face. 'You will obtain no greater help in Königsberg, I promise you.'

'What are you hiding here?' I demanded.

'Sweep it away,' he said to the soldiers without answering me.

As the men removed the snow with their bare hands, I stood simmering with rage. Was this why I had been placed in charge of such a delicate investigation? To be guided, manipulated, frustrated? Had I no effective power?

'Shift him here,' Vigilantius instructed, and the workmen revealed what had been referred to so obliquely. 'Now, get out!'

The soldiers obeyed him willingly, leaving us alone with Vigilantius.

I drew close and looked down.

'Who was he?' I asked.

'*Was?*' the grating voice challenged. 'This *is* Jeronimus Tifferch, fourth victim of the killer terrorising Königsberg.'

I had seen corpses in France. I knew what the slicing blade of a freshly oiled guillotine could do. But that did not prepare me for the sight of Lawyer Tifferch. He lay on his back in a wholly unnatural position. Trunk curved upwards, knees bent to form a high pointed arch above the table, arms stretched out and reaching downwards. The life seemed to have been ripped out of him. His skin was glassy, unnatural, the ivory-yellow colour of mummified Italian saints. Cheeks sucked inwards, his mouth gaped wide open. He was the picture of puzzled innocence. His hair had frozen stiff, and was so very white I thought it to be ice. A long straight nose led down to a thin pair of twisted black moustaches which Tifferch appeared to have cultivated with more than usual care. His suit was olive green and well cut with narrow gold piping around the collar, hem and buttonholes. Biscuit-coloured stockings hung limply away from slim calves which had contracted with the cold. Both kneecaps were heavy with caked mud. There was no evident mark of death on him. Nothing to explain what had brought Lawyer Tifferch to such an end.

'How did he die?' I asked, more to myself that to anyone else.

'We will soon discover *that*,' Vigilantius replied darkly, as he began to go about his work. It was like a Roman Catholic ritual. I had attended the mass in Rome some years before and been fascinated by the pagan ceremonial that the priests employed there. Placing a hand on either side of the dead man's face, the doctor closed his eyes and touched his forehead to that of the corpse like a priest consecrating bread and wine at the Offertory. He remained like this for some time, silent and stiff like the dead man beneath him. Suddenly, he began to sniff noisily, wildly at the nose and mouth of the corpse. Sweat rolled down off his brow in a torrent. He quivered violently, all his limbs shook, he seemed to be possessed of a frenetic energy that he could not control.

'Jeronimus Tifferch,' he intoned in a loud voice. 'Jeronimus Tifferch. Return from the shadows. I, Augustus Vigilantius, command you . . .'

A rattling growl rang to the stony vaults and ran skittering around the room, dissolving in a long agonised howl.

'Someone else is hiding here,' I said aside to Koch.

Koch stared back at me. His teeth were clenched, eyes aflame with the firelight from the torch. 'There's nobody, sir,' he said. 'Just him, us, and the body.'

Vigilantius swayed wildly back on his heels.

'*Let me be. Let me rest in darkness,*' he hissed. His mouth was huge, twisted, formless, the strange disembodied voice sharp, clear. There was an infinite sadness in it which I would not have imagined Vigilantius capable of evoking. His breathing became troubled, laboured, and – my God, I wish to deny it! – his voluminous cloak began to rise up of its own accord like a malignant black cloud which threatened to engulf him whole. Everything happened so fast. We were like men adrift in the middle of a raging torrent or a howling storm.

'Take energy from me!' screamed Vigilantius, as if an unseen hand were ripping the heart from his body. 'Who *are* you?'

'*I am no longer I,*' the voice replied in a shrieking howl, and I felt Koch's hand grasping at my sleeve for comfort. There was silence for some time, then the wind began to moan and wail again. '*I am . . . I . . . no more . . . no more . . .*'

'Who took you into the darkness?' Vigilantius asked calmly, as if it were the most natural question in the world.

'*Murder . . . murder . . . murder . . .*' the wind raged back a dozen times, like a hammer blow repeated over and over again. It echoed and resounded in my brain. In the flickering light, I seemed to see the stiff frozen mouth of the corpse open and close in speech. Vigilantius quivered from head to toe. Mangled words and rent phrases rushed from his lips in an incomprehensible avalanche.

Then, there was a sharp cry of pain.

'Who did this, Spirit?' Vigilantius stormed. 'Who murdered you?'

I heard the hoot of an owl, the sound of pigeons cooing, the howl of a cat, the wild babbling of a tuneless song, then that wind-like rush again.

'*A tongue of flame. A fire at the back of my sku . . .*' The speech slurred suddenly, then picked up more clearly with a snatching, nasal sibilance which was quite distinct. Was this the true voice of Lawyer Tifferch? '*Dark . . . dark . . . a voice . . .*'

'Which voice?' Vigilantius shouted against a babble of disconnected sounds like the tuneless mangling of a hurdy-gurdy when the handle is turned the wrong way. 'Who spoke to you? Describe him, I command you!'

I saw, or thought I saw, the lips of the dead man move in answer. '*The Devil's . . . is a face . . . no more,*' the corpse said, and silence fell as if a tomb-slab had been dropped in place. Time stood still, but questions rattled in a swirling vortex through my brain. What had I just seen? What jiggery-pokery had I just witnessed? Sweat ran cold along my spine. The performance had certainly been impressive, my heart was still heaving like a bellows. I gasped for air, and had to clear my throat for fear of choking. In that instant, I realised, Doctor Vigilantius was watching me. The *real* Vigilantius, if anything could be called real in that dark place. Suddenly, his upper lip curled, his black eyes sparkled, and he grinned fiendishly from ear to ear.

'You heard it, did you not?' he said. 'The human corpse is the receptacle of vital sensations. My *magister*, Emanuel Swedenborg, taught me how to tap them long ago. Open your blinkered mind to mystery, Herr Procurator. More illustrious men than you have learnt to see without using their eyes.'

He took a step towards me, blocking the body from my sight. His sense of his own powers was absurd, unquestioning. Arrogance oozed from his person, sweat rained from his brow, rivulets ran down his face and his neck. 'Make the most of what you have just been privileged to witness,' he said, waiting for my reaction, the smile slowly fading from his lips.

I took a step forward.

'Impressive, sir,' I said, my pulse thumping rapidly. 'You've missed your calling. You should have been an actor. But what remains of the play when the curtain falls?'

I stared into his eyes for some moments, but he did not reply.

'You have told me nothing useful,' I went on, my anger mounting. 'How did this man die? What weapon killed him? And why could he not describe the face of his murderer? You are a ventriloquist, sir, a conjuror. I have heard not a single word of truth from the dead man's lips. Nor from yours. You are wasting my time, obstructing my investigation. The King will have a report of what is happening here.'

The necromancer's coal-black eyes stared defiantly into mine, and that annoying, self-satisfied smile twisted his thin lips once more. 'What has the King to do with this, Herr Stiffeniis?'

'Surely, you remember him?' I replied sarcastically. 'Our monarch? King Frederick Wilhelm III? The person who entrusted this case into my hands? I have his letter of authority here in my . . .'

'You couldn't be more wrong,' Vigilantius interrupted, waving his hand in the air as if to dismiss a bothersome fly. 'King Frederick Wilhelm knows nothing of you, or me. A person of eminence whom His Majesty trusts has promised to solve these mysteries for him. With your help, and with mine. Your letter of authority isn't worth the paper it's written on. It was signed and sealed by some faceless secretary in Berlin, I'd wager. A pretext to bring you here.'

My hands began to shake with rage, and I thrust them deep inside my cloak, trying to keep my voice cool and sharp when I spoke. 'An eminent person? A person whom the King trusts? And this great man has promised the King to solve these murders by means of sleight-of-hand and conjuring tricks. How remarkable! I am eager to meet this Professor of Chicanery. The city of König-berg could not be in better hands.'

Vigilantius stared at me in silence, that mocking smile fading into a stiff and brooding glare. 'You are insulting a great man, Herr Procurator. I hope that I am present when you meet him.'

'In this world, or the next?' I muttered, staring down at the corpse, before turning to Koch. 'Help me. I wish to examine the empty shell of this man now that the *spirit* has departed!'

We bent over Jeronimus Tifferch. There was not a drop of blood on his clothes, nor any bruising of the skin, no evidence of a blow or strangling. The tip of his tongue protruding between his yellow teeth was a clear pink, neither black nor swollen. I put both hands flat on his chest and pushed against the ribcage. All was sound. I opened his shirt and found no sign of stabbing or assault. What kind of murder was this? Which closed door had the robber, Death, unlatched to enter Lawyer Tifferch's body?

'Help me turn him over, Koch.'

I forced myself to lay my hands on the stiff, cold corpse again, and together we levered the dead man onto his left flank. His clothes crackled as we shifted him, the skin hard to the touch like wet stone. In times past, doctors of medical science must have felt as I did then, while they practised the forbidden art of anatomical dissection. The place was fitting enough, a secret room in the stinking bowels of the earth. Outside, it was night. Inside, it was night too, but of a far darker hue. Was it possible to imagine doing what we were engaged in beneath the unforgiving light of day? There was something desecrating in the action.

'Do you have a knife, Sergeant Koch?'

'What do you intend to do with it?' Vigilantius objected.

I ignored him, taking the pocket-knife from Koch's hand, and scoring a line from the collar of the dead man's jacket down to the hem. With a rent I tore the stiff cloth away and repeated the cut through his linen shirt. We both stared in amazement at what was revealed.

'Good God!' Koch exclaimed in a whisper.

I replaced my gloves to avoid contamination. The dead man's

upper back was a mass of ancient weals and recent cuts. Had Tifferch been a living-room carpet, one might have thought he had been recently beaten and combed with an iron brush. Slowly, carefully, with the tip of my finger, I rubbed away the crust of congealed blood to reveal the frozen flesh beneath.

'Whipped,' Koch murmured.

'There can be little doubt of that,' I said, my eyes racing over the flayed skin as if it were an ancient scroll written in a mysterious language that I had still to decipher.

'Could this have caused his death, sir?' Koch asked, gesturing uncertainly at the man's tormented flesh.

'He told you himself!' Doctor Vigilantius erupted. 'He spoke of flames. Of fire in his brain. That must be your starting point.'

'I'll decide where I will start!' I snapped back.

'Those wounds are *not* the cause, Herr Stiffeniis,' the necromancer insisted. 'Your stubborn incredulity is the poisoned fruit of dogmatism. Logic is only one of many systems of understanding. Can you not see? There are a hundred paths to Truth.'

'This man has been beaten,' I replied forcefully. 'I know that the beating did not kill him. But it may explain why he was killed. I cannot ignore that fact. The investigation must begin with this.'

Augustus Vigilantius smiled broadly. Facts, apparently, did not diminish him. 'Tifferch himself has just told us a different story. You would not be wise to ignore his words.'

'If they *were* his words,' I countered.

'My information is not the result of physical examination of the body,' he replied stiffly. 'My concern is with the vital energies imprisoned inside the fragile human shell. I am merely the drum, the sounding-board.'

'Hocus-pocus!' I sneered. 'I'm surprised that you haven't produced a rabbit from the dead man's hat!'

The arrow bit home.

'When the moon is at its height,' the necromancer spat back, 'the flux of the human spirit waxes to its fullest power. Then, it may be tapped by any scholar learned in the art of divination. His body was preserved here for that purpose. But the vital moment has passed, it will come no more. You intoxicate yourself with external appearances, Herr Stiffeniis.'

'Help me turn him back, Sergeant Koch,' I said, pointedly ignoring the mountebank.

'You should be grateful to me, Herr Procurator,' Vigilantius insisted at my shoulder. 'Do not disdain the help I can offer you.'

I did not answer, but in the silence which followed, I heard the same disgusting noise that had given me the shivers only minutes before. As I turned, I met the necromancer's mocking eyes. His nostrils twitched open, then closed, sucking at the air with greedy energy. His head was close to mine, and he was sniffing me.

'Are you a dog, sir?' I snarled, standing back. 'This trick may work with the dead. But I am alive.'

He drew further off, but nothing could wipe the smirk from his face.

'Only on the surface, Herr Stiffeniis. Beneath, I smell the death you carry with you everywhere.' He tapped the side of his nose. 'It stinks. There is a dark, stagnant pool where a carcass lies rotting. A dead thing is poisoning your mind and your life. Am I wrong, Herr Procurator? What stalks you in your nightmares? What secrets do those murky waters hide? You are afraid of what might float to the surface at any moment.'

His words resonated and echoed beneath the vault.

'Thank you for your invaluable opinions,' I murmured. 'There's nothing more to keep us here, Koch.'

Vigilantius's eyebrows arched with surprise. 'But I have one thing left to show you. Something even more important may be got from this corpse.'

'I've had my fill of corpses and their keepers,' I snapped.

'But, sir!' he opposed, and there was something two-faced in his way of doing so which contrasted sharply with the honeyed entreaty which followed. 'There is another aspect of my *art* which may be of use to you.'

'Your arts do not interest me,' I sneered.

'As you wish, then, Herr Procurator,' he said with a bow of exaggerated courtesy. 'I cannot force you to stay against your will.'

I strode out of the room with Sergeant Koch hard on my heels, and we retraced the dark and musty passages through which we had come. We climbed the staircase to the surface without exchanging a word, our matching footsteps ringing along the narrow corridors and across the claustrophobic courtyards.

'What an impertinence! Talking to you like that, sir?' said Koch with feeling as we emerged into the central courtyard. 'What do you think he's up to?'

'That's anybody's guess,' I said dismissively. I felt no desire to imagine what Vigilantius might be doing down there with the dead body. A stiff wind had swept away the clouds, and I raised my eyes to gaze at the stars which dotted the dark sky like precious grains of sugar accidentally scattered across a table, drawing the fresh air deep into my lungs. 'Did you have any idea that some other person than Procurator Rhunken was involved in this investigation, Koch?'

The Sergeant did not reply at once.

'No, sir,' he said at last. 'None at all. But can you wonder that the city fathers would appeal to any person that they thought might be able to help them out in their trouble?'

If there was one irrefutable good quality to be found in Koch, it was his sound common sense. I took comfort in it and had to smile.

'The coach is waiting,' he reminded me.

'Let it wait,' I said. 'Take me to Herr Rhunken's office. We have wasted time enough this evening. The investigation must begin in earnest. Sniffing dead men's bones will get us nowhere fast.'

Chapter 6

If the basement cellars of the Fortress of Königsberg had reminded me uncomfortably of the lower reaches of Hades, the upper floors were as confusing as the maze of Crete. Gloomy, ill-lit passages shot off left and right of the main corridor, no feature distinguishing one way from any of the others.

'The building was erected in the twelfth century by the Teutonic Knights, sir, as a stronghold during their long struggle to capture Prussia from the pagans,' Sergeant Koch explained with obvious pride as we trod the labyrinthine corridors. 'It has been enlarged in recent times, of course. Now it is an impregnable fortress. Bonaparte himself could not hope to storm it successfully.'

'How many men are stationed in the garrison?' I asked.

'Three thousand soldiers, as a rule,' the sergeant reported, though we met not a single one that night.

'So, where are they all?'

'General Katowice has sent them out on defensive manoeuvres.'

At that point, we were obliged to pass across a wooden walkway laid over iron gratings which had been let into the stone floor. Rough voices snarled curses beneath our feet as we clattered across this makeshift bridge, while others cried out for food and water. The clinging vapour of sweat and stifled breath rose all around us in drifting clouds, like steam from a kettle on the hob. We might have been crossing a marsh. The air was rank, fetid, the noise little short of demonic – Alighieri's harrowing vision of Hell came unwillingly to my mind. Had the Italian poet, I asked myself, been to visit the prisons of his native Florence in his search for inspiration?

'What's happening down there, Sergeant?'

'Prisoners awaiting transportation,' Koch informed me.

He paused for a moment and inclined his ear towards the grating as a fine female voice rose high above the hubbub, wailing a keening lament. I knew the ballad well enough. It was one that my own grandfather often crooned. He had learnt it, he said, during the Seven Years War, and it was the only song that he ever sang. When he had no voice for singing, he whistled the tune beneath his breath. There was a pining, nostalgic note in the woman's voice which added a new, tragic dimension to the soldier's tale: *The snow will feed me, the snow will sate my thirst, the snow will warm my bones when I am dead.*

'Mezzo-soprano,' said Koch with a smile and a shake of his head.

We moved on, and shortly after, having climbed a newel staircase to the floor above, stopped before a heavy wooden door no different from a hundred others that we had passed along the way.

'Here we are, sir,' Koch informed me. 'This is Herr Rhunken's office.'

I was too stunned to speak. There was no nameplate on the door, no symbol of the authority that Herr Procurator must surely have enjoyed, nothing to indicate that the owner of the capable hands to which the peace and safety of the city had been entrusted was to be found inside that room.

'So close to the squalor down below?'

'Procurator Rhunken was in charge of Section D, sir. If you'd rather be somewhere else . . .'

'I wouldn't think of it,' I replied quickly. 'If this room was good enough for him, I will make the best of it.'

'The felons destined for Siberia are kept in those cages. Herr Rhunken was still working on the list. There are places left on board the ship. Once the ice-pack begins to break up . . .'

There had been a raging debate about deportation over the last three or four years. King Frederick Wilhelm III had decided to rid the nation once and for all of recidivist criminals, despatching them to some remote penal colony for life, under sentence of death if they should ever dare to return. His Majesty's overtures to many distant foreign powers with colonies or unpopulated territories, including the United States and Great Britain, had been rejected, but finally, the Russian Tsar had declared his willingness to take them for a substantial fee. There was still a great deal of lingering controversy among liberal thinkers concerning the Royal decision. Criminals do not occasion much sympathy in Prussia, or anywhere else, but the notion of selling them into Russian slavery had met with much opposition in Enlightened circles. The Noble Savage was still a popular catchphrase, and the French government, and the Americans before them, had declared all men to be equal. Still, on 28 February 1801, an agreement had been signed. Prison governors throughout the land had been ordered to select the most serious and incorrigible offenders in the land for banishment.

'Herr Rhunken chose this room himself, sir,' Koch reported. 'This is where he carried out interrogations. Those cries and screams down below had a certain effect on the person being questioned.'

'I can picture the scene,' I said with an involuntary shudder.

'Herr Procurator was held in great respect for the severity of his methods,' Koch concluded, drawing a large key from his pocket, and opening the door.

He stood aside to let me pass, and I waited in the darkness with growing impatience while he struck a damp flint again and again, eventually managing to light a candle. The apartment was large with a high ceiling and grubby grey walls which needed a fresh coat of paint. A large rust-stained iron stove filled the far corner, though it had not been lit. Narrow window-slits looked out over the prison-gratings on the floor below. Four lanterns had been hung on the walls to provide illumination, and Koch hurried to light them all, but the flames of a dozen more would not have done the trick.

'Two smaller rooms adjoin this one, sir. One is the Procurator's archive. In the other one, there's a cot where Herr Rhunken sometimes took his rest when he was obliged to work late.'

This is where I should have been put up in the first place, I reflected. Not in a quayside inn, comfortable as The Baltic Whaler undoubtedly was. In the austere and inhospitable Fortress of

Königsberg, my newly gained authority as the magistrate-in-charge of the investigation would be clear for all to see. I made myself comfortable at a heavy, elaborately carved desk which stood in splendid isolation in the centre of the room. This piece of furniture alone spoke of power and status. A wine carafe and cut-glass goblet had been provided for refreshment during the hard hours of labour. Now the decanter stood empty, its stopper thick with dust, and a large, dead spider lay imprisoned beneath the upturned wine glass.

'I want to see Procurator Rhunken's reports and files concerning the murders. They should be here somewhere, Koch. The ones you showed me in the coach are incomplete. Ulrich Totz told me he had been interrogated personally by Procurator Rhunken soon after the murder of Jan Konnen. I wish to read what he had to say for himself.'

Koch glanced around uncertainly.

'I've no idea where they are kept, sir. Papers the Procurator gave me are locked up in my own desk. The rest are stored in the archive, I suppose. But my master would allow no one to enter there.'

'You have *my* permission to enter, Sergeant.'

I stood up and walked to the window to cut short any objection he might have made. Wiping the dust away from the filthy pane of glass with the hem of my cloak, I gazed down onto the floor below with its iron gratings and the hum of imprisoned misery. In the darkest corner, one of the guards, the first I had seen, was squatting in the gloom, his white trousers down around his ankles, defecating. The memory of my own pleasant office in Lotingen returned to me in a blinding flash of light and warmth. With its cheerful flower beds and clipped green lawns, mothers and nursemaids brought their charges to play beneath my windows in the spring and summer. The soldier finished his business, hauled up his pantaloons, then adroitly covered the mess with his boot before going on his way.

I turned back to the room once more, but I felt little in the way of comfort. The dismal rumbling of the prisoners down below was inescapable. I hoped to go at least one step further than Rhunken had gone. Despite his vast experience, Herr Procurator Rhunken had been as helpless to stop the murders as any of those who had died directly at the hands of the killer. Could I dare to hope for success where he had failed?

I paced out the length and the breadth of my predecessor's professional tomb, preparing myself for the work that lay ahead, until Sergeant Koch returned some minutes later.

'I found this lot, sir,' he reported, the papers in his hands pitifully few. 'They were stacked on one of the shelves.'

'Nothing more?' I asked incredulously.

Koch shook his head. 'Nothing, Herr Stiffeniis. Except for this letter, which I placed on top. I thought that you would wish to examine it.'

'A letter? From whom?'

'It is addressed to Procurator Rhunken,' he said, placing the papers on the desk. 'I would not presume to open it. You did tell me to bring everything, sir.'

I sat down again, and took up the thin sheaf of papers. Despite the lack of more substantial documentation, I felt a deal of satisfaction. At last, I thought, I am sitting in Herr Rhunken's chair, resting my elbows on his desk. His papers and his reports are in *my* hands. His sergeant is now *my* assistant. For the very first time since arriving in the city, I began to feel at ease. I began to enjoy the sense of power that attached to my new position. It was my first taste of real executive power, and it made a mockery of the shallow civic authority I had been permitted to exercise in Lotingen. I would, I realised, be responsible for the lives of the inhabitants of Königsberg. Whether they lived or died would depend on myself and General Katowice. Or on Napoleon Bonaparte and the Army of the Revolution, should he decide to invade Prussia.

Picking up the first document, I began to glance through the long list of names of condemned men and women who were destined for transportation to the distant borders of Siberia and Manchuria.

Sergeant Koch noisily cleared his throat. 'I could not help noticing, sir,' he said, pointing with his finger, 'that letter is from Berlin.'

I snatched up the missive and looked it over, noting the presence of the same large Hohenzollern seal which had turned my own ordered life upside-down.

'Sir', I read,

In view of the imminent danger which the country faces, vis-à-vis, the upstart, Bonaparte, and the growing risk of French invasion, this spate of murders in the city of Königsberg has been allowed to go unchecked too long. To remedy this deplorable situation, a highly qualified person of the most particular talents has been recommended to Our attention. His task will be to conclude the investigation which you began – with all possible haste. You are commanded to resign your commission and surrender all relevant documents to the magistrate in whom Our hope now resides, and return to your former duties. As of this moment.

The edict was signed with a flourish by King Frederick Wilhelm III, and it was, I noted, a distinctly different flourish from the letter which had been sent to me.

Was Doctor Vigilantius right?

Was my summons to Königsberg a fake?

This letter had been sent from the Imperial capital three days previously, so Rhunken had received it two days before. And that very day, his health had taken a turn for the worse. What I had mistaken for a natural illness – the trembling face, quivering limbs and stench of physical decay – had been provoked by the shock of receiving that letter. Rhunken had suffered a crippling apoplexy as a direct result of the humiliation that the announcement of my arrival had occasioned.

I recalled the shattered wreck of a man I had confronted in his bedchamber only hours before. How that curt letter must have soured his opinion of me! I had no illusions now about how he viewed me. The magistrate appointed to replace him – 'a highly qualified person of the most particular talents' – the man who had ousted him and won the patronage of the King, was not only young, he was also totally inexperienced. And he came from Lotin-

64

gen, a tiny *village* on the extreme border of the western circuit. Rhunken had been expecting a serious rival, a senior magistrate, a member of the secret police, or the Security Council, some gifted doyen from Berlin. What he had got was me!

'The statements of the witnesses should be there, sir,' Koch prompted, his voice intruding on my thoughts.

I shuffled through the miserable bundle of papers and found with ease the declaration that the innkeeper of The Baltic Whaler had made to the police. It was short, and added nothing to what Ulrich Totz had told me in person. Jan Konnen had been drinking in the saloon bar that night, though not excessively. He was in the company of a group of foreign sailors, who may, or may not, have been playing cards for money, but Totz refused to be drawn on that subject. In the past, it seemed, there had been fierce objections to the renewal of his liquor licence after fierce fighting between gamblers over allegations of cheating. The sums involved had been quite substantial, and one man had lost two fingers in a knife fight. 'But no one had been gambling that night,' Totz claimed. I skipped down the page and read:

> *Herr Totz declared that he had made no immediate connection between the man seen in his tavern that night, and the body found further down the quayside the following morning. When first approached by police, he denied all knowledge of the victim.*

No mention was made of the strange goings-on at The Baltic Whaler, which the prying serving-boy had mentioned so particularly to me that very afternoon. Indeed, the name of Morik did not appear in the report at all. Evidently the boy had made no claim to superior knowledge when the opportunity presented itself. I was surprised that he had said nothing to excite the interest of the gendarmes who must have filled the tavern that morning with their conversation about the dead man. Morik had, after all, made such a fuss of my own presence at the inn. He had risked a flogging from his master in doing so. Had he been absent that day? Or might the Totzes have prevented him from speaking? Did they have something to hide? Why else would Morik fail to approach Procurator

Rhunken when he interviewed the landlord and his wife?

The wife . . .

Three lines at the bottom of the affidavit confirmed that Frau Totz had served short beer and hot sausages to Jan Konnen. She declared that she had never seen the man before, and that he had made no particular impression on her. She thought he had left the inn alone at ten o'clock, or thereabouts, though she could not be certain. In her opinion, the murdered man had visited their inn in search of wholesome food and good ale, and for no other reason.

A single sheet of paper, the next in the sheaf, drew a verbal portrait of the first victim. The information, such as it was, could have been chiselled with ease onto his tombstone. Jan Konnen, blacksmith, fifty-one years old, lived alone. He had never wed, and had no known living relatives. A taciturn and secretive man, Konnen was a complete enigma even to his closest neighbours. On this account, Rhunken had ordered the police to make extensive enquiries into his private life, but nothing untoward had been discovered. Konnen had no debts, no friends, he did not mix with women of low repute, nor belong to a political faction. He held no known grudge against any man, had never committed a crime, never been arrested. To all appearances, he was a blameless innocent who had been in the wrong place at the wrong time, and he had paid with his life for that mistake. At the bottom of the page, Rhunken had written a note: 'Enquiries made regarding possibility that victim might have had foreign political connections – no evidence found.' The last words Procurator Rhunken had written made me gasp: 'victim – category C – protocol 2779 – June 1800, I. M. O., Berlin'.

Like any other young magistrate just setting out on his career in the very first year of a new century, so soon after the revolution in France, and the rise of Napoleon, I had read that particular protocol. It warned of the possible infiltration of spies and revolutionaries who aimed to undermine the stability of the Nation and introduce Republicanism. Rhunken appeared to have convinced himself that the investigation should proceed in that direction, and he had given Konnen a low, but significant grading, as a potential danger.

I turned the page in search of more, but the following sheet referred to the case of Paula-Anne Brunner, second victim of the murderer. A statement taken from her husband related that his 'poor missis' had done more or less the same thing the day she was murdered as she always did, which amounted to feeding her hens, collecting their eggs, and selling them to her neighbours and to one or two shops in town. 'The only new thing she did,' the bereaved spouse complained, 'she went and got herself killed!' Frau Brunner was a sociable woman who went to the Pietist Temple twice a day, three times on a Sunday. She was renowned for honesty, moral rectitude and good works, and she was immensely popular with all the neighbours. She had no known enemies. Indeed, it was believed that she had never argued with any single person in her entire life. Clearly, Rhunken had suspected the husband of the crime. Heinz-Carl Brunner had been held in prison for two days and subjected to 'severe interrogation'. In short, they had beaten him until he screamed for mercy, then let him go when he said nothing incriminating. At the exact time of the murder, as several rival farmers had noted, Brunner had been working in his field with two of his helpers, and this alibi could not be shaken. So, *he* was in the clear. Once again, Rhunken had added a note which seemed to sum up the direction which his enquiry was taking: 'No political ties or radical affiliations reported or found. Prot. 2779?'

I suppose I must have let out a groan.

'Is everything all right, Herr Stiffeniis?' Koch enquired.

'Was Procurator Rhunken collaborating with any other magistrate? I mean, might someone else have been helping him to collect evidence or take statements from these witnesses?'

'Oh no, sir,' Koch replied at once. 'Herr Procurator always worked by himself. I know that for a fact. He trusted no one.'

I nodded and turned my attention to the next sheet of paper, a report concerning the third murder in the series. As I read the name of the victim, a jolt of electricity raced through my veins. *Johann Gottfried Haase?* How I cursed myself for my ineptitude! While travelling towards Königsberg in the coach that day, I had purposely skipped the name of the most important man to die at the

67

hand of the assassin. Johann Gottfried Haase was a scholar of wide international fame, and a frequently published author. Some years before, I had read a pamphlet he had written. A Professor of Oriental Languages and Theology at the University of Königsberg, Haase had caused a sensation when he asserted that the Garden of Eden was by no means fictional. Adam and Eve had, indeed, been tempted by the Serpent, the scholar claimed, more or less on the very spot where we were standing. According to Haase, the city of Königsberg had been built on the original site of the Biblical garden. Who would dare to kill such an eminent man?

Looking down the page, eager for details, I had to laugh. Indeed, I laughed out loud, while Sergeant Koch regarded me with an expression of serious concern.

'What an idiot I've been!' I said.

'Sir?'

The victim's name was Johann Gottfried Haase, but he was not the person I had been thinking of. It was a simple case of two men sharing exactly the same name! The Johann Gottfried Hasse who had been murdered was a destitute halfwit. He eked out a miserable existence begging crumbs of stale bread and cake from the city bakeries, and asking for money on the streets from casual passers-by. Everyone in the city knew him by sight, but no one knew him well. Procurator Rhunken remarked that no written record had been found regarding his birth – he was not so much as related to the scholar. No one could say whether he had ever been to school, passed a night in a poorhouse, a month in an orphanage, or a year in jail, though enquiries had been made by the police on all of those questions. Herr Haase was, to all effects, an utter nobody. 'NOT OPENLY POLITICAL', Rhunken had noted. He had not even made the obvious connection with the unknown victim's eminent namesake. Still, the perplexing question that I had asked myself before returned to my mind, and even more forcibly this time. Why kill such a poor and apparently useless creature? An Oriental linguist-theologian might provoke animosity in some quarters, but a penniless beggar? Again, the protocol number '2779' appeared at the foot of the page.

It was a recurrent theme. I could only ask myself what had prompted Procurator Rhunken to decide that the murders were politically motivated. The only common factor that I could find was the absence of anything even remotely political in the victims' lives. Had their apparent indifference to politics seemed to him to be a blind? He had made a note to the effect that Konnen might be a secret agent. Did he believe the same of the others, too? And if so, which foreign power did he suspect them of spying for? Perplexed in my own mind, I turned slowly to the next sheet of paper.

Though not in sequential order, I found it to be the deposition of the midwife who had discovered the body of Jan Konnen. In all that I had read before, this witness had been referred to only in terms of her trade and but never by name, which was very odd. I glanced quickly through the information. Again, no name was given. Early that morning, this mysterious midwife declared, while on her way to minister to a fisherman's wife who lived on the quayside, she came across the body of a man who appeared to have slumped against a wall. The only detail which added to the scant account that I had read in the coach was of some importance. 'I knew that there was evil in it,' she declared. 'Satan used his claws.'

I paused. Sergeant Koch had used the same expression when first he told me of the crimes, but what exactly was *she* referring to? This superstitious woman had seen the dead body with her own eyes. Why use those particular words to describe what she had observed? The Devil's name, I realised, was never far away in Königsberg. I had heard Satan invoked already with great familiarity by Koch, by the maid of Herr Rhunken, by Doctor Vigilantius, and by the soldiers remaining in the Fortress. Was it nothing more than a superficial reflection of the fierce religious sectarianism for which the city was renowned throughout Prussia? The Pietists were a dominating influence in Königsberg; the University was packed with members of the sect. Their reading of the Bible led the Pietists to believe that eternal salvation could only be achieved by personally wrestling with the Devil and his temptations. They had even invented a specific term for it. *Busskampf*, they preached, was a necessary battle that every true believer must fight and win if he hoped to enter the kingdom of Heaven.

I shook my head, and read on to the end. Lublinsky and Kopka, the two officers who had countersigned the woman's statement and based their own report on it, had not pressed her for precise details. Indeed, they had not asked her much at all. Not even her name! Then again, neither had that most excellent magistrate, my predecessor, Procurator Rhunken . . .

'Your master kept few notes, Koch,' I said, as I replaced the sheet.

'True, sir, very true. Kept it all in his head, he did.'

I made no comment, reflecting only that Procurator Rhunken's way of going about the investigation left much to be desired. A degree of professional jealousy might explain his determination to tell me nothing more at our interview than the scant information which his papers contained, but it did not speak well for him, and it made my task all the more difficult.

Finally, there was a brief note about the latest victim, Jeronimus Tifferch, the notary, whose body I had examined in the cellar not an hour before. In his case there was a notable and remarkable difference. Regarding his personal history and habits, there was absolutely nothing. Merely a statement of his death. No other word had been consigned to paper. No person had been questioned, no detailed examination had been made of the corpse. So far as I could tell, no doctor had even been called to verify that he was actually dead, nor to sign a certificate to that effect. As a result, no possible cause of death had been hazarded. As in the notes I had read in the coach the day before – I was getting used to the omission by now – no mention was made of the nature of the weapon which might have been used to kill him, nor of the sort of wound it had inflicted. Indeed, the normal process of legal investigation seemed to have been suspended in Tifferch's case. In anticipation of my coming, perhaps?

There was a knock at the door. Without lifting my head from my work, I heard Koch murmuring with someone on the threshold.

Above all, I reasoned, there was one glaring omission in all that

I had read so far. The name of the 'eminent person' who had called Vigilantius and myself to investigate the string of murders in the city. I could find no reference to it in what Rhunken had chosen to record. Did he not realise that some rival authority was conducting a parallel investigation?

'Herr Stiffeniis, sir?'

Koch's voice interrupted my considerations. I looked up and found him standing stiffly in front of the desk, his linen handkerchief close to his mouth, his glaring eyes red and puffy.

'What is it, Koch?'

'His Excellency, Herr Procurator Rhunken, sir. A guard just brought the news. My master is dead.'

I have rarely seen such naked sorrow on a human face. Instinctively, I looked down at the pile of papers scattered on the desk.

'When will the funeral take place?' I asked.

'He's been entombed already, sir,' he said, slowly passing a hand over his eyes. 'An hour ago, apparently.'

'But that's impossible!' I protested. 'Herr Rhunken was an authority. The city will want to pay its tribute to . . .'

'It was his final wish, sir. He wanted no one present at his burial.'

I looked away to the farthest, darkest corner of the room. Koch had been greatly attached to the magistrate who had died. Still, he could hardly reproach me for Rhunken's death. And yet, I sensed a hidden vein of condemnation in his voice. I could not help myself, a feeling of discomfort crept up on me. Half an hour before I had been congratulating myself on the fact that I was sitting at Herr Rhunken's desk, that his assistant was standing stiffly to attention in front of me, that the Procurator's personal archives were at my complete disposal, that his own sparse accounts of his investigative methods were in my hands to be rifled through, criticised and challenged. But now, suddenly, he was dead.

In some indefinable manner, I felt as if I had been the cause.

Chapter 7

It was past ten o'clock when Sergeant Koch left me at The Baltic Whaler that night. The tavern was busy when I entered, so I sat myself down at a table in the quietest corner, that is, the one furthest removed from the fire, to pen a note to my wife before calling for my dinner. But what should have been a simple task proved far harder than I had anticipated. What should I tell Helena about what was happening in Königsberg? What could I say of the investigation that could reassure her, and what, instead, was better kept to myself? I mused for a moment, took up the quill once more, dipped it in the inkpot and went on:

Believe me, my love, when I tell you that I am <u>not</u> doing this in the vain hope of winning back my father's affection. What has happened will never – ever – be erased from his mind, no matter what I try to do, or fail to do. I have lived under that shadow far too long, and have forced you to share the seclusion of Lotingen with me. It is time to forge a better life – for ourselves, and for our little ones. Lotingen has been a safe haven, but now the storm is over. I refuse to hide away any longer. This investigation opens a doorway . . .

I stopped, uncertain how to go on. I had no desire to tell my wife of the difficulties that I had been obliged to face that day, nor of the horrors that I had seen. What could she do to help me? I swirled the point of the duck-quill in the ink, and turned my thoughts to brighter matters.

Herr Koch and I arrived safe and well in Königsberg this after-

*noon. I am writing from my lodging near the port. The air is
fresh here, I can tell you! But my bedroom is warm, clean and
welcoming. It is almost a home from home, indeed . . .*

'Sir?' a honey-sweet voice recalled me to my immediate surroundings. A buxom woman in her mid-forties with a moonlike
face and large, bright, green eyes stood before me, holding an
empty tray in what seemed to me to be a parody of servitude.

'I am Gerta Totz, sir,' she announced with a hideous, mincing
smile, 'wife of the landlord. Are you ready for your dinner? Would
you care to try something in particular?'

'Anything at all will do,' I said, quickly folding up the letter to
my wife. I had not eaten since my arrival in Königsberg six hours
before, and the smell of fine cooking which filled the room was suf-
ficiently enticing to whet my appetite.

'I'll bring the best we have, then,' she said, bobbing and removing herself in the direction of the kitchen. As she moved away, I
noticed that she stopped to say a quiet word to three prosperous-
looking gentlemen who were sitting in a tight huddle at a table
quite near to my own.

Something in her manner of addressing them caught my attention, and I followed her progress across the room, wondering
whether she would be equally deferential to all the other customers
in the place, but she disappeared into the kitchen without saying a
single word to anyone. My interest awakened, I looked around at
the assembled company. Beyond those gentlemen with whom Frau
Totz had just spoken, closest to the fire, sat the same plump, dark-
skinned man wearing the red fez and bright oriental naval garb
that I had noticed in the afternoon. He sat peering intently into the
darting flames, as if to evoke the warmer lands of his home. In the
far corner of the room, a knot of fishermen were drinking strong
ale and singing sea shanties. Other less notable customers were
scattered around the room in groups of two or three. A couple of
women with brightly painted lips and rouged faces sat with a
group of foreign navy officials whose uniforms I could not place.
The men were drinking and playing cards, the women watching

the movement of money around the table with sparkling eyes and animated smiles. There could be little doubt where their interest lay, nor of the means they would employ to procure it. In short, it was the sort of scene one might find anywhere along the Baltic seaboard on a cold, winter night, and I soon grew bored of looking.

I had just unfolded my letter again and primed my pen, when a shadow fell over the page. Surprised at such remarkable alacrity, I glanced up, expecting to find Frau Totz with my dinner. Instead, Morik, the serving-boy, was standing over me, his hands firmly clasped behind his back like a common footsoldier waiting to address a confidence to a superior officer.

'What can I do for you?' I asked him.

'Those men at the next table,' the youngster hissed out of the side of his mouth. Leaning closer, eyes wide and staring, he added, 'They meet in the cellar at dead of night, sir. Pretend to order something, or they'll catch on.'

I attempted to look past him, but the boy was standing hard up against my table, blocking out the prospect. 'Now, listen here, my lad,' I began sternly.

'Please, sir!' he whispered urgently. 'Do it loud, or my goose'll be cooked.'

I sat back, perplexed. Then, in a voice that was calculated to wake the dead, I announced to the inn at large: 'Bring me another quill, boy. And be quick about it! The point of this one's ruined, I am unable to finish my letter.'

Morik leapt to attention.

'Right away, sir,' he shouted.

He was gone in a flash.

I looked more attentively at the three men seated close by. Each one smoking a long clay pipe and quaffing ale from an ample *stein*, they were the picture of respectability.

The landlady appeared again from the kitchen, and came bustling across to my table, though there was still no sign of my dinner arriving.

'Is everything in order, Herr Stiffeniis?' she enquired, smiling still. 'Has our Morik been bothering you?'

'I needed a quill,' I said. 'The boy is seeing to it for me.'

'Oh, you should have asked *me*, sir,' she said, wiping the back of her hand across her face. I got the impression that she seemed relieved by what I had just told her. 'He is such a nuisance, that lad! Can't be trusted to do a thing! Be sure and tell me if he gets up to any mischief, won't you, sir?'

'I most certainly will,' I assured her.

'I'll be a-getting back to the kitchen, then,' Frau Totz announced, trotting off and nodding silently to the men at the next table as she went.

I put aside my letter, my attention now engaged by the three strangers, my curiosity heightened by this odd exchange with the landlady. Could Morik be telling the truth? There was something decidedly staid and measured in the behaviour of the three guests that was out of place in a quayside tavern. They did not joke, or laugh, and they seemed to speak to each other in unnecessarily hushed tones.

On impulse, I rose from the table and moved towards the blazing fire, as if to warm my hands. As I passed close by their table, I caught a phrase in French. Was that what had tickled the serving-boy's fancy, the fact that those men spoke the language of Napoleon Bonaparte?

'Your quills, sir!' Morik called loudly from my table, holding them up for me and everyone else in the room to see. I returned to the table, recalling what both the landlady and her husband had said of the lad's untrustworthy nature.

'I've sharpened them to your satisfaction I hope, sir?' he said out loud. In a whisper he added: 'Those men are French. They arrived three days ago.'

'So? What of it?' I said quietly, taking up one of the quills and trying the point against the paper, playing my part in the charade.

Morik raised his voice again. 'Right, sir! A sharp knife in case they split again.'

But he made no move to leave me in peace as the landlady passed by, taking four more pints of frothing ale to the fishermen who were merrymaking in the far corner. As soon as she had gone, Morik lowered his voice again. 'Stop them, sir! Before they strike again.'

75

I stared hard at the boy. He stood looking around the room, a stiff smile engraved on his lips. I could see quite clearly that he was afraid.

'Stop *who*?' I asked.

'Those Frenchmen, sir! Two nights ago that man was killed. They've been here before, they'll murder again.'

'Why should they wish to kill anybody?' I asked quietly, holding a pen up to the light and examining the point, playing my part with more care now.

'Let *me* try, sir,' Morik said aloud, grabbing the pen from my hand and a scrap of paper from the pile I had placed on the table. He wrote something, his hand shaking as he did so, then glanced up to gauge my reaction.

'Napoleon intends to invade Prussia,' I read.

Before I could speak, he picked up the paper, rolled it into a tight ball, strode across to the fire and thrust it deep into the flames. He did not return to my table. Instead, Frau Totz appeared at my side. Morik must have seen her coming.

'Here's your dinner, sir,' she said, laying a large, full plate on the table. 'I hope I have not made you wait too long?'

Her sharp eyes followed Morik as he moved away from the fire and through a door that led into the kitchen.

'Did Morik serve you as he ought?' she asked.

'He seems a most accommodating fellow.'

'He always makes a fuss of new guests,' she explained. 'But he's far too nosy for his own good, that lad! Drive my poor sister to her grave, he will. He's all she's got. Working here in the inn, with all these sailors passing through, has turned his silly head. He's interested in everybody's business but his own. Enjoy your meal, sir.'

Was that the true explanation of the boy's behaviour? The coincidental fact that the first victim of the unidentified murderer had spent his last night on earth in the bar of The Baltic Whaler might be at the root of the boy's gossip. But then another aspect of the situation struck me forcibly. If the mysterious person who had had me called to Königsberg had been behind all that had happened so far, had he also decided that I should be lodged at The

Baltic Whaler? Did he suspect that something illegal was going on there? And if so, what was I supposed to do about it?

I determined to do two things. I would speak privately to Morik about his absurd accusations. Then, I would question Innkeeper Totz more closely with regard to the statement he had made to Procurator Rhunken. But first of all, I had my empty stomach to care for. I took up my fork and spoon and set to with a will, dining on a rich vegetable broth, roasted chicken and an abundant helping of those tiny turnips that are stored under ice through the winter. The wine was white, a fruity vintage imported from the Nahr region, and it was surprisingly good.

As I ate my dinner, however, I did not lose sight of the three men who had aroused Morik's suspicions. One of them in particular caught my attention. He was taller, older, more heavily built than his companions. Detached and watchful, seemingly aloof from the general conversation, he appeared to be more alert than the other two concerning what was going on in the inn. Every now and then, he would lower his head and say a quiet word to them in confidence.

French spies conspiring against Prussia? Murdering innocent people in the streets? It took an incredibly wild stretch of the imagination to credit what Morik had said of them. What military objective could such a devilish strategy serve? The victims were men and women of no civic importance. Their deaths would not affect the city and its defences, except, perhaps, by spreading panic. But would the spread of panic help Bonaparte invade Prussia if it was happening in Königsberg alone?

I did not realise until too late that the three foreign gentlemen were looking in my direction. While I had been mentally analysing them, they had been paying more careful physical attention to me. Suddenly, the tallest one – the leader, as I described him in my own mind – rose from his seat and came across to my table.

'Good evening, sir,' he began with a polite bow. 'My name is Guntar Stoltzen. I hope I'm not disturbing you?'

'Not at all. I have finished my meal, Herr Stoltzen,' I said, sitting back in my chair and looking up at him. 'What can I do for you, sir?'

'My friends and I are jewellers,' he began, nodding over his shoulder in the direction of his companions. 'The serving-boy told us yesterday that there have been a number of murders in the city, sir. He said that you are here to investigate them.'

So, Morik had been at work with them as well.

'Forgive me, sir,' he continued, 'I would not have you believe that I am more interested in the affairs of other men than of my own, but we are concerned for our safety. We've still a long way to go and . . . well, you understand, of course. We're carrying precious gems to Tallinn. What we heard alarmed us. Being robbed is one thing. Being robbed *and* murdered is quite another!'

I sipped a little wine and gathered my thoughts. Clearly, this Morik was a scandalmonger. He had frightened these innocent travellers, and awakened my own suspicions with ease. Frau Totz was right about him. The boy was definitely a troublemaker.

'You are French, are you not?' I asked.

'German, sir, my companions are French. We have travelled through East Prussia many times before and nothing unpleasant has ever befallen us. But this news is alarming. If these murders were committed by robbers, we might easily be in danger. Do you not agree?'

'Where did you hear that these crimes had been committed by thieves?' I enquired, expecting Morik's name to be raised again.

'What other reason could there be for killing innocent people?'

'Why kill, if not for gain? Is that what you mean, sir?'

Herr Stoltzen smiled and nodded his head.

'Would you be happier to believe that the murders had been committed for political reasons?' I probed.

'Politics?' He frowned, evidently surprised by the suggestion. 'Is that why these people have been murdered, sir?'

I shook my head. 'You have formed one opinion, I offer an alternative which would guarantee the safety of you, your companions, and the valuables you are carrying.'

'A political plot?' he mused. 'For what purpose, sir?'

I shrugged my shoulders and put a piece of bread in my mouth, chewing slowly for some moments before I replied.

'Imagine that someone wished, for reasons still to be determined, to spread terror here in Königsberg. A spate of apparently random murders would do the trick, don't you think?'

'If your investigation points that way, I wish you all success. But now, sir, I will leave you to digest your meal in peace,' he said with a warm smile and a bright twinkle in his eye, as if meaning to return to his own table.

'A political coup does not worry you, then?' I said, unwilling to end the conversation.

He stared at me intently. 'Of course it does, sir, but such an explanation would mean that commercial travellers like myself and my friends could go about our business undeterred. One government is very much like another where trade is concerned.'

'I am glad if I have set your mind at rest,' I replied with a smile.

Herr Stoltzen bowed his head and smiled back. 'My friends and I will toast your good health. With your permission, sir?'

He clicked his heels lightly, returned to his companions and spoke to them quietly. All raised their beer mugs and smiled at me convivially.

I raised my glass to return the courtesy.

I have just interrogated my first suspect, I thought.

I drank my wine to the lees. Then, wishing good night to the three men with a nod of my head, I rose from the table and retired upstairs to my bedroom. The fire had been banked up for the night, a copper jug of water was warming on the hearth. Despite feeling deathly tired, I sat down at the desk to finish the letter to my wife.

Reading over what I have written thus far, my dear, I find that I have failed to report the progress of my investigations. I may have found a trail to follow, and hope that I will not be staying very much longer here in Königsberg. And so, my darling wife, with this good news I wish you a fond farewell.

I added a few tender words of love for the children, then sealed the envelope and set it to one side. Leaving the candle on the table by the window while I put on my night-clothes, I glanced casually out of the window to see if it were still snowing. The sky was a mass of heavy swirling clouds, the moon barely visible. I was just about to turn away and take myself to bed, when a sudden movement in a window on the far side of the courtyard caught my eye. Peering through the misty glass, I observed a dark figure in the far room holding a hooded candle, his head turned to one side as if he were eavesdropping. In the flickering candlelight, the face was grotesque, the eyes two dark, gaping, black holes, the forehead and nose monstrously distorted by the shadows. The figure placed the candleholder on the window ledge, and in that moment, I recognised him. It was Morik.

What was the boy playing at?

He looked up and waved his hand. The lad knew the room in which I was lodging and he appeared to be trying to attract my attention. My thoughts flew to the three travelling merchants. Was he daring to spy on them? The serving-boy truly was a pest. I decided that I had better speak to him about his behaviour the very next morning. Sooner or later, the boy was going to get himself into serious trouble.

I snapped the curtains shut and blotted his figure out, determined to have no more to do with Morik and his foolishness. It had been a long, hard day and I was thoroughly exhausted. Quickly, I washed my face and hands, then I retired to my bed. The crispness of the fresh linen sheets, their heady perfume of blubber soap and starched cleanliness, induced a strong sense of well-being as I nestled down beneath the heavy eiderdown coverlet. Soon, I knew, I would be sound asleep. But in those delicious moments before gentle Morpheus had fully narcotised my senses, I suddenly tensed with fright. Had I dreamt it, or had I actually seen a moving shadow lurking at Morik's back? A pale apparition glimpsed so fleetingly that my conscious mind had not fully registered it?

I sat up with a start, jumped out of bed, and darted over to the window. Throwing back the curtains, I looked out across the yard. All was dark on the other side of the court. There was nothing left to see.

No candle. No Morik. No sign of man, or ghost.

Chapter 8

The first pallid intimation of the dawn caressed the curtains around my bed, but I had been wide-eyed and awake for an hour already. The ritual nightmare had brought me choking from my sleep, hair plastered to my forehead, limbs rigid, my heart in my mouth. And yet, somehow, the frightful dream had been less painful, less vivid in its gruesomeness than usual. The rock had barely penetrated his skull. The grass had not been red with blood. His glassy eyes had seemed to be less fixed, less accusing than they had been on previous occasions. For the first time, in those dreams that had plagued my sleep for seven years, I had not been frozen with fright. I had *moved*. I had tried to reach him, skipping down from the towering height of the rock, holding his salvation clasped in my hand. I could not be blamed for neglect this time. I had taken the vial from my pocket, the glass cold against my fingers, a flash of sunlight making the contents gleam and glisten like melted amber . . .

I dismissed the memory as I jumped up from my bed, shivering in the cold as I agitated the grey embers of the fire, adding wood shavings and some larger chips of wood which Morik had left behind for that purpose the previous evening. The first flame crackled into life, and I swung the copper pot over the fire to reheat the water I had used to wash myself the night before. Crossing over to the window, I looked out on the day. There had been more snow during the night, but the pearl-grey sky was free of further threatening clouds. A freezing day to come, I thought, noting the extraordinary length of the icicles that dangled from the guttering of the roof above my room. The window on the far side of the yard where I had seen Morik the night before was dark, reflecting only the gleam from my candle. What had the boy been doing there? Had somebody been watching him, an accomplice, perhaps, or had I imagined the entire scene?

I wrapped the top coverlet from the bed around my shoulders, and sat down at the desk to make a list of all the things I would need to do that day. The name of Lawyer Tifferch was at the top. He had been dead three days already, so the trail was already growing cold. Today my work would start in earnest. I had wasted time enough with the necromancer, Vigilantius, the night before. I had not been long at my task, however, when I heard someone clumping about in the hall outside my door.

'Morik!' I thought, rising quickly and striding to the door, intent on catching the little sneak off his guard. The boy was spying again. On me, this time.

With a sudden wrench, I threw the door wide open.

Frau Totz was on her knees in the hallway, staring hard where the keyhole had been but a moment before. She fell backwards onto her large bottom, her legs seesawed into the air, and she let out a yelp of surprise. A second later, raising herself to her normal height again as if nothing untoward had happened, she fixed me with that mincing smile she habitually wore. It appeared to have been painted on her face.

'Good morning, Herr Procurator,' she chimed brightly. 'I hope I haven't disturbed you? I thought I saw a glimmer of light beneath your door, and did not know whether to knock. I was wondering if you would care for something special for your breakfast.'

'I told you last night what I want, Frau Totz,' I answered sharply. 'Bread, honey, hot tea.'

That smile did not fade or flicker, despite my rudeness. It was fixed, immovable, dreadful in its intensity, especially so early in the morning.

'We have fresh cheese and some choice cuts of ham in the cold-room,' she went on smoothly. 'I was wondering whether you might like to try . . .'

'Another time,' I said, cutting her insistence short. The landlady had been spying on me. Morik had been spying on the other guests the night before. And someone else had been spying on Morik. Was spying a contagious disease in the Totz household? I could not suppress a note of sarcasm when I added, 'Your great concern for my well-being is most reassuring, ma'am. Send Morik up at once, if you please.'

Her head was covered with a linen bonnet a size too small from which her reddish-brown curls seemed stiffly intent on fighting their way out. The bonnet drooped towards her right shoulder and that grotesque smile slowly faded away until it was a poor, pale shadow of its former self.

'Morik?' she murmured. 'That boy should have been busy down in the kitchen an hour since, but I haven't heard a peep out of him. I thought that he might have come up here to wake you, sir.'

'Morik, here?' Was that her true motive for peeping through the keyhole? I hesitated, wondering what sort of a vile bawdy-house I had been lodged in. 'His bedroom stands on the far side of the courtyard from mine, does it not?'

A frown flitted across her brow. 'Oh no, sir, no,' she said. 'Morik sleeps down in the kitchen behind the stove.' She let out a sigh. 'I'd better go and see what's got into him. With your permission . . .'

'Who *is* staying in that room over the way, then?'

'That room, sir?' she said with a puzzled expression, glancing across the yard. 'No one, sir. It's been vacant since two business gentlemen from Hanover left last Thursday.'

'But I saw someone in there last night. I'd have sworn that it was Morik.'

'You must be mistaken, sir,' she replied quickly, and the smile reappeared like a carnival mask, but it was tense and rigid, ever more patently false. 'If you'll excuse me, I'm needed downstairs in the kitchen.'

'When you find him, Frau Totz, send Morik along with my breakfast, will you?'

The woman's lips pursed like those of an insolent child suppressing a remark for which she knew she must be scolded. Whatever she might have been intending to say, however, she simply said: 'As you wish, Herr Stiffeniis.'

I returned to my desk and added a few more items to the list of things I had to do, then I washed and shaved with care, dressed myself in a clean linen shirt and my best brown suit and took out my periwig from its travelling-box. Lotte had remembered to pack it for me, despite the fret of my departure. I disliked wearing the wig – it made my scalp hot and itchy – and generally I avoided doing so, but in the present circumstances I was not a private citizen: the people of Königsberg would expect formality of the man who had been entrusted with the salvation of the city. That mass of silver curls would, I hoped, lend an air of authority to my person which my youth might seem to deny. It would also, I reflected, protect my ears from the cold . . .

There was a knock at the door, and Frau Totz appeared again, carrying my breakfast on a tray.

'He's nowhere to be seen, sir,' she announced grimly. This time she did not attempt to smile. Her green eyes glanced away from mine and darted swiftly around the room, almost as if she thought the boy might be playing hide-and-seek, almost as if *I* were a party to the game.

'Do you think he's hiding under my bed?' I asked her.

'Oh, no, sir. What an idea!'

Nevertheless, she did glance towards the four-poster again. 'He ought to be down in the kitchen getting breakfast ready,' she murmured slowly.

'He has probably gone out on an errand,' I said to put an end to the subject. 'Now, can I have my breakfast?'

Frau Totz blushed bright red and cried: 'Oh, dearie me! Forgive me, sir!'

I took the tray from her hands and looked her squarely in the eye. Tiny beads of sweat had begun to break out on her forehead along the line of her ginger hair.

'What, precisely, are you afraid of, Frau Totz?' I asked.

'Well, sir, I'm not . . . not afraid exactly,' she muttered uncertainly. 'But Morik's such a hothead. His noddle's full of strange ideas.'

I found her manner of speaking allusive and annoying at the same time.

'Strange ideas about *what*, Frau Totz?'

'I did tell you, sir. An' I tried to warn you last night, too. He invents things.' She fixed her eyes on her meaty hands; they seemed to be engaged in a nervous tug-of-war over which she had no control. 'Always up to no good, that lad,' she went on. 'My Ulrich was saying just last night that my nephew's been acting odd since you arrived, sir. Asking questions about who you are, why you're here, that sort of thing. Morik seems to think that if you're staying here, instead of in town, it's because you are watching the inn.'

She looked nervously around the room again, then back at me, and I had the distinct impression that my arrival at The Baltic Whaler had whetted the curiosity not merely of Morik the serving-boy.

'There is no reason for you to worry, Frau Totz,' I said, intent on being rid of her. 'Your house is far more comfortable than the Fortress. Now, if you'd be so kind, I would like to enjoy your excellent breakfast while the tea is still hot.'

She jumped as if she had been jabbed from behind with a sharp needle. 'Oh, pardon me, sir!' she exclaimed. 'Wasting your time like this when you have more important things to do! If you need anything, just ring the bell. You're right about Morik, sir. He'll be back in his own good time, no doubt.'

She bowed herself out as if I were the King. Ten minutes later, my breakfast done, my toilet completed, I went down to the lounge where Amadeus Koch was standing before the fire.

'Good morning, Koch,' I said with energy. 'I am glad to see you.'

And indeed I was. I could not have imagined the day before that I would be so happy to see his severe, pale face again.

Koch bowed deferentially. 'I hope you slept well, sir? I delivered your note to Herr Jachmann's house half an hour ago,' he reported at once.

'Did he send a written reply?'

'No, sir.'

I was surprised.

'A message by word of mouth?'

'Nothing, sir. I'd have told you if he had. His servant took the note, then closed the door. I waited five minutes or more, but without result.'

'Of course, I . . . Thank you, Sergeant.'

I stared at the fire and asked myself what this silence on Jachmann's part might signify. I had stated my intention to call at his home at twelve o' the clock that morning. Was I to conclude that the absence of any message implied consent?

'The coach is waiting,' said Koch, breaking in on my thoughts. 'D'you wish to go to the Fortress, sir?'

'Is Kliesterstrasse far from here?' I asked.

Koch looked at me curiously. 'A mile, sir, no more. It's in the business part of town.'

'The weather is better this morning, is it not?'

'It ain't snowing, if that's what you mean, sir.'

'Let's go on foot then, Koch. A walk will do us both good, and I need to learn my way about town,' I said.

Frau Totz was hovering near the kitchen door, her eyes fixed on me with an intensity that I could not fathom.

'I'm sure that Morik will turn up soon,' I called across the room.

The rigid smile materialised once more like the horrid grimace on the face of an Etruscan figurine. 'He certainly will, Herr Stiffeniis,' she replied, and instantly bowed her head. For a moment, I thought that she was about to cry. But with a shrug, she turned and disappeared through the door to the kitchen.

Out in the street, we turned away from the ice-bound port and set off up the long rise of Königstrasse hill, Sergeant Koch walking in dutiful silence at my side. Shops here and there on either side of the thoroughfare were beginning to open their shutters for the day's business, though there was no one in the street apart from ourselves, and a boy with ringlets and a white skullcap whom we met halfway up the hill. He was kneeling with a bucket and cloth, attempting to scrape the paint off a wall, where some night-creeper had daubed the Star of David and a slogan in large letters using whitewash: *Blame the sons of Israel!*

I looked away, not daring to think what might happen if bigoted hotheads chose to take that accusation seriously, as had happened in Bremen three years before. Twenty-seven Jews had lost their lives there, and thousands more had been forced to flee.

'Since these murders began, sir,' Koch confided, 'there's been no lack of threats against the Hebrews. Hostile pastors openly blame the Jews for murdering Our Saviour. The killing of a churchgoer in Königsberg might provoke a bloodbath . . .'

He fell silent as we approached a tobacco shop.

The owner, a tall, thin man wearing a soiled brown apron and black skullcap, was idling against the door-post, smoking what must have been his first pipe of the morning, studying us attentively, nodding in an inviting sort of manner. He let out an audible growl of contempt as we walked on past his emporium without so much as stopping. Glancing in at the dusty window, the sort of trade that he attracted was evident. Twists of dusty, rough, black tobacco-shag dangled from hooks; short cob-pipes, and even shorter ones of white clay, yellow with age, lay scattered in a heap beside a pile of mouldy cheese roundels. Situated so close to the port, I chose to speculate, the sort of customer who frequented the area was rough and ready, neither choosy nor particularly extravagant in his tastes. They would be sailors for the most part, or soldiers from the garrison, men in search of cheap, strong smoke and the sort of pipe that would suffer any number of hard knocks.

Jackets made of stiff canvas hung suspended on rails outside the next shop. They were ugly garments stained with sea-salt and clearly second-hand. Koch's pea-coat, I noted, was of heavy grey wool, and it was almost new, while my own black mantle of imported English wool – fashioned by Helena on the occasion of an invitation two months earlier to a Christmas dinner at the home of Baron von Stiwalski, whose estate of Süchingern was less than a mile from Lotingen – was a trifle light for the season, perhaps, but no one could possibly doubt the quality of the material. Even so, the owner came running out onto the pavement, bowing and inviting us to step inside and try on waterproofs 'guaranteed to resist the rigour of the very coldest seas,' as he proclaimed with a certain pomp. We might have been the only customers he had seen in a month or more.

I smiled, and said: 'Thank you, no.'

'Half-price to you, sirs!' the man called after us.

'Business does not seem to be booming,' I said to Sergeant Koch, as we continued on our way, our progress continually monitored by the shopkeepers all along the street.

'It's a problem, sir. Not just here, almost everywhere in town. The shops open first thing in the morning,' he replied, 'then close by three o'clock, most of them. No one goes out after dark. The vegetable market near the cathedral has a bit of a crowd around midday, the fish market down in Sturtenstrasse is still pretty busy, depending on the state of the tides, but not the way it used to be. Just look, sir!' Sergeant Koch observed with a sweep of his hand as we turned the corner into a broad cobbled street marked 'Baltijskstrasse'.

I noted two well-dressed gentleman fifty yards ahead, walking in the same direction as ourselves. On the other side of the street, a maid in a linen cap and a red-and-white striped apron was furiously sweeping the snow from the steps of an elegant town-house. Another maid in a similar garb, carrying a covered basket under her arm, hurried into a house further down the row, slamming the door at her back. Otherwise, the street was empty. No horses, carts or carriages disturbed the peace. There was nothing remarkable to be seen.

'What do you mean?' I asked.

'Baltijskstrasse was the busiest street in Königsberg, sir,' he said excitedly. 'A year ago, you couldn't take here a step without bumping into someone.'

'Where have all the people gone?'

'They're barricaded in their homes, sir,' Koch replied. 'Waiting for the killer to be caught.'

'You may be right,' I allowed with a sigh of discomfort. I had never imagined that accepting the investigation would require me to re-establish normal life in Königsberg, and safeguard the lives of potential sacrificial goats.

'What news is there this morning, Koch?' I asked, suddenly aware how silent, how aloof, I must have appeared to my assistant.

88

'All men under the age of thirty-five with military experience have been recalled to active service by General Katowice, Herr Stiffeniis,' Koch replied with his usual vigour. 'That's another reason why the town's so empty. The general wants a close watch to be kept on all known agitators, foreign residents and other aliens.'

'Is there a list, Koch?'

'I suppose there must be, sir.'

'Can you get a copy of the names for me?'

'I'll try, sir. God knows how complete it will be. The hotels will be easy enough to check' – Koch panted with the pace I was setting, letting out little puffs of steam as he spoke – 'but the dock area is another matter. You'll have noticed that yourself, sir. There's much coming and going, but if they made you sign the visitors' book at The Baltic Whaler, it's only because they know who you are.'

'I want the names of all visitors who have slept in the city in the past two weeks, Sergeant,' I returned with force. 'And The Baltic Whaler would make an excellent place to start the hunt for the killer. There are two Frenchmen and their German companion – travelling salesmen, they call themselves. I would like to know more about them.'

Koch said nothing for some moments.

'Do you want them interrogated, sir?' he asked gravely, as if he thought he might be putting into words what I had lacked the courage to say.

'For God's sake, no!' I exclaimed. 'I share General Katowice's fear of the mob. We must exercise control without being heavy-handed. If these crimes are politically motivated, the important thing is to lull the terrorists into a false sense of security. Interrogate anyone and the whole city will know what we are about. When I say check on them, I mean by talking to the hotel owners in a confidential manner. Sound out their suspicions, ask them if anything out of the ordinary has happened. The police are capable of that sort of strategy, are they not?'

'Is that the line you mean to take in these investigations, sir?'

'What do you mean, Koch?'

'Politics, Herr Stiffeniis. The mere thought of invasion by French cut-throats is enough to frighten the life out of anyone living here in Königsberg. If such a possibility exists, General Katowice should be informed at once. The King too . . .'

I pulled up short and turned to him. 'What can we tell them, Koch? We have nothing to communicate. Bonaparte has not chosen to show himself as yet. Local agents may be at work to undermine the government, using the tactics of terrorism to scare the populace, but this hypothesis needs to be verified. There may well be other alternatives.'

Koch blew into his handkerchief. 'May I ask what other alternatives, sir?'

The question caught me off guard. What alternatives, indeed?

'Well, Sergeant,' I began, walking on, 'you voiced one yourself just yesterday in the coach.'

'Did I really, sir?'

'You mentioned the Devil.'

'And you, sir, laughed at the suggestion,' Koch objected, scrutinising my face as if uncertain whether I might be joking.

'I cannot afford to exclude any avenue, Koch,' I smiled. 'No matter how abhorrent the idea may be to me personally.'

We walked on in silence, Koch occasionally indicating the geography of the place as we went along. 'This is Kliesterstrasse,' he announced at last. 'Which house are we looking for, sir?'

I did not reply, but began to walk along the dark, narrow alley of uneven cobblestones. Dwellings of different shapes and heights were clustered on either side of a shallow sewage ditch which ran stinking down the centre of the street. Some of the houses were fashioned out of faded wood-and-wattle daub, while others dotted here and there among the leaning terraces were of ancient wind-worn sandstone. They might have been put there to hold the frailer buildings steady in their places. The upper floors on either side seemed almost to touch, closing out the grey sky. Leaded windows, like a honeycomb of stacked wine bottles, gave light, but prevented the curious from looking into the ground-floor rooms. There was a listing, drifting, slanting air about the place, as if a violent puff of wind might bring the whole lot crashing down.

'Procurator Rhunken left his work unfinished at this point, Sergeant,' I explained. 'Let us see if we are able to discover what the man we examined last night on that anatomical table has left behind to help us solve his murder.'

A bronze plate was fixed to the door:

JERONIMUS TIFFERCH, NOTARY AT LAW & RECORDER OF OATHS.

Chapter 9

The door swung open framing a diminutive stunted figure in the entrance. Her face and hair were hidden by a lace cloth of the same sombre hue as her plain black gown. 'Office closed,' the woman chimed in a high-pitched, sing-song voice. 'Herr Tifferch is no more.'

'Frau Tifferch?' I asked, jamming the door with my foot as it began to close again in our faces.

Suddenly, the door flew back, the veil began to nod from side to side, then jerked as a cackling whoop escaped from the woman's lips. 'Ooh, no! Do you wish to see my lady? Expression of sympathy, is it?' Throwing the shroud back over her head as she spoke, the ancient exposed a lantern jaw of singular extension as she glared up at Koch and myself. Two yellow fangs protruded from the centre of her shrunken gums like the ravaged teeth of an aged buck-rabbit.

'This is not a social visit, ma'am,' I corrected her. 'My name is Hanno Stiffeniis. I am an investigating magistrate and I wish to speak to your mistress about her late husband.'

The woman cackled again, and said quite plainly, 'You won't have much luck there!'

She did not seem put out by the fact that her master had been murdered, her mistress widowed. Despite the mourning weeds, her attitude was most irreverent in the circumstances. 'What d'you want to see her for?' she asked.

'I need to look through Herr Tifferch's things,' I said.

'Help yourself,' she shrugged. 'What's stopping you?'

'I wish to ask permission of your mistress *first*.'

The maid stepped back, and waved us in, nodding towards a closed door on the right of the entrance hall. 'Her ladyship's in there. In all her glory! Ask her all you want.'

I was puzzled by this cryptic description. Her Ladyship? Was Frau Tifferch a member of the *Junker* aristocracy? Certainly, the surname she had acquired by marriage had nothing noble-sounding about it. Before I had the chance to ask, however, the maid had slammed the door to the street, and taken herself off along a dark corridor to the left without another word, her pattens clacking noisily on the floor tiles as she went away.

'Not the sort of maid I'd have in *my* house,' I muttered, remembering my father's terrified domestics and our own compliant Lotte, as I tapped my knuckles gently on the sitting-room door.

'Go on in!' the maid screeched from the end of the corridor. 'She'll not answer, though you wait all bloomin' day.'

Koch pushed the door open, and I followed him into the room. It was dark and gloomy, more like a funeral parlour than a suburban sitting room. Wide black swathes of ribbon had been tied to all the candlestick holders, and the tapers were lit. Black shrouds glistened everywhere, hiding the furniture, the fittings, and even the pictures on the walls, though a plaster statue standing almost three feet high on a table in the far corner had not been covered from view. It represented Jesus Christ. A sort of shrine reigned over there. Red votive lamps burned beside His pierced and naked feet, and Our Saviour held His vestments open wide in a most unseemly fashion, His heart exposed for the careless world to see. This organ was crowned with golden tongues of flame, bright red, pulsing with blood. I looked at Sergeant Koch. And Koch held my gaze. We had entered Roman territory. In the centre of the room sat a woman in a high-backed chair. Dressed like the maid in black from head to toe, her finery was of an earlier generation, richer by far, costly silk with trimmed flounces and ribbed fustian. She wore a magnificent jet necklace which covered her breast, while matching jet bracelets weighed down her slender wrists. Death seemed to have figured prominently in this woman's history.

'Frau Tifferch?' I asked, advancing across the room. 'May I offer my most sincere condolences on your unfortunate loss?'

The woman looked at me. That is, she lifted her face at the sound of my voice. Bright pinpoints seemed to glint at me from beneath the veil, but no word of greeting or gratitude issued from her lips.

'Your husband, ma'am,' I hinted, pausing to hear the sound of her voice.

Frau Tifferch did not move. She appeared not to breathe.

'I am leading the enquiry into the circumstances regarding his murder,' I was obliged to continue. 'I must ask you some questions about your husband. I'm interested in any business he might have been engaged upon when he was killed. He was out of doors after dark, it seems . . .'

The woman reached out a hand. Her bracelets tinkled as she took a black handkerchief from a small table at her side, carried it beneath her veil, and began to sob.

'Frau Tifferch?' I pressed gently.

Silence answered.

'Frau Tifferch?' I repeated.

Koch crossed the room on tiptoe and stood behind the lady's chair. Leaning forward, he whispered in her ear, 'Frau Tifferch?'

Standing to his full height at the woman's back, he raised his forefinger, touched himself twice on the temple, then shook his head.

'Call the maid back in,' I said, waiting in silence until the servant traipsed noisily into the room a minute later, followed by Sergeant Koch.

'What do you want?' she muttered. Her ill disposition had not softened in the least in the interval.

'Is your mistress feeling unwell?' I asked.

'You could call it that,' she said. 'Out of her wits. That's what *I* would say. Frau Tifferch's in a world of her own. Never says nowt, she don't.'

'What's wrong with her?'

She shrugged. 'I've no idea. No one told me, did they? I'm just the nursemaid. It happened four or five years ago, I believe. I wasn't working in this house then. But this I *was* told by the neighbours. It happened out of the blue. She was strong and active before.' She pointed at her charge and shook her head. 'It must have been something fearful, that's all I can say.'

I frowned. 'What do you mean?'

She shrugged again. 'You don't become a turnip for no good reason, do you?'

I stiffened, fighting off the sudden overlapping of images in my mind. I saw my own mother sitting there before me in the place of that heavily veiled widow, her eyes fixing themselves on mine while she asked a question for which there was no simple answer: 'How could you do it, Hanno?' That was the last coherent sentence she had ever uttered. A spasm had wracked her body and she collapsed apparently lifeless at my feet. Her tomblike silence endured for days. The doctors were called, but no remedy could be found. The pastor came to pray, and stayed to read the Last Rites. And all that time, my father said not a single word to me. But in his gaze I saw my mother's question. 'How could you, Hanno? Why did you do it?'

I closed my eyes to free myself from those painful memories, and opened them again on the gaping lantern jaw of the housemaid.

'What is your name?' I asked.

'Agneta Süsterich.'

'How long have you been working here, Agneta?'

'Too long.'

There was nothing subservient about the old woman. Words like 'sir', phrases such as 'by your leave', did not figure in her already limited vocabulary. She was brusque to the point of rudeness. Had Lawyer Tifferch never taken the surly drudge to task for her foul manners?

'Be more precise!' I insisted.

'Two years,' she replied in a forced fashion. 'An' curse the day I came! Once this lot's over, I'll be on my way. I should have left him to it . . .'

'Does your mistress have anyone else? Sons or daughters?' I pressed on.

'No one,' the woman replied. 'No relatives. I never seen a soul all the time I been a-staying here. No one visits this house. No one . . .'

She paused significantly, as if inviting me to complete the sentence.

'Except for *whom?*' I said.

'Priests!' she flared. 'Catholic priests! Blasphemous vermin! An' now, the police messing around . . .'

'You are not of that religion, I take it?'

The maid's eyes narrowed, as if I had just accused her of the most heinous crime under the sun. 'I am a Pietist!' she protested. 'Everyone in Königsberg's a Pietist. I goes to my Bible reading every night to cleanse my Christian lungs of the foul Catholic air I am forced to breathe in this house. I told the master. Told him straight, I did. I goes to Bible meetings, Herr Tifferch, I said, or else. But now there's no one to look after her. What am I going to do?'

'Did you light all those candles?' I intervened, trying to stop the angry flow before it became a raging flood.

'I had to, didn't I?' the woman muttered. 'Only way to keep her quiet. She likes her candles. All them Catholics do. Heathen rubbish, I say!'

'What are your duties here?' I asked with all the patience I could muster.

'Everything.' She started ticking items off on her fingers as she spoke. 'Wash her, clean her, dress her, comb her, feed her. I decked her out in black in case one of them bloodsuckers came.'

'Has a "leech" been called?' I asked.

'Papists!' she spat. 'Stayed clear so far, they have.'

'Your master was murdered three days ago,' I ploughed on. 'Late in the evening. Did he tell you where he was going when he left the house?'

The woman lifted her eyes, stretched her jaw, and grinned. 'Master allus kep' his counsel to hisself. Never knew what was going on in *his* mind. He was a dark horse, all right.'

'He carried on his business from this house,' I persisted. 'Which clients came to visit him that day?'

'I've no idea. None at all. That front door was allus open. Seven 'til five, Monday to Sat'day. They come, they go.'

I tried another tack. 'Did you hear anyone shouting, or quarrelling with Herr Tifferch?'

'I keeps meself to the kitchen,' she replied. 'It's warm out there.'

'Do you know if your master had any enemies?' I asked.

Agneta Süsterich thought this question over for some moments. Then she looked at me with a smile, and my expectations rose.

'Only the missis,' she declared. 'Used to scream every time she saw his face. Does that answer you?'

It most certainly did not. Whoever had produced those livid cuts and scars on Lawyer Tifferch's body, it had undoubtedly not been his wife. 'Did anything out of the ordinary happen the day he died?' I pressed on.

Agneta Süsterich sighed aloud, her annoyance growing more visible with each new question.

'He worked in the morning. As usual. Had lunch with his wife. As usual. Sat in his office 'til five. As usual, I went to Grüsterstrassehaus . . .'

'What's that?'

'The Pietist Temple. I left a cold supper out for them. As allus. I was back at half past seven to put the mistress into bed. As usual. I never seen *him* at all, but that was nothing new. He went out every night . . .'

'And where did he go?' I interrupted.

The woman's ugly face twisted with disgust. 'I can only imagine,' she said. 'I seen him staggering down them stairs that many times of a morning. Pain was writ all over his face. As if he just been kicked in the bollocks by an 'orse. Can't hardly stand on his own two feet some days! Them Catholics like to sin, all right. The priest absolves 'em quick enough for a thaler or two.'

'Do you hear him return at night as a rule?' I asked, coughing to stifle a laugh at this lurid description of the rival faith.

'I says my prayers and I goes to sleep. Ain't no use waiting up for the Devil. More so that night, 'cos he never come home, did he? Night Watch knocked us up afore the first crow of the cock.'

'So, where is his office?'

'There are four doors out in that hallway,' the woman said.

'One's mine, one's hers, one's his. The other goes upstairs to the sleeping quarters.'

'Show me to your master's workroom,' I said.

Before leaving the sitting room, I turned to the widow again. She was as still and silent as the plaster idol in the corner. She had given no sign of life since we entered the room, and she showed no sign as we left it.

Agneta Süsterich pointed to a closed door on the other side of the hall.

'That's where he worked,' she said. 'It's locked.'

'Do you have the key?'

'Master kept it,' she replied.

'But surely you cleaned the room for Herr Tifferch?'

'He cleans it hisself. Herr Tifferch let no one in, except when he was here. Customers, an' that. Go on, break it down,' she challenged. 'You're the police, ain't you?'

Koch stepped forward with his clasp-knife. 'Shall I try my luck, sir?'

I nodded and the sergeant dropped on one knee, thrusting the blade into the ancient lock. He prodded away and twisted, while the maid stood watching him, as if he were a thief, shaking her head with the disgust she seemed to reserve for the world at large. With a sudden crack, the door swung back on its hinges.

'You have a talent for the work, Koch!' I exclaimed.

'I just hope he can close it again,' the maid muttered, as if Herr Tifferch might come back and berate her for the ruined lock.

Larger than the sitting room we had left, there was only one desk in the centre of the room. Two straight-backed chairs were set out in front of it. The notary kept no clerk, the maid reported, but handled all his business for himself. Glass-fronted bookcases lining the walls held tight scrolls of documents bound up with ribbons of diverse colours. Laid out in alphabetical order, they gave an impression of industriousness.

'Mistress needs a-changing,' the maid announced from the doorway, gazing into the office as if it were a forbidden land. She disappeared without waiting for permission, and shortly after, we heard her shouting in the room across the hall. In answer, the lady of the house began to scream. The high-pitched keening went on for quite some time.

'Herr Tifferch's situation was not a comfortable one,' Koch observed.

'Light some candles, Koch,' I said. 'I hope to know a great deal more about his life before we've done.'

For the next two hours, we sifted through the dusty documents in that room, rolling them up again and putting away what was useless or irrelevant. Some were thirty years old, the paper yellow and brittle with age, legal transactions of every imaginable sort: marriage contracts, bills of purchase, receipts of sale and lading, inheritances resolved and claims disputed. Anything in those papers might have been important, I suppose, but nothing came to light that could be directly linked with the lawyer's death, no indication that might serve to connect his murder with any of the other recent killings.

The last case on which Tifferch had been working was laid out neatly on his desk. Arnolph von Rooysters, a rich burgher, had left all his moveable property to his butler, a man named Ludwig Frontissen. Apparently, the relatives had tried to reverse this decision, but Tifferch had a sworn testament in the hand of the dead man in favour of the servant which settled the argument. I had sat myself down at Tifferch's desk to read these papers; Koch was busy on the other side of the room with the last of the scrolls.

'Herr Stiffeniis,' Koch said, 'there's a cupboard here that's locked.'

Having noticed a large bunch of keys in one of the desk-drawers, I took them out and tossed them across to him. 'See if one of those will fit,' I said.

I heard him jangling the keys uselessly against the lock while I continued reading a sequence of letters and declarations relating to the quarrel between von Rooysters' relatives and the butler. The descendants of the deceased had appealed to a certain Minister in Berlin who had written to Tifferch to know exactly how things stood in the case. Tifferch maintained that the law was undeniably on the side of the fortunate butler. Minister Aschenbrenner, who was a distant relative of the von Rooysters, agreed with Tifferch, but proposed a compromise to put an end to the squabble. Accordingly, Tifferch had offered the family members one half of the inheritance, which, it seemed, the butler was well disposed to share with them. The dates on some of these documents went back a couple of years, and Tifferch had most recently concluded the dispute to the advantage and the satisfaction of all parties. There was absolutely nothing that might suggest a possible reason for his murder.

'It's no good, sir,' Koch's voice broke in upon my thoughts. 'None of the keys fits.'

'Well, then,' I replied, 'do as the housemaid suggests.'

'Sir?'

'Force the lock, Sergeant. If he hid the key, he probably kept money and valuables in there.'

With a nod Koch set to work on the lock. Some minutes later, he let out a grunt of triumphant satisfaction. Then, silence followed.

'Well, Koch?' I asked impatiently, dragging myself away from the paper I was reading. 'What have you found?'

'You'd better come and see for yourself, sir,' he replied.

I clapped my hands to remove the dust, then joined him on the far side of the room. Koch had placed a candle on one of the chairs to light the cupboard, which was deep and dark. On the top shelf stood a grinning porcelain bust of Napoleon Bonaparte. I stretched out my hand to pick the statue up, and almost dropped it as my fingers closed upon the base. The pressure of my thumb had triggered a hair-spring: the Emperor's hat flipped up and two satanic horns popped out of the flat hair on his head.

'What a remarkable toy!' I exclaimed with a laugh. 'What else is there?'

On the shelf below was a stack of pamphlets and broadsheets, which Koch and I examined with mounting curiosity. They were ribald and even erotic in their contents, and referred in the most scabrous terms to the Emperor of France. If the anonymous cartoonists were to be believed, Bonaparte showed a marked sexual preference for the animal world. Donkeys he particularly favoured, though in one instance, he was portrayed in amorous coupling with a female elephant. As Koch was quick to point out, the satirical comments beneath these drawings were in the German language, and the obscenities appeared to have been printed on a hand-press using wooden print-blocks, a system long out of commercial fashion.

'I wonder where he bought these,' I said, glancing through the pages.

'Do you think he might belong to a political group, sir?' Koch asked.

'A scurrilous circulating library, more like! You could be right, though. It seems as if Herr Tifferch led a busy secret life.'

Were these seditious materials, I asked myself, the cause of his domestic problems? Had his wife chanced upon those disgusting images, the shock proving too great for her health to withstand? The sudden knowledge that one's apparently respectable husband was, instead, a radical pervert might quite easily transmute a woman of over-strong religious ideals into a living statue.

A *living statue* . . .

My mother's image rose to my mind once more. Sweat broke out on my forehead, and a nervous tic in my throat brought on a coughing fit.

'It is dusty in here, isn't it, sir?' Koch responded diligently. 'Would you like me to get you a glass of water?'

'That won't be necessary,' I replied, and really it was not. The maternal ghost with her desolate air of constant accusation had fled at the sound of his voice.

'Do we need to go through all of these pamphlets, Herr Procurator?' Koch asked, his dislike for the task quite evident.

'I am afraid we must, Koch,' I said. 'We cannot afford to leave any avenue unexplored.'

'I see, sir,' Koch replied, and made haste to do what he had so hastily wished to abandon not a moment before.

Still, I tried to make it easier for him. We examined the leaflets front and back, looking for names. None was found, of course, except for *noms-de-plume* of an evidently fantastical and francophobic origin: *Cul de Monsieur, Seigneur Duc de Porc, Milord*

Mont du Merde, and so on. We returned this material to its shelf, then moved on down the cupboard. A large, brown velvet box on the next shelf was closed by a small padlock. Applying himself to the key-ring again, and finding no help there, Koch removed the padlock with his knife on my orders. The box opened up to reveal a domestic tableau in wax and wood: Bonaparte and his paramour, Josephine Beauharnais. The Emperor was standing, the Empress sitting on a stool, and they were facing one another. There was an odd expression on the woman's pretty face, her mouth open, her eyes gaping wide, as if she were in a state of shock or terror. At the jerk of a rod on the base of the model, Napoleon's trousers slid down around his ankles, his third leg rose stiffly into the air – it was as long as the other two – and hovered close to the mouth of the lady. A lever on the other side of the automaton caused the woman's head to lean forward and do perverse and beastly things that no self-respecting French Empress ought to do in public.

'A most . . . unusual sense of humour,' Koch murmured uncertainly.

Without looking at his face, I knew that he was blushing.

Could Herr Tifferch have been murdered by Napoleonic sympathisers in Königsberg? A man might keep such toys a secret from his wife and maid, but surely he would share them with his friends. And friends in times as dangerous as ours need to be handled with care. Since the revolution in France, not every man in Prussia is as patriotic as he ought to be.

'How strong are sympathies for France in the city, Sergeant?'

Koch stroked his chin before he answered. 'Prussia has been isolated by the political events of the past few months, sir. We have so few allies, and Bonaparte intends that we shall have none. Then, he will attack. But he *does* have followers in Königsberg. He has supporters all over Europe . . .' He stopped, and looked at me. 'But do you really think that some fanatic killed Herr Tifferch for his ribald attitude towards the French Emperor, sir? What about those scars on his body? How do they fit in?'

'I don't know,' I said with a sigh. 'I can't see any link. Rhunken's reports make no mention of whip marks on the other bodies, but he seemed to believe that the connection between the murders was political. He suspected that there was a conspiracy of some sort behind all of these deaths, although he could not say what *sort* of plot it was. This,' I said, indicating the collection of items in the cupboard, 'appears to lead us in the same general direction.'

Just then, a ray of sunlight entered the room. Like a beam piercing the dark interior of a *camera obscura*, the light settled for an instant on a rolled-up bundle of dark purple silk pushed to the back of the bottom shelf. Uncertain what Herr Tifferch's next posthumous trick might be, I retrieved the bundle carefully and held it up in both hands for Koch to see. It was as long and thick as a spicy Danish dried sausage.

Setting this object down on the top of the notary's desk, I carefully rolled it open. Koch and I looked at the contents in silent disbelief for some moments.

'This may explain the pained expression on Tifferch's face when he came down to breakfast,' I said.

'I've never seen such a thing,' said Koch in a hushed voice.

I took up the dark leather stick, and shook it in the air. Three long tails with knotted tips waved free in a sinister cascade. 'At least we know what made those lacerations on Tifferch's body, Koch. Old scars, new wounds . . .'

Koch struggled to find his voice. 'Do you think he did it to *himself*, sir?'

'There can be little doubt,' I said. 'But whether to punish himself for his sins, or as a source of sexual pleasure, we cannot even begin to guess. Perhaps both?'

'That such a thing could exist in Königsberg!' It was clear from the expression of shock on Koch's plain, honest face that he found himself in a new and disturbing dimension. 'In France they do such things, I've heard. In Paris. But here in Prussia?'

'Put everything back where you found it,' I said quietly, watching as he returned each object to its allotted place in the cupboard. He handled them as if they might corrode his fingertips, closing the door again with gusto.

As we took our leave, Agneta Süsterich was preparing to feed her mistress. Frau Tifferch was seated in a stiff-backed chair without her veil, a white linen cloth spread protectively over her finery. Her round face was puffy, white, expressionless, her pale blue eyes two empty blanks fixed on the bowl of gruel on the table before her.

'I hope you've found what you need to catch Herr Tifferch's murderer,' the maid huffed sharply over her shoulder, the only note of sympathy she had offered for her master since we stepped into the house. 'You know where the front door is. Her pap's the only blessed thing the lady's interested in. She won't be kept a-waiting.'

Outside in the street I felt a grey blanket of depression fall upon my spirits. What sort of life would Frau Tifferch lead without her husband? What future did she have, a helpless woman in the company of a bitter maid in an empty house? Then again, I thought, what was Agneta Süsterich's lot? A Pietist forced to live in a Catholic shrine she hated, she was bound to discover the secrets of her master's cupboard sooner or later. Would the stark revelation make her less caring of her mistress, more resentful of her sinful master? Would she continue to nurse Frau Tifferch? And if she did not, who would? The person, or persons, who had killed Jeronimus Tifferch had brought distress into that household. How much havoc had been caused, and how much more had been swept away forever, with the deaths of Jan Konnen, Paula-Anne Brunner and Johann Gottfried Haase? I knew from my own personal experience the immense distress that a single thoughtless action could unleash on the lives of the people close to a family tragedy.

'Sir?'

I looked up, and took stock of my surroundings. The winter sun shone weakly above the almost-touching roofs in a narrow strip of blue sky. Packed ice flashed as blue as steel on the cobblestones. The cold wind cut deeper than a sharp knife as it whistled in from the sea.

'What are your conclusions, Herr Stiffeniis?' Koch asked cautiously as we made our way to the end of the street.

'We have found a whip in a cupboard,' I said. 'But we still do not know exactly how or why Herr Tifferch died. And neither have we been able to find any connection between him and the others who were murdered. I hardly have room in my head for conclusions.'

I lapsed into a dejected silence as we emerged from the street into a small snow-filled square with a huddle of leafless trees in the centre. I had hoped to discover a great deal more.

'Do you think that a war with France is inevitable, sir?' Koch asked suddenly.

'I certainly hope not,' I returned promptly, 'but there isn't much we can do about it. Russia hovering on our right flank; France on the other, and all this idle chatter about Bonaparte! Who's for him, who's against him. And whether King Frederick Wilhelm can keep Prussia out of it. And will the Frenchman let him? The argument never seems to end. In such a climate of mounting suspicion and intrigue, these murders aren't helping things one little bit.'

General Katowice had warned me that whether the country went to war, or not, might depend on how I managed the criminal investigation. The memory of his alarm set my head spinning once again. Nervously, I unhooked my fob-watch and glanced at the face. It was almost ten to twelve.

'Is Klopstrasse far from here?' I asked briskly.

I had no wish to be late. Herr Jachmann was a stickler for watching the clock. He was very like his oldest and dearest friend in that respect.

'It's just across the square, sir.'

'Good!' I exclaimed.

Before Koch could say a word, I struck out across the snow-filled square.

Chapter 10

The house in Klopstrasse stood out from its brightly coloured neighbours like a rotten tooth. The once-green paint was peeling and grey. A dead ivy vine grasped the facade like a skeletal hand intent on throttling the life out of the building. A rusty balcony running the length of the upper floor seemed likely to collapse with the next winter storm. The shutters, half-closed and broken, hung sadly from their hinges. It was not a pretty sight. Herr Reinhold Jachmann's days of gracious and fashionable living seemed to be long past.

'Shall I go in with you, sir?' Koch asked.

'No, Sergeant,' I said quickly. I wanted no witness to the conversation I was about to have. 'Go to the Court House, and see about that list of aliens I mentioned. Send the gendarmes out to check it.'

Koch bowed stiffly. Was it my impression, or did a look of disappointment flash across his face? I watched him march away with all the haste that the fresh-fallen snow would permit, then I turned towards the house. The wrought-iron gate protested loudly when I pushed to open it. A loud shriek gave way to a long painful groan as I forced back rusty hinges which had not tasted whale-oil in many a month. Apart from the crusted footprints that Koch himself had left there earlier that morning as he came to deliver my message, no other impression had been made in the snow. No visitor or tradesman had called before or since.

I let the iron knocker fall against the door, and the sound seemed to echo and rebound on the icy air as if the house and garden were enclosed within a vacuum. A lone blackbird flew away, twittering angrily. That sudden noise shattered the silence which reigned supreme in the garden. The motionless shrubs and bushes hidden beneath the deep coverlet of snow might have been forgotten tombstones in an abandoned graveyard. I was looking around forlornly as the door opened silently at my back.

'You have come then, Stiffeniis.'

I recognised the deep, resonating boom of Reinhold Jachmann's voice, though I did not recognise the man as I turned to face him. A cold, unearthly winter had blown over him, too. His thin hair was as white as bleached bed linen, his eyebrows large snowdrifts above piercing, coal-black eyes. His stiff seriousness alarmed me. I remembered a warm friendly man during our first and only meeting seven years before, but the suspicious stranger glaring down at me from the top of the steps was the very opposite. For one moment, I thought he would refuse to allow me to enter his house. We stared at each other in silence.

'This way,' he said at last, and led me through the hall and into a sparsely furnished sitting room on the ground floor. Pointing to a sofa before a cast-iron fireplace where a single log smoked and smouldered, he asked me to be seated. It was more an order than an invitation. He watched me sit without a word, then he walked to the window and looked out over the garden.

'What brings you here?' he enquired without turning around.

'A matter of the greatest urgency, Herr Jachmann,' I replied. 'A Royal commission.'

'So you mentioned in your note,' he said. 'Can I know its nature?'

I had hoped he would not need to ask.

'I have been appointed to investigate the recent spate of murders in the town,' I said quietly.

With a sudden movement, he turned to look at me, some of his former energy returning. 'You, Stiffeniis? Investigating murder?'

He appeared to be stunned by what I had just told him. 'I thought that Procurator Rhunken was in charge of the case?' he said.

'He died, Herr Jachmann.'

He shook his head and looked confused. 'I have heard nothing of his death, nor of his burial.'

'It happened just yesterday evening,' I explained. 'Herr Rhunken was buried immediately. There was no funeral. It was his final wish.'

'Gracious me! What has become of Königsberg?' he whispered, turning again to the window. He remained there for quite some time, peering out at the snow.

'I warned you, I *told* you, never to come here again,' he growled over his shoulder, his face livid with anger, as if I had brought these new disasters along with me from Lotingen.

Another brooding silence followed his outburst.

'I was very surprised to be assigned the case,' I ventured to say at last. 'I accepted the commission with trepidation, sir. For the sake of . . .'

'Have you seen him yet?' Jachmann interrupted gruffly, his eyes still fixed on the garden and the street.

'Oh no, sir,' I replied. 'I would never dream of doing so without consulting you.' I paused for a moment, then blurted out, 'Your letter came as a great shock to me, Herr Jachmann. I have not gone back on my word, sir. His peace of mind is as precious to me as it is to yourself. I've not forgotten your warning.'

He turned to face me. 'But you intend to visit him now, do you not?' His voice had risen again, the blood rushed to his cheeks, and he stared at me with evident distaste.

I shifted uncomfortably in my seat. 'Not if I can help it,' I said, 'though there is the possibility that we might meet by accident. I thought I ought to warn you, sir. That is why I am here.' I stopped for some moments, but then curiosity got the better of me. 'How is he, sir?' I dared to ask.

'He is well enough,' Jachmann returned brusquely. 'His valet reports to me on a regular weekly basis.'

'His servant?' Now it was my turn to be surprised.

'His servant,' he confirmed sharply without adding anything more.

'But you are his closest friend, Herr Jachmann . . .'

'I *was* his closest friend,' he interrupted, his voice cracked, broken. 'I am still his domestic administrator, but I have not seen him in the past twelve months, or more. He has become secretive, almost a recluse. I go to his house no longer. All essential communication passes through his valet.'

'How can this be, sir?'

He waved his hand dismissively. 'There was no quarrel, no argument, if that is what you mean. The professor has no time for old friends. His door is closed to all and sundry. His servant is instructed to say that he is busy, and does not wish to be disturbed. Work and study, as you know, have always been the mainsprings of his existence.'

He twirled away and paced up and down the room in silence, then came to rest once more in front of the sofa. He bent close, the deep lines of age in his long face etching themselves even more sharply with the effort to control his emotions or his temper.

'Why would any responsible person want *you* to conduct this investigation, Stiffeniis?' he enquired.

I know what I would have liked to reply. That the King had recognised my qualities, knowing that I would succeed where all other investigators, including Procurator Rhunken, had failed. But I was obliged to concede the truth.

'I do not know, Herr Jachmann.'

'I expected an angry reply to that harsh letter of mine,' he said suddenly. 'I knew that you would return to Königsberg unless I managed to stop you. Had you answered telling me to mind my own affairs, or asking me to explain the motives that obliged me to write to you in such a manner, I would not have been in the least surprised. But when your answer came, stating meekly that you would comply with my wishes, I was more than surprised, I can tell you. I was alarmed.'

'I took you at your word,' I began to say, but he was not listening.

'You knew *why* I did not wish to see you ever again,' he continued angrily. He paused, drew a deep breath, then added: 'I have tried many a time to fathom what passed between you both that day in the fog.'

I stared into his accusing eyes and held my breath, recalling the day seven years before when I had been privileged to speak in private with the most famous man in Königsberg, Jachmann's friend and colleague at the University, Professor of Philosophy, Immanuel Kant.

'You ordered me to avoid the city for the good of Professor Kant,' I whispered. 'I had no idea why, but I saw no reason to question your integrity. You were his dearest friend. You knew what was good or bad for him, and . . .'

'*You* were bad for him!' His white face suddenly blazed with resentment. 'That is the point. Don't you see? Why should there have been any need for me to forbid you to see Kant? What other reason could there be to make me fear for the mental stability of the most rational man on Earth?'

'You are unjust, sir,' I protested, but Jachmann rode over me.

'I realised that something was amiss whenever your name was mentioned afterwards,' he continued with great intensity. 'It had such a marked effect on him. There was agitation in his manner, wild distraction in his eyes. It was out of character, totally unlike him. This madness began the day that he invited you to lunch. In itself, *that* was an event without precedent.'

'Why do you say so, sir?' I asked.

'He had never invited a stranger to his home before. Not once!' He looked at me inquisitively. 'Something in you triggered his interest. Something that you had done, or something that you had said to him.'

'But you know why he invited me,' I replied with passion. 'I had just come back from Paris, Professor Kant was interested in what I had seen there.'

Jachmann nodded grimly.

'I recall your speech about what you saw the day the Jacobins executed their legitimate ruler . . .'

I closed my eyes to block out the memory. Would the image of that moment never leave me in peace? How long would it haunt me? The sight of human blood on the ground. The stench of it in the air.

' . . . Paris, January 2nd, 1793,' Herr Jachmann intoned pedantically.

The scene flashed before my mind's eye. The bubbling gaiety of the crowd. The condemned man in his soiled finery proudly climbing the steps to the block. The oiled blue triangle of steel shimmering in the early morning light. The sound of grating metal as the blade fell. Then, blood! Oceans of crimson blood, spurting out of that severed neck like water from one of the ornamental fountains that the King had built for himself at Versailles, drenching the faces of the onlookers. Falling like rain on my own face, on my mouth and my tongue . . .

'They murdered the King that day.'

A king? A man had been butchered before my eyes. A flick of a lever, and a shadow had been cast upon my soul. A hidden part of myself had risen up with the mob and taken possession of my confused mind.

'Kant had met others who had been in France,' Herr Jachmann continued. 'Others who were involved in those tragic events. He was not upset by what they had to say. But you, Stiffeniis! *You* brought a malignant plague to his house that day.'

He stared fixedly at me.

'Whatever happened between the two of you, Stiffeniis, it changed him. It changed him totally. And it all began with that conversation about the effect of electrical storms on human behaviour.'

'It was not *I* who raised the subject,' I spluttered in my own defence. '*You* started it, sir.'

'But it was you,' Jachmann replied, his finger pointing accusingly, '*you*, Stiffeniis, who led the discussion in such an unsavoury direction. You froze the blood in my veins!'

He turned his gaze to the fire. 'How many times have I regretted that odious conversation! Kant was studying the effects of electricity on the nervous system in that period, he was interested in little else. And the night before, there had been a terrible storm.'

Every single detail was still vivid in my mind.

'Looking out of your window,' I murmured, 'you found a stranger in your garden. Careless of the lashing rain, the thunder and lightning, he was staring up at the sky in a trance. You'd been disconcerted by his behaviour, and you asked Kant if static electricity might provide an explanation for it.'

'And he replied by saying it was not the electrical discharge, it was the unbounded energy of Nature which had fascinated the man,' Jachmann went on. 'The destructive power of the elements had mesmerised him. Kant referred to the *incantamento horribilis*. Human Kind, he said, is fatally attracted by Sublime Terror.'

He sat down heavily in an armchair, his forehead couched in his hand. 'I was shocked. Unable to believe my ears. Immanuel Kant? The Father of Rationality celebrating the powers of the Unknown? The dark side of the human soul?'

'I remember, sir. You objected that such power belongs to God alone. That Man is bound by moral ties which he should never question . . .'

'Then *you* spoke up,' Jachmann interposed, still shading his eyes, avoiding my sight, 'and suddenly the pleasant young student who had won our respect with his good manners and his sound reasoning appeared in a different light.'

'I just said . . .'

He held up his hand for silence. 'Your words are indelibly printed on my memory. "There is one human experience which may be equal to the unbridled power of Nature," you said. "The most diabolical of all. Cold-blooded murder. Murder without a motive."'

Jachmann stared at me, his eyes narrowed and resentful. I felt as if my body had been stripped away, my soul exposed to view.

'When Professor Kant shifted the discussion elsewhere,' he went on, 'I felt grateful to him. But the ghost that you evoked that day had not been laid to rest. He insisted on taking a turn around the Castle Walk alone with you, though he had not been out of doors all winter, except to go to the university. The fog was dreadful, you remember. But I knew that he would wish to talk with you again.'

'You are curious to know if we talked further of the same subject. Are you not?' I asked, on the defensive.

'You are wrong, Stiffeniis,' he replied. 'Totally wrong! I do not wish to know what was said. But let me tell you what happened as a consequence. When Kant returned to the house, I was waiting for him. Long before I saw him through the fog, I heard his footsteps. And what I heard was enough to convince me that something was wrong. Very wrong. Kant was running. Running! But from whom?

From what? I rushed out to meet him, and the expression on his face was frightful to behold. Rather, I was frightened by what I saw. His eyes sparkled with nervous energy. I thought he had taken a fever. I expressed my concern, but he announced that he had work to do which could not wait an instant. In short, he sent me about my business! And the very next day, he told me that he had begun to compose a new philosophical treatise.'

I frowned. 'I have not heard of any new book,' I said.

Jachmann shook his head dismissively. 'It has not been published. That is why you've never heard of it. No one has read a single line. Indeed, I am inclined to believe that the work does not exist. At that time, he was under great mental strain. Some younger philosophers accused him of ignoring the deeper resources of the soul. Emotion, they suggested, was more powerful than Logic, and Kant was ruined by the bitter controversy. His classes were empty in the last years of his tenure. The young did not want to pay to listen to him.'

'So I heard,' I said.

'It was very sad. He was all but forgotten. "Old-fashioned" is the new-fangled term, I believe. Things had got to such a state that one of his former protégés, a bright young fellow named Fichte – you've heard of him, I'm sure – described Kant as the "philosopher of spiritual idleness" in a book which sold very well throughout Europe.'

'That must have been humiliating.'

'Remember his legendary timekeeping?' Jachmann reminisced. He seemed calmer as he recalled the distant past. 'How the people in Königsberg used to set their clocks by Kant's coming and going? Well, the new generation of students thought it such a clever joke to interrupt his lessons, coming in one after another, watch in hand, saying, "Late, sir? Me, sir? Your timepiece must have stopped, sir." It drove Kant to a premature retirement.'

'I can imagine his distress.'

'I doubt it!' Jachmann snapped. He was rambling now with the frantic energy of an old man for a lost cause. 'But the person who was most distressed was Martin Lampe.'

'His valet?' I asked in surprise.

'I had to dismiss him. After thirty years of faithful service! He'd been the perfect servant. Mental order and discipline may produce fine thoughts, but they do not make for the efficient running of a household. Kant has trouble putting on his own stockings! Lampe looked after him, while the master concentrated on his books.'

'So why did you send him away?'

'For Kant's own good, Stiffeniis!' He looked at me intently, as if searching for the correct tone of voice with which to say what followed. 'I no longer trusted Lampe. More to the point, I was afraid of him.'

'Afraid, sir? What do you mean?'

'Strange ideas had found their way into Lampe's mind,' Herr Jachmann went on. 'He had begun to behave as if he were Professor Kant. Why, he told me once that there would be *no* Kantian philosophy if not for him! The new book on which Kant was working, he claimed, was his, not his master's. When the students started deserting Kant's lessons, it was Lampe who had the most violent reactions. He became quite vehement, shouting, saying that Kant must show the world what he could do.'

'He had to go,' I agreed. 'But who is looking after the Professor now?'

Jachmann cleared his throat noisily. 'A young man named Johannes Odum manages the house and he seems to be doing it well enough.'

He fell silent. Indeed, there seemed to be little left to say, and I stood up, reaching for my hat, preparing to take my leave, having said what I had come to say.

'Why in the name of heaven did you choose the law of all subjects?' he asked me quietly.

I paused before replying. I ought to have been insulted, I suppose, but there was a measure of satisfaction in what I was about to tell him. 'That day I came to Königsberg, Professor Kant himself advised me to become a magistrate.'

'Did he really?' Jachmann frowned, evidently puzzled. 'Given the wild opinions you expressed, I can only wonder at the soundness of his judgement!'

'It was during our walk around the Fortress after lunch,' I hurried on, ignoring the sarcastic jibe.

Herr Jachmann shook his head sadly. 'That walk! Everything seems to have started out there in the . . .'

There was a sharp rap at the door, and a man in dowdy brown serving-livery poked his head inside without stepping into the room.

'That person's here again, sir,' he announced, surprise writ large on his face, as if his master were unused to receiving visitors, and my own visit had been more than enough for one morning. 'To speak with Procurator Stiffeniis, he says.'

Koch was waiting out in the hallway, his face ash-white, his expression drawn and tense. 'I'm sorry to disturb you, sir, but it's a question of necessity.'

'What is it?'

'The boy at the inn, sir.'

'Morik?' I said sharply. 'What about him?'

'He's been found, sir.'

I glared at him for a moment. 'I am glad of that, Sergeant, but I do not see the urgency . . .'

'I'm sorry, sir,' Koch interrupted forcefully. 'Perhaps I didn't make myself clear. The boy is dead, sir. Foul play's suspected.'

Chapter 11

Wild, angry shouts exploded suddenly all around us.

'The King! Where's the King?'

'Napoleon will slay us, no one seems to care!'

'Down with the King! To the scaffold! *Vive la revolution!*'

Our coach rumbled onto the long wooden bridge that spanned the River Pregel, scattering a furious crowd of cat-calling men and screeching women who jostled towards the scene of the crime. In that barrage of noise and derision it was impossible to isolate the individuals who were fomenting the protest. Perhaps there were no leaders in that rabble. I had the unpleasant impression that the coach was a fragile boat forced to run between converging reefs, which threatened to sink us at any moment.

'They blame the authorities for what is happening,' I said, as we trundled on and left the raving mob behind us.

'Their fears feed on each new corpse,' Koch replied. 'It's just as General Katowice feared, sir. Rumour, unruly gatherings, riots. These murders will lead to trouble. Rebellions have a way of spreading.'

'Terror is what they aim at,' I said, feeling the enormous burden of the delicate task with which I had been entrusted. 'But what were you saying before we were interrupted?'

'About the eel-fisherman, sir. He found the corpse while setting his traps. The troops brought him to the Court House, then they called me. I spoke to him, but he had nothing much to add, beyond the macabre discovery. If you wish to interrogate him, sir, I made a note of his name and address . . .'

'We'll see him later, Koch. How far is The Baltic Whaler from here?'

'Half a mile, sir. No more.'

I thought back to what Morik had told me the previous night, and to the scene that I had witnessed later from my bedroom window. What further proof did I need that the boy and all the others had been murdered by terrorist infiltrators?

'Were the landlord and his wife taken into custody?'

'They were, sir.'

'As soon as we've seen the body,' I said, 'I will interrogate them. Then, perhaps, I'll be in a better position to report my findings to General Katowice.'

The coach slewed and skidded suddenly, rolling and jerking to an uncertain stop at an angle to the bridge-rail.

'Get back there! Go on, get on with you!' Soldiers were blocking the way, their muskets pointed in a menacing fashion at our driver. Sergeant Koch jumped down and some minutes later the coach was allowed to pass through the road-block on my authority. For once in my life, I must admit, I felt reassured by the bullying behaviour of the troops.

Having crossed the bridge and turned to the left along the far bank, the vehicle pulled up a hundred metres further on beside a long, slippery flight of slime-covered stone stairs, by means of which we reached the rutted, muddy bank of the river. It was a vile, salt-smelling sort of place. The river was low, the weeds dank and black, flattened by the force of the retreating tidal waters. We hurried on beside the stream to where a knot of soldiers stood braced in a tight circle, facing outwards, firearms at the ready. They waved us away with bayonets fixed to the muzzles of their guns.

'I am the new Procurator. Make sure that no one else approaches,' I ordered sharply, glancing across the river as the troops fell back. The far bank was packed with idle onlookers. Half the town had gathered there, as if to see some gruesome public spectacle or welcome a travelling circus. With a feeling of disgust for Mankind in my heart, I turned to my task, but I pulled up suddenly. A figure was down on his knees in the mud, his trademark wig glistening with damp, the corpse of Morik visible only as a shapeless, twisted heap of mud-stained clothes and pale flesh beneath him. Like a wild beast poised to feast on fresh blood and warm flesh, Doctor Vigilantius was sniffing and slobbering over the body.

'In the name of Heaven!' I cried.

Vigilantius did not look up. The blasphemous ritual continued unchecked.

'This is an outrage!' I erupted. 'Who called him here?'

'I did, Stiffeniis.'

The voice at my back was feeble, but I recognised it even before I turned.

'*I* sent for Doctor Vigilantius.'

A three-cornered hat sat low on Immanuel Kant's head, his face almost hidden beneath it. He wore no wig. A fine mesh of silvery-white hair graced his deformed left shoulder. Wrapped up against the weather in a shimmering, waterproof cloak of dark brown material, he held on tightly to the arm of a young man so tall, robust and protective that they might have been a father and his son, age reversing the roles that Nature had assigned them.

His unexpected arrival there on the banks of the river robbed me of the power of speech. Of course, I realised, it was inevitable that I would meet him sooner or later in Königsberg. But not in that place, nor in such doleful circumstances. Who had told him of the finding of the body of Morik? Had Jachmann informed him of my presence in the city, and of the reason for my being there? Herr Jachmann had warned me of the changes advancing age had inflicted on the philosopher, but I could only compare what I saw with what I recalled as we parted that afternoon seven years before, and Kant made his way home alone, limping painfully as the swirling fog swallowed him up. He did not seem a day older.

'My dear Hanno, how happy I am to see you!' he said warmly.

My first impulse was to take his hand and press it to my lips, but natural reserve stopped me. 'I did not expect you, sir,' I said, attempting to hide my confusion and embarrassment.

'I expected nothing less of you,' he returned with a welcoming smile. 'You made the acquaintance of Doctor Vigilantius last night, did you not?'

He did not wait for me to reply, but shuffled forward, still clutching the arm of his servant, and cast his eyes on the horrid spectacle. 'He has not wholly finished his examination, I see.'

Vigilantius was on his knees beside the dead boy, grunting like a pig over a mountain of offal. At the sound of his name he looked up quickly, acknowledged Kant with no more than a nod, then returned to his business. The scene was vile, nauseating, revolting, but Professor Kant did not appear to be in the least disturbed by what he saw.

'I hope the doctor will be able to tell us something useful,' he confided quietly, looking over his shoulder at me. His passionate concern spoke all the louder for a lack of violent animation. The keen intelligence shining from his eyes seemed to suggest that he had lost none of his renowned intellectual powers. 'You are wondering what he is doing here, are you not?'

Kant remained silent, waiting for me to reply.

'He is a follower of Swedenborg,' I said, carefully measuring my criticism. 'He claims to speak with the dead, sir. You condemned his master as a fake and a cozener.'

'Oh, that!' Kant returned with a tinkling laugh. '*Dreams of a Spirit Seer* is the only book of mine for which I have ever apologised. Do you disapprove of my having called on Swedenborg's spiritual heir in my search for the murderer?'

'*Your* search, sir? Indeed, I am puzzled,' I admitted.

'Were you not impressed by what he had to show you at the Fortress?' he asked, a thin smile tracing itself on his pale lips.

I hardly knew how to respond. 'The séance, sir?'

Kant frowned. 'Séance? Is that all you saw last night?'

'What else should I call it, sir? A man asking questions of a dead body, the corpse supposedly speaking back. I left Vigilantius knowing nothing that my own eyes did not tell me when I examined the body.'

'Ah!' Kant exclaimed with a smile. 'You ran out of patience and did not stay until the end. I should have foreseen that possibility,' he murmured. Then he looked at me attentively. 'So, you *are* surprised to see Vigilantius here, but you are *not* surprised to have been nominated in the place of Rhunken. Am I correct?'

His open irony regarding my appointment struck me like a slap in the face.

'It seems that I have you to thank for the honour, sir,' I began, but a louder voice than mine cut in.

'This death is not like the others, Herr Professor.'

Vigilantius was towering over Morik's body. 'This is the work of another killer,' he said.

'Another killer?' I repeated, appealing to Professor Kant. 'In God's name, sir, what is he talking about?'

Kant ignored me. Turning to Vigilantius, he said: 'Explain yourself.'

The doctor smiled triumphantly in my direction before he spoke. 'This corpse does not confirm what we know from the other bodies, Herr Professor. The scent here is . . . entirely different. The energy with which the soul left this body is distinct from what I have divined in other instances. They were taken unawares; this boy was not. He realised what was about to happen. He saw the blow before it fell, and he was terrified.'

Kant was silent, absorbed in his own thoughts.

'I see,' he said at last. 'And does this corpse tell you anything more?'

I was lost for words. What devilry could induce him to speak in such a deferential manner to an infamous necromancer? Kant had formulated a code of social ethics and rational analysis which had dragged Mankind out of the Dark and into the Light. And was he now inviting a smooth-tongued quack to reveal what a dead body had told him during a vulgar spirit-raising?

'Professor Kant!' I burst out, unable to contain myself. 'Herr Tifferch's corpse revealed what was obvious to any man with two eyes in his head. His back was covered with wounds, old and new . . .'

'I told you how he was murdered,' Doctor Vigilantius sneered. 'He did not die of those wounds. You would have had the proof if you had had the courtesy to wait last night.'

Kant turned and fixed me with a stare.

'Indeed, Herr Procurator, what did you make of those wounds?' he queried, like a falcon that has spotted a limping hare.

'I know they did not kill him,' I muttered. 'They were self-inflicted.'

'Self-inflicted?' Kant interrupted me. 'What do you mean?'

'I searched his house first thing this morning,' I began, 'and there I found evidence of how he had procured those wounds . . .'

I stopped, embarrassed to speak to Kant about such things.

'Well?' he insisted.

'A goad was carefully hidden in a cupboard, sir,' I murmured. 'Herr Tifferch had quite an eccentric private life.'

'How interesting!' Kant exclaimed. 'Rip the mask from any man's life, and what do we find? A black heart behind a smiling face, the bent wood of Humanity. Do you think that this is the motive behind his murder?'

'Not at all, sir,' I replied. 'There is another element which may indicate a common factor in all of the other killings, too.'

I took a deep breath before continuing. Immanuel Kant was the person that I admired above all the intellectual authorities in the Enlightened world. His learned meditations upon the topsy-turvy broomstick that was Man had marked out the path of Rational analysis and Enlightened behaviour. He had summoned me to Königsberg to assist in solving a mystery, and I did not intend to disappoint him.

'Herr Tifferch had a secret hoard of anti-Napoleonic trash hidden away in a cupboard,' I announced. 'He may have been assassinated by the political enemies of the State. Procurator Rhunken held the same opinion. I've read his reports . . .'

'But *how* did he die?' Kant spat out the question like an angry adder. 'That is the question which interests us, Stiffeniis.'

'I . . . I do not know yet,' I admitted hesitantly. 'He might . . .'

Kant was no longer listening. Curtly, he turned to Vigilantius.

'Is there any trace of the claw on the child's body?' he asked.

I was stunned. Professor Kant had used the term employed by the woman who had found the body of Jan Konnen. *The Devil's claw.*

'No sign, sir. Not this time,' Vigilantius replied gravely.

'What are you talking of?' I cried in frustration, excluded from their conversation by the cryptic intimacy of this exchange. Had

Jachmann been right to express concern for Kant's mental health? 'No trace of *what*?'

'I'll show you later,' Kant replied with a flash of impatience. 'If there are two murderers, we don't need paranormal powers to see the problem that it poses for the authorities. Come, Stiffeniis, let us take a closer look at the physical evidence.'

Laying his slender hand on my arm, pulling me forward, we took a step towards the body. Vigilantius moved aside with a sweep of his cloak like an actor who has successfully recited his lines and I forced myself to look down. I did not see the dead boy from The Baltic Whaler. I saw another body lying there on the wet ground, the skull crushed, bone splinters white and stark against the mess of blood and brain, eyes staring at me through a glassy veil. I fought to cancel out the unwanted vision, struggling to concentrate all my attention on what was, in that moment, before my eyes.

'This is him,' I mumbled. 'Morik.'

Signs of terrible violence were written on his face, or what was left of it. The left side of his skull had been crushed like a fragile eggshell. Slivers of brain and spots of congealed blood were splattered on his hair, temple, forehead and cheeks. His left eye stared up at the cloudy heavens from the corner of his mouth, as if it had crawled there of its own accord like some hideous slug.

Kant might almost have read my mind.

'Does this sight disturb you?' he asked, looking intently at me, studying my face, rather than the disfigured face of the dead child on the ground. 'Of course, it must. Your brother suffered similar wounds to the cranium, I suppose?'

I swallowed hard. Kant's concern had quite unmanned me.

'It . . . the crushing . . . was on the other . . . the right lobe,' I managed to reply.

'Were you obliged to examine his body?' Kant asked, scrutinising me closely. 'I don't remember having heard of a criminal investigation afterwards.'

'No, sir,' I murmured. 'There was no investigation.'

He hesitated a fraction. 'Let's get on with the business, then.'

'It . . . This, I mean, was a fearful blow,' I said, struggling to direct my attention to the dreadful sight before me. 'Death must have been instantaneous.'

'And the boy saw it coming,' Kant added. 'His fists will be clenched, I'd wager. Move his clothes away, will you?'

Before I could react, Koch had dropped to his knees and pulled the sodden clothes away from the boy's hands to reveal the accuracy of Kant's intuition.

'Sergeant Koch is my assistant,' I explained quickly, having completely forgotten his presence just a few steps behind me. 'He used to work for Procurator Rhunken.'

'His name is not new to me,' Kant replied, eyeing Koch curiously. He drew closer and followed every movement, his hand still on my arm, the other gripping his silent manservant for support.

'Note the look on the boy's face, Stiffeniis,' he said, his voice quavering with emotion. 'Physiognomy teaches us much regarding that expression, does it not?'

I could only stare at the dead boy's face, unable to frame a single thought.

'Can't you see?' Vigilantius snapped. 'Everything is different here.'

'Note the position of the legs,' Professor Kant continued, ignoring both of us, completely absorbed in what he was doing. 'The others were kneeling when they were murdered. This boy was not. You saw the position of the body of Herr Tifferch last night. Now you have room for comparison. I instructed the soldiers to conserve his corpse under the snow for you and the doctor to examine.'

So, there it was. The answer to the question with which I had been plaguing Koch. Professor Kant had been behind it all. He had arranged and orchestrated every move that I had made since reaching Königsberg. He had sent me to see Herr Rhunken, who was not expecting me. Then, I had been directed to the horror chamber of Vigilantius. Kant had decided that I ought to lodge at The Baltic Whaler. The police had had no say in the matter. Nor had the King. Immanuel Kant knew more about those murders than any man in Königsberg.

'Let's see if Vigilantius is right,' he said. 'Turn the boy on his stomach, Herr Koch. If you would be so kind?'

Koch lay Morik gently face-down in the mud. The boy's hair and neck were caked with blood and mud. 'Bring water, Sergeant,' Kant urged, and Koch sped off towards the bridge, returning with a metal water bottle he had taken from one of the soldiers.

'Douse his head,' Kant instructed. 'Pull back the hair. Remove that mud.'

He directed Koch's attentions with the firmness he might have used to guide the hand of his laboratory assistant at the University. 'More water. Clean the neck. Yes, there, there!' Kant pointed with impatience.

As the blood and the dirt drained away, white flesh emerged. Kant leaned forward and stared intently at the bumpy vertebrae of the boy's neck. 'There is no wound here. No sign of it at all. The injury to the skull was done with a hammer, or a heavy object. It ought to have bled copiously, and yet I see no sign of blood here on the ground.'

'The cold might have staunched the bleeding,' I suggested.

'The temperature cannot explain the absence,' Kant snapped with a flash of irritation.

'What would you suggest then, sir?' I asked.

'He was not killed here. Nor by the person that we are seeking. The evidence is quite plain,' he replied. 'This boy was killed for a different motive, whatever it may have been.'

I was bewildered. Kant had reached the same conclusion as Vigilantius.

'But there *cannot* be two murderers in Königsberg!' I protested. 'Morik was killed at the inn. I saw him there. His body was left here to throw me off the trail. I have every good reason to believe that he knew something about the other murders. Why, I spoke to him last night!'

Kant's eyes sparkled with excitement. 'You spoke to the boy? Do you mean to tell me that you arrived at the inn and immediately won his confidence? Well, that is truly remarkable! I was right to choose you, and correct again in sending you to The Baltic Whaler.'

For a moment, I believed he was teasing me. Then, I thought, perhaps he *was* genuinely impressed. He had placed me there for no other purpose, after all. 'That tavern is a hotbed of spying and sedition,' I said. 'But you knew that already, sir, didn't you?'

Kant looked at me, and I'd swear there was a mischievous twinkle in his eye.

'Your arrival must have caused some tension,' he observed quietly.

The events of the previous evening at the inn flashed before me. The anger on Herr Totz's face, the suspicious behaviour of his wife, the boy's terror of them both. I told Kant everything that Morik had revealed about the foreigners staying there, and added what I had seen from my bedroom the night before.

'It's just as Procurator Rhunken suspected,' I said. 'Insurrection. Foreign agitators. What better motive could explain these murders?'

'I could postulate a hundred,' Kant replied immediately. 'One certainly comes to mind.'

He gazed at the River Pregel, as if the dark waters were an aid to concentrated thought.

'I beg your pardon, sir?' I asked timidly.

'The sublime pleasure of killing, Stiffeniis,' he replied slowly, carefully separating his words.

I was amazed. Had I heard him right?

'Can you be serious, sir?' Sergeant Koch burst out. 'Excuse me, Herr Stiffeniis,' he apologised, 'I did not mean to interrupt.'

'I appreciate your frankness, Herr Koch,' Kant replied. 'Go on, Sergeant. Say what you feel compelled to say.'

'Could any sane person kill for such a reason?' Koch demanded. He did not seem to be the least intimidated by the mighty reputation of Immanuel Kant. 'For pleasure, and nothing more?'

Kant studied him quizzically for a moment. 'Have you ever been to war, Sergeant?'

Koch blinked and shook his head.

'But you do have friends or acquaintances in the army?'

'Yes, sir, but . . .'

Kant raised his hand. 'Bear with me, Koch. If you were to object that killing an enemy on the field of battle is a question of duty, I would not dispute it. But there is an ambiguity in doing the deed

125

which may be worthy of our consideration. I have met few soldiers who are ashamed of their murderous capacities, or reticent in claiming to have perpetrated the most exquisite savagery in the sacred name of duty. And not on the field of battle alone. Duelling is common among the officers in our army.' He nodded down at the corpse. 'A man who possesses these lethal skills may find untold pleasure in using them.'

'A soldier, sir? Is that your theory?'

Kant directed his attention to me, as if Koch had never opened his mouth.

'Imagine the power of life and death in the hands of this person, Stiffeniis! He chooses the victim. He chooses the time, and the place of the execution.' He counted off these circumstances on his thin white fingers. 'Only God has such unbridled power on this Earth. The act of killing may be a source of immense power, of gratification in itself, but that is not the end of it. Look over there,' he said, pointing across the river at the crowds lining the opposite bank. 'Look at the soldiers manning the bridge. Consider our presence here, the terror that moved the authorities to summon us. Whoever he is, whatever his motives may be, this person has unleashed Chaos in Königsberg. *He* commands us all!'

'Power, sir?' Koch insisted with a frown. The hypothesis seemed to alarm him more than any other possibility.

'A power which accepts no human limits, Sergeant Koch. A Deity. Or a Demon, if you like.'

A cold wind swept over the waters of the River Pregel. When Doctor Vigilantius spoke, his voice sounded as sharply as the first crack of the polar ice-cap in Spring.

'Professor Kant,' he said. 'I can do no more for you, sir. I have urgent business to attend to. If you need me again, you know how to contact me.'

'Your assistance has been of incalculable value in this affair, sir,' Kant replied with all the respect he might have employed if David Hume or Descartes had been present. 'Stiffeniis will make good use of your findings.'

With a final, dismissive glance in my direction, Augustus Vigilantius, that glowing meteor of the Swedenborgian universe, turned and walked away along the river bank, never to appear again in Königsberg while I was there, except in the columns of *Hartmanns Zeitung*. His 'urgent business' turned out to involve a conversation with a billy-goat, the animal having been possessed by the soul of the farmer who had once been its master.

Kant smiled warmly at me. 'I hope we'll have no further need of him,' he said. 'Now, regarding your conspiracy theory, Stiffeniis. You should verify it.'

I was taken back. 'I thought you did not share my opinion, sir?'

'It is your theory, Stiffeniis,' he said warmly. 'You must put it to the test. That is the essence of modern scientific methodology. Go at once to the Fortress and interrogate those people from the inn. When you've finished, there is something I would like to show you.'

'Excuse me, Herr Stiffeniis,' Koch intervened. 'What about the fisherman who found the corpse? You'll need to speak to him, sir.'

Before I could reply, Kant turned sharply on Koch.

'Don't waste your master's time! That poor fellow knows nothing, I am sure. I'll pick you up at four of the clock,' he said to me as he turned away towards the bridge. After a few halting steps, he looked back with an enigmatic smile. 'Aren't you curious to know more about the Devil's claw, Hanno?'

He did not wait for my answer.

'I am at your disposition, sir,' I murmured, watching in silence until he had safely reached the stairway to the road. Then, I gave orders for the body of Morik to be removed, waiting while the soldiers went about the sad business. As they covered his face, I recalled the fawning smile of Frau Totz and her pretence of concern for the child that morning. A wave of anger swept over me.

'To the Fortress, Koch,' I snapped. 'It is time to loosen some tongues.'

Chapter 12

Koch glanced around the room with a show of concern. 'I had your personal belongings brought here from the inn,' he said. 'It was the best I could do at such short notice, sir.'

The accommodation on the first floor of the Fortress was tiny. There was just space enough for a narrow bed and a wooden chair on which my travelling-bag had been placed. The acid taint of stale urine from a cracked porcelain night-bowl peeping beneath the cot hung heavily in the air. A window high in the wall provided next to no illumination, and it was icy cold in there. No one had taken the trouble to light the stove. The screaming and shouting of the prisoners down below was muted, which was a relief, but had a turnkey come along and locked us in for the duration, I would hardly have been surprised.

'It will do well enough,' I said with less animation than I truly felt. I had taken possession of Procurator Rhunken's private chamber, the room he used for resting when the pressure of work denied him the comfort of returning to his own house. I glanced at the four walls as if to familiarise myself with their grey drabness. 'This is where I should have been lodged in the first place,' I added with the conviction of an anchorite examining the cave in which he was destined to spend the rest of his penitent life.

'You did make some important discoveries down at The Baltic Whaler, sir,' the sergeant reminded me.

'We should be thankful for small mercies, I suppose.'

'Professor Kant seemed pleased,' Koch continued, though his tight-lipped manner gave the lie to the compliment.

'Is something bothering you, Koch?'

He did not try to deny the suggestion, tugging at his shirt collar as if the room were ten degrees warmer than it was. 'A couple of things, sir,' he began with some hesitancy. 'I was wondering about Professor Kant, sir.'

'What of him?' I asked brusquely.

'I was most surprised to find the gentleman down by the river this morning, sir. At his age, it seems rather odd that he should take such a . . . morbid interest in murder. Don't you think so, sir?'

'He is not vulgarly interested in murder, Koch, if that is what you mean,' I replied quickly, for the sergeant had given voice to a perplexity which I shared. 'Herr Professor Kant cannot countenance the disorder that crime brings, that's all. He fears for Königsberg and would suffer any inconvenience for the city that he loves.'

'Nevertheless, he did not seem to share your theory about a revolutionary conspiracy being the cause of these crimes,' Koch went on.

'Professor Kant is neither a magistrate nor a policeman,' I explained. 'He did concede that it seems to be the most obvious explanation. He is the supreme theorist of Rationalism in Prussia. He wants a hypothesis that can be confirmed by solid evidence. When we meet him again this afternoon, I intend to provide the definitive proof that he seeks.'

'Indeed, sir,' said Koch. He did not sound entirely convinced.

'And the other matter?'

Koch placed a hand on his vest as if to calm the beating of his heart or apologise in advance for what he was about to say. 'It concerns your brother, sir,' he said. 'Herr Kant spoke of him in connection with that boy this morning. Was your brother murdered, sir?'

I half turned away, opening my bag, pretending to look for something.

'Not murdered,' I snapped. 'As I told him, Sergeant, it was an accident. A most unfortunate accident.'

I rifled through the contents of my bag to avoid his gaze. When I looked up again, I thought I caught an expression of bewilderment on Koch's plain face. Brushing past him, I strode through to the connecting room.

'Where are the prisoners?' I asked.

'Officer Stadtschen is waiting on your orders before he brings them up, sir,' Koch replied, straightening his jacket, his face a neutral mask once more.

'Ask him to step in on his own first, would you?'

As if I had called the Devil, the Devil came. There was a sharp rap on the door, and Stadtschen presented himself with a stack of papers in his hands. He was an enormous man with a bloated red face, resplendent in an immaculate dark blue uniform with white stripes on his sleeves and along the seam of his riding-breeches. 'Foreign visitors in Königsberg, sir,' he said with a bow, handing me a copy of the list of names that had been drawn up for General Katowice.

I took the paper from him and scanned the names.

'Twenty-seven persons? In the whole of Königsberg?'

'We don't get many outlanders these days, sir,' the Officer replied. 'There are sailing-ships, of course, but they come and go the same day, most of them, or the crews sleep aboard. Casual visitors avoid the city, sir. No sensible man wants to get himself murdered.'

'Are any of the names on the list known to the police?'

'No, sir. I checked them myself.'

I noted the names of the three gem-traders who had been at The Baltic Whaler the night before. 'You searched the inn, did you not?'

'Indeed, sir,' he said, placing a large bundle of papers on the desk before me. 'This is a sample of the material we discovered there.'

'Where was it hidden?'

'In a secret room, Herr Procurator. A trap-door beneath the carpet in one of the upstairs bedrooms.'

The image of Morik spying came back to me. Was that what he had been trying to communicate to me the night before? That a seditious meeting was going on in that room opposite my window?

'Papers and maps, sir,' Stadtschen went on.

'Maps?'

'Of Königsberg, sir, and other places, too. And pamphlets written in French. The name of Bonaparte figured large in the texts.'

'Did you find any weapons?'

'None, sir,' Stadtschen replied with a grin, 'except for an old pistol in the bedchamber of Totz. It's as rusty as a lost anchor and would blow up in the face of anyone rash enough to fire it.'

'How many persons did you arrest?'

'The landlord and his wife only. Those tradesmen that Sergeant Koch said you were interested in had left the city early this morning. They may have left by sea. The gendarmes are trying to trace them now.'

'Did Totz or his wife say anything at the moment of their arrest?'

'I didn't pay them much attention, sir,' Stadtschen replied. 'I had more important business to attend to.'

'What do you mean?'

'Well, sir,' Stadtschen wiped his hand across his mouth. 'The lads have been under a lot of pressure since these murders started up. I had a tough time keeping them in order. I didn't want them taking justice into their own hands, if you know what I mean.'

'Very good,' I said. 'We may as well begin.'

Stadtschen snapped to attention. 'First, sir, General Katowice wants the prisoners in Section D to be separated from the rest.'

'Section D?' I queried.

'The deportees, sir. The General wants them to be moved to Pillau port, sir. Ready for immediate embarkation. If there is a French plot, the prison will start to fill up with political agitators and terrorists. Königsberg Fortress could turn into the Prussian equivalent of the Bastille, sir. That was how the General put it. Sixty deportees left Swinemunde jail yesterday aboard the *Tsar Petr*. It should dock in Pillau some time tomorrow, sir. Procurator Rhunken had drawn up a provisional list' – Stadtschen took a deep breath, and dropped his eyes – 'but, well, he didn't have the chance to sign or seal it, sir.'

He handed me a document written in italic script on heavy parchment. I knew the Royal Edict referred to in the title. A copy of the original had been sent to my office in Lotingen some months before. Fear of a Jacobin revolution had taken hold in Prussia; all prison governors had been ordered to compile a list of 'men who pose a threat to the security of the commonwealth, using every violent expedient to free themselves from captivity, having frustrated the mission of the penal institutions to reform and chastise them.'

'Procurator Rhunken had selected six names for deportation, sir. General Katowice has added two more. He requests you to finalise the procedure.'

I took a rapid glance at the names inscribed on the parchment.

Geden Wrajewsky, 30, deserter
Matthias Ludwigssen, 46, forger of coin in base metals
Jakob Stegelmann, 31, evil disposition, 53 convictions for
    drunkenness and brawling
Helmut Schuppe, 38 . . .

'Good God!' I exclaimed with horror as I read the charges against him. 'The wolves of Siberia won't have much of a chance with men like these.'

'Aye, sir,' Stadtschen said with a grim smile. 'They're a bad lot, all right.'

Andreas Conrad Segendorf, murder and abduction
Franz Hubtissner, 43, cattle thief
Anton Lieberkowsky, 31, murdered his brother with an axe . . .

My heart began to race. How many years of hard labour, flogging, ice and biting wind would be needed to punish such a Cain?

'If you want to add Totz and his wife to the list, sir,' Stadtschen added, 'I'll have them moved to Section D straight away.'

I dipped the pen in the inkwell and drew a line beneath the names. As I wrote my signature, I asked myself how many extra days of life this decision would grant to the murderer, Ulrich Totz, and his partner in crime. Prisoners condemned to hard labour in Russia were unlikely to last more than two or three months.

'I wish to complete my investigation before deciding what to do with them. Excellent work, Stadtschen. You have done well,' I said, handing him back the document. His face flushed with pride. Winning my favour, he could hope to accelerate his advancement. 'Now, we'll have Gerta Totz in first.'

I was eager to begin. Had the landlady known of Morik's fate that morning when she declared herself to be so concerned for the boy's safety? Would she be so keen to smile now that Morik was dead, and she found herself facing a charge of murder?

The prisoner was ushered into my office some minutes later.

'Come forward, Frau Totz,' I said, pointedly ignoring her, shuffling through the papers Stadtschen had left upon the table: red rags intended to foment political discontent, intermingling Bonaparte's name and catchphrases I had heard in France – Liberty, Equality and barbarous violence. 'Now, let us . . .'

I looked up. What I saw froze the words on my tongue. The woman had been more roughly handled than Stadtschen had admitted. Her face was swollen, bruised and puffy, the lower lip split and bloody. Nevertheless, she still managed a lopsided version of the sugary smile with which she had greeted me earlier that morning.

'Herr Procurator?' she said, clasping her hands together in a servile manner, as if waiting for me to order my food and drink.

'Sit down,' I said, avoiding her eyes.

Stadtschen placed a heavy hand on her shoulders and sat the woman down with such force that it made the chair creak. I was about to reprimand him, but the memory of the crushed skull of Morik, the eye dangling at the corner of his mouth, flashed through my mind.

'Well, Gerta Totz, what have you to say for yourself?'

She looked up with a pitiful grimace of hideous concern. 'Herr Stiffeniis, I humbly beg your pardon,' she mumbled, stifling tears with bunched fists. 'They closed the inn, sir. What will you do now? Where will you stay?'

'That is the least of your worries,' I replied. 'You told me this morning that you were looking for Morik. Did you know that he was dead?'

'Oh, Herr Stiffeniis! What are you saying, sir? I was fretted out of my mind. That boy's a blessed nuisance. I thought he might be bothering you . . .'

'Why should he bother me?' I interrupted.

'He knew you were a magistrate. He . . .'

'Is that why he was killed?'

133

'What an idea, sir!' she mumbled. 'I was right to worry, was I not, sir?'

'There have been some devious goings-on in your house,' I continued. 'Morik uncovered the plot. He knew that the murders in Königsberg had been planned and carried out by you, your husband, and other persons who frequented the inn.'

She did not contest what I said. Not directly.

'Is that what Morik told you, sir?' she replied. She joined her hands like a child at prayer and leaned towards my desk, struggling against the restraining hand of Officer Stadtschen, blood trickling freely from the split in her lower lip and running down her chin and throat. 'My Ulrich feared as much. He saw Morik hovering around your table last night. We both did, sir. I warned him off. And then I warned you too, sir, didn't I?'

I did not trouble myself to respond.

'I did, sir. Really, I did. But that boy had a wild imagination,' she went on. 'He was a danger. Who could tell where the truth started and the lies ended with him? When my husband was told of your coming, the first thing he said was this: "We'll have to send that lad away, Gerta." Ulrich was afraid no good would come of it if Morik got to know about your business in Königsberg. But we couldn't afford another lad.'

'The Baltic Whaler is a notorious haunt for foreign conspirators,' I pressed on. 'There were three of them present at dinner yester-night, two Frenchmen and a man of German origin, who claimed to be merchants in precious gems. What have you to say about them?'

'Those travellers, sir? It's not the first time they've stayed at the inn. Very righteous, hard-working gentlemen they are. Always paid their bills on time.'

'They are Jacobins,' I insisted. 'French spies.'

The woman blinked at the violence of my reaction. 'I don't know what's got into you, sir,' she protested. 'They're honest men, I'd swear!'

'You and your husband plotted with them, Frau Totz,' I persisted. 'That is why Morik was murdered.'

134

'It isn't true, sir,' she whined. 'It isn't. My Ulrich was glad about what happened in France, I won't deny it. Who wasn't? The Revolution was what the French went and done because they had that terrible king of theirs, not a gentleman with fair laws and respect for the people like our dear King Frederick. Them French ideas aren't so very terrible, sir. Liberty, Equality, Frat . . .'

'We are not talking about ideas,' I insisted. 'There was a plot against the government, Frau Totz.'

'A plot, sir?' she whimpered, raising her hands to heaven and shaking her head from side to side in denial. 'Is that what Morik told you?'

'I told you that I had seen Morik in a room across the courtyard from my own. You denied the fact this morning. Yet, in that room, the very *same* room, the gendarmes discovered this hoard of subversive material.'

'It's nothing but a storeroom, sir!' she cried. 'I denied its existence, 'cause I didn't want you worrying over the silly things in that boy's head.'

'The boy is dead!' I shouted. 'Murdered for those *silly things*!'

'We all use that cellar, sir,' she moaned desperately. 'All of us. Me, my husband, Morik. Yes, Morik, sir! It's crammed with broken furniture and all the summer linen for the inn, plus stuff that people leave behind without thinking. We never throw nothing away in case they come and ask for them back. Whatever was found, if it isn't used in the inn, it isn't ours, sir. I swear to you.'

'Stadtschen, where exactly was the subversive material found?'

'Well hidden in a trunk beneath some blankets, sir,' the officer confirmed.

'Those papers aren't ours, sir,' Gerta Totz protested. 'I've never seen them. And as for Morik, I only took him in to help my sister. He wasn't right in the head. And these murders didn't do him any good at all. It's quite possible that he believed the murderer was hiding in our house, but surely you don't think so? Not *you*, Herr Stiffeniis? Ulrich and me have been as scared to walk the streets as any innocent souls in all these months. It hasn't been easy, we've had a dropping-off in trade. Since that man was found dead out on the quay, we've been hard-pushed to keep the place going.'

All of this came out in such an impetuous rush that I had diffi-culty in writing it down. The brazen woman was lying, but I would need to break her resistance if I hoped to incriminate her and Totz.

'These lies are enough to condemn you,' I stated, staring at her coldly.

I saw a different Gerta Totz before me, a perverse, criminal ver-sion of the homely, comforting and all too inquisitive landlady I had met for the first time the night before. It was the fixed grin on her face that did it. Its mincing falsity gave me the shivers. She was accused of murder, yet she insisted on smiling, as if that smile were her most tried and proven resource. It haunts me still.

'You're going to torture me, aren't you, sir?'

I froze.

Had she read my thoughts, interpreted some malign expression on my face? Though King Frederick Wilhelm III had formally pro-hibited its use, the Royal Decree had not put an end to the practice. Karl Heinz Starbeinzig, a prominent Prussian jurist, had recently published an essay in favour of its reintroduction, which had been extremely well received at Court. 'Torture is fast and cheap,' he argued. 'It embodies those two essential principles of the modern state: economy and efficiency.' To obtain precise details of how and why Morik had been killed, torture might prove to be useful.

Frau Totz let out a whimper of fear. 'You have the power to kill me and Ulrich, sir. But what's happening in Königsberg won't end with us.'

'We'll see about that. Do you have anything more to add at this time?'

She wept aloud and tore her hair, but said not a word. I nodded to Stadtschen to take her out of the room. But as he tried to pull her to her feet, the woman threw herself forward onto my table. The bloody slobber from her lips dripped onto my notes. She stared up at me with defiance, the hideous smile still there, but twisted now with rage.

'Why did you come to The Baltic Whaler?' she snarled. 'What did you want from us?'

I pushed back from the spray of blood and bile.

'Somebody sent you. To catch us in a trap.'

Stadtschen had her by the neck and attempted to drag her from my desk.

'Somebody who holds the city dear,' I snapped.

'Someone who wants to destroy us,' she screeched back, hanging on by her nails to the desk. 'The Devil sent you! The Devil!'

'You'll never know how wrong you are.'

'*You* killed Morik!' she spat the words into my face. Blood splattered my hands and the linen cuffs of my shirt. 'You, and whoever sent you to the inn!'

'Stadtschen, take her out,' I shouted, but Frau Totz grasped the table like a fury, and pushed towards me.

'I knew you'd bring destruction on us. The instant I saw your face. You started Morik off! He told his stupid stories, and you believed them. There was nothing to discover in our inn. *You* came, and Morik died. *You* slaughtered him, Herr Stiffeniis. And now you're going to butcher us . . .'

It happened so quickly, I took myself by surprise. Before I knew it, my bunched fist shot out and hit the woman square on the nose. It was not a terrible blow, but sufficient to make the blood spurt from her nostrils. Her body jerked with pain as she slid to the floor.

'Take her down,' I ordered.

Both Koch and Stadtschen stared at me in silence.

'Stadtschen, take her down to the cells,' I repeated.

Officer Stadtschen blinked, then stepped forward and lifted the woman up from the floor. He cuffed her on the back of the head as he pushed her out of the door. 'They ought to string you up, you shameless whore!' he shouted. 'We'll give you a welcome here you won't forget!'

I sat down at my desk, took a long, deep breath, then carefully wiped away the spots of blood from my person and my papers with a bit of rag cloth I used to clean my pens.

'They'll hurt her, sir,' Koch warned in a low voice. 'The guards will do her serious harm.'

I did not look at him. Nor did I reply. What cruel thoughts passed through my mind in that instant? What punishment did I believe she merited for what she had done to Morik?

I picked up my quill, dipped it deep into the inkwell, then signed and dated the woman's deposition with great deliberation. I melted wax in the candlelight and carefully affixed my seal.

Then, and only then, I turned to Sergeant Koch.

'Tell Stadtschen to bring up the husband,' I said.

Chapter 13

Gerta Totz had told me the name of Morik's killer. Despite the absurdity of the accusation, I could not shake off the sense of responsibility and even guilt that it involved. Had I been the unwitting cause of the boy's death? Had the mere act of speaking to me been enough to provoke his killer?

I tried to displace these sombre thoughts with others of a more resolute kind. I would need to be more incisive if I hoped to confirm my suspicions of a political plot at The Baltic Whaler. I had learned little from Frau Totz. Unless her husband were more forthcoming, I would be obliged to resort to torture. Whether I felt happy with the idea or not, the worsening political situation would oblige me to use hot irons and crushing weights.

Officer Stadtschen entered the room a moment later, pushing Ulrich Totz before him. The innkeeper appeared to have been more liberally treated than his wife. He had suffered a dull, dark bruise high on his forehead, but nothing worse. There were no open wounds. No blood to spatter my papers and my clothing.

'Sit down, Totz,' I said, waving him to the chair.

'I'd rather stand,' he replied.

Stadtschen jabbed him in the back.

'Do as you are told,' he growled.

I observed Ulrich Totz from the corner of my eye while I organised fresh paper, and prepared myself to question him. A supercilious smile played about his surly lips.

'Does something amuse you, Herr Totz?' I enquired.

'With your permission, Herr Stiffeniis,' he began, 'that cell stinks. It's full of rats. You found comfort under my roof.'

'It is cosy compared to the unmarked grave of a murderer,' I snapped.

He answered this with a lazy shrug. 'Very well, Herr Procurator Stiffeniis,' he said, 'let's get down to business. It won't take long. I admit my crime. I killed our Morik with these here hands.'

He held them up to me for examination. They were large and meaty. I saw them picking up some heavy object, and smashing open the side of Morik's head. How many blows had it taken, I wondered with an inward shiver, before the boy's eye popped out from its socket and the skull poured forth its bloody pulp? Despite the feeling of revulsion, my heart leapt with excitement. The murderer was ready to confess.

'I want the facts, Totz,' I said calmly.

He nodded, then spoke for ten minutes without a pause, describing all that had taken place at The Baltic Whaler the night before. Such an ample confession should have pleased me, yet there was something mellifluous and practised in the telling that disconcerted me. Only the temptation to believe that these bare-faced admissions would soon release me from the investigation stilled the objections I might have raised. I let him go on unchecked, my hand racing over the page as I recorded his admissions.

'I've always supported what happened back in '89,' he declared proudly. 'Kings and nobles prancing around, while we slave day and night like dogs over the bones. I'm a Jacobin, all right, Monsieur Robespierre's my god. I don't give a hoot for religion. That's more bloodsuckers for you. Priests! Chop their stinking heads off, and good riddance, I say. Not just in France, but here in Prussia too. Damned Pietists! Just you wait 'til Napoleon gets here! He'll show 'em! I knew the inn was being watched by the police, but no one could prove a thing against me. Not 'til you arrived.'

Totz wiped his mouth on the back of his sleeve, and stared back at me with nonchalant indifference. 'The minute you turned up, I knew the danger we were facing,' he continued. 'Well, two can play at that little game, thinks I, and I played my part well enough. But then Morik had to go and stick his nose in the pie. I caught him spying again last night. He would have told you soon enough . . .'

'Is that why you killed him?'

Totz's eyes blazed with hatred. 'Revolutions have their victims! You might almost say you killed him yourself, Herr Procurator. If you hadn't come along when you did, no one here in Königsberg would have given Morik a second of his precious time.'

'Where was he killed?'

Ulrich Totz let out a long, weary sigh. 'I don't know why you're bothering to ask,' he sneered. 'You saw him from your window, Gerta told me. God knows how you didn't see me as well! I caught him lurking outside the store-room, so I just pushed him down the stairs.'

So, it was Totz's face that I had seen at Morik's back the night before. The admission should have banished any lingering doubts from my mind. So why did I have the feeling that he was telling me exactly what I wanted to hear?

'Pushed him down the stairs, Totz? You did much more than that!'

'When I found him snooping there, I knew for certain he'd tell you. I had to kill him, didn't I? He was courting you like a big, fat maggot on a tasty bit of red meat.'

'Let's be more precise about what happened, Totz,' I interrupted. 'You grabbed the lad and you pushed him down the stairs. Is that what you are saying?'

'I saw you blowing out your candle and closing the curtain to go to bed. That was when I decided to act.'

'Very well. You pushed him down the stairs, and then?'

'I ran down after him and struck him dead.'

'What did you hit him with?'

'The first thing I laid my hands on.'

'*What*?' I insisted.

He did not hesitate. 'A hammer we use for opening barrels. It was easy. He was that scared. But you knew that already, didn't you? He told you himself that his life was in danger.'

'You are not here to question me, Totz,' I warned.

'What do you want to know then, sir?' he replied with a shifty look.

'I want to know why you killed the boy there in the cellar. In your own house. Why not lure him out of the inn?'

Totz shrugged. 'He'd never have come with me. And sooner or later, you'd have paid attention. What else could I do? I had to silence him. And quick.'

'You could have sent him out of Königsberg. Home to his mother.'

'And you'd have been more suspicious than ever! No, better another victim of the Königsberg killer. Another dead body in the streets.'

'And your wife was a party to it?'

'Gerta don't know nothing,' he added quickly. 'She wouldn't hurt a fly.'

'You killed him by yourself, then? No one helped you?'

'That's right, sir. One proper blow and the boy was dead. There was blood all over the place.'

'If I may speak, sir,' Officer Stadtschen intervened, 'I can confirm that an attempt had been made to clean up the mess, but there were traces of blood everywhere.'

I turned back to Totz. 'Why did you take the body to the river?' I asked.

Ulrich Totz smiled that slow, dreamy smile once more.

'I wanted him to be found, sir. Like all the others. But not outside my own door again. Konnen brought trouble down hard on me. We lost a lot of business after that. The river's only a couple of hundred yards away from the inn through the back streets.'

'How did you carry the boy, Totz?'

'In a sack slung over the back of my old packhorse. He didn't weigh a mite. I threw the rags I'd used to clean the blood into the river. Ten, fifteen minutes, it didn't take no more. We come back unseen, and . . .'

'*We?*' I raised my head sharply from the words I had just transcribed. 'You, and who else, Totz? Your wife? One of the guests?'

'Me and *the packhorse*. Don't insist, Herr Procurator. Gerta knows less than nothing about all of this.'

'She knows that you killed Morik, does she not?' I countered, uncertain whether some vestige of humanity might be leading him

142

to shield his wife from her part of the blame in their nephew's death.

'She does not, sir. She'll ne'er forgive me. Morik was her sister's only son. She's always felt a duty to help that boy.'

'But who helped *you*, Totz? I can hardly believe that one man . . .'

'Herr Procurator, I've already told you,' Totz replied forcibly. 'I did it all on my own. By myself. No one helped me.'

'What about those foreigners who were staying at the inn last night?'

He shrugged. 'The Frenchmen? They were customers, paying guests. No more, no less,' he answered squarely, his eyes blazing fiercely into my own.

'I don't believe you,' I said.

He looked at me coolly for a moment, then an ugly smirk erupted on his face. 'Believe whatever you like, Herr Procurator. I'll not tell you any more about my private affairs.'

'We will see about that,' I replied, eyeing him coldly, letting the threat dangle. 'We have proven methods of making the recalcitrant talk.'

'Torture, sir? Is that your game? I bet you enjoy seeing 'em stretched out on the rack, screaming their guts out, don't you, sir?'

If Ulrich Totz was trying to taunt me, he succeeded. As a consequence, I felt less hesitation about the idea of subjecting him to pain. Indeed, I almost enjoyed the prospect. He would laugh from the other side of his insolent mouth.

'Give over with your threats, Herr Procurator,' he stared back at me with that look of open hatred I had seen before. 'I'm a dead man, you can't scare me with talk of torture. I don't mind dying for what I believe in.'

'They were harmless people, Totz,' I hissed. 'There is nothing noble in the murders that have embroiled Königsberg. Do you really believe that rebellion will automatically follow on because you have slaughtered a few innocents?'

'It serves the purpose!'

'Purpose?'

'Revolution, sir.'

I ignored this barb. 'Apart from Morik, how did you choose the other victims, Totz?'

He did not reply at once, but sat so long in silence that I thought the question had gone over his head. And all the while, he stared at me fixedly in what I took to be sullen reproach. Only later did I realise that there was crude calculation in his behaviour. He was trying to figure out how much I knew, while I was more than convinced that this was the devil who had unleashed mayhem in the city. The fact that he showed no remorse reinforced my belief.

'I will repeat the question, Totz,' I said more slowly. 'How did you choose the victims?'

'The time, the place,' he murmured. 'The fact that there were no witnesses hanging around. It was all a question of opportunity. That was the beauty of it. I'd seen Konnen in the inn the night I first got the idea . . .'

'There was no political reason behind your choice?'

Totz sat up straighter in his chair, his mouth drawn in a stiff-lipped smile, but he said nothing. I thought he seemed intent on outfacing me.

'You knew Herr Tifferch, didn't you? He was a prominent lawyer, a well-known hater of Napoleon . . .'

'All Prussians hate Napoleon!' he seethed, his face a mask of hatred. 'Any one of the buggers is a political target as far as I'm concerned. That lawyer was a parasite! Living off the *Junkers*! Helping to buy and sell for them, sending their tenants to jail for debts and unpaid rents. I'll get even with the lot of them!'

'You will hang from the gallows,' I stated coldly.

I added a note in my report to the effect that the anti-French sentiments of the penultimate victim had been the probable cause of his murder. Everything seemed to me to be suddenly sharp and clear, like a magic-lantern projection when the lamp is lit, the lens is turned and the first slide comes into focus. With one reservation only.

'Were you not afraid of being recognised?'

Ulrich Totz seemed to relax more comfortably in the chair. 'People here know me. That made things easier. I'm an innkeeper, see?

I know everyone. It was normal enough for me to walk up to someone, stop them, chat for a bit, see that no one else was around, then strike. They didn't have time to take in what was happening.'

'Very good,' I said. 'Now, tell me about the weapon that you used.'

He stared at me. 'I've told you already,' he said.

'You used a hammer to kill Morik, you say. But what about the others?'

Despite his readiness to confess, I still had no idea how the other victims had died.

Ulrich Totz rubbed his knuckles and eyed me warily.

'I used whatever came to hand,' he said slowly. 'The hammer, stones, my own hands.'

'How did you kill Herr Tifferch, for instance? He had no visible wounds. What weapon did you use on him?'

For the first time, Totz was silent.

'What about this Devil's claw that all the town is talking of?' I insisted.

Ulrich Totz looked from me to Koch, then back again. He smiled, weakly at first, then with growing confidence. 'Oh, I can see your point, sir,' he said with a flash of cunning. 'I tell you all I know, you pack your things and go back home. Got a wife and bairns waiting for you, is that it? I've told you more than enough already, Herr Procurator. The rest you'll have to discover for yourself.'

Suddenly, he leaned forward and rested his forearm on my desk. I held up my hand to stay Stadtschen and Sergeant Koch. They had made to pounce on him to protect me.

'Well, Totz? What more have you to add?'

He eyed me without speaking for some moments.

'Listen, Herr Stiffeniis, and listen good,' he said in a low, surly voice. 'You can torture me if it pleases you. You can make me scream, but I'll tell you nowt. You can torture my wife, and she'll agree to any words you care to put into her mouth, knowing nothing for a fact. But that's the end of it. I don't intend to say another word to you, or to anyone else, 'til they lead me to the scaffold.'

'This is not the end of our conversation, Totz,' I returned, staring into his half-closed eyes. 'I will interrogate you again, and you will tell me everything. Every single thing! About the pamphlets and those foreign agents who helped in your conspiracy. Next time, there'll be no holds barred.'

'Do your worst, Herr Stiffeniis,' the innkeeper replied in a low murmur. 'That's your job. Mine is to resist.'

'We'll soon see which of us is the better at his task,' I said dismissively, pulling out my watch. It was almost four o'clock. Time for my appointment with Professor Kant. I had made enough progress for one day.

'Take him away, Stadtschen.'

The room seemed suddenly empty. Ulrich Totz had filled the space with his anger, his cruelty and his undisguised hatred for authority. Koch remained silent, and I was certain that he was waiting for me to make some comment. I stood up and walked across to the window. Outside, the daylight was fading. My throat was dry, and I felt light-headed. Ulrich Totz had confessed to killing Morik. My theory of a political plot aimed at creating terror had been confirmed, the murderer had a name. I should have felt proud of myself, and yet, for some niggling reason, I was not entirely convinced. Wasn't it all just a mite too easy? Could the mystery of Königsberg be such a simple thing? Surely, a magistrate of Procurator Rhunken's vast experience ought to have arrived at such a conclusion months before.

'If I may make a suggestion,' Koch spoke out, 'a public whipping in the square outside the Fortress would not go amiss, sir. I could request permission from General Katowice, if you wish. Procurator Rhunken was a great believer in the efficacy of the rod. Two years ago, a man was whipped for murdering his father. He was, of course, beheaded some months later. But the example made a lasting impression on the populace.'

Should I follow the lead of Rhunken? Corporal punishment and physical mutilation were still admitted within the *Constitutio Criminalis Carolina*, though it had been formulated in the sixteenth century by Charles V.

'Times are changing, Koch,' I replied. 'King Frederick Wilhelm is an enlightened monarch. He believes, quite rightly, that public cruelty may arouse the sympathy of the watching crowd, and thus frustrate the intended purpose of the punishment. If Totz and his wife are members of an active group of Jacobins, a public whipping may inflame the spirits of the other members. In attempting to douse the flames, we may succeed in fanning them. I will speak to the suspects first, and warn them of the danger. We have time a-plenty.'

I collected my papers together, and began to put them away in my bag.

'In any case,' I said, looking at my watch, 'we have an appointment to keep. Professor Kant and the mysterious Devil's claw await us.'

'Is there any point, sir?' Koch returned. 'I mean to say, you seem to be well on the way to concluding the case without his help.'

He was right, of course. I ought to have pressed on, there and then, with my interrogation of the Totzes. 'Beat the iron while it's red and hot, the people say in Lotingen. But Professor Kant would never forgive me if I let him down.

'Since the case is so clear-cut,' I said with a smile, 'we can afford to indulge an old man's whims for an hour.'

As we left the room and hurried down the stairs together, I began to compose in my head the letter which would announce my success to Helena, and the prospect of my early homecoming.

I could not have imagined in that moment of heady euphoria the difficulty I would experience before the day was out in holding a pen, or in trying to form the letters with my shaking hand.

Chapter 14

A smart black coach was waiting for me outside the Fortress gate.

I could not avoid smiling as I made my approach. Professor Kant was busily consulting his pocket-watch behind the closed windows. His insistence on punctuality was maniacal, and all the world knew it. But as I raised my fist to tap on the glass and announce my arrival, a hand touched me fleetingly on the elbow, and a voice whispered, 'May I speak with you, sir?'

The servant who had been solicitous of Kant's safety that morning on the river bank was peeping from the rear corner of the coach. His large, strong face, which had appeared so expressionless then, now seemed tense and drawn.

'Johannes Odum, isn't it?'

With a pointed glance he indicated that I should join him behind the coach.

'Your master will not condone time-wasting,' I warned him.

'A word, sir, no more,' he insisted. He gestured towards the vehicle and its passenger with his thumb. 'Recent events have been a trial for him, sir. What we saw this morning down by the river is good for no man, sir, least of all a gentleman of his age and delicate nervous disposition.'

'You were there, you saw him yourself,' I whispered. 'Professor Kant may be frail, but he seems to be holding up.'

Perhaps I ought to have warned the servant that the danger was past, and that the case was closed, but I had no intention of wasting such momentous news on Kant's valet before I had told it to the man himself.

'He's been working night and day at this investigation, sir,' the servant replied. 'All night sometimes . . .'

'All night?' I interrupted. 'Doing what?'

'Writing, I believe, sir.'

I thought of the treatise that Herr Jachmann had mentioned, his incredulity regarding its existence. 'Do you know *what* he is writing?'

Johannes Odum shrugged his broad shoulders dismissively.

'He's in danger, sir,' he insisted. 'Real danger. He was seen with you this morning by the river. Now, you'll be seen travelling in his coach. And before we left the house this morning, I found something that you should see . . .'

'Johannes!' The fretful shout made both of us start. 'Where is Procurator Stiffeniis?'

I signalled to the servant to run around the other side of the vehicle, while I stepped out and attracted Professor Kant's attention.

'Here I am, sir,' I said brightly. 'I left some papers behind in the office, and had to go back for them. Do you mind if Sergeant Koch joins us?'

I nodded to Koch to stand forward.

'Of course not,' Kant replied with impatience. 'We must hurry. The way is long, and it is extremely cold.'

'Off to Siberia, are we, sir?' I joked. I knew I could not fail to hit the mark. Kant's hunger for information and gossip was as renowned as his clock-watching. The news of the ship that was about to moor in Pillau port could not have escaped him. It had featured prominently in all the recent Prussian papers.

'Not so far,' he replied with a smile, 'but just as cold.'

I laughed heartily. I was in an excellent humour. The case was over, except for the red tape. Even if they managed to escape the hangman, Ulrich and Gerta Totz would be deported to the frozen wastes. I had no idea where Professor Kant was taking us, nor what he intended to show us. Whatever it might be, I thought, humouring the old gentleman would add nothing material to the investigation. But nor would it detract.

As the coach sped forward, I expected him to ask me about the progress I had made that afternoon. Was he not curious to know what had happened? He had been so openly sceptical that morning, yet he had urged me to interrogate Ulrich and Gerta Totz. Surely he would wish to know what they had said?

'Do you like your new lodgings?' he asked suddenly. 'They hardly compare with the delights of The Baltic Whaler, I'd wager. Frau Totz is renowned for her roast pork.'

Was he teasing me? Was my ex-landlady's cooking all that interested him?

'The inn was certainly comfortable,' I conceded uncertainly.

'I knew you'd feel at home there,' Kant said with a warm smile. 'Of course, the Fortress of Königsberg is another matter altogether.'

Was this the behaviour that had so disturbed Herr Jachmann? Kant seemed to be absorbed in details which were of no importance, concerned about matters of which he could have no personal knowledge. He had dined in his own home and nowhere else for the last twenty years, as all the newspaper sketches of his doings habitually reported. Celebrity has no secrets from the intrusions of the press.

'What a depressing building the Fortress is!' he said next, his mood shifting suddenly. 'The sight of it used to put the wind up me when I was just a little child. Mother and I were obliged to pass each morning on our way to the Pietist Temple. The fear I felt, she said, was naught compared to the fear I'd feel the day I had to stand before my Maker and look into His eyes!'

Professor Kant looked out of the window like a lost child. The Fortress had fallen far behind, but it might still have been visible before his eyes. 'Will you be able to sleep in there tonight, Hanno? They say that the place is haunted by the victims of the Teutonic Knights who died in the dungeons.'

What could I reply? Koch and I exchanged glances, but neither dared say a word. As our coach clattered and rattled over an ancient wooden bridge, dense fog swirled in twirling clouds above the still waters of a dark moat. Only the towering keep of the Fortress on the hill above was visible in the fading afternoon light. The battlements seemed to peep over a solid wall of low clouds.

Kant glanced in my direction. 'Nearly there!' he exclaimed gaily as the coach turned sharply right and crossed another bridge. Clearly, he was excited by the prospect of what lay before us. 'I suppose that you have been counting the bridges?' he said.

'Bridges, sir?' I had no idea what he was talking about.

'Surely you know the problem?' he replied. 'Before he died, the great mathematician, Leonhard Euler, questioned whether it were possible to trace a route through Königsberg which crossed the nine bridges spanning the River Pregel without ever using the same bridge more than once. You ought to try it while you are here.'

I began to remind him of the reason which had brought me to Königsberg, but he had no mind for me. 'When I began to teach at the University,' he went on, 'I won a bet with a colleague who had been a great friend of the mathematician. He told me that, in fact, Euler himself didn't know the answer! Well, I provided two solutions to the problem . . .'

He did not finish. Turning to me instead, he laid his hand on my arm, and asked urgently: 'What have you to tell me about the Totzes?'

For some moments, I knew not how to reply. Should I tell him that the case was solved, the guilty closed in their cells, awaiting judgement? That the Devil's claw, whatever it might prove to be, was irrelevant?

'The husband confessed, sir. And quickly too,' I replied. With care, limiting myself to the sequence of events, suppressing the cry of victory which hovered on my lips, I related the facts to Kant as neutrally as possible.

'So, that's that,' he said. 'A political plot is at the root of all the evil which has poisoned Königsberg. Acts of terrorism aimed at . . .'

He halted abruptly, and looked at me.

'Aimed at *what*? Did the culprits reveal their final objective?'

'Not in so many words, sir,' I admitted. 'Ulrich Totz seems to believe that the fear generated by these murders will weaken the faith of the people in their rulers and provoke some sort of a revolution. I suspect that he targeted people who were known for their opposition to the French.'

Professor Kant sat back in his seat. He beamed with delight.

'Oh, I see! How clever of him! And he described the weapon that he used to kill Morik, I suppose?'

I shifted uneasily on the leather bench.

'A hammer, sir.'

My answer seemed to amuse Kant even more. 'A large hammer, Stiffeniis, or a small one?' he asked.

'It . . . it was only a preliminary interrogation,' I stammered. I had thought to win his praise. Instead, his penetrating mind had laid bare the limits of my method of proceeding. 'Totz did admit that he had used various weapons to kill the other victims.'

'Not one alone?' Kant frowned.

'Whatever came to hand, he said,' I added quickly. 'Of course, sir, I will question him until all the details emerge.'

'Details are of the utmost importance,' Kant confided. 'The King will want to know the exact strength and number of his enemies.'

Was he being sarcastic? I felt like a student who has just been handed back an essay by a tutor and told that the work was good, very good, though it should have been a great deal better. Suddenly, Kant laughed out loud. He did not say what amused him. This mercurial humour of his was new to me, and I was not reassured by it. Nor was Koch, as I could see quite clearly by the expression on his face.

'I am glad that you have found the high road to Truth,' said Kant. 'Did you, by any chance, ask Ulrich Totz about the Devil's claw, as the people call it?'

'Herr Procurator cannot be expected to complete his investigations in a single day, sir,' Sergeant Koch interrupted. His deference to my authority was as pronounced as his loyalty to Procurator Rhunken had been. The bureaucracy here in Prussia is famed for producing such men. They are obedient and subservient to a fault. And sometimes they are blunt, too.

'Whatever this Devil's claw may be,' Koch went on, 'whatever the common people say about it, it hardly seems relevant, Professor Kant. Procurator Stiffeniis has unmasked the plot.'

'Dear Sergeant Koch,' Kant returned mildly, 'do not presume too far. In my experience, there is more truth in the common voice than anywhere else on Earth.'

'Ulrich Totz admitted killing the boy,' Sergeant Koch replied staunchly. 'He admitted murdering the others. Herr Stiffeniis has caught his man, sir.'

To my surprise, Professor Kant showed no resentment at this rebuttal. He nodded thoughtfully. 'I can understand your reservations about the utility of what I intend to show you, Herr Koch,' he continued. 'And I appreciate your openness where my young friend shows only dutiful reticence. I am certain that Stiffeniis shares your opinion. I would ask you both to be patient for a short while longer. What you are about to see is the fruit of the most original research that I have ever undertaken in my life.'

My heart beat faster. Was Immanuel Kant going to show me what he had been hiding from his best and closest friends?

'A masterpiece, I am sure, sir,' I said with warmth. 'Any book from your pen . . .'

'A book?' Surprise was evident on his hollow face. 'Is that what you are expecting to see, Stiffeniis?'

'The world has waited too long for a new opus, sir,' I answered.

He made no immediate reply. When he did speak, he seemed even more animated than before. 'A book . . . A book! Why not?' he said, resting his chin on his bunched fist. 'And what could be the title? Why, given the circumstances, a *Critique of Criminal Reason*, I think.'

'I am eager to read it,' I enthused, as the coach laboured up the hill.

Kant was smiling gleefully, his lips drawn back tightly to reveal the few yellow, pointed teeth he still possessed. I must confess, it was not a pleasant sight.

'You have taken possession of Rhunken's office, I imagine. Have you read the reports that he cobbled together regarding these murders?'

'I did so yesterday,' I began eagerly. 'They have been most useful, sir. Indeed his theory seems to be confirmed by what Totz, the innkeeper, confessed this afternoon . . .'

'A political plot? Is that what you think lies behind these deaths?' Kant interrupted me with a dismissive wave of his hand. 'Vigilantius came closer to the truth!' He uttered these words with an energy which was very close to rage. 'You lost patience with him last night. You should have stayed until the end. Herr Rhunken is a magistrate of the old school. He is an information-gatherer, nothing more. He hopes to frighten the truth from people, and sometimes he succeeds. But not in this instance. His dull imagination is no match for the killer's. Vigilantius has discovered a great deal more, but you refused to take his insights into consideration.'

I glanced at Koch. His face was taut, the muscles clenched and stiff. Clearly it cost him a great deal not to speak out in defence of the dead man he had served so faithfully and for so long. But one thing was certain: Professor Kant had not been informed of the magistrate's death.

'Well?' Kant niggled. 'Why didn't you stay?'

'I considered it a pantomime, sir,' I protested uncertainly.

'Pantomimes sometimes represent a truth,' he replied. 'I expected you to be put off at the beginning, but I hoped that you would learn something useful from Vigilantius. I sent Rhunken's official reports to you for the same purpose.'

'I beg your pardon, sir?'

I could find no thread of coherence in his arguments. What could be the connection between Vigilantius and the police reports that I had been allowed to read on the journey to Königsberg?

He leaned close and spoke quietly. 'I knew that I could rely on your sense of duty. Who can refuse a commission from the King? Especially a magistrate who has chosen to hide himself away in a tiny village near the borders of West Prussia. What is the name of the place? Lotingen?'

For a moment I feared that he might be about to ask me why I had chosen never to return to Königsberg after our first meeting seven years before, why I had never made the effort to write to him. The possibility that he might know about Jachmann's interference in our affairs threw me into a panic. What could I tell him? In frenzied haste, I searched for excuses, ranging from my own bad health, to – God forgive me! – serious diseases that Helena or the children might have suffered.

But he did not bother to ask. He had other matters on his mind.

'I tried to whet your appetite for the obscure side of human behaviour with the help of those reports, Hanno,' he went on. 'I hoped that you would be intrigued by the strangeness of these deaths. I remember well at our first meeting, you showed a natural inclination for . . . how shall I call it, *mystery?*' He leaned back in his seat. 'I hoped that you would be puzzled. Not so much by what you'd read, but by what you did *not* read in those reports.' He started to number off the items on his fingers.

'Why was there no explanation of how the victims had died? Why was no mention made of the weapon used? Why was no hypothesis offered which might suggest a common motive behind all those murders? There was no question of theft or of passion, no apparent connection linking one victim to another. You cannot fail to have realised that what was happening in Königsberg had something peculiar about it. A magistrate of Herr Rhunken's fame was unable to resolve the enigma. Oh, I'd not deny that Rhunken did his job. He did what he was capable of doing. But his heavy feet never left the ground. His plodding intelligence was no match for the killer's. Sometimes such magistrates are fortunate, I have no doubt, but not in this instance.' He looked at me inquisitively.

'If you want to understand what is going on here, my young friend, you must learn to soar. You must pay attention, even to the most obscure and mysterious of sources available to you. Even to the likes of Vigilantius. If you continue to dig for reasons, to look for explanations, to chase proofs – as you began to do the minute you arrived in Königsberg – you'll get no closer to the truth than your predecessor did.'

His voice gradually faded away as he spoke. He was disappointed, I could tell. I had failed him in some way, though I was unable to say exactly how I had fallen short of his expectations. But suddenly, he shifted in his seat and changed his course, like a fish you think you have safely caught in your bare hands that darts away in another direction, leaving you with just an empty swirl in the water.

'By the way, how is your father?' he asked.

It was dark inside the carriage, and I was glad of that. I felt the blood drain instantly from my face. It was the second time that he had referred to the tragedy in my family. What strange association of ideas brought the question to his lips just then? And why was he so lacking in curiosity about the *new* family I had made? Were my wife and my children of no interest to him? I had baptised my only son in his honour. It was as if that part of my life did not exist. Instead, he harked back continually to the old life, the old me, the Hanno Stiffeniis that he had helped to exorcise seven years before.

'I have heard, sir, that he is somewhat better,' I replied, though Kant did not appear to be listening. He seemed to be following a delicate pattern that his mind had already traced out for him. He waved his forefinger in the air, following the movement with his eyes, as though his mental and his physical states were wholly separated, and equally fascinating, the one to the other.

Just then, fortunately, the coach began to slow down.

'At last! We have arrived!' he exclaimed, interrupting his private reflections with sudden animation. 'Let's waste no more time.'

Johannes pulled down the folding steps, and helped his master into the dark lane. I had no idea where we were, but then I caught a glimpse of the towering bulk of the Fortress again. We seemed to have circled around the defensive walls and come at the Fortress from another direction, standing beside a miserable hovel that flanked an approach road to the portcullis. The building might have been used centuries before as a customs post. It was in a remarkable state of dereliction and ought to have been pulled down. I was baffled, wondering what had driven Herr Professor Kant to choose such a forlorn place to work upon his final masterpiece?

With an eager nod from his master, Johannes Odum produced a large key from his pocket, and proceeded with some difficulty to unlock the ancient, worm-eaten door.

'Wait here,' Kant said to his man. 'Now, Stiffeniis, if you lend me your arm, perhaps Sergeant Koch could step inside and strike a light? There's a lantern hanging just inside the door.'

The cobbled road was slippery underfoot with packed ice and snow and a thin top-sprinkling of frost, as treacherous as a road could be. If I needed proof of Immanuel Kant's age and physical frailty, I had it then. He rested his feather-like weight on my arm as we stepped inside the door, where Koch was waiting with a storm-lantern raised high above his head.

'Do not touch anything,' Kant warned.

We were in an abandoned store-room of some sort. Broken armament boxes had been dumped in a large, careless heap on one side of the room. Cobwebs hung like shimmering shrouds from the ceiling. Dust lay in a thick blanket over everything else. In the centre of the room, a large rat caught by the neck in a trap had been stripped to a skeleton by its luckier fellows.

'Go ahead, Koch,' Kant ordered. 'We will follow you.'

He pointed towards a narrow, vaulted tunnel, whose once-white walls were stained and black with mould and smoke. Dropping my arm as if possessed of a demonic energy, he set off at a shuffling trot behind Sergeant Koch, and I was obliged to accelerate to keep pace with him. Our passage through this tunnel was made more difficult by the lowness of the brick vault, which grazed the top of Kant's three-cornered hat, whilst Koch and I were obliged to stoop. My nose tingled with the pungent odour of rot, and there was a sharp, acidic smell underlying it. If Doctor Faustus and his familiar, Mephistopheles, had leapt out to welcome us in the gloomy depths of the place, I would not have been in the least surprised.

As we entered a large room at the end of the corridor, and Koch held up his light, I caught my first glimpse of the voluminous alembic jars and the serpentine glass-tubes which gleamed upon the shelves, together with a neat pile of boxes set in an orderly stack on a workbench.

'Feel the cold,' Kant enthused. 'Siberia is closer than you think!'

He ordered Koch to take a spill from his lantern and light the lamps which were hung at intervals around the walls. As the sergeant added light to light, the objects assembled in that room began to stand out more clearly from the gloom.

Professor Kant turned towards the far wall.

'Now, Stiffeniis, let me introduce you to those who are obliged to dwell down here in this unwholesome twilight world,' he said.

From the darkest corner of the room, vacant, watery eyes stared fixedly back at us in the pale, flickering glow of the lamplight.

Chapter 15

'Can you guess who they are, Stiffeniis?'

Immanuel Kant's voice was hoarse with the cold. There was a strident, triumphant note in it which robbed me of the power of speech. I could not drag my eyes away from the large glass jars lined up on the shelf, where four human heads floated in a pale, straw-coloured liquid.

'Draw closer,' Kant invited, taking me by the arm. 'Now, let me introduce you to Jan Konnen, Paula-Anne Brunner, Johann Gottfried Haase and this one here, a newcomer that you probably recognise, having seen him last night in the cellar at the Court House. Would you bring down the exhibit on the far left, Sergeant Koch, and place it on this table?'

Stunned horror written on his face, Koch obeyed without a word.

I was incapable of forming any coherent thought as I stared at the gruesome contents of the glass jar that Koch set before us on a table, while Kant was the soul of affable sociability. He might have been arranging the chairs for a tea party.

'Bring another lamp, Sergeant Koch. That's it, yes. And place it there. Just there!' Kant's voice battered painfully on my inner ear. 'Now, tell me, Stiffeniis. What can you see inside this jar?'

The lights on either side threw the human lineaments into sharp relief.

I swallowed hard, my voice little more than a whisper: 'It is a . . . a head, sir.'

'This was Jan Konnen, the first victim of the murderer. Now, I would like you to describe precisely what you are able to observe, and with all the accuracy at your disposal. Come, come, Stiffeniis!' he encouraged. 'A head?'

'A human head,' I corrected myself, 'which belongs . . . that is, which *used* to belong to a man aged about fifty. Despite the distorting effects of the glass jar, the facial features are regular, and . . .'

I stopped short. I knew not what to say next.

'Describe what you can *see*,' Kant pressed. 'I ask no more. Start at the crown of the head, then slowly work your way down.'

I attempted to shake off the numbing sense of inadequacy which had taken possession of me. 'His hair is tinged with grey. It is thin on top, almost bald, and worn long around the ears.'

'Covering the ears,' Kant corrected me.

'Covering the ears, yes. The forehead is . . .'

I baulked again. What in the name of God was I supposed to say?

'Don't stop! Go on!' Kant prodded impatiently.

'The . . . forehead is broad and it is without wrinkles.'

'And that vertical split where the eyebrows meet? Was it there before the man died? Or did it appear at the moment of his death?'

I took a step forward and peered closely.

'I have no way of knowing, sir,' I mumbled.

'Use your intuition!'

'It looks like a puzzled frown,' I suggested, examining the furrow closely.

'Would you not expect such a frown to fade away after death?'

'But it has not,' I said at last.

'This was the final expression on his face. It appeared at the moment of his death. The victim's facial muscles were paralysed in that precise expression. This is a well-known phenomenon. Any soldier with experience on the field of battle has seen a similar expression a hundred times before. It is of some importance,' added Kant. 'Now, what have you to say about the eyes?'

I looked into the unseeing eyes inside the jar. If Man has a soul, the ancients say, its light is visible there. If the body has a vital spirit, the ghost manifests itself through those windows. What so disconcerted me about the detached head of Jan Konnen was the sensation that he was watching us as intently as we were studying him.

'The victim's eyes have rolled up in their sockets, exposing the whites,' I forced myself to say.

'Could there be an explanation?'

I was bewildered. 'There is no literature on such matters, sir. I . . . Anatomy texts exist, of course, but not in a case like this one. Not concerning murder.'

'Very good, Stiffeniis. You see the tricky ground we are on? We have no authority to guide us. We must use our eyes, trust our observations, and make the deductions that logical inference suggests. This will be our method.'

'Perhaps the blow came from above?' I suggested. 'He glanced up when he was struck?'

Kant made a sound of approval. 'Did the blow come from above, or from behind? We are uncertain as yet, but we will not allow ourselves to be distracted by the question. Now, look at that nose, Stiffeniis! What can you read in it?' he quizzed, though he did not wait for an answer. 'That it is long, thin, and utterly undistinguished? And so we come to the mouth. How would you describe that?'

'Open?' I offered.

'Wide open?'

'Not entirely,' I said, defending my choice of word.

'Would you say that he was screaming when he died?'

There was something in Professor Kant's hungry expression that caused me to quake. For a moment, my head began to spin and I thought I was about to faint.

'Screaming, sir?' I echoed.

'An open mouth suggests that he was screaming in the instant that he met his death, wouldn't you say?'

I forced myself to look more carefully. 'No, sir, I would not. I would say that he was not screaming.'

'What was he doing, then? What kind of sound could have come from his mouth?'

'A gasp of surprise? A sigh?'

'Would you say that something dramatic and violent happened to produce that expression?' Kant went on.

'No, sir.'

'And I would agree with you. Now, Stiffeniis, the cause of death. Can you suggest what might have been the death stroke?'

'There is no unsightly wound to the face itself,' I floundered.

'Was clear evidence found elsewhere on the body?'

'The body does not interest us. It is the head, the *head*, which has its story to tell. Would you turn the jar, Sergeant?'

The candlelight cast a jaundiced sickly glow as the head rolled lazily in the cloudy liquid. 'Observe, Stiffeniis. Here at the base of the cranium. There was no resistance. The instrument went in like a hot knife cutting lard. But it was not a knife . . .'

These were the words with which I originally began this narration. At that time, I intended to celebrate the incredible versatility of the genius of Immanuel Kant, and hoped to reflect my own small part in the resolution of a mystery which held the city of Königsberg in thrall. But those words marked the first clear signpost on my personal road into the maze of corruption, treachery and evil that had been so carefully mapped out for me.

'Can you see it?' Kant bent close and pointed. 'The mortal stroke was delivered here. Death came quickly and it was unexpected. It was not a violent blow, there is no unsightly penetration. Something sharp and pointed entered Konnen's neck just here, and he was dead on his knees before he even realised what was happening. This tiny spot is all the evidence that remains of the attack.'

He paused for an instant, as if to emphasise the vital importance of what he said next.

'If I have understood you well, among the variety of weapons that Ulrich Totz claims to have used, he made no mention of anything which would leave a mark such as this.' His eager eyes darted quickly at me, and I felt a drowning sense of nausea, as if I had just received a violent blow to my own head.

'Koch, bring down another. Any jar will do.' Professor Kant's voice was tremulous with excitement as he picked up the nearest lamp and moved it closer to the second severed head. 'The same mark is evident here,' he said, rapping his forefinger sharply on the glass. 'Do you see it now?'

The scalp of Paula-Anne Brunner had been shaved away at the back, long red hair remaining on the crown and at the sides only. To my young eyes, there was something foul in such a desecration, the bare nudity of the woman's skull somehow suggestive of the stealthy violence by which she had met her death.

'There is an identical mark on Tifferch's neck,' he concluded flatly. Then with a sigh he added, 'If you had stayed to watch Vigilantius at work last night, you would have known straight away that Morik was not killed by the person you are here to chase. Totz is not the killer we are looking for.'

'Is this the work of Vigilantius?' I asked in a whisper.

In the dim light I thought I saw an expression of satisfaction settle on Kant's hungry face. 'The doctor is the *crème de la crème* of European anatomists!' he confirmed with pride, as if he had done the disgusting work himself.

The ingratiating smile on the necromancer's lips flashed before my eyes, taking on a new and more sinister significance. 'You may have finished *your* business, sir,' he had said with scorn the night before. 'But I have something more to do.'

I imagined him, pulling out the instruments from beneath his large mantle. What could they have been? Sharp knives, a medical saw, pointed scalpels, as he bent over that anatomical table and assaulted the corpse, cutting mercilessly away at the vulnerable remains of Lawyer Tifferch.

My anger flashed at Kant's lavish praise of the man.

'This proves that he's a charlatan, sir. He had no need to ask the spirit of the dead man to tell him how he had been killed. He knew the answer already!'

Kant placed a pacifying hand on my sleeve. 'You are unjust, Stiffeniis. The doctor had not performed the first dissection when he suggested in that histrionic and slightly irritating manner of his that the cause of death was to be found at the base of the dead man's head. The corpse had already spoken to him. The cutting came later.'

The dead man spoke?

'Professor Kant . . .' I began to protest.

'How did you guess, sir?'

Koch's question took us both by surprise.

'Excuse me, Professor Kant,' the sergeant said, and flushed with embarrassment, 'I did not mean to interrupt your speculations, but I am puzzled. How did you understand so quickly the significance of the murder of Jan Konnen? At that time, there was no way of knowing that similar crimes would follow on.'

Kant half closed his eyes, a contented smile illuminating his face.

'I have been collating vital information regarding the incidence of death in Königsberg for many years, Sergeant,' he said. 'About a year ago, I received my weekly report from the local police. A corpse was mentioned for which no evident cause of death had been identified. Now, that was *most* irregular. The physician called to certify the death had failed to notice that tiny perforation in the neck of Konnen. Cause of death – unknown. How was I to include such a death in my statistics? Had the man died, or had he been killed? I asked for the body to be donated to the University, and, by a fortunate turn of events, Doctor Vigilantius was lecturing at the Collegium Albertinum that very week. Having learned in conversation that he was also an experienced anatomist, I took advantage of the circumstance in two ways. Firstly, I was curious to see how a Swedenborgian communicates with the spirits of the dead. Secondly, I wished to preserve the evidence that you have just seen. When a similar murder occurred some months later, I saw the link, asked for the corpse, and sent for Doctor Vigilantius to repeat the operation.'

'Did Procurator Rhunken know of this place, sir?' asked Koch, making a sweeping gesture with his hand to indicate the whole laboratory.

Kant dismissed the idea with a flash of annoyance.

'Your master was not prepared to consider the utility of the evidence I was assembling here. He ridiculed my findings as the ramblings of senility! By using standard police procedures, he would never have caught the killer. The murderer's taste for his work was gaining in momentum, terror was mounting in the city, the King was worried about a possible French invasion, and he wanted the case to be solved without delay. *I* suggested to His Majesty some weeks ago that Procurator Rhunken be removed from his post. Special talents were needed here. Talents such as those of Augustus Vigilantius . . .'

'And myself,' I added.

Kant placed his hand on my arm and smiled warmly. 'Now you know why I sent for you, Hanno,' he said. 'Only someone who has visited the land of shadows can cope with what is happening here in Königsberg. As you are well aware, the darkest impulses of the human heart go far beyond Reason and Logic.'

Impulses of the human heart which go beyond Reason . . .

I froze. I had used that very phrase myself, the first time that we had met.

'That's why I sent you to The Baltic Whaler,' he said, his eyes sparkling mischievously. 'It seemed to be the obvious place to start. That inn had been the scene of the first murder, and rumours were rife that the owner was a sympathiser of Bonaparte. Morik, the serving boy, aroused his master's suspicions, I'm afraid. Now, that I did *not* foresee,' he added thoughtfully. 'Still, Totz killed him, and he used a hammer to do the deed, as he confessed to you. In doing so, he eliminated himself from our investigation. That must be clear to you by now, I hope.'

'Why did you not tell me at once, sir? You let me go blundering on in the name of Logic.'

I had been too easily persuaded of a political cause. That is, I had too easily convinced myself of it. Everything had fallen into place: the lurid contents of Herr Tifferch's cupboard, Morik's idle gossip, all that I had seen and heard at the inn, Ulrich Totz's confession, his poor wife's smile! I had twisted the facts to suit my theory. And in doing so, I had proven myself to be a mindless fool in the eyes of the very person who had trusted so much in my good qualities.

'You believed that you had definitive proof,' Kant continued. 'You would not accept anything else to the contrary, even when it was as plain as the nose on your face. Remember what I told you, Hanno. Your investigation must aim to reconstruct *how* things happened. It will not tell you *why* they happened in that way. The motivation is still hidden in darkness. Logic and Rationality do not guide the human heart, though they may explain its passions.'

He extracted a document from one of the files, and laid it on the table.

'Look at this,' he said.

Koch and I bent close in the flickering light. It was nothing more than a sheet of paper, on which an image had been sketched. There was not a trace of art in the drawing, just a vague outline of a kneeling body propped against a wall. There was a ghoulish contrast between the technical imperfection of the picture, and the simple figure that it portrayed. As if a child, distracted from daubing flowers and fairies, had chanced upon a scene of the most irresistible horror and innocently tried to capture the image on paper.

'What is it, sir?' asked Koch uneasily.

'Two gendarmes were sent to the scene of the first murder by Rhunken. I had already begun to conduct a parallel investigation using my own methods, of which I had privately informed the King. I instructed the same two gendarmes to sketch what they remembered having seen at the scene of the crime. This became a standard procedure for each of the following murders. The other drawings are in those files over there if you need them,' Kant pointed. 'They portray the exact positions in which each of the bodies was found.'

'You sent soldiers to *draw* dead bodies, sir?'

Kant laughed shrilly before replying to Koch's question.

'Unusual, don't you agree? One of the soldiers proved his worth. Whenever a suspect corpse was found, I told Lublinsky to make a sketch of the scene for me. I paid him for his efforts, of course.'

'A cross on a pay chit's more than most of them can manage,' Koch returned with surprise. 'May I ask another question, Professor Kant?'

Koch's eyes darted anxiously around the room.

'All this, this . . .' he muttered nervously. 'Bodies without heads! Why, it's . . . it's a monstrosity, sir. What do you hope to achieve by it?'

Kant turned to me and smiled as if Koch had never opened his mouth.

'The dead *do* speak to us, you know, Hanno. Now, do not misunderstand me. I have not been converted to Swedenborg's way of thinking. In this room, in this instant, a murdered man is the object of our scrutiny. By examining the physical evidence and scrutinising the circumstances, we can draw reasonable conclusions about where and when his murder was committed. These factors may help us in their turn to understand how the crime was enacted, and what was used to do the deed. Finally, if our intuitions have not played us false, we may even be able to conclude who his killer is. Morik was killed by Totz, and no one else. Now, the body of *this* dead man can tell us a great deal about the person who killed *him*.'

'You aim to reconstruct conditions at the scene of the murder, do you not?' asked Koch before I could speak.

'That is my intention, Sergeant. You have witnessed the usefulness of this 'monstrosity', as you choose to call it. Without these glass jars and their contents, Procurator Stiffeniis would have proceeded blithely on in the wrong direction and accused Ulrich Totz of crimes that he had never committed. Now, he can correct that error,' Kant said with quiet satisfaction.

'I call this place my laboratory,' he continued, 'though I have not yet found a suitable name for the science that I have been exploring here. This material will be of use to a mind trained in investigative procedures. If Herr Stiffeniis can work out how these crimes were perpetrated, he may anticipate the murderer's modus operandi and apprehend him. Of one thing we may be absolutely certain. This person will kill again!'

'Totz had no idea how these people were murdered,' I admitted. 'But why should he have lied to me?'

Kant touched my sleeve lightly, as if to encourage me.

'Morik was killed for a political motive, Stiffeniis,' he said. 'Totz told you the truth in that respect, at least. He must have thought his conspiracy was about to be discovered. Hence, he murdered the one person who had direct knowledge of the facts, the one person he could not trust. Morik.'

'But why accuse himself of the other murders?'

Kant shrugged. 'Would you wish to appear in the pathetic guise of a ruthless murderer of defenceless children? Ulrich Totz may simply be trying to fashion a more attractive image for himself as a revolutionary, a pitiless local Robespierre. You'll have to force the truth from him.'

'I will!' I said, feeling a weight of anger building inside me.

Again, Professor Kant placed a restraining hand on my arm.

'Before you go,' he continued with great animation, 'there is something else for you to see. It was the pretext on which I invited you here. I am truly surprised that you have not asked about it already.'

Like a stage magician pulling a rabbit from a hat, he set a folded grey cloth down on the table. 'The Devil's claw! Its presumed existence inspires more fear in Königsberg than any tangible fact could do. Uncover it, Stiffeniis.'

I held back.

'It won't bite,' he said with a brittle laugh.

The wrapping was thin. My nervous fingers felt a tiny form cocooned within. Whatever it was, the object was small and weighed next to nothing. I unfolded the material on the table-top to reveal a tiny pointed fragment measuring less than two centimetres in length. It seemed to be made of ivory or bone.

'What is it, sir?' Koch whispered.

Kant shook his head before speaking. 'Part of the murder weapon. The tip, I presume. It was probably longer when the murderer jabbed it into the base of each victim's skull. Vigilantius found this fragment impaled in Jan Konnen's neck. We can assume that as the killer attempted to pull it out, the point snapped off.'

'In the night officers' report, the woman who found the body spoke of seeing the Devil's claw,' I noted. 'Obviously, she couldn't have seen this tiny piece. Does the discrepancy suggest that she actually *saw* the whole weapon sticking out of the dead man's neck?'

'It's a point worth investigating,' Kant suggested with a vigorous nod.

'I must speak to her. Lublinsky's reports are vague on this particular point.'

'Lublinsky might know where she is,' Koch added, picking up the fragment from the table and studying it with the sort of avid concentration a botanist might apply to an exotic fruit he had never seen before. 'If this one snapped and broke, the killer seems to have had no trouble obtaining a replacement, sir. I'd wager that they are easy to procure.'

'And to hide,' said Kant. 'No sensible man stands close to the butcher when he swings the cleaver in his hands.'

He turned to me, an amused glint in his eye.

'Do you see the way ahead now, Hanno?' he asked.

I looked at the glass jars, the files and the boxes stacked on their shelves.

'Everything here is new to me, sir,' I said with a shiver of excitement. 'But I promise to use these remarkable objects to the best of my ability.'

I might have been swearing a solemn oath.

'Here is the key,' said Kant with a kindly smile. 'The heads are there, the clothes the victims were wearing at the time are stored in those boxes. Each box is marked with the name. Sketches of the corpses are in those folders.' Kant pointed everything out with methodical calm. 'All you need, I believe, is in this room. The exhibits are yours, Stiffeniis. Use them as you think fit.'

Kant appeared to shrink before my eyes as he placed the key in my hand. I had the feeling that it had not been an entirely natural performance, though it had certainly been memorable. His nervous strength was utterly consumed.

'Take Professor Kant home in his coach, Koch,' I said. 'I will make my way on foot to the main gate. I want to speak to Lublinsky at once.'

'Oh no, sir. No!' Koch replied with force. '*You* take the Professor home. I will return on foot to the main building of the Fortress. You'll get lost, sir, while I know precisely where to find Officer Lublinsky.'

'It could be dangerous,' I replied, puzzled by the fierceness of Koch's opposition to my proposal.

'I'll keep my wits about me,' the sergeant replied, glancing in the direction of Professor Kant. In a flash I realised what was troubling him. He was not afraid of the dark, the fog, or the unknown criminal stalking the night. He was frightened of Immanuel Kant.

'Very well,' I conceded. 'Find Lublinsky and see what he has to say about the woman. I will join you shortly at the Fortress.'

Outside, night had fallen. The fog was even denser than before, and cut visibility on the dark stretch of road beneath the Fortress to nothing. Johannes Odum leapt forward to open the door while I assisted Professor Kant to mount the carriage-steps.

'Will you be coming home with Professor Kant, sir?' Johannes asked, a note of caution in his voice. I suddenly recalled that the valet wished to show me something at the house.

'Of course, I will,' I replied, handing Professor Kant into the coach, and again I was moved by his frailty and the effort of will that it cost him to match the incredible energy of his mind.

'Be careful, Sergeant,' I warned, as I climbed up behind Professor Kant, and Koch slammed the door. 'Take no risks.'

The coach pulled away and proceeded slowly. Neither I, nor Professor Kant spoke for some time. At last, he turned to me. 'I hope you'll join me in a warming glass of Bischoff's cordial? It has been a tiring day, and we both need something strong to fortify our spirits.'

'With the greatest of pleasure, sir.'

The promise seemed to content him. A few moments later, he was snoring lightly, his head reclining against the seat. I leaned back myself, thinking of the letter I had intended to write to Helena announcing my success in hunting down the killer. Thanks to Professor Kant, my days in Königsberg were not to be so quickly counted off.

Chapter 16

Professor Kant slept all the way home. The driving energy that had sustained him throughout that day seemed to have left him utterly spent. Only minutes before, eyes sparkling with excitement, his movements had been swift, unburdened by age, his mind quick, speech animated. But slumped there beside me on the carriage seat, that glistening cape of his looked like an empty cocoon left behind by some recently hatched creature which had taken wing to find its way in the cruel world.

But I was not in the least tired. By an inexplicable law of osmosis, the energy that had left my mentor now passed to me. That morning on the muddy banks of the River Pregel, I had seen the corpse of a boy, his head smashed beyond repair. I had just emerged from a sinister chamber of horrors which was barely conceivable in a howling nightmare. The streets of Königsberg were dark and dangerous. A killer was lurking there, a ruthless being who thought nothing of taking human life, leaving tragedy in his wake, promising worse violence to come. But my heart was singing. I might have been returning from a walk through the idyllic woods of Westphalia. As we left Professor Kant's laboratory far behind us, my mind was filled with sensations that any other man might have reserved for a refined and precious collection of *objets d'art*. Was I disgusted by what I had seen in that dark and gloomy place? Quite the opposite!

I held the key to Kant's laboratory tightly in my hands, which shook with awe and fascination. Those exhibits were remarkable, but more remarkable was the fact that Kant had entrusted the custody of his collection to *me*. To me, and to no one else! It did not surprise me to learn that Herr Procurator Rhunken had not been privy to the secrets of the place. Poor, loyal Koch had been shocked by the news, but I was elated by it. Now I knew why Kant had chosen me instead of any other magistrate. Other men might be more experienced in the traditional ways of criminal detection, but Kant believed that I alone would be able to comprehend the utility of the exhibits and appreciate the macabre *beauty* – there was no better word for it – which his incredible mind had conceived and created in that place. Seven years before, Kant had advised me to become a magistrate. And now he was offering me the opportunity I had purposely sought to avoid in Lotingen. He had placed the material in my hands and invited me to prove that I was the first of a new breed of investigative magistrates, that I was capable of employing a totally revolutionary technique involving methods that had never been used before in the fight against the worst of all crimes. Crimes that could endanger the very peace of the Nation.

This was the reason that had impelled him to call Vigilantius, and use both his anatomical knowledge and his arcane skills to assist the law. Was there a magistrate alive who would have dared to employ such a stratagem? That was why he had wanted me to watch the necromancer at work the night before. Suddenly, I saw the doctor's skills in a wholly different light. Kant's aged mind was drifting towards some dark and final shore, but the great philosopher had not lost his grip on reality, nor his ability to apply logic and sound reasoning to the resolution of a conundrum. He was teaching me to do what he was physically no longer able to do for himself. He was my Socrates, he was leading me towards a completely new way of looking and doing. Investigating a criminal act was not simply a matter of gathering circumstantial information and worming the truth out of a reluctant witness, as Rhunken thought. As I had thought myself, I reflected, with a flash of honesty.

Kant had been preparing me for what I had just seen, training me to use such knowledge for the good of Mankind, warning me not to discount any evidence in the light of its perversity or *monstrosity*, as Sergeant Koch had called it. Surely, that was how Rhunken must have viewed Kant's way of doing things. As recently as the night before, I would have agreed with Rhunken. In a trice, I realised what I must do. When the case was over, when the murderer was caught and condemned, I would write a learned treatise of my own to celebrate the incomparable genius of Immanuel Kant. He had ventured further in this field than any other man before him, and I was thrilled by the prospect of learning from the inventor of this new procedure. I turned to watch the Professor sleep, my soul crushed by waves of emotion and gratitude. I owed everything to him. He might have been my father. Indeed, I realised, I owed him more, far more, than I had ever owed my own father.

My head was spinning with the immensity of these considerations. I had to close my eyes to regain equilibrium, and did not open them again until the coach lurched suddenly and stopped. Outside, the fog was thicker than before. I glanced again to Professor Kant, but he slept blithely on. Beyond the window-glass, a face materialised in the milky darkness, and the ghostly apparition of Johannes Odum signalled me to step down into the road. I opened the carriage door with all haste and quiet.

'We can go no further, Herr Stiffeniis,' the valet announced as I stood beside him. The fog became an impenetrable wall at the point where a rippling stream ran beside the road. 'I'm very afraid of driving the coach into the ditch.'

'I'll walk ahead and lead the horse on,' I offered.

'Take one of the carriage-lamps, sir. Be careful, the way is treacherous here,' he advised.

I set off quickly in the direction of the house, but was forced to slow down. Beneath my feet the snow was tightly packed. Behind, the horse shied with fright. Johannes had him tightly reined in, fearing for the worst, but I was forced to plod on for an age before Professor Kant's residence finally loomed up out of the fog.

Johannes lifted Kant from the coach like a sleeping babe, while I held up the lamp and helped them by opening the door. Standing in the hall, I watched as the valet carried his master effortlessly up the stairs to his bedchamber, waiting there while Johannes made him good for the night. The operation took no more than ten minutes.

'He's truly worn out. Thank God for a moment's peace!' Odum

whispered, as he reached the bottom of the stairs. 'But now, if you follow me, sir, I'll show you what I found this morning.'

Taking up the carriage-lamp, he opened the front door and led me with difficulty to the rear of the house. The kitchen garden was enclosed all around by tall trees. Snow lay in knee-deep drifts and folds, and the going was difficult.

'This is Professor Kant's private study,' he said, stopping by a darkened window. He lowered the lamp closer to the ground. 'But look here, sir. This is what scared me this morning.'

I looked down. The snow gleamed like diamonds in the beam of light. Dark imprints etched like stepping stones in the frozen mantle led all the way from the window to a wicket gate at the far end of the enclosure. I examined these vague footprints in the snow for a moment, wondering to myself what Johannes was so concerned about. Had the responsibility of looking after Professor Kant begun to wear on his nerves?

'Is this what you wished to show me?'

He glanced at the ground, then back to me. 'After we returned from the river this morning, sir, I opened the curtains in the study. And there they were!'

'I do not follow, Johannes.'

'No one's been out here since summer.'

I felt the muscles tense in my jaw. 'Are you certain? A neighbour, perhaps? A beggar, or a tradesman?'

Johannes shook his head with energy.

'There's only one possibility, sir,' he said with great seriousness. 'Some person has been spying on him. Or trying to enter the house.'

There was something lumbering, heavy – almost stupid, I might say – about the man. The cold air seemed to have dropped an appreciable number of degrees, and I shivered violently despite the heavy woollen cloak that Lotte Havaars had providently seen fit to pack for me.

'Or worse, Johannes,' I said with far more calm than I felt.

'Worse, sir?'

'The killer may have followed him here.'

173

'Oh, God!' Johannes exclaimed with a groan. 'I told Professor Kant he was becoming too involved in those murders. I warned you, sir. Being seen down there by the river was dangerous. Now, you must . . .'

I held up my hand to stop this flow of recrimination, concentrating on the measures which would need to be taken straight away. 'We will protect him,' I said. 'Make sure to bar the doors and lock all windows, Johannes. I will call the gendarmes to guard the house and watch the road.'

As I spoke, I stared at those footprints in the snow. What would Kant do in such circumstances as these, I asked myself. The answer came in a flash. My mind turned in the direction that Professor Kant had so carefully plotted out for it.

'There's something we must do first,' I said with decision. 'Herr Professor himself would have done it. Hold up that lamp, Johannes.'

'You'll not bring Professor Kant out here, I hope, sir?' Johannes cried with fright.

'What are you saying, man?' I replied. 'I would not dream of disturbing him. What I mean to do is apply the analytical method that Professor Kant has just been showing me in his laboratory.'

'Sir?' Confusion glistened in the servant's eyes.

'We need to find a specimen which is whole and compact,' I said, looking around me.

'A specimen? Of what, sir?'

'Of a footprint, Johannes. Keep that lamp close to the ground.'

The wind had made the top surface of the snow as brittle as glass. As I bent closer and studied the surface of the snow, I could see that some attempt had been made to cancel the prints. Whoever had been lurking outside that window had let his feet drag as he walked, to avoid leaving the very evidence that I was seeking.

'Follow the tracks across the garden,' I said.

Johannes mumbled some complaint or protest to himself, then held up the lamp and led the way.

'Do not step on the imprints,' I warned him. 'There's confusion here enough already.'

The tracks led to the hedge and a wicket gate in the far corner of the garden. They seemed to have been left by a person who was in a hurry, and they had all been distorted. Not one was whole. We passed out into the lane at the rear of the house, but the footsteps of the passers-by combined to render the task impossible.

'This is a hopeless task, sir!' Johannes burst out nervously.

I led him back to the garden in silence, examining the trodden area beneath the window once again, then moving on to the three stone steps which led up to the back door of the house.

'He's been here, you see? And here . . .'

A cry of triumph erupted from my lips. On the top step, springing into sharp relief as Johannes raised the flickering lamp, was the reward for all my stubborn persistence: a footprint in its entirety.

'He tried to enter by this door,' I said, beginning to search for drawing paper in my bag.

'D'you think he got inside, sir?' Johannes asked, a note of fear in his voice.

I carefully examined the solid barrier of dark pine and the large metal keyhole. Everything was neat, intact, untouched. 'There is no sign of an attempt to force it open. The door seems to be locked from inside,' I said, trying the handle.

'I barred it myself, sir.'

'He must have abandoned his plan. At least, for the moment,' I said, my voice catching in my throat. What would happen, I thought, if he found the way to break in next time? 'Come, Johannes, we must determine if this is the murderer's footprint.'

'But how, sir? How can you do that?' he said, an expression of blank incomprehension on the servant's face.

'By comparing this print with the tracings of footprints made where the murders took place,' I replied, realising even as I spoke that I was using the new investigative language of Kant, which could mean nothing to the servant. 'This is what your master would have done,' I explained. I had found a sheet of paper in my bag, and was searching in vain for a pencil. 'But what am I to draw with?' I murmured, looking around as if I expected a quill and a pot of ink to materialise before my eyes.

'Draw, sir? I don't understand you.'

'Those prints. I want to copy them. Is there a pencil in the house?'

'In my master's room, sir. But I wouldn't want to wake him.' He glanced around the garden. 'One moment,' he said, breaking a brittle twig from a leafless rosemary bush beside the kitchen door. He opened the lantern, burned the wood in the flame, extinguished the lighted stick in the snow, then handed it to me.

'Charcoal, of course!' I exclaimed with a smile.

Daily contact with Kant's genius had evidently worked its magic on the uneducated valet. Never was such a simple instrument more useful. I laid the paper down on the snow next to the footprint to mark off the extension, then rested it on my knee and drew in the figure. There was a distinctive crosscut on the sole of the shoe – the left foot of the pair – which would be useful for the purpose of comparison. Warming to my task, I sketched out a plan of the garden and drew arrows to indicate the direction of the intruder's coming and going, while Johannes watched in silence.

'You heard nothing out of the ordinary last night, I suppose?' I asked him, as I was completing my sketch.

'No, sir, I . . . I did not,' he faltered.

I lifted my head and stared at him. His eyes shifted away from mine.

Had he let someone into the house, someone of whom his master might not have approved? But that was illogical. Would he have shown me the footprints if he knew for certain who had left them?

'Nothing at all, Johannes?' I insisted.

Might he have taken unfair advantage of the fact that his aged master was sleeping? Johannes was thirty years of age, no more. He might have a sweetheart or be married.

'Hold up that lantern,' I said, searching his face as he obeyed reluctantly. 'Believe me, Johannes, anything you choose to tell me, your master will know nothing of the matter. Did you invite someone into the house without asking the permission of Professor Kant?'

'Oh no, sir. No!' His denial was immediate. 'I would never dream of taking such a liberty. I give you my oath on it, sir.'

176

Despite this fervent plea of innocence, Johannes seemed to be on the verge of tears. I waited, watching in silence. It is a trick we magistrates favour.

'In truth, sir,' he added, 'I do have a . . . a minor confession to make. It means breaking faith, but . . . I . . . well, you ought to know of it.'

He set the lantern on the ground, rubbed his hands together, bunched them over the flaps of his pockets in tight fists, then stared unhappily into my face.

'Professor Kant could be in grave peril,' I reminded him.

'I . . . I was afraid to tell anyone, sir. Especially Herr Jachmann. I thought I'd lose my place if I told him. Herr Jachmann instructed me never to leave Professor Kant alone.'

'Quite right,' I said.

'And I have followed his instructions to the letter, sir. Except . . .'

'Except for what?'

'Except for Professor Kant himself.'

'What do you mean?'

'He asked me to leave him alone for an hour last night, sir. He gave me permission to visit my wife. You might say that he . . . insisted.'

'Alone, Johannes?' I was shocked. 'Why should he wish to send you away at night?'

'He's working on his book, sir. He said that he wanted no distractions. I tried to dissent, but he told me to make the most of the opportunity. Indeed,' he added, 'it has happened a number of times, sir.'

'When was the last time?'

'Why, yester-night . . .'

'Before *that*!' I hissed.

'A week, ten days ago, sir. He has released me from his service five or six times in the past month.'

I trembled to think of the mortal danger to which Professor Kant had exposed himself. I imagined the murderer spying on him alone in the house. Like a spider watching the fly that had fallen into its web. 'How could you?' I seethed. 'Alone in the house at night? At his age?'

Johannes was now in tears.

'What was I to do, sir?' he protested, wiping his eyes on his sleeve. 'Herr Professor was so kind to me. It would have been ungrateful to refuse him. I can't deny it, sir, living in this house I miss my wife and children.'

'You should have informed Herr Jachmann,' I said. 'It was your duty. He administers Professor Kant's domestic affairs.'

'I know it, sir. But Herr Jachmann comes no more.' He hesitated for a moment, then with peasant practicality he insisted, 'And Professor Kant *is* my master, sir. I had to obey *him*. It's put me in a very difficult position.'

He bowed his head and began to sob again like a child.

'You know what is happening in Königsberg,' I said, placing a hand on his shoulder to calm him. 'There is a murderer in the city. You must never forget it!'

Johannes bit his lip and choked back his emotion.

'I swear to you, sir! I'll never leave him alone again . . .'

'He is alone at this moment, is he not?' I said. 'Go back inside, Johannes. I will finish here. I'll send a squad of soldiers from the Fortress the instant that I arrive.'

He turned to go, then stopped. 'You won't tell Herr Jachmann, will you, sir?' he begged, looking back over his shoulder.

'I expect to hear from you at the first sign of danger,' I said, making no attempt to reassure him. 'Do not hesitate. Call the soldiers!'

I watched him return along the path to the front of the house. As I followed him some moments later, I heard the entrance door close behind him, the heavy bolts sliding into place. As I hurried away in the direction of the town, the urgency of danger prickled at my scalp. Servant and master were alone in the house, while a killer was stalking the streets of the city. He had set his sights on Professor Kant, and the soldiers had yet to be sent. Again, I felt the overwhelming burden on my shoulders. Before it had concerned the safety of the whole of Prussia. Now, the person that I loved and admired more than any other in the world. Except for my wife and my children.

I left Magisterstrasse, and turned down the dark lane which led towards the city centre and the Fortress. As I strode purposefully through the deserted, tree-lined streets, I was aware that the person who had dared to violate the *sancta sanctorum* of Immanuel Kant must have followed the same route that I was now treading. He could be hiding behind any one of those trees. I glanced around anxiously and increased my pace, the image of a large glass jar flashing before my eyes, my head floating inside it, while Doctor Vigilantius casually washed my sticky blood from his hands and put his knives away.

Slipping and falling on the icy surface more than once, my frantic progress matched the furious thundering of my heart. I did not pause to catch my breath until the flickering lanterns outside the Fortress appeared through the gloom on the far side of Ostmarkt-platz. But as I began to advance again, more slowly now, a sudden movement in the shadows caught my eye.

A man was standing near the main gate in the freezing cold.

He looked up, saw me, and began to run in my direction, mindless of the ice and the snow which covered the cobblestones.

A sensation of helplessness possessed me then. I felt like a wooden puppet with a human brain. And an unknown, malignant hand had just jerked tightly on my strings.

Chapter 17

Sergeant Koch came slithering to a halt in front of me. His face was pale, drawn, his mouth gaping, puffing out clouds of milk-hued air as he fought to catch his breath.

'What's wrong?' I gasped, my heart racing like a cornered hare. My nerves were raw. The mysterious footprints in Kant's garden. The palpable sense of danger in the city which came with darkness. Each new fear was greater than the last.

'There's been a mishap, sir.'

'What's happened?' I shouted, catching at the lapels of Koch's pea-coat and shaking him.

He grasped my wrists with a strength that I did not expect and lifted my hands away. 'We could do nothing to save them, sir,' he said.

'To save *whom*?' I cried.

'Totz and his wife, sir. Half an hour ago. They killed themselves.'

The implications of this news flashed upon me. Two people whom I had accused of murder, conspiracy and sedition, two people whom I had thrown into prison, intending to torture the truth out of them, had taken the final decision into their own hands.

'I gave instructions to keep them apart,' I managed to say.

Koch took me by the arm and led me towards the gate. 'And so they were, sir. I spoke to Stadtschen. He vowed that your order had been obeyed to the letter. When Totz was taken down, he was obliged to pass the cell where his wife was being held. They must have exchanged some sign, a signal. It was all decided in an instant.'

Koch banged on the entrance, the gate swung open, and we stepped into the torch-lit inner court. 'I instructed the guards to bring the bodies up before the other prisoners catch on,' he said. 'They have six senses down there, they smell death like starving wolves. At all costs, we must avoid a riot. General Katowice won't stand for it. He'll hang the lot of them. Fortunately, the ship that's taking them to Siberia is on its way, Herr Procurator. It should arrive tomorrow, depending on the weather. Stadtschen is making arrangements for the Section D prisoners to be taken to the port in Pillau. They'll pass the night there. It'll be a darned sight safer than keeping them here in the Fortress, sir.'

I nodded, unable to find my voice.

'We have been lucky. Really, sir, if the word might be permitted,' he went on. 'Totz was in a cell by himself. His wife was with two women, and they were both asleep when she took her life. She didn't make a sound. A guard found the husband first, then went to check . . .' He stopped suddenly and looked beyond my shoulders. 'But here they come.'

Soldiers were crossing the courtyard with two heavily laden, grey blankets slung between them.

'They'll be buried in the morning,' Koch added.

The fixed expression on Gerta Totz's lips flashed through my mind. Had she smiled in that same ingratiating fashion while taking her own life? The urge to see was irresistible. I strode across the courtyard.

'Lay them on the ground!' I ordered. 'Throw those blankets off.'

The signs of violence were written clearly on the corpses. Gerta Totz's face was black, swollen to bursting, her eyes popping out, as if she had just been told something very rude. The strip of dress she had used to hang herself was tightly knotted round her throat, sliced above the knot when they had cut her down from the cell-grating. Her nostrils were still ringed with the blood that my punch had drawn. Otherwise, the distorting hand of death had wiped everything familiar from her features. That hideous grin was gone forever.

Ulrich Totz's face was a bloody mask.

'He smashed his head against the cell wall with extraordinary violence,' Koch explained.

'More than once to produce such devastation,' I added with a shiver.

A river of dried blood cascaded from his crushed nose to his white linen shirt-front. He had succeeded in smashing his pate or breaking his neck. I stared at the bodies for some moments, then turned away. How should I consider them? As the fifth and sixth victims of the monster of Königsberg, or, like Morik, were they the victims of my own bungling?

'Take them away,' I murmured. I watched the soldiers frog-march across the yard with their burden, and struggled to shake off my depression. 'Send a patrol at once to Magisterstrasse, Sergeant,' I ordered. 'Someone has been prowling in Professor Kant's garden. It could well be the murderer.'

Koch knit his brow. 'Kant's not been harmed, I hope?'

'He's well. But not safe. He won't be out of danger until this affair is over,' I muttered, grinding my teeth. 'It seems that the killer is growing bolder.'

'Do you really think he'd try to kill the Professor, sir? This monster has always chosen his victims at random. That was his strength. No one knew where or when he would strike next. So, why decide to attack a specific target all of a sudden?'

'Perhaps he has changed his strategy,' I replied helplessly. 'The killer is faceless, hidden by anonymity, yet he knows who we are. Clearly, he knows that Kant is involved, and also where he is to be found at any hour of the day or night. He rarely leaves the house.'

'I'll give orders to the duty officer, Herr Procurator,' said Koch. He ran away across the yard and an armed patrol left by the main gate at a half-trot a few minutes later. Relief swept over me like a massive wave, but I felt no better when that sea subsided. All that had happened that day in Königsberg, and all that might still happen, seemed to weigh on me like a granite tombstone. Darkness crowded in upon me. Darkness, and a terrible sense of responsibility. Three people were dead, and the fault was mine. I closed my eyes to block the awful vision out.

'You do look pale, sir.'

Koch was standing before me, an expression of concern on his face.

'You must keep your strength up. It's been a long day, sir, there's food in the regimental kitchen. You have not eaten a bite since breakfast.'

'Thank you, Koch,' I said, and attempted to smile. 'You are better than a wet-nurse.'

His imperturbable face relaxed a little. 'Follow me, sir.'

I was beginning to think that, if nothing else, I had made *one* wise decision in the past two days. Sergeant Koch had shown the better side of himself after the difficulties of our first few hours together. Throwing open a door, he led me into a large, vaulted room which was excessively heated by a ceramic stove of gargantuan proportions.

'The garrison refectory,' he explained.

Human sweat and the odour of boiled mutton hung ripe in the air, but I felt at home with the stench. After the pungent stink of methyl alcohol and human decay in Kant's laboratory, this smell was healthy. It came from living beings doing vital things: working, eating, drinking, protecting the city and its inhabitants.

Koch sat me down, then went out again, returning some minutes later with a young soldier in a white apron who laid a tray on the table before me. A bowl of mutton broth with knobs of fatty gristle, black bread, red wine. A soldier's repast. I fell on it with appetite, while Koch stood looking on like a proud restaurateur.

I felt brighter almost immediately.

'Not for a delicate stomach, Koch,' I said between mouthfuls, 'but the most invigorating dish I ever ate in my life. Now, what have you to report about this woman who found the first corpse and about the gendarme who spoke to her?'

I gulped another spoonful of broth. 'What's his name?'

'Lublinsky, sir.'

'Did you speak to him?'

He nodded. 'A most singular person, Herr Procurator,' Koch replied.

I stopped eating and looked up at him. 'What do you mean?'

'You'd better see for yourself, sir,' he smiled uncomfortably. 'It was a mistake to leave such delicate business in the hands of rough soldiers, in my opinion. Give them a battle, they know exactly what to do. Ask 'em to speak to a woman, you cannot guess what might come of it.'

'Is he quartered here?' I asked, sipping wine.

'He's in the infirmary, sir.'

'Is he ill?'

'Not *ill*, as such. One of the walking wounded.' Koch jabbed a finger at his cheek. 'Just about here, sir. He looks as if he's been stabbed.'

'Been duelling, has he?'

'Lublinsky would probably deny it. Soldiers deny everything as a rule.'

'I want to speak with him straight away.'

Koch indicated the tray. 'Don't you want to finish your meal first, sir?'

'He is one of the investigators, Koch. The sooner I see him, the better.'

'I'll go and get him from the Infirmary, sir.'

Koch went away, while I finished what was left on my plate. I felt like a new man by the time he returned in the company of Officer Lublinsky.

I did not pay the soldier any immediate attention as he entered the room, but poured myself more wine and drank it down, the warm liquid melting the cold of a dreadful morning and a worse afternoon from my frozen bones.

'Stand there,' I heard Koch saying. Then, he came around the table to stand at my shoulder like a guardian angel.

Lublinsky clicked his heels and stood to attention. Only then did I glance up, and my stomach churned on the food I had just consumed. A cry of revulsion rose to my lips, though I managed to stifle it. Never in all my life have I seen a man more horrible to behold. Every inch of his rough, red skin was pitted, potted with lumps, holes, every sort of excrescence that distemper could inflict. From his forehead to his chin, he had lost any resemblance to Nature. Among the peasants working on my father's land I had seen what smallpox could do to a human being. What it had done to Lublinsky was beyond description.

His uniform had a collar cut high to cover the livid pockmarks and festering boils which plagued his neck and his throat. A black, blood-ringed wound gaped in his left cheek. He deliberately wore a forage-cap two sizes larger than he required, in order to cover his face.

'Take off your cap in the presence of Herr Procurator,' Koch ordered brusquely. The man obeyed, and his baldness came to light with all the starkness of harsh deformity, the crown of his head as pocked and cratered with boils and scars as his face. Had it not been for his height and build, and his ability as a soldier of the King, he would have found employment in a travelling freak-show and nowhere else. He glanced beyond me, challenging Koch to meet his eye. Those eyes were large and black, and darted around with fiery energy. He would have been handsome if Fate had dealt him a better hand. With those high cheekbones, aquiline nose, square jaw and strong chin, he might have been an artist's model or the lover of a baroness in a better world.

'Shall I remove the plates, sir?' Koch enquired.

'Leave them be.' I had no wish to diminish Koch in the eyes of this man. 'You have been assisting in the investigation of the murders under the direct supervision of Professor Kant, have you not?' I said, addressing Lublinsky.

His eyes darted from me to Koch, then back again, and he opened his mouth to speak. If I had been shocked by his face, his voice horrified me. A spluttering wild baboon seemed to have been let loose in his oral cavity, a beast he had great trouble in taming. I must have shown my difficulty, for he suddenly stopped short, then started up again, pronouncing his words more slowly to avoid the nasal and guttural emissions that made his speech so difficult to comprehend.

'Professor who?' he whined, the words whistling from a severely cleft palate. 'I did what I was told. Reports, they wanted. Reports, they got.'

'But you were also paid to make drawings for Professor Kant.'

'Oh, *him*!' he exclaimed. 'Was he a professor?'

'Who did you think he was?' I asked.

Lublinsky shrugged. 'I wasn't paid to think, sir. I didn't care. I gave him what he asked for. The world is full of old men with strange tastes.'

I forced myself to look at him, and tried to imagine what was going though his mind. Everything in Königsberg seemed to be tainted, sick, removed from the normal light of day. In that instant I felt oppressed by the necessity that obliged me to be a part of it. What 'talent' had Professor Kant divined in this improbable man?

'Tell me about yourself,' I said, and soon I wished I had not asked.

A great deal of patience was needed to make sense of his babble. His name was Anton Theodor Lublinsky. He was a native of Danzig. He had enrolled in the light infantry ten years before, and seen fighting in Poland. For three years he had been stationed in Königsberg, where, he chose to specify, he'd been happy until quite recently.

'Are you not content here, Lublinsky? What changed your mind?' I asked, thinking that he had a perfect right to be unhappy wherever he might happen to find himself.

'I'd rather be fighting, sir.' He seemed to smoulder at the idea, then added gruffly, 'On the battlefield you see your enemy face to face.'

His coal-black eyes blazed defiantly, then looked away.

What had he seen to induce him to prefer military action and the risk of being killed? I leaned across the table, slammed my fist down hard, then stared into his eyes. The sharp odour of his person mingled with the stench that had impregnated the room. I had to force myself not to look away.

'I have read your official reports, Lublinsky,' I said. 'I found them less than complete. Tell me exactly what you observed at the scene of the murder near The Baltic Whaler. You were the first to see the body, were you not?'

He shook his head.

'That's not exact, sir. I was with another gendarme. Then, there was the woman . . .'

'One year ago,' I recapped, 'you were sent to the scene. You spoke with the woman who had found the body. Is that exact? I want to know precisely what was said on that occasion.'

Lublinsky began to speak in a gabble. Had I closed my eyes, I might been listening to some mysterious Greek oracle, or a voice conjured up from beyond the grave by Vigilantius. I studied the man's lips in the hope of understanding, while Koch prodded, corrected and interpreted.

That morning, he reported, a cold wind was sweeping in from the sea. He had risen at four to assume command of the guard. As he was relieving the night officer, word came in that a body had been found near the port. He and Kopka, his second-in-command, went off to examine the find, leaving the night-officer at his post. They both welcomed the opportunity to be out and about, instead of hanging around at the Fortress with nothing to do. At the scene, they found a corpse and a woman. There was no one else. The sun had not yet risen, the streets were still deserted.

'What did you see there, Lublinsky?'

He was silent for some time.

'I've stared Death in the face a thousand times, sir,' he said suddenly, glaring fiercely at me. 'Oceans of blood, fearsome wounds, the agony of grapeshot. There was none of that in Merrestrasse. But I felt no better on that count.'

He and Kopka had found no sign of violence, nothing to indicate how the murderer had dealt the *coup de grâce*. Even so, it was obvious that the victim had not died of natural causes.

'Obvious, Lublinsky?'

The body of Jan Konnen had pitched forward on his knees, the head resting against the bare stone. It was the same position Muslims adopted when they prayed to their God, he said. As nothing was to be learned from the corpse, they had turned their attention to the woman. A midwife on her way to deliver a baby. The woman refused to say a word. She was shaking with fright. Then, Kopka had a bright idea. He went to procure a pint of gin from a nearby inn.

Lublinsky paused, and seemed to think long and hard before he continued. 'She wasn't the killer, sir. That was clear enough.'

'Clear? What was clear about it?'

He sucked in a mighty gasp of air through his mouth like a suffocating animal. 'She was terrified.'

'What was this woman's name?'

He hesitated again.

'I want to know the midwife's name,' I repeated firmly. 'You failed to record that in your report.'

A cloud of emotions seemed to tear at his face and mouth.

'Withholding information is a criminal offence,' I warned him.

'Anna, sir,' he said, after some moments of brooding silence. 'Anna Rostova.'

'Did she tell you this while Kopka was away?' I asked.

Lublinsky's large hands began to trawl nervously over his uniform, adjusting his buttons, straightening his collar, rolling his cap up tightly into a tube. At last, he glanced at me and nodded.

'And why would she do that? How did you win her confidence?'

He flushed bright red. 'I don't know, sir,' he said. 'I . . . that is, I thought she might have taken a fancy to me.'

That a man so ugly might take advantage of the promise of sexual favours from a woman extravagant enough to offer them did not seem far-fetched. I could almost sympathise.

'For no other reason?'

An expression of pain took possession of Lublinsky's face. Of all the sordid details of this story that recur most frequently to my mind, Lublinsky's ruined face most disturbs my sleep and dreams. His eyes darted around the room, his mouth opened and closed like a carp beached on a fouled hook.

'It was pity, sir. Her only child had died of smallpox, she said. She knew what I had suffered. That was the reason she gave.'

I looked at Lublinsky long and hard. His laboured breathing was the only sound in the room.

'What *exactly* did this woman propose?' I asked, preparing myself to hear a squalid confession of sexual degeneracy.

Before he chose to answer, Lublinsky played with his fingernail at the hole in his cheek until the blood flowed. Then, resentment burst from him violently, as if some private dam of reserve had suddenly given way.

'She told me that the Devil had murdered him.'

'The Devil,' I repeated mechanically.

'She had seen his claws, sir.'

'Did you see them too?' I asked with all the ingenuity at my disposal.

'No, sir. There was nowt to see. I examined the corpse. There was nothing. No wound, no weapon. Only Satan could have done it, she said.'

'So, you saw nothing, but you believed her. Why did you not include these details in your written report?' I objected.

Lublinsky did not respond. Instead, a violent quivering shook his limbs. I did not comprehend the battle going on in his head, the invisible enemy that had him by the throat.

'She said . . . she'd . . . help me, sir,' he murmured at last.

'A midwife, Lublinsky? How could a midwife help you?'

He raised a hand to his scarred and blistered face. 'She promised to cure me. I caught the fever in Poland. I should have died, but didn't. I wish I had. I was engaged to a lass from Chelmo. She ditched me when she saw my face. And that was just the start of it. My mates in the regiment avoided me. Called me Son of Satan, they did. Five years this has been going on. Five years, sir! Anna said she'd save me. She swore I'd have skin like a baby's arse, and I believed her. She was the first female . . .' He gulped for air. '. . . to look at me in all that time. Before Kopka came back, I sent her on her way. I had her address . . .'

'One thing remains unsaid. Two things, to be precise,' I interrupted him. 'What had Anna Rostova seen that you did *not* see? And how did she intend to cure your ills? You risk prison for not having done your duty, remember.'

He needed no threatening. 'I'm as badly off as I was a year ago,' he said with anger, holding his face up to the light. He seemed almost to glory in the ruin Nature had made. 'Anna said the Devil would end my suffering. That was why he'd left his claw behind.'

I tried to keep calm. 'You've seen it, haven't you?'

Lublinsky shrank back in silence.

'Don't make things worse,' I warned. 'Describe this . . . claw.'

189

'A long thing like a pointed bone,' he declared at last. 'The claw of Lucifer. It has great powers. That's why she took it from the body.'

'Powers, Lublinsky? Which powers are you talking of?'

'To cure . . . To kill, sir. She said she'd cure my face with that object from Hell. It was charged with the life of the dead man. He'd been the sacrifice. His life was to be my healing.'

I sat back as Lublinsky leaned across the table, his misery turning to anger.

'Look at me, sir. Just look at my damned face!' he cried. 'Wouldn't you have done the same?'

I stared at the ravages of his illness, steeling myself against compassion.

'Your face is horridly disfigured,' I said, coldly. 'Am I to understand that you never saw this kind-hearted woman again?'

Lublinsky lowered his gaze.

'You know the answer, Herr Procurator.'

'What did she do to help you?'

'This, sir. She did this.' He touched the black hole in his left cheek, his voice tingling with rage. 'She pricked my face with the Devil's claw.'

'Were you not wounded in a duel?' I said, throwing a glance in Koch's direction.

'No blade could do this. Only a witch,' he replied in a whisper, slouching on the bench, wishing to appear less large a man than he actually was.

'How long has this been going on?'

'Since the first murder, sir.'

'The woman still has the claw in her possession, then?'

'Yes, sir.'

'When did you see her last?'

He turned his face away and stared at the wall.

'Yesterday, sir,' he whispered after some moments.

I understood at once what he meant. 'There was a murder the day before yesterday. You saw her whenever another innocent died. Correct?'

Lublinsky bunched his fists and turned to face me. 'Each murder made that thing more powerful. I'd be a step nearer healing. That was what she told me.'

I looked directly into his eyes, and made no effort to stifle the distaste I felt for him. The smallpox had deformed his mind as surely as it had ruined his once-handsome face.

'Why you are telling me this now?' I said.

He shifted uneasily. 'What do you mean, sir?'

'You *know* what I mean. You didn't write a word of this in your reports. You said nothing to Procurator Rhunken, nor Professor Kant. And yet, you have decided to tell me. Now! You know that she is lying, don't you? She cannot help you, no matter how many people die. You are handing her to me as a form of revenge. You want Anna Rostova to be caught and punished because she fooled you. Isn't that true?'

He did not answer.

'What happened to Kopka?' I pressed him. 'Where was he when the other bodies were found?'

Lublinsky wiped his nose on his sleeve.

'He deserted, sir.'

'Why would he have done such a thing?' I asked in surprise.

'I've no idea, sir. He ran away. That's all I know,' he said, staring fixedly ahead, his face as dark and vengeful as a demon's mask in a Lenten morality play.

'Very good,' I said, jumping to my feet. 'Now, you will take us to see this woman without any more delay. Come, Koch.'

Aboard the coach, travelling in silence, each locked in his own thoughts, towards the address that Lublinsky had given the driver, I found myself unable to look at the man sitting before me in the gloom without a sense of overwhelming physical revulsion. Of all the victims of the events that had taken place in Königsberg, and of those that had still to unfold, Anton Theodor Lublinsky aroused the most pity in me.

Now, that feeling is mingled with the taint of moral disgust.

Chapter 18

Königsberg . . .

The first time I heard the word, I was barely seven years old. General von Plutschow was returning to his country home when he called on us in Ruisling one day. My father's oldest comrade at the military academy was a national hero. He had been the guest-of-honour at a ceremony in Königsberg the previous day commemorating the twentieth anniversary of the glorious battle of Rossbach, which had taken place in 1757. General von Plutschow had led the charge of the Seventh cavalry that day, and secured the national victory. As a special treat, my younger brother, Stefan, and I were allowed to attend the guest in the visitors' salon. We listened open-mouthed to the colourful account that the general gave of the magnificent gala event at which the King himself had been present. And all the while the visitor was speaking, I could not drag my eyes from the place where his right arm ought to have been. General von Plutschow's empty sleeve was folded up and pinned to his silver epaulette with a gold medal.

'Königsberg is the essence of all that is most honourable, most truly noble, in our great nation,' my father enthused when the general had finished speaking, and my mother had dabbed the tears from her cheeks. Henceforth, the glorious name of Königsberg and the lost arm of General von Plutschow were inextricably linked in my mind long before I ever saw the city. To my way of thinking, Königsberg was a place where only glorious things could happen, and where the very best of people lived. Despite the murders that had brought me there, despite the killing of Morik, and the suicide of the Totzes, I still cherished the fond belief that Königsberg was a blessed place, and that it could be restored to its rightful peace with the help of Immanuel Kant.

But that evening, as the carriage followed the directions that Lublinsky gave the coachman and we left the centre of the city far behind, I began to see the other side of Königsberg, the dark under-belly of a wretched beast, a world of misery and poverty that I could never have imagined existing in the place where General von Plutschow had been honoured, where Professor Immanuel Kant had been born, a city that he praised as a sort of earthly paradise.

We were going to a district called The Pillau. It was a port of sorts, Koch explained, a shallow, shelving beach where whalers landed their catch, cutting up the meat and drying it on the windswept shore. Even with the windows closed, the stench that entered the coach was abominable. The rot of blubber and the decay of gutted carcasses fouled the air as the vehicle progressed along the eastern branch of the Pregel estuary towards the Baltic Sea. The way was dark, the dwellings few and miserable. An atmosphere of imminent danger seemed to lurk in every rut and pothole of the muddy track down which we jolted. The mingling of the cold salt water of the sea and the warmer waters of the river produced a dense fog, which seemed to thicken with every fateful turn of the carriage wheels.

'Are we going in the right direction, Sergeant?' I asked. I had no wish to lose our way in that forsaken place.

'I've only been out here a couple of times myself, sir,' Koch replied, peering intently out of the window. 'But I doubt that Lublinsky wishes to mislead us.'

Wrapped up in silence inside his dark military cloak, his disfigure-ment concealed by his oversized cap and high tunic collar, Officer Lublinsky stared fixedly out of the window as if to keep the sight of his unhappy face from our intrusive eyes.

I followed his gaze into the darkness, and thought of the fisher-men hard at work out there on the boundless sea. If the fog were to swallow their boats and our coach, would anyone know where to start looking for us? Far off, a foghorn let out a mournful groan, but there was no comfort in the sound.

'This is it,' Lublinsky broke the gloomy silence, leaning even closer to the window and staring out, his nose pressed flat against the glass. The swinging carriage-lamp lit his deformed profile, and a strangely ambiguous feeling welled up inside me. Distaste for the part that he had played in helping the woman hide the murder weapon, embarrassment for the humiliation he was now undergoing on her account. But there was no time for idle sentiment that night. Everything happened at a rush. Koch tapped on the roof, the coachman stopped, and we jumped down. The fog was like a wet sponge, my face was damp in an instant, and Lublinsky set off briskly towards a row of lean-to hovels which loomed up out of the gloom. A feeble glow lit one of the dirty windows. At the porch of the cottage, he turned, looked at me for an instant, then began to hammer a military tattoo on the narrow door with his fist.

The door creaked open almost at once and the dark figure of a woman appeared in silhouette, her hair a fuzzy halo about her face, which was hidden in the shadow.

'You, Lublinsky? Here again?' a husky voice purred.

I stepped from behind the officer's bulk and the words froze on the woman's lips. Her eyes sparkled with fright, flashing from me to Lublinsky and back again.

'Who's this?' she hissed.

Koch appeared on the other side of Lublinsky and the woman let out a stifled scream.

'What do you want?' she snarled. 'I'm not working tonight.'

I pushed Lublinsky forward and we followed him into the cottage, the woman backing away in front of us, bumping into a low table before she stopped in the centre of the room. She picked up a candle and waved it in our faces like a shepherd trying to scare off wolves with a firebrand. She was tall, shapely, her dress a faded red, low-cut, revealing a deep, dark chasm between her breasts. By the quickness of her movements and the sharpness of her voice, I guessed her age to be around thirty. In the candlelight her glistening skin was so pale as to seem transparent, her eyes of the same ghoulish hue. Silvery-white hair cascaded over her shoulders in a bewildering mass of curls and ringlets. Meeting her in the street at night, one would have thought she had been sculpted from a solid block of ice. I had never seen an albino before. There was a riveting beauty about her doll-like face, her lips pursed in a distrustful bow of firm white flesh, cold eyes as wide and penetrating as an Oriental cat's above strongly defined cheekbones.

'I'm resting tonight,' she said, a coy smile on her lips. 'Unless you gentlemen want to make it worth my while, of course.'

'We are not your usual clients,' I said. 'I am investigating the murders in Königsberg.'

The smile faded. 'What do you want from me, then?'

'Bring a chair. You have much to tell me.'

With a resentful flash of white-lashed eyes, the woman went to drag a rickety stool with a frayed wickerwork seat out of a dark and dusty corner to the centre of the room. I looked around by the light of the candle. We might have been inside a pagan temple, or the tent of one of those indigenous medicine men described by travellers in the Americas. The walls were hung with animal skulls, whalebones, objects cast up on the shore, and stranger things whose nature and use were hard to comprehend. On one smoke-blackened wall, graffiti etched with a blade in the plaster showed matchstick men and women coupling in a variety of beastly postures. As I shifted the candle, the figures seemed to thrust and jerk together in wanton lust. I turned away quickly, my face burning with I know not what emotion, until the stool was brought.

The woman gestured to me to be seated.

'It is for you,' I replied. 'Sit down, Anna Rostova. That is your name, is it not?'

She sat herself down, though she did not bother to answer my question.

'A year ago, you discovered a body,' I pressed on. 'Jan Konnen, the blacksmith, was the first of four victims of a still unidentified murderer. Officer Lublinsky tells me that you found something at the scene of the crime, something important, and that you carried it away with you. You have shown him this object, I believe, on more than one occasion since.'

'You know what this means?' she spat like a venomous snake at Lublinsky, who looked away sheepishly.

'Address yourself to me,' I snapped, 'and to no one else.'

'No wench will ever look at you again, soldier,' she went on, heedless. 'They'll throw up in your filthy face!'

'What did you find on the body of Jan Konnen?'

'Mothers will scold their babes,' she intoned, her glistening, transparent eyes fixed on Lublinsky. 'That monster with the face of shit will kiss you if you don't go straight to sleep, they'll say. He'll come . . .'

I raised my hand and slapped her hard on the cheek.

'Shut your mouth!' I shouted. I don't know what provoked me, but there was something so barefaced, wild and intimidating about the creature.

Her eyes locked into mine, she touched her face, caressing the inflamed flesh as if she took great pleasure in the pain. 'Hmmm, that was *nice*,' she cooed with a smile. 'You like to hurt a girl, don't you, sir?' A wet, pink tongue snaked swiftly over her lips, then retreated to its lair again. 'Have me whipped, is that your plan? Enjoy yourself at my expense?' she sneered. 'They gave me thirty lashes last time. You should have seen the lumps in their trousers! Got all excited when my white flesh started bleeding, they did. Is that what you like to see, sir?' She laughed aloud. 'Prussia, home-land of the whip and the cane!'

The woman's glassy eyes never left my own for an instant. I had to look away, and I caught the glance of Koch as I did so. I saw puzzlement written on his face, too. By then, Lublinsky had retreated to the far wall and there he huddled, head bent low, shaking as if a violent fever had taken possession of him as the woman spoke.

'What did you steal from the body?' I insisted, struggling to master the tremor in my voice.

The woman stared defiantly up at me, a shaft of light gleaming triumphantly in her dilated grey pupils, as if the situation amused her. 'If that idiot already told you, what need have I to repeat it?'

'I have the power to make you talk, Anna Rostova.'

She giggled then. The sound started deep down in her throat and gurgled out in a crescendo of ridicule. 'Oooh, you are a *rough* young one, sir! I can see that. Does your missis like it?' The expression on her face was lustful, smiling, evil. 'Stroke your oar with the Devil's claw? Is that what you want? D'you fancy it, sir? Its touch killed that man on the dock, and other men too, but there are far pleasanter ways to die . . .'

Her cat-like eyes shone brightly, the pupils needle-sharp points of light. I had never been so intimately involved with a woman of that sort. She was so different from my wife. So distant from any woman who moved in Helena's sphere. Lechery seemed to crackle and spark from her pores like electricity. I ought to have been disgusted. But I was not.

'You have naught to fear if you tell the truth,' I lied, struggling to control my emotional confusion.

She laughed again shrilly. 'The truth, sir? Well, let me see now. That night, I was dossing down in Lobenicht.'

'What's that?'

'A hellhole,' Koch clarified. 'A slum down near the city port, Herr Procurator. It's ten minutes from The Baltic Whaler.'

Having seen The Pillau, I could only shudder at the thought of Lobenicht.

'A woman in Wassermanstrasse was going into labour, but her time had not yet come, so I went to see this friend of mine that lived close by. I stayed with her some hours, then I left to finish off the business.'

'What time did you leave your friend's house?'

'It was after three. I'd drunk to fortify myself. It was cold that night. Like a tipple of something strong yourself, do you, sir?' Before I could reply, she went on: 'I knew what was waiting for me. A screaming hag, a half-cut husband, a blood-soaked, wailing wean, if the Lord saw fit. I was praying for success as I hurried down the road.'

'Praying?'

The word sounded like an obscenity on her lips.

'I pray to God,' she smiled. 'And to the Devil too. There's a tussle 'twixt 'em two when a child is born. Sometimes one wins, sometimes t'other. But first, I pray to God. Things don't go well for me when He loses. If a baby dies, I have no work for a long while after. It wouldn't be the first time that I have suffered on the Devil's count. I've seen hard times. In this trade, reputation's everything.'

'What did you see as you walked through the streets?' I cut her short.

She held my gaze for some moments. 'There was no one, sir, not even a drunk, nor the gendarmes on their rounds. I saw no living soul 'til I came to the port. The lights along the quay were almost all blown out by the wind. There, I saw a man on his bended knees. At first, I thought he must be praying like I was doing. Still, it was a funny time and place to go down on your knees and say your prayers. First light was breaking, that's the coldest time of night. As I drew close, I saw that something wasn't right. Then, I smelt the evil.'

She wrinkled her nose and bared a perfect set of pearl-white teeth.

'What do you mean? What did you smell?'

'Brimstone, burning. The Devil's stink . . .'

She stopped abruptly, twitched her nose, and looked around the room, as if she had caught the first whiff of that infernal stench again. She was acting and she was good at it. The harlot was more than capable of entrapping a fool as desperate as Lublinsky.

'Don't waste my time,' I warned her. 'Just tell me what you saw.'

'The man was dead, sir.'

'You smelt evil. The man was dead, yet you approached the corpse. Why didn't you call for help first?'

She stared at me for some moments.

'The dead are special, sir,' she murmured at last, and she seemed in awe of them as she said it. At the same time, she seemed to be strangely intent on reading my own mind. 'But *you* know that, sir. Don't you? The dead . . . you've seen a corpse. Their bodies here in this world, their souls wandering in another place. You've got the knowledge, I can tell . . .'

'One minute, a dramatist; the next, a poet,' I said, cutting her short. More roughly, I added: 'Tell me what you stole from the body.'

She twisted in her seat to Lublinsky. 'Damn your soul!' she cursed.

I grabbed at her hair, and twisted her face around towards my own. 'I will shut you up in a cell if you persist,' I shouted.

'You'll do it anyway,' she replied with a shriek, 'but *he* will roast in hellfire. That *bastard*! I'll ask Satan . . .'

'Forget Satan!' I shouted, twisting her hair until she screamed. 'What did you *take* from the body of the corpse?'

She clenched her teeth, looked up at me and hissed. 'It was sticking out of the back of his head. A poniard quivering in the air. Or so I thought. Then I saw what it was.'

'Go on,' I urged.

'Let me be! Let go of me!' she screeched, her hands locked around my wrists as she tried to free her hair. 'I'll tell you all, sir. Honest . . .'

She looked at me directly as I released her, the fierce anger she had directed at Lublinsky gone. As if possessed of some unbridled terror, the woman seemed to physically shrink in size. 'The most powerful of charms,' she whispered. 'That man was dead, stone-cold, the weapon jutting out of him, but there wasn't a single drop of blood. Not one, sir. No blood was spilt. Who could have done that, if not the Devil? I'd been invoking God a minute before; the Evil One was answering. It was an omen. Satan wanted me to find that body, to show me His power over Life and Death. If a babe was to be born that night, a life had to be taken. The wheel comes round. It was a symbol of the Devil's power. A gift from Satan, so I took it.'

'You didn't inform the police?' I insisted.

The woman shrugged, then shifted the cascading mass of silvery curls from one shoulder to the other, flashing her sparkling eyes at me. 'The Devil's claw was meant for me,' she said. 'Others would find what was meant for *them*.'

'But the murders continued,' I countered. 'You knew that the police were searching for the weapon.'

She glanced at Lublinsky. 'I had other fish to fry.'

'You informed him,' I said. 'You used the power you claimed the

Devil's claw gave you to divert Lublinsky from his duty. You promised to cure his face. Am I correct?'

Anna Rostova returned my challenge with a derisive laugh. 'His own good looks were more important than Justice. I told him what I had found. He chose not to make it public. That's for him to square with his conscience.'

'Show me this object, Anna Rostova.'

She stared at me uncertainly. 'Believe me, sir . . .'

'Bring it here,' I said sharply.

As I stood over her, a strange transformation took place. The subdued expression gave way to one of seductive compliance. Her fingers lightly brushed the bare white flesh of her breasts, she flashed another dazzling glance into my face, and a cunning smile lit her lips.

She stood up, leaned towards me. 'With your permission,' she whispered in my ear. Her hair brushed my cheek and seemed to give off a sudden jolt of energy. Then, withdrawing to the darkest corner of the room, she disappeared behind a tawdry curtain. Koch and I exchanged glances. We could heard her rummaging about, cursing to herself. A few moments later, she came back into the pale circle of light, carrying something in her hands. Like a vestal priestess, she bowed and placed the bundle in my hands. If the material had ever had any distinct colour, it was now entirely washed out. Mould had penetrated and stained the fibre.

Fumbling to unwrap the strings, I was obliged to remove my gloves. The inner folds of the cloth were spotted with ugly-looking, rusty brown stains. As I unfurled the wrapping, a nerve pulsed frantically in my cheek. And then, I held it in my hands. Twenty centimetres long, the colour of bone, straight and slender, like no weapon I had ever seen before. I passed it to Koch, who held it up to the light as if it were a specimen of some exotic beast.

'A needle, sir,' he said, down-to-earth and practical as always, before he handed it back to me. 'There is no eye. And the point has gone.'

I turned the thing in my fingers. Here was the weapon that had terrorised a city. The fragment in Professor Kant's possession was the broken tip of the same object, there could be little doubt of it. In a woman's workbox you would hardly have noticed it. Sticking from a dead man's neck, it possessed an awesome power.

'That night, my charge gave birth to a pretty little boy,' Anna Rostova murmured with satisfaction. 'While she was in her labour, I pricked her with it, three times on the face, three more on her belly. That babe survived, though he was choking on her cord when he came into the world. Satan saved him. That soul was worth the winning. I used the power of the claw to cure all sorts of ills that doctors wouldn't touch. Wenches came flocking to me when they had a baby coming . . .'

A moan escaped from Lublinsky.

'You knew it would do me no good,' he cried, his back to the wall like a cornered beast. Suddenly, he sprang at Anna Rostova.

'Beware, Lublinsky! You are an officer of His Majesty,' I warned, stepping forward to block him, laying my hands on his chest and pushing him away.

'She'd only help me if I kept my mouth shut,' he howled like a frenzied beast. 'She milked them dry. Pregnant women, old men that couldn't get it up, crippled babes. The White Witch, they call her. Look in that back room of hers, Herr Procurator. It'll turn your stomach. See for yourself what Anna Rostova does for money!'

I placed the needle on the table, grabbed up the candle, crossed the room, and threw back the curtain that served as a door. Dust flew into the air, and an abominable stench assailed me. Some reeking beast might have been closed in there since the dawn of Time. Covering my nose with my cloak, I raised the flickering flame above a kitchen table pressed against the wall. It was caked with dirt, spotted with the unmistakable dark, rusty stains of dried blood. Knives of different lengths were laid out in order of size on the table as if for a surgical experiment. Blood had dried on the blades in a dull, orange film. In the candlelight the metal gleamed and sparkled, despite the filth. On a narrow shelf above the table stood a row of filthy pots and pans. Brass glistened dully. A kitchen to all appearances, but not the sort of kitchen any decent housewife would keep.

I took down one of those pots and glanced inside. It contained something that looked like a large mangled radish, or some strange algae, and it gave off a dreadful smell of putrefying sweetness. I had never seen anything similar before. A large fat maggot, perhaps, congealed beneath a layer of gelatine, a worm with sprouting protuberances, a pale white worm. I swung the lantern close and almost dropped the pot. It was no algae, no radish decomposing in its fetid broth. It was a barely developed foetus, the tiny arms stretching out, the unformed head larger than all the rest, curving in towards the chest. I did not need to open the other dishes, nor ask myself what happened in that house.

I closed my eyes with disgust, and backed out of the place.

Lublinsky greeted me eagerly, the light playing on one side of his face, the rest in darkness. 'Abortion, sir! That's her trade. Got a pie in the pot, girls? The Devil's claw will solve your problem! That's what she says. That's how she lives. Ask the whores out on the Haaf! They come here snivelling when Nature plays them a foul hand . . .'

'You lying prick!' the woman screeched, leaping at Lublinsky, her clenched fist tracing a wide arc in the air. 'You'll carry the plague to Hell along with that rotten, stinking face of yours!'

Lublinsky screamed like a pig being butchered. Then the squeal choked in full pitch, and he fell back on the floor, his hands clasped tightly to his face, the Devil's claw protruding like a massive sting from between his clenched fingers. Blood flowed in rivulets over his hands, cheeks and neck.

Koch dropped to his knees beside Lublinsky, who lay flat on his back, crashing his heels hard on the floor against the pain. With a determined grunt, Sergeant Koch leaned over and jerked the needle out. A red fountain of blood spurted upwards, drenching his face and hands. Lublinsky spluttered and spasmed, then his body went limp. Koch called wildly for the coachman to come in, and between them, they carried the injured officer out of the house at a run. Like Lot's wife staring back at the ruins of Gomorrah, I watched them go, unable to move a muscle.

When I awoke from this trance, Anna Rostova was nowhere to be seen. Alone in the room, I seemed to breathe freely once more.

But outside in the street, Koch was calling frantically to me to run and open the carriage door.

'We need a surgeon, sir!' he urged. 'He'll bleed to death without help.'

We tumbled aboard the vehicle and galloped back along the dark road to town, lurching and bouncing over the ruts and the potholes. As the first lights of Königsberg began to appear, Lublinsky lay motionless on the bench seat, his face covered by his cloak.

'Is he still alive?' I shouted, as the coach thundered and clattered over the cobblestones, sparks flying from the horses' hooves.

Koch did not reply before we had entered the Fortress. As the gates closed behind us, he turned to me. 'We'll carry him to the Infirmary. Run across to the guard-house, sir. Call out the soldiers. That witch must be taken!'

Did I reply? Was I capable of forming a phrase to show that I was still the master of myself? Koch had taken command. He decided, he disposed, giving orders as the coach skidded to a halt and we manhandled Lublinsky down to the ground.

'That way, sir,' Koch pointed. 'Over there, Herr Procurator. Tell Stadtschen to send the troopers out.' He turned back to the coachman, dismissing me. 'Help me, man!' he ordered.

I ran as I had been told to do, advancing blindly through the fog, praying that I was running in the right direction, stumbling forward in the cold, drenching void. And as the edifice loomed up above me out of the swirling mist, a phrase that Koch had used rang loud in my ears.

'You've found your killer, sir.'

I realised that I was clutching the needle tight in my fist. I did not recall picking it up, my fingers sticky with Lublinsky's blood. All the way from The Pillau to the town, I had held the Devil's claw clasped in my grip like a talisman of Truth.

Chapter 19

I sat in the guard room and sipped a fortifying glass of wine set a-sizzling with a red-hot poker while the officer-of-the-watch was sent for. I was still in a state of physical shock and emotional confusion when Officer Stadtschen came barging in through the door. I told him quickly what had happened, then ordered him to send out armed patrols.

'What does this woman look like, sir?'

I began to pace slowly up and down the room at his broad back, carefully measuring my words as I recalled what Koch had said earlier that evening about 'women and rough soldiers'.

'She is tall, Stadtschen. Thirtyish, as regards her age. And she is wearing a . . . red dress,' I began slowly, soon stuttering to a halt. Why had I begun with such tiny and secondary details? Why hold back information that would make her immediately recognisable? 'She . . . this woman's name is Rostova,' I added, reluctantly. 'She is an albino.'

'A *what*, sir?'

'She is white, Stadtschen. White all over,' I explained somewhat foolishly. 'Her skin, her lips, her hair. White as fresh-milled flour.'

'I know the freak you mean, sir,' he said with a sly grin. 'They call her Anna, that one.'

I did not bother to ask him where or when he had met her. I was able to imagine the circumstances all too easily, and an unwanted vision flashed before my eyes. As it faded, fear took its place. Fear for the chain of unpleasant events that I was about to unleash on the woman. The freak, as he had called her.

'Tell your men not to touch a hair on her head,' I said sternly. 'I hold you personally responsible, Stadtschen. Gerta Totz took her own life yesterday after the rough treatment she got from you and your troops. Bring Anna Rostova here unharmed. Without a single mark on her body. Do I make myself clear?'

Stadtschen stiffened. 'These things happen, sir. The lads give all the new prisoners a bit of a welcome, so to speak. To soften them up. There's nothing wrong with that, Herr Procurator. Guilty or innocent, they'll get another good thrashing before they're released.'

I winced at the thought of Anna Rostova falling into their hands.

'*Prussia, homeland of the whip and cane!*' she had laughed in my face not two hours before. If the soldiers had been so hard on a creature as submissive and docile as Gerta Totz, how kindly would they react to exotic beauty, a sharp tongue and the certain knowledge that the woman was a common whore?

'*. . . thirty lashes last time. They got excited when my white flesh started bleeding, those animals did.*'

She would provoke them to the worst excesses, I had no doubt.

Had it been possible to call back the accurate description I had just given to Stadtschen, I would have done so. But it was too late for lies. He knew her. Could I tell him now that I had make a mistake? Would he believe me if I informed him that the woman I was chasing was, in fact, small, dark, fat and very ugly? All I could do to protect Anna Rostova was to lock her up within my own custody, and the sooner, the better.

'I know the barbarous things that go on in Prussian jails,' I said to him sharply. 'I do not want anything similar to happen in this case.'

A half-smile traced itself on Stadtschen's face. 'You gave that Gerta Totz a proper welcome yourself, sir. A right good punch, if I may say so.'

'I sincerely regret it,' I snapped.

'If she died, sir,' Stadtschen looked down, avoiding my gaze as he spoke, but accusing nonetheless, 'it was because you gave us no specific instructions.'

'I am giving them *now*!' I stressed. 'I mean to be obeyed. Anna Rostova must not be harmed.'

Stadtschen clicked his heels to signify that he had understood, though perplexity was written openly on his face. Anna Rostova was a criminal in his eyes. He knew how such people should be handled. I could only envy him for the clarity and the absoluteness of his judgement. The simple fact that she had put an officer's eye out was all the proof that he needed. In that respect, Stadtschen was transparently honest in his prejudices. I, by comparison, felt far less certain, more inclined to doubt. The fact that I had probably identified the assassin should have been grounds for rejoicing, but I was still without definitive proof.

'One more thing before you go,' I said, giving the fugitive a few extra seconds to make her escape, as I hoped she would do. 'A man named Kopka deserted from the regiment some months ago. I want to see his service records.'

Stadtschen frowned, then cleared his throat noisily. His face betrayed a look of concern that the prospect of hunting down Anna Rostova had not aroused in him. His eyes flashed away from mine, and when his voice came, it was hesistant, halting. He might have been walking barefoot on broken glass.

'I . . . I'll need to check the battalion files,' he said. 'It might not be easy, sir. You know what deserters are like. They leave few traces behind them. None at all, if they can get away with it. What exactly were you wishing to know about this fellow, Kopka, sir?'

I peered up into his face. It was large, chubby, as red as raw beef. His small black eyes crossed as he squinted down his nose at me. He appeared to be holding his breath, an effort that brought a flush of white to his rosy cheeks. Did his *esprit de corps* hold deserters in such contempt, or was he hiding something from me?

'I want to know who he was, and why he ran away,' I said. 'And just you remember one thing, Stadtschen. I will report any failure to cooperate here in the fortress of Königsberg to the authorities in Berlin. "Dumb insolence" is the military term for hindrance, I believe. I will report any such behaviour. Names, dates, all the details will be included in my report. I make no exceptions. Now, send your men out after that woman, tell them how they are to behave, and bring me any information which exists regarding

Kopka. I'll be waiting in my lodging. Send Koch up to me the instant he returns. If Anna Rostova is taken, I'm to be informed at once. Do you understand me?'

'Yes, sir,' Stadtschen barked. He spun on his heel and marched to the door.

'At the double!' I called after him.

Out in the corridor I heard him break into a trot.

I drained my glass of sweet, lukewarm wine, then retired upstairs to my quarters with an oil lamp. I could do no more. As I opened the door, I caught immediate sight of a letter. It was neatly folded, sealed and propped against a candlestick on the table. I recognised the hand that had written it at once. In other circumstances, I would have rushed to break the post-seal with joy in my heart. But that night, I hesitated, blinking like a convalescent who feels the heat of sunlight on his face for the first time after weeks in a sick-room with the shutters tightly closed. I sat down before opening the envelope.

Helena had taken it into her head to visit Ruisling. She had left the children with Lotte for the day and taken the morning coach alone. Ruisling was fifteen miles from Lotingen, a journey of a little more than an hour, though we had never made such an excursion together. Her purpose in going, she explained, 'was to lay an unhappy ghost to rest'. Helena has always been determinedly sentimental. She has a tender nature, as open and sincere as the day is long. Her sensibility to the needs of others, her passionate concern for all creatures, great or small, for myself and for her children, had always made her shine in my eyes. If something had to be said, she said it. If some other thing were to be done, she did not hesitate to do it. I had always loved and admired those sterling qualities. Her heart was her compass.

Suddenly, this goodness grated on my nerves. I would have preferred to read the vapid letter of a less enterprising wife. The idea of Helena standing before my brother's tombstone was unbearable. Had she not felt the abyss opening up at her feet? Had she not understood the mystery of the place? That grave was the dark pit in which my own soul was buried.

'I wished to say a prayer over Stefan's grave,' she wrote. 'I wanted to ask him to watch over you in Königsberg. What better way to close with the past, I thought, than to leave a sisterly kiss upon his grave!'

I knew what followed before I read the words. My father, hat in hand, dressed in black, had been meditating before the monument of a weeping angel which marked the family tomb. He kept a lonely vigil there, rain or shine, every morning from eleven 'til the clock struck noon.

'I guessed it was him the instant I saw him. I went to him directly, told him who I was and why I had come. I told him where you were, and that His Majesty had called you to His service. "You ought to be proud of Hanno," I said. "Your son has been given a most important commission. He is a feather in your cap, sir."'

I stopped reading. I could picture the scene. Sweet animation and simplicity of manner on the one side; on the other, the granite face of the man who had made me, the man who had rejected me for ever, the man who blamed me for the deaths of his dearest wife and his favourite son. My father had listened to Helena's plea for reconciliation in silence. Then, he had uttered one sentence before he turned and walked away from the graveside.

'"Leave Hanno while you can," he said.'

I stared at the words inscribed on the paper. My father's voice echoed hard, bitter and unforgiving in my ears.

'I cannot imagine the cause of such hatred in a father,' she continued. 'What does he think you have done, Hanno?'

I screwed the letter into a ball, and dropped it on the table. My heart might have been pickled in vinegar. I did not feel a thing, I am ashamed to say. I seemed unable to find the strength to react to the bitter news. Nor could I answer Helena's question.

What does he think you have done . . .

My father's attitude, my brother's early death, the demise of my mother, Helena herself, our children, all seemed to belong to another life. I knew that I was linked to them, but my memory of them was fading fast. Königsberg was like a rapid-turning kaleidoscope, the glittering images changed from one instant to the next, and it was difficult, nay, impossible, to hold fast to any single one of those coloured pictures.

I needed rest, restorative sleep, but the dark cell in which I found myself offered little comfort. The bare, stone walls were as cold as ice, the stove unlit in the corner. How I regretted the loss of the blazing fire in The Baltic Whaler, the hot water Morik had provided for my ablutions, the fine cooking of Gerta Totz, the well-stocked cellar that Ulrich Totz had kept. Unlatching my pantaloons, I took advantage of the one facility which was at my disposition, the chamber-pot peeping out from beneath the bed. After relieving myself, I took the Devil's claw from my pocket, unwrapped the filthy rag and laid it on the table next to the lamp. I must have sat there for quite some time, unable to remove my eyes from that object, questions rolling around my brain like echoing thunder in a fjord. What was it? Where had it come from? Why had the killer chosen such an unusual weapon? And all the time, like lightning breaching the dark clouds, the voice of Sergeant Koch rang in my ears: 'You've found the killer, sir.'

Was Anna Rostova that person? If she truly were the murderer, then Königsberg's troubles and my own would soon be over. I ached to discover the culprit, of course, but I did not ache half so much to catch Anna Rostova. Totz and his wife had died, and the fault was surely mine. Stadtschen had defended the actions of his men, as any officer must. It was true, too true, I had not protected the prisoners as I ought. I should have guessed the inevitable consequences of such slackness. Koch had warned me of the danger of indifference, but I had chosen to ignore his wisdom. The soldiers had pushed Ulrich Totz over the edge, and his wife had followed him faithfully off the cliff. And now I had set the same hounds loose on Anna Rostova. Wherever I turned – I thought of Morik, of Lublinsky, of my father, mother and brother – I had brought devastation.

Just like the murderer I was hunting . . .

I saw the albino woman in my mind's eye. Her wild silken tresses, her skin as white as frost, the lights in her eyes as she spoke, the sensuality of her full lips. The way she caressed herself so openly, running her fingers wantonly down into the deep, warm chasm between her ample breasts. Those same fingers had seized the Devil's claw and drawn Lublinsky's blood. I had struck her, I had touched her flesh. And with what pleasure of coy delight she had accepted my show of anger! There was perilous beauty in her. Anna Rostova . . . there was even something magical in the name. Evil and attraction, equally mixed. I sank down onto my bed, images of her coming thick and fast. And I was aroused by them. My pulse was quick, my breathing quicker. Struggling to wipe this alien invasion from my senses, I tried to conjure up the face of Helena – I was caressing her, she returned my love, my life, my darling wife . . . But the Devil's claw lay there on the table. What had Anna said? *Shall I stroke it for you, sir?* I turned on my face, willing myself to see Helena's hair, to smell my wife's skin and feel her mouth on mine. But other carnal images raged within my troubled mind and poisoned my soul.

I sat up suddenly and pressed my knuckles hard against my eyelids. Anna Rostova was evil. *Evil*! Lublinsky claimed that she was a witch. Was that it? Had she enchanted me? Why else would I wish to protect her?

'Proof,' I said the word out loud, over and over again. Proof was what was needed. Proof of her guilt. Until I had such proof, no harm should come to her.

I went across to the table, sat down, and began to pen a letter to Helena. I have no clear memory of what I wrote, nevertheless I wrote with a frenzy. As if by doing so, I could unburden my mind of the restlessness that troubled me. My hand shook as it moved over the page. That hand might have belonged to another man. I signed the letter, sealed it, then opened the door and called to the guard on duty at the end of the corridor. He came running and halted in front of me. The hands holding his gun were blue with cold, his green eyes watered with the wind which whistled out in the passageway.

'Orders, sir?'

I nodded and held out the letter. 'This message must be delivered to Lotingen. It is urgent.'

Was it, really? I wanted to reassure Helena, to tell her that the investigation was making progress, that I would soon be home with her and the children, that everything would be back to normal again, the slate wiped clean. That there would be no more murders, Königsberg a memory, Vigilantius and his jars of human heads, Lublinsky . . . all a dream, all left far behind. And what of Anna Rostova? If she truly *were* the murderer, I would sign her death sentence with a happy heart.

If, if, if . . .

'Sir?'

The soldier was staring at me. How long had I kept him waiting, the letter held out in my hand, his fingers gripping it, pulling gently against my reluctance to let it go?

'This message is very urgent,' I repeated, and relinquished the letter.

I watched him walk to the end of the corridor, then I closed the door and lay down on the bed again. But still sleep would not come. My mind was troubled and sore. Despite what Lublinsky had told me, despite what the woman had done to him, despite the weapon in her possession, I was less than certain that she was the killer. Anna Rostova was no fool. Lublinsky might believe that the Devil's claw would cure his ills, but did she? She was too worldly-wise and knowing. An abortionist, a harlot, a creature of the Underworld, Anna lived by manipulating the gullible. Why kill the hen that laid the golden egg? She made her living from the likes of Lublinsky, from child-getting, child murder. A murderer will often kill for gain, rarely at a loss. Would spreading terror on the streets of Königsberg serve *her* purpose?

And if it did, what might that purpose be?

Koch had suggested human sacrifice as a motive, trading lives with the Devil for power and wealth. But superstition, charms and magic were the tools of Anna's trade, she made money from them. Death would not profit her directly. If gold were not the cause, I concluded, only Evil remained to explain her behaviour, and I would just have to face up to the fact. I would be required to publicly accuse her of consorting with Satan. I would be cast in the odious role of a Springer, or an Institoris. I had read their *Malleus maleficarum*. In the Dark Ages, those two blinkered magistrates had condemned numberless women to the trials of the ducking-stool, and sent them to the flames in public squares in the hallowed name of Religion. I would be obliged to do the same in the name of the Prussian State. Would I be immortalised to future time as 'Stiffeniis, the witch-hunter of the Age of Enlightenment?'

A knock shook the door, and an immediate sensation of relief swept over me. At that moment, any distraction was better than the leaden weight of my own thoughts.

Chapter 20

The bulk of Officer Stadtschen blocked the doorway, his face an inscrutable mask in the gloom. As he stepped into the light, the expression on his face was no more reassuring.

'Have they caught her?' I asked quickly.

He shook his head, then drew a brown paper file from behind his back and held it out to me. 'Kopka, sir,' he said.

'You had no trouble finding the information, then?'

He looked away. 'I didn't need to look very far,' he murmured.

'So much the better,' I said.

He bowed his head as we stood facing each other in the cramped room. 'I knew where to look, sir,' he said quietly. 'I knew Rudolph Kopka. I would have known where to find those papers in any case, sir, once you said that the man was a deserter.'

The sombre expression fell away from his face. The muscles in his jaw seemed to pump and pulse with tension.

'Where might that be, Stadtschen?'

'"Dead Soldiers", sir. His file was there.'

'Dead? I thought that Kopka had deserted from the regiment?'

'He did, sir . . .'

'A court martial, I suppose?'

He shook his head and smiled wanly. 'It doesn't work that way, sir.'

I took the file from his hand, and sat down on the bed to read the notes he had given me. There were three sheets of paper in the folder, and I examined the first.

REPORT

On the morning of the 26th inst., Rudolph Aleph Kopka,
absconder from the 3rd Gendarmerie, was captured by a search
party in the forest to the south-west of Königsberg. He had
been absent without leave for four days. No motive for his
absence has been ascertained. Although questioned before
incarceration in the holding-cell by the receiving officer, Lieut.
T. Stauffelhn, Subalt. Kopka could offer no defence for his
actions. After physical examination, the prison doctor, Colonel-
Surgeon Franzich reports that the prisoner's larynx has been
crushed by a violent blow to the throat. The capturing officer
reports that during chase and arrest the prisoner fell from his
horse after being struck about the head by a low tree-branch.
Kopka will be remanded in the Fortress Infirmary until a state-
ment can be taken, and a court martial convened.
    Signed. Capt. Ertensmeyer, Company Commandant.

The second sheet confirmed the medical diagnosis: 'Crushed larynx caused by a severe blow to the throat.' It was signed by the regimental doctor.

The third, a death certificate, had been signed by the same doctor
and witnessed by Captain Ertensmeyer: 'Prisoner died of wounds.'

Once again, I was struck by how incomplete these documents
were. They were like a mosaic with important pieces missing. Who,
in the first place, was the mysterious capturing officer, the man who
had led the search for Rudolph Kopka and witnessed the accident
that had muted him and eventually caused his death? Why was he
not identified?

'Who led the hunt for him, Stadtschen?'

'I've no idea, sir.'

'Did Kopka die in prison?' I asked, setting the papers aside.

Officer Stadtschen leapt to attention, but his reply was slower
coming. 'In a manner of speaking, sir,' he said.

'Well? Did he, or didn't he?' I burst out.

'Indeed, he did, sir.'

'That wound to the throat?' I asked. 'Or was it something else?'

Stadtschen looked first at the wall, then his eyes rose towards the ceiling.

'Something else, sir,' he said without expression.

I left him to simmer while I paced up and down the room in silence for some time. 'What actually happens when a man deserts, Stadtschen? When I mentioned a court martial before, you said yourself that it doesn't work that way. How *does* it work exactly?'

Stadtschen continued to stare at the ceiling as if his own larnyx had just been surgically removed.

'I will not warn you again,' I said sharply. 'Tell me everything you know. This is not an investigation into military comportment. I have nothing at all to say on that matter. Murder of innocent civilians is my only objective. What happens to a deserter who is caught?'

Stadtschen coughed uncomfortably. 'He is not disciplined by a military tribunal, sir. He has shamed his uniform, and he is punished by the members of his regimental company who are proud to wear the colours.'

'*How* is he punished? That's what I want to know!'

Stadtschen emitted a loud sigh. 'The company is assembled, two close lines facing one another. Then, on some pretext – like going to the jakes, or changing cells – the traitor is forced to pass between the rows.'

'It sounds harmless enough,' I prompted when he said no more.

'Each man has a large stick,' Stadtschen added slowly. 'And he doesn't hesitate to use it.'

I scrutinised him for some instants. 'In a word, Kopka was beaten to death. Is that it?'

Stadtschen said nothing. He now stared fixedly ahead, his eyes dull flints. Then, he slowly nodded his head.

'And is the capturing officer the one who oversees this final punishment?'

The answer to this question came quickly. 'It's likely, sir. In cases such as this one, names are rarely mentioned.'

'The authorities know about this unlawful practice, I presume,' I stated, picking up the papers again and glancing over them.

Stadtschen's mouth creased into a hollow smile. 'Not officially, sir. And in the army, if it ain't official, it never happened.'

I closed my eyes, and rubbed my eyelids. The death-roll in Königsberg seemed to be endless. Four people had been murdered in the streets for a reason that no one could divine. Morik's death made five. The Totzes, six and seven. Rhunken made eight. And now, I could add Rudolph Aleph Kopka to the list.

'Go away, Stadtschen. Get out,' I said, dismissing him with a wave of my hand.

As the door closed and his footsteps receded quickly along the corridor, I threw myself down on the bed, my head a whirlpool of conflicting thoughts. And that confusion is all I remember. Somehow, I must have drifted into sleep. A dark void opened up before me, a dreamless vacuum untroubled by the spirits of Morik or the Totzes. Lublinsky was nowhere to be seen. Kopka might still have been alive, attending to his duty in the rowdy company of his fellows. No intruder marred the snow in Professor Kant's garden. Helena's pretty face cancelled out that other face with its pale skin and silver hair.

When I awoke, the first glimmer of dawn illuminated the narrow window-slits, and the long, pale face of Sergeant Koch hovered above my bed like a ghostly impersonation of the early morning sun. He was sitting on the chair beside my cot. 'I'm glad you managed to get some rest, sir,' he said quietly.

The cold inside the room was less intense.

'Did you light the stove, Koch?' I asked. 'I didn't hear you enter.'

'I've been here a while, sir. Made myself useful while I was waiting. I did not wish to disturb you. It would have served no purpose.'

I sat up quickly. 'Is Lublinsky dead?'

Koch shook his head. 'He may lose his sight, according to the doctor. The wound's deep, and there's a danger of infection, but that can't be helped. He'll live.'

'Where is he now?'

'There's an isolation ward in the infirmary here in the barracks.'

'Anna Rostova?'

Koch shook his head.

I lay back on the pillow, breathing more easily. 'You think that she's the killer, don't you, Koch?'

The sergeant looked down at his hands. He might have been mixing a pack of playing-cards, looking at each figure, searching for a particular one before he spoke. 'Many things point that way, don't you think, sir?' he said. 'We know that she's done harm to more people than Lublinsky with that filthy Devil's claw of hers. Remember what she was doing in that back room, sir? That's prison, that is. A long spell, too.'

'But did she commit these murders, Koch?'

Anna Rostova was an abortionist, a prostitute, she had blinded Officer Lublinsky, harmed and tricked any number of people, but if no incontrovertible proof of her involvement in the murders came to light, I would be able to go more easily on those lesser crimes.

'Kopka's dead,' I said, my mind skipping to the latest horror. 'They made him run the gauntlet.'

Koch frowned. 'Who's Kopka, sir?'

'He and Lublinsky were the officers who were sent to guard Jan Konnen's body. They also wrote the reports and drew the sketches of the second murder. But some time later, Kopka decided to desert. What could have made him do it, Koch? He knew what his fate would be if they caught him. All the soldiers know, apparently. Lublinsky, too. That's probably why he never tried to run away . . .'

'Goodness!' Koch murmured. 'D'you think Lublinsky set him up?'

I shrugged. 'If Anna Rostova were the killer, and Lublinsky was her partner in crime, it would make some sense. Perhaps Kopka realised what was going on, and fled in fear of what Lublinsky and Rostova might do to him? It's just a possibility, of course. Until we catch her . . .'

My voice faded to a whisper, and we remained in silence for some time.

'I don't believe any clear-cut, rational motive will ever explain these crimes, Herr Stiffeniis,' Sergeant Koch said at last with great deliberation.

I studied his face. It was furrowed, wasted, mirroring my own confusion and frustration.

217

'I do not follow you, Koch.'

'I'm coming round to Professor Kant's point of view, sir,' he said with an attempt at a smile. 'Do you recall what he said about the pleasure of killing? He said that pure evil exists as a fact, and that it doesn't require any explanation. To be sure, a simple motive would make things crystal-clear and we'd all feel better for that, but what if no such justification exists?' He stared unhappily down at his hands, then glanced up again.

'Anna Rostova is evil. There can be no doubt of that, sir. And you don't need *any* proof to condemn her. The Prussian Law Code of 1794 has never been repealed, it is not subject to *habeas corpus*. Napoleon's army could come sweeping through the country at any time, Minister von Arnim was quite clear on the necessity for martial law. I remember reading the circular, sir.'

'But what would be the *charge*, Sergeant? Witchcraft?' I interrupted him angrily. 'Because the woman claims to invoke the Devil? Not so very long ago, an accusation such as yours would have lit a raging bonfire beneath her. If I am going to accuse Anna Rostova of anything at all – even trafficking with the Devil – I need to be quite certain in my own mind what it is.'

'Herr Professor Kant would not be so put out by the absence of a motive for murder as you appear to be, sir,' Koch replied at once.

'*What?*' I expostulated, shocked by the gravity of the accusation.

'Forgive me, sir,' the sergeant said with a shake of his head. 'But there seems to be no rational motivation for anything happening here in Königsberg. Kant's sudden interest in murder, for example. Would you call that rational?'

Koch knew of my respect for the philosopher, he had witnessed the special relationship which existed between us. Even so, I realised, his personal aversion to Professor Kant was stronger than his sense of duty in my own regard.

'Kant's interest in murder, as you call it, may well prevent a war, Koch. Surely, you have not forgotten our conversation with General Katowice? He was champing at the bit, and I almost gave him the excuse that he was looking for. I was convinced there was a terrorist plot behind all this. But it was Kant's help and the contents of his laboratory that corrected my mistake.'

'Nevertheless, sir,' Koch replied quickly, 'here in town there are many people better qualified to handle the situation than Professor Kant. Perhaps I ought to say, there *were* . . .'

'Procurator Rhunken, you mean?'

'Aye, sir,' he said, studying my reaction. 'Professor Kant had him removed because he wanted you to lead this investigation. But, if you'll permit me to speak freely, sir, that was altogether most irregular. You had no experience in cases such as this one. You told me as much when I first presented myself in your office in Lotingen.'

Only someone who has travelled in the land of shadows . . .

How could I make Koch understand the motive that had induced me to become a magistrate? Or explain the part that Immanuel Kant had played in the decision?

'I thought philosophy was at the root of it,' Koch went on thoughtfully. 'You share his interest in a rational method of analysis. Maybe *that's* what makes them different, I thought. But does philosophy drive a man to conserve human bits and pieces in glass jars? Does philosophy push a man to order soldiers to do things that would revolt them more than anything they've ever had to do on the battlefield? What sort of philosophy asks a common soldier to take up a pencil and draw the dead? Or store dead bodies under snow in a stinking cellar while they wait for the moon to rise? Lublinsky's mind has been affected by it, I'd wager. All this talk of the Devil! There's no clear cause or logical explanation that I can see in the whole affair.'

I stopped him there. 'All of this may appear odd, out of place, even motiveless to you, Koch. But what Professor Kant has created in that laboratory is a new method, a new science, I would say. It represents a revolution in our way of thinking. New ideas always surprise us. He is acting in pursuit of Clarity and Truth.'

Koch held up a finger, as if asking permission to speak. A deep frown creased his troubled forehead. 'May I finish what I was saying, sir?'

'Please, go on,' I said, suppressing my defence of Kant.

'Another idea came into my head at first light, sir, and I cannot shake it out. Professor Kant is unwholesomely interested in the mechanics of Evil. He's not in the least concerned about police business. That eel-fisherman down by the Pregel this morning, for instance. He should have been questioned. Instead of doing which, we sent him on his way. Professor Kant has more important things on *his* mind. He's trying to slip inside the skin of the killer, attempting to penetrate Evil, learn its secrets. That laboratory is just about the most diabolical place that I have ever been.'

The land of shadows . . .

'I was revolted by what we saw there,' Koch continued, 'while you two were in your natural element. You share a knowledge which goes far and away beyond my own comprehension, sir. If *that's* philosophy, I thought, I want none of it.'

If Sergeant Koch was horrified, I was dumbstruck at this description of what he believed Professor Kant and I were doing in the hallowed name of Philosophy.

'D'you really think that Kant believes in the powers of reasoning, sir?' Koch ploughed on, pulling a wry face of disbelief. 'After what we've seen in that room?'

'Clearly you do not, Koch,' I said bitterly.

He did not react to the jibe.

'I was shocked, to be honest,' he continued. 'He was hovering like a vulture over the body of that poor murdered boy on the river bank. He seemed to gather strength from what he saw there. Any decent man would shrink at the sight of such a thing, but *he* did not. His mind was charged with supernatural energy by the spectacle of that lad's corpse. I had the same impression in that room. Did you see the burning light in his eyes, sir? Wild with excitement, he was. His voice grew stronger, his whole expression changed. Why, he's eighty years old . . .'

Koch broke off for a moment, and rubbed his hands as if to purify them.

'His behaviour gave me quite a turn, sir. He seemed to revel in the fact of death. He's not diminished or humbled by it. No, I would say that he is fascinated by the subject in a manner that is not entirely . . . healthy.'

Koch paused before pronouncing the final word. Then, he waited for me to reply. But I had no reply to make. He had not specifically mentioned my own way of behaving, but he made no secret of the unwholesome fact that he thought that I shared Kant's unhealthy interest.

'Don't waste your time trying to explain what drove Anna Rostova to it, sir. Leave the explaining to Professor Kant. He'll come up with an answer.'

How could I defend the philosopher from such a perverse misreading of his intentions? Immanuel Kant had assembled the evidence in his laboratory in the interests of understanding and science. For the same reasons, he had made his way down to the River Pregel. He was not 'hovering like a vulture' over the corpse of Morik, sucking energy from the dead like a vampire. He was seeking Truth, regardless of the harm he might do to his own great mind and fragile body. And I was the only man alive who understood his working method to the extent that I could help him. Was this not patently clear to Koch?

Searching frantically for some winning argument to counter the sergeant's jaundiced view, my eyes darting hither and thither, I suddenly spotted a sheet of paper lying on the floor. It must have fallen from my pocket. The sketch that I had traced the evening before of the footstep enshrined in the snow behind Professor Kant's house. In that instant, profound peace descended on my troubled mind. I might have been walking through a vast and silent forest from which the chattering songbirds had taken wing with the first onset of winter cold.

'I will demonstrate to you that Professor Kant is not fascinated by Evil, Koch. I will prove it!' I said in a flash, wondering how in heaven's name I had forgotten such an important piece of evidence. 'Call the coach at once. Our own eyes will tell us whether Anna Rostova is the killer, or not. Thanks to Professor Immanuel Kant, I should add.'

Chapter 21

As I turned the key and pushed open the heavy door of Kant's dark *Wunderkammer*, my nerve-ends were tingling. At my side, Sergeant Koch appeared to be untroubled. Calm and detached, apparently in full control of his faculties, he might have been Professor Kant's most convinced advocate. We seemed almost to have exchanged roles. Koch looked steadily ahead, while I glanced anxiously here and there, examining the sandglass clock in its wooden frame, the lidded crucibles and the clay retorts that Professor Kant had used to conduct his scientific experiments with a good deal more attention than they deserved. I had reason enough to be uneasy; I was not entirely certain that I would find what I was searching for. Would I be able to confound Koch's doubts, and silence my own?

Neither one of us was so wholly unguarded in his motions, however, as to direct the lantern at the shelves lining the far wall. We seemed to have reached an unspoken pact on that score: those jars did not exist. Even so, we were aware of the glitter of light on the curved glass surfaces just beyond the edge of our vision. I could not shake off the notion that some unspecified 'thing' might take shape and step out of the dark shadows. Something evil and ominous. Had Kant really frequented that place alone? Or with Doctor Vigilantius, cutting and carving what the murderer had left in one piece? Koch's suggestion that Professor Kant found some morbid satisfaction in handling those distressing objects forced its way into my mind, but I shrugged it off.

'We must find the sketches that the Professor asked Lublinsky to draw,' I said, shifting an alembic jar from the worktop and taking my own drawing from my pocket. 'If any footprints were found beside the dead bodies, I intend to compare them with the partial print that I traced last night in Kant's garden.'

'Do you think that it belongs to the killer, sir?' Koch asked.

'That's what we are here to find out. If it does, we'll be able to match it against Anna Rostova's shoes.'

'The gendarmes will have to catch her first,' Koch objected.

'When they do, I want to be ready,' I stated guardedly. 'I must be sure in my own mind whether she is innocent or guilty before I proceed.'

Lifting down the fascicles from the shelf where Immanuel Kant had left them, I placed them on the table while Koch held up the lantern to assist me.

'Our job must begin in this room,' I said, splitting the bundle of papers into two roughly equal piles. 'Those are for you to check,' I said, moving the first pile towards Koch. 'These are mine.'

I did not need to encourage him. He shifted a large alidade measuring-instrument out of harm's way and bent over the table-top in silence, concentrating on the stack of documents I had placed in front of him. On the other side of the table, I began to sift through my own portion of the papers, and I was soon equally absorbed in the work. Not least for the meticulous order which Kant had brought to the task. My admiration for his methodology knew no limits. Each item in the first file I examined had been separated from what followed by a sheet of paper which noted the time and the date at which the report had been compiled, together with a short comment regarding the reporter and the weight to be attached to the evidence that he had supplied. The brilliant, organisational nature of Immanuel Kant's mind was precisely reflected in the physical disposition of his papers. The first file consisted of the finding-officers' reports. There was nothing new to me in any of them.

The next bundle was captioned 'Doctor Vigilantius' in Kant's distinctive handwriting. As I digested the first few lines that he had written, every distraction flew from me. It was the original tran-script of the necromancer's communication with the departed soul of Jan Konnen:

I have been dead for two days now, the sights I've seen grow dim.
Be quick for I belong to light no more. Darkness consumes me,
my mortal spirit seeping from that perforation . . .

Clearly, Professor Kant had witnessed a séance like the one I had attended shortly after my arrival in Königsberg. *Were you not impressed by what you saw last night at the Fortress?* But what had the philosopher himself been thinking, as he watched Doctor Vigilantius at work? I sought some clue which might reveal his own most private sensations, but no hint was given away. Kant had transcribed the spoken words alone and had left no testimony regarding his intimate impression of their veracity.

I put the first file back on the table and took up a bulkier one. It was marked 'Spatial Characteristics of the Murders in Königsberg'. As I began to read, my heart tightened in my chest. Who but Immanuel Kant could conceive of a systematic enquiry into murder which might easily have been an additional chapter to the *Critique of Pure Reason*? Who but Professor Kant could maintain a semblance of calm enquiry when face to face with outrageous facts that would have driven any sane man to quaking terror?

I turned another page and let out a sigh of satisfaction. Drawings of the positions in which all the victims had been found were collected together and catalogued in a portfolio. A connoisseur of prints or a collector of anatomical drawings could have done no better. Professor Kant had inspired the hand of a rough, untaught soldier to replicate the sort of evidence that the untrained police ignored as a rule. The schematic reporting of such invaluable details opened up prospects regarding the nature and execution of crime which no man had ever contemplated before myself. I laid the drawings out on the table in the order in which the murders had taken place, and called for Koch.

'Just look at these,' I said, my voice echoing around the vault.

'What are they, sir?'

'The precise positions in which the bodies were discovered.'

The pencil lines were faint, uncertain. They had been gone over more than once as the amateur sketcher tried to get closer and closer to the horrid truth before his eyes. 'These doodles are Lublinsky's work. Now, let us see if the footprints left in Kant's garden match anything shown here.'

We began to study them together, Koch's intensity matched by my own, glued to those drawings, analysing every line and every mark until our poor eyes ached. But there was nothing to suggest that the sketch I had made the night before was similar to anything that Lublinsky had ever drawn.

'What about these smudges, sir?'

Koch's finger indicated some odd cross-hatchings traced near the body of Jan Konnen. We stared at them for some moments. They might have been marks in the form of a cross like those that I had found in the snow, but the scale was wholly different. I had drawn a shoe in its actual proportions, and nothing else, while Officer Lublinsky had attempted to sketch the entire scene of a murder.

'I don't know, Koch. It could be a cross. Indeed, I am inclined to believe that it is, but it might be something else,' I admitted reluctantly, picking up another sheet of paper. 'We must consider the possibility that the artist was not equal to his task. In trying to represent everything, he may have included too much. Still, this looks like a cross, don't you think?' I indicated the drawing with my finger. 'Officer Lublinsky may have excluded a great deal of vital information in pursuit of what he thought was clarity. Too much, too little? In either case, the drawings are not conclusive.'

'So, until we find Anna Rostova and compare her shoes with the drawing that you made,' Koch concluded, 'we'll never know for sure if it was she who entered Professor Kant's garden, will we, sir?'

The image of Anna Rostova flashed before my eyes. I saw the gendarmes chasing her, catching her, throwing her to the ground, doing her harm. It ought to have been my most fervent wish. Instead, it was my greatest fear. I had let the hounds loose before, and caused unnecessary suffering. Now, I wavered between extremes. If she were the killer, the case would be over, she would be condemned. But what if she were innocent of murder? She would escape execution, but not imprisonment for abortion, and the inevitable abuse of incarceration and forced labour. I hardly knew which I preferred.

'And yet,' I murmured, my eyes nailed to those sketches, 'they were all kneeling. Lublinsky is consistent in that respect. Each one fell down in more or less the same position.'

'Just like Tifferch, sir. He . . .'

'Herr Tifferch was lying on an anatomic table,' I interrupted. 'He was an isolated object without a context. Concentrate on the *drawings*, Koch. Here, you see, the victims are located in the real world. This is the world in which the killer moved. I . . . I had not fully understood the implications before. I had thought it a mere coincidence that they were kneeling . . .'

I paused, deep in thought.

'Perhaps, is it just a coincidence, sir? The violence of the attack may have knocked them off their feet.'

'Oh, no, Koch. No,' I insisted, shuffling quickly from one drawing to the next, then back again. 'You see? A man struck from *behind* would fall flat on his face if death were instantaneous, but that was not the case. These people are all *kneeling*. We have the entire sequence of murders here, as Lublinsky sketched them. It's as if we can see the crimes being committed one after the other. Each victim fell just so, and his or her forehead came to rest against something, a wall, or a bench in the case of Frau Brunner. So *why* did they not fall flat, Koch?'

'You seem to believe that there *is* a reason, sir.'

'There is, indeed. Because they were already kneeling when they were struck. That is, they knelt down in front of the killer, then they were despatched.'

Koch looked up and stared at me in wonder.

'But that's impossible, sir! Would any sane person do such a thing? I can't imagine . . . An execution, sir? As if they were being put to death.'

'Precisely, Koch. An execution. But how did he get them to kneel?'

Koch glanced from one drawing to the next. 'Why didn't Herr Professor Kant point this detail out to you, sir?' he asked. 'He cannot have failed to notice the fact.'

'He has done much more,' I replied vigorously. 'He has placed the evidence before my eyes. Kant made sure that Tifferch's body was preserved under ice and snow for me to see. Then, he made an issue of the fact that Morik's corpse had not been found in the kneeling position. It is not his way to point things out, Koch. He shows you the available data, then he invites you to explain the obvious. I ought to have understood all this before.'

'That's all very well, sir,' Koch objected, 'but Professor Kant had no way of verifying the *truth* of what Lublinsky had drawn.'

I was silenced for a moment. It was a reasonable objection, after all. But the answer came to me in a flash: 'Tifferch's trousers!' I exclaimed.

'Sir?'

'There we have the proof, Koch. In Tifferch's trousers. The knees of his breeches were caked with mud. Do you remember? If my theory is correct, all the victims' knees should be dirty, if Lublinsky has drawn precisely what he was told to draw.'

I glanced around the room.

'Over there, Koch!' I said, pointing to the upper shelf against the far wall. 'Shift that vacuum pump out of the way, and bring down a box. Any one will do. To verify Lublinsky's evidence, all we have to do is examine the clothing.'

Koch hauled down a long, flat, pressed-paper box, the sort used by tailors to deliver suits and gowns. With mounting excitement we removed the lid. A cloud of dust flew into the air and into our lungs.

'Paula-Anne Brunner,' Koch announced with a splutter. The woman's name was written on a slip of yellow paper listing all the items in the container. I could not fail to recognise Kant's neat handwriting.

'A thin, green cloak of braided cotton,' Koch began to read. 'A long-sleeved white blouse. A grey gown of thin, indeterminate fabric. One pair of heavy, grey woollen stockings. One pair of wooden clogs with worn heels . . .'

'The gown, Koch.' I interrupted the litany. 'Let's see the gown.'

Koch spread the garment out on the table-top, then stood back. I moved closer and bent over the woman's gown, flipping it over, then turning it back again, my anxiety mounting.

'There are no stains,' I spluttered, the words choking in my throat. 'Not a single spot of mud on the knees.'

Koch's voice was a low murmur close to my ear. 'What does it mean, Herr Stiffeniis?'

'I have no idea,' I admitted, my head spinning with confusion.

'Hold on a moment, sir,' Koch declared with energy.

Without a word of explanation, he picked up the list, read it again, then began to search through the items in the garment-box. I watched in silence, fighting the impulse to stop him, resentful of the rough way he was rummaging among the articles that Professor Kant had so carefully arranged there.

'Now, let me see,' he said quietly, pulling out a pair of woollen stockings. 'Frau Brunner possessed this gown, I presume, and no other. The stuff is thin for the season, which made it precious. If she had to kneel down on the ground, she'd have done what any other lady would. She lifted up her best gown and soiled her stockings. You see, sir?'

There was no hint of triumph in his voice.

Like Doubting Thomas, I stretched out my hand and touched the rough, grey worsted with my fingertips. There were holes in the toes and heels. The stockings had been darned and mended more than once. And on the knees were two large, dark stains.

'She put more trust in those heavy stockings to protect her from the winter,' Koch continued, 'than in the light gown she was wearing.'

'So simple, so logical,' I murmured. 'And quite conclusive. We may assume from this that all the victims knelt down voluntarily before the person who intended to butcher them. They seem to have helped the killer.'

The words I had read from Vigilantius's macabre colloquy with Jan Konnen flashed into my mind, and I felt a tingle of excitement. Could there be a grain of truth in what the necromancer called his 'art'?

Darkness surrounded me after I knelt . . .

'A ritual was being acted out, I'd say, sir. The victims were being sacrificed to some pagan deity, perhaps. This certainly strengthens your case against Anna Rostova,' said Koch excitedly.

I stopped him quickly. 'Put everything back in the folders. Replace those boxes. We still do not know if Anna Rostova really is the killer, but I am pleased to hear that you now appreciate the value of this room and its contents.'

Koch made no reply until he had packed everything away.

'What now, sir?' he asked as he turned to me.

'Let us feast our eyes on the stars!' I said.

'The stars, Herr Stiffeniis?' Koch stared hard at me. 'It isn't lunchtime yet!'

'I have not gone wholly mad,' I explained with a smile. 'An Italian poet used those very words to describe his escape from Hell and his safe return to the real world. You and I have been forced underground by this investigation, Koch. First, in the basement of the Fortress with Vigilantius, then in this laboratory. It is time for us to return to the "Realm of Light".'

Outside, sunbeam shafts filtered weakly through a web of gossamer clouds which extended in flimsy strands to the very rim of the earth. Occasional flakes of snow swirled in the air like autumn leaves on the wings of a piercing cold wind. Spread out below us lay the glistening slate roofs and the soaring church spires of Königsberg. Beyond, the sea stretched to the horizon in thousands of acres of rumpled grey silk. I stood gazing out on the scene for some moments, filling and refilling my lungs with the fresh morning air.

'I need to speak to Lublinsky again,' I said, as we boarded the coach and began to descend the hill in the direction of the centre of town. 'But there is something else that I must do first.'

'What's that, sir?'

'I must call on Professor Kant. We must pay our homage to him, Koch. He needs to know that his faith in me has not been entirely misplaced. I'm afraid that I have not been the best of students.'

Chapter 22

'*Now, let's see who'll be the first. Older does not always mean wiser. Remember that, Hanno! Don't let your brother beat you once again. He has a good head on his small shoulders . . .*'

The images of childhood that remain most clearly fixed in my memory are those associated with my father, Wilhelm Ignatius Stiffeniis. A martinet by natural inclination, religious to a fault, our father had no time for indolence or tantrums. But oftentimes, he would amuse himself at the expense of my younger brother and myself with a conundrum of his own devising. As with all the things my father did, there was a serious purpose in his games. He wished to impart a lesson which would serve Stefan and me in our adult lives.

The family house still lies in the drear hill country out beyond Ruisling. A large and rambling mansion, all the rooms were cluttered with knick-knacks. My father would delight in hiding a well-known trifle. Then, he would call us in, and invite us to speculate which object had been shifted from its usual place. Our memories became prodigious as we grew accustomed to cataloguing the entire contents of the house. Indeed, we knew the material and the substance of our inheritance by heart before we were out of the nursery.

'*Now, lad, what d'ye have to say for yourself? A curlicue paper-weight of French glass? Bravo, my boy!*'

The winner was inevitably rewarded with a slice of brown bread coated thickly with the rich, dark honey from my father's hives. That was the prize. The chestnut-scented honey had brought renown and wealth to the house of Stiffeniis. To Stefan and myself, it represented a sort of condensation of all that our father stood for: the authority which he exercised with knowing severity, the promise that hard work would bear rich fruit, the notion that generosity would inevitably reward the effort required to overcome an arduous test. To taste my father's honey meant admission to his world. It signified his acceptance. And for no other reason than that he had decided that it should be so. The severe glance reserved for the loser was a sufficient punishment in itself. And that severe glance had left its mark on my less than perfect infancy.

Though younger by two years, Stefan was more competitive than I would ever be. Blessed with a quick intelligence and powers of intense concentration, he was the victor more often than not. And when our father was too occupied with the business of the estate, Stefan threw out challenges of his own, which became ever more physical and daring as we grew. Again – invariably, I should say – I was the loser. Stefan was taller, Stefan was stronger, Stefan was destined for a brilliant military career. Yet that military career would last less than six months. Father took me aside when his favourite son was brought home in a carriage and told me of the doctor's diagnosis. 'No more games,' he ordered. 'No physical trials of any sort, Hanno. I hold you responsible for your brother's life.'

In a word, he commanded me to treat my brother as an invalid. And so I did until the day that Stefan proposed a challenge that I was unable to refuse.

As the coach trundled slowly on towards Professor Kant's, I began to wonder whether my mentor had been playing his own sly variant of my father's game at my expense. I had the persistent feeling that Kant had been trying to test my abilities, perhaps to gauge how I might react to the provocation. On more than one occasion he had challenged me to reconsider something that I had failed to notice. But why did he wish to measure and probe my investigative capacities? Was he critical of my lack of attention to detail? Or was he more concerned about the superficiality with which I analysed the available evidence?

Just then, the carriage turned the corner at the end of the Castle Walk into Magisterstrasse. The cobbled street gave way to pebbles and the horse broke into a liberating trot. Glancing out of the window, I realised with a start that something was not as it ought to be at the house: black smoke was billowing in the wind from the tallest chimney at the gable-end. As I had read with interest in a colourful biographical sketch which had been published in one of the more popular literary magazines, Professor Kant forbade the lighting of fires before noon, both in summer and in winter. And the upstairs curtains were still drawn fast! As the writer had described the facts, Immanuel Kant insisted that they be thrown open with the first light of dawn. 'The slightest change in the mechanical regularity of the Philosopher's daily life', the writer concluded, 'means that something has occurred to prevent it from running its course in the manner which he has set for himself, and that it is a matter of some importance . . .'

I jumped down from the coach and ran swiftly up the garden path with Sergeant Koch hard on my heels. Before I had touched the knocker, Johannes opened the door. The expression on his face seemed to confirm my worst fears. His eyes flashed with what I took to be fright.

'What's wrong, Johannes?'

'You are very *early*, Herr Stiffeniis,' he said with a theatrical shake of the head, raising his forefinger to his lips. He nodded over his shoulder, and spoke out far louder than was necessary. 'Professor Kant has not yet donned his periwig.'

Could this simple fact distress the servant so much?

'My master is not yet ready to receive visitors,' Johannes explained, pointedly turning his head towards his master's study as he took my hat and gloves.

'But the fire is lit. I saw the smoke . . .'

'Professor Kant has a head-cold this morning, sir.'

Beyond Johannes's shoulder, the study-door was ajar. I could see only the writing-table set hard against the wall, an elbow resting on it, and a slippered foot extended beneath. I felt reassured to know that Kant was safe, out of bed and well enough to sit at his desk, though what he might be doing, I had not the faintest idea.

Following the direction of my glance, Johannes stepped quickly across the hall and gently closed the study door. 'I am attending to him just now, sir.'

'What's going on?' I whispered.

The servant glanced nervously over his shoulder again, then told me something that I would rather not have heard. 'Thank the Lord, he's safe, sir! He had a visitor this night.'

'Explain yourself,' I said sharply.

'I slept in the house, sir, as you ordered,' he continued. 'Professor Kant said he had some work to finish, and could do it all the better if he were left in peace. He asked me if I wished to have an evening free to visit my wife. Of course, I replied that I did not, sir. I informed him that I had much work to do about the house.'

'Thank the Lord, indeed!'

'I have learnt my lesson, sir. I told him that I'd be in the morning room if he needed me. He retired to his study, while I prepared a chair next door. I decided to stay on guard all night, but . . .' He swallowed a bitter sigh of mortification. 'I must have fallen asleep. Suddenly, something woke me. It was the French window to the garden, sir, I'd swear.'

'At the rear of the house?'

He nodded. 'It makes a creaking noise like no other.'

'What time was this?'

'Not long after midnight, I suppose.'

'Go on,' I urged him.

'Well, I thought at first it was Professor Kant, sir. He sometimes opens the window to change the air in the room. But then I heard, that is, I *thought* I heard something else.'

'Come to the point, Johannes!'

'Murmurs, sir. Voices. I jumped up and scraped my chair loudly on the flagstones. If some thief had broken in, I wanted him to know that Professor Kant was not defenceless and unguarded.'

'Had someone forced an entrance?'

'I knocked and ran into the study at once, but Professor Kant was alone. Then I heard a noise in the adjoining kitchen, and would have given chase, but . . .'

'But what, Johannes?'

His eyes opened wide and he stared at me for some moments. 'Professor Kant prevented me, sir.'

233

'He stopped you?'

'He was as pale as ash, holding his hand to his heart, clearly disturbed by whatever had happened. I couldn't leave him on his own, could I, sir? Not even to chase off the robbers. He was gasping for air as if about to suffocate. He was in a frightful tizzy!'

'He had seen the intruder, then?' Though shocked by the risk that Professor Kant had run, I was excited by the possibility that he might have seen the face of the murderer.

Johannes again shook his head. 'I don't think so, sir. I gave him a drop of brandy to calm him down, and the first thing he did was to thank me for waking him up.'

I looked at him with a frown. 'Forgive me, I don't follow you.'

'A nightmare, sir. He said he'd probably called out in his sleep. Well, I saw no point in alarming him further. If there had been any danger, it was past.'

'But you *did* hear a noise?' I asked.

He shook his head uncertainly. 'The kitchen door was open,' he blurted out. 'Either I had forgotten to lock it, or someone had let themselves out that way. But I'd swear I locked it from the inside, sir.'

'I am sure you did,' I reassured him. 'Did you call the soldiers?'

'First, I helped Professor Kant up to bed. I did not wish to frighten him even more. Then, I went to talk to the soldiers, but they had seen nothing, nobody. The fog last night was a real pea-souper.'

'How was your master this morning?' I asked.

Johannes looked down at his boots and mumbled, 'He seemed well enough, sir. I brought him tea in bed, and he smoked his usual pipe, but then he fell asleep again. I did not have the courage to open the curtains, sir. He's not himself this morning. He wanted the fire lit in his room, complaining of a chill which had risen to his head. And his bowels . . .'

'Tell him that I am here,' I said.

Johannes bowed and turned to go, but I placed my hand on his arm. What the servant had told me at the beginning came back in all of its importance.

'Wait a minute! He was working last night, you say?'

'So he told me, sir.'

'And what was he doing exactly?'

'He was writing, sir.'

'*What* was he writing?'

'I do not know.' The valet's eyes narrowed. 'And when I put away his implements this morning, there was no sign of the paper I'd set out for him last evening. Not a single page! His quills were worn, the inkpot dry, but whatever he'd been writing has disappeared . . .'

The study door opened with a creak and Professor Kant stepped out into the hallway. 'A *most* successful evacuation, Stiffeniis!' he exclaimed with a radiant smile. 'A finely formed stool, substantial in its density of faecal composition, and with a minimal liquid content. I hope that you have managed something of the sort yourself this morning?'

'Oh, decidedly, sir,' I managed to reply. The first time I had met him, he had spent a good half-hour discussing the workings of his bowels with his close friend, Reinhold Jachmann, over lunch. It was, apparently, a subject of which he never tired. 'Did you sleep well, Professor?'

'Never better, never better,' he replied dismissively.

And he did look to be in fine fettle. With the exception of two details. The first was his periwig. He must have donned it himself at the sound of visitors out in the hall. The mass of powdered curls sat uncomfortably far back on the crown of his head, his own silken hair, as fine and white as the gossamer threads of a spider's yarn, exposed beneath it. For the rest, as always, he was immaculately dressed in a padded three-quarter-length house-jacket, made of crushed satin the colour of Burgundy wine, brushed linen trousers reaching down to the knee, and pink silk stockings. The second anomaly, slightly ludicrous in the circumstances: he was still wearing his bedroom slippers. As a rule, Kant received guests as if, at any moment, he might be called to leave the house with them. He pointed down at his domestic footwear with an apologetic smile, and said, 'I was late in rising from my bed this morning.'

'I did not intend to disturb you, sir,' I apologised.

'Nor have you. I am sure you have much to tell me,' he replied, leading Koch and me into his study, where he took a seat in an upright wooden chair with wings. It was, I realised, a commode. Placing his elbow on the arm of the chair, he rested his head delicately on his upturned hand. There was a lingering smell of warm humanity in the room, and his nose twitched appreciatively. He looked like a silkworm wrapped up within a warm cocoon of his own making, though his ice-blue eyes were as sharp and wide awake as ever. Everything in his aspect seemed to deny the nocturnal drama that Johannes Odum had just narrated. For all his physical fragility, Kant appeared to be the very axis of a world that turned simply because he wished it to turn.

'Well?' he said.

'I have found the weapon used by the murderer, sir,' I began.

A lightning bolt of energy seemed to rocket around the room. Kant sat up straight in his chair. 'Have you really?' he said.

I drew the Devil's claw out of my pocket. Unfurling the filthy rag in which it had been kept by Anna Rostova, I held it up to his view.

'Goodness gracious me!' he exclaimed. I had hoped to impress him, and I was not disappointed. As he held out his hand to touch the object, I noticed that his fingers were trembling. 'What is it, Stiffeniis?'

'Sergeant Koch thinks it may be a knitting needle. It appears to be made of bone.'

'Would there not be an eye for the yarn in that case?' Kant asked, taking the needle in his hand and bending forward to study it more closely.

Koch had been silent, standing stiffly at my back all this while. 'It's been cut short, sir,' he said suddenly.

'Of course,' Kant nodded sagely. 'The murderer has fashioned a tool to meet his own precise requirements.'

'This needle was stolen from the body of Jan Konnen,' Koch went on, apparently warming to his tale. 'The piece that you found, sir, was the tip of this very item. It must have broken off as the murderer was trying to extract it from the corpse. We may deduce from this that the killer has a supply of them.'

'Equally, Herr Koch,' Kant responded sharply, as if he were

annoyed by something the sergeant had said. 'we may deduce that there is a precise reason why he chose this peculiar object, and no other, for the task. Where did you find it, Stiffeniis?'

'A person I have been interrogating gave it to me,' I began to say, spinning my triumph out, but Kant was impatient for details.

'A person involved in the killings?'

I nodded. 'I believe so, Herr Professor, though I wish to be certain before I make another arrest. She . . .'

'*She?*' He looked up quickly. 'A woman?'

'Indeed, sir.'

'Are you assuming that the owner is a woman because of the feminine nature of this object?' he asked, his eyes darting to the Devil's claw couched in the palm of his hand, as if it were a rare and precious butterfly he feared might fly away.

'That's why I came, sir. I needed to confirm my line of reasoning with you.'

Kant turned to me with a grimace of mad irritation on his face.

'Do you persist in believing that Logic can explain what is going on in Königsberg?' he snapped.

I blinked and swallowed hard. The oddity of the remark did not escape me. Professor Kant had spent his entire life defining the physical and moral worlds of Man by means of Logic alone. Did he now deny that vital principle?

'I see that I've disconcerted you,' he continued with a conciliatory smile. 'Very well, then, let us summarise the uncomfortable position in which we now find ourselves and see where *your* Logic leads us. The killer – a woman, if your suspicions are correct – has chosen a most unusual weapon. It is not a gun, or a sword, or a knife. Nothing that we would recognise as a weapon, but something banal and apparently innocuous. And with this domestic instrument, this woman has brought the city of Königsberg to its knees. Am I correct?'

He paused and looked at me. 'My first question, Stiffeniis. What can be her purpose?'

'There's reason to believe that witchcraft is the cause, Herr Professor.'

'Witchcraft?' Kant pronounced the word as if it were an insult addressed personally to him. He shook his head, and his face became a mask of malevolent sarcasm which, for a moment, shocked and entranced me. 'I thought you said just now that you had come here to be guided by Reason?' he went on with merciless irony.

I struggled to compose a reply. 'The woman describes *herself* as a familiar of the Devil, sir,' I said, attempting to justify my position. 'Witchcraft may well be a motivation for the murders, but I have no conclusive proof as yet that she is actually the killer.'

'So you still presume that there are rational motivations in this case,' he continued. 'My second question. Do you think that witchcraft will supply them for you? Not so very long ago, you believed that a terrorist plot was the cause.'

'That was my mistake,' I admitted. 'I don't deny it, sir. For that reason, I wish to make sure of her guilt before I arrest her. "We must bring light where the darkness reigns . . ."'

'How I detest being quoted!' he interrupted in a tone that was very near to rage. 'You have faced the turmoil which dwells within the human soul. You know it is a more powerful driving force than any other. Perhaps you ought to consider its role in this specific case.'

He leaned towards me, his musty breath invading my nostrils, throat and lungs, like a sour, suffocating wind. 'Once before, I seem to recall, you found yourself in similar uncharted territory, and what you saw there frightened you. You told me yourself, you had no idea that such passions could exist. Well, they do! You know your way through this labyrinth. *That* is why I sent for you. I thought that you would be able to put your own experience to good use.'

Against my will, I stiffened.

'Don't take it ill, my young friend,' he continued with a complicit smile. 'I assembled the evidence in that laboratory for someone with an open mind, a man who would be able to use it, and reach conclusions which are not so unthinkable as they appear. But come, tell me why you suspect a woman of the murders.'

I spoke of Anna Rostova with relief, describing the steps that had led me to her. I was careful not to mention the footprints that Johannes had found in the garden the day before. Nor did I tell him that although I had sent the soldiers out to search for Anna Rostova, I hoped never to see or hear of her again.

'So, this instrument has truly done the Devil's work,' said Kant with gravity when I had finished. 'The woman may, or may not, have committed the murders with this needle, but she has certainly put out Lublinsky's eye. I'm sorry to have been the cause of his involvement in this case. He's seen his share of ill fortune.' Kant shook his head. 'Lublinsky served me faithfully, or so I believed. But the money I paid him for those sketches came second to the desire to cure his good looks. And where did this lead him? He was an ugly brute before. He'll be uglier now. Goodness gracious!'

I listened in silence to this monologue, but I was not blind to what I could see, nor deaf to what I could hear. Kant showed no sense of pity for the man, no real sorrow for having involved Lublinsky in an affair that had pushed him into an abyss from which there was no coming back. There was no compassion in the Professor's voice. Nor in his eyes, which sparkled greedily over that instrument which lay exposed in the palm of his hand.

'It is about those drawings that I have come, sir,' I said, interrupting the silence that had fallen. 'Concerning the kneeling position in which the victims were found. You pointed out that missing detail when we examined Morik's body. I must apologise for my blind stupidity. Of course, I had seen the position of Herr Tifferch's corpse, but I only recognised its significance when I saw the sequence of drawings in your laboratory. As I understand it, the assassin induced the victims to kneel down before striking them. This is the mystery within the mystery. How do you think it was done, sir?'

'I hoped that you would find an explanation,' Kant said with a shrug. 'I have not been able to resolve this enigma. Nor could Doctor Vigilantius provide any clue, whether anatomical or paranormal,' he added thoughtfully, raising his hands to cover his eyes as if to isolate himself by excluding the sight of everything and everyone around him. He remained in silence for an unconscionable time. Then, suddenly, he looked up at me and a smile spread over his face like the sun coming up to illuminate the dark Earth. 'Do you recall the first thing I said to you about the weapon when we went to examine the jars in my laboratory?'

Could I ever forget those words? I inscribed them on the very first page of this testimonial. '"It went in like a hot knife cutting lard,"' I recited.

'Precisely,' Kant confirmed. He held the Devil's claw close to his right eye, which was less clouded by cataracts than the left, and peered at it. 'The ease with which this needle could be handled was the reason it was chosen. It requires no physical strength, no undue manipulative skill. The only thing needed is a little knowledge of anatomy. Knowing the most vulnerable point to enter the seat of the brain, the cerebellum. This is the key to its efficacy. And yet, it is not so easy to deliver the death-blow as it may seem.'

'What do you mean, sir?'

'The victim may not cooperate,' Kant replied with a mincing smile.

'They offered themselves up to be murdered?' I asked. 'Is that what you are suggesting, sir?'

Kant did not reply.

'It sounds like the Devil's own way of going about the business to me,' I heard Koch murmur dubiously, though I paid him no attention. Instead, I recalled a phrase that Doctor Vigilantius had spoken in the name of Jeronimous Tifferch: 'When asked, I felt no fear . . .'

What had Tifferch been asked to do? Had the necromancer sensed something vital concerning the modus operandi of the murderer?

'It was all done in a fraction of a second,' Kant said in a whisper. 'Before the victim realised what was happening, it was too late. The chosen one had to be immobilised. He, or she, had to acquiesce in some way. But how? If the needle struck an inch to the left or to the right, there was the risk of failure. The killer certainly foresaw this possibility. He – or *she* – must have thought long and hard about the danger before finding an answer.'

'An expedient that would prevent the victim from moving,' I murmured. 'Some stratagem that would convince the prey to pause long enough for the killer to strike. The murderer induced Paula-Anne Brunner to lift up her gown and kneel in the wet mud in her stockings.' Mounting excitement almost overwhelmed me. 'Why did she do so? Because . . . because the face we are convinced is hideous and evil was familiar to her. She did not feel threatened. "The Devil's is a face, no more," Tifferch said through Vigilantius.'

'A face like any other,' Kant added with conviction.

'She could have been obliged to kneel at pistol point,' Koch objected.

'Why not shoot her, then?' Kant's hand dismissed the suggestion with a quick flight through the air. 'No, no, Sergeant. The use of one weapon to compel obedience, and another to ensure death, defies common sense. There was no sign of a struggle, no testimony that cries for help were heard. The deed was done quickly. And there was compliance in it.'

'A weapon that excludes the need for strength, the use of a stratagem to distract and immobilise the victim, a face with nothing exceptional or frightening about it.' I listed the evidence. 'All this suggests that the psychological need to kill is greater than the killer's physical capacity to commit the crime. Cunning is used in the place of physical force. May we deduce that the murderer is unable to act in any other manner?'

Kant looked at me for a moment, and his thin lips drew back in a smile.

'A person who is weak? Is this what you are theorising, Stiffeniis?'

I nodded.

'What sort of person has no alternative to strength?' Kant continued. 'A person who is frail by congenital nature. A person sick or infirm. A woman. An old man . . . Is that what you're suggesting, Stiffeniis?'

Was he trying to steer me towards Anna Rostova?

'Many elements point to this woman,' I said.

'You mentioned witchcraft,' Kant reminded me.

'I need to verify it, sir.'

'It is a start, Stiffeniis. At least we now know that the terrorism theory was a red herring.'

So, there it was. I had convinced him. Kant had sneered at the notion of witchcraft, but I had brought him round. I had his blessing for the new line of investigation that I was about to take. Just then, the doorbell tinkled loudly, and Johannes entered the room a moment later.

'Herr Stiffeniis, there is a man outside to speak with you,' he announced.

In the hall, a young gendarme was vigorously rubbing and blowing on his large hands, which were blue with cold. I knew what he was about to say before he opened his mouth, though I have always refused to believe in presentiments. Such coincidences are part of the general incoherence of Life, not emanations of the hidden design of God, or any other Supreme Being. Even so, it was a strange sensation.

'Anna Rostova?' I asked, the blood pumping quickly in my veins as he stepped forward and told me what I both wished and feared to hear.

'Yes, Herr Procurator. She's been found.'

Chapter 23

'Good news at last, Stiffeniis! They have found her. The efficiency of our police force offers you a second chance to question the woman and find the proof that you lack.'

'Indeed, sir,' I replied, though Kant's enthusiasm sounded strangely fulsome to my ears. I was troubled by a ringing note of irony in his voice.

But then his thoughts veered like a sailing boat in a squall. Looking out of the window, he said with equal passion: 'It must be *freezing* out there! Bring me my waterproof cape, Johannes.'

The valet threw a worried glance in my direction as he left the room.

'You are not thinking of going out, sir?' I asked, but Kant did not reply. He remained by the window, studying the formation of the dark clouds with boundless interest, while I stood waiting, awkward and embarrassed, fully aware that I ought to have been rushing away on more important business.

Johannes returned some moments later, bearing the large waterproof overgarment with its distinctive sheen of beeswax, which Professor Kant had worn on the banks of the River Pregel the day before.

'This is for you, Stiffeniis,' Kant announced. 'It was designed to my own specifications. That wrap of yours may do well enough in Lotingen, but here in Königsberg the climate is unforgiving.'

I did not dare to protest. Nor did I wish to waste another minute. I let the valet help me on with his master's cloak, then thanked Professor Kant profusely for his kindness. And with my own mantle bundled under my arm, I hastened out into the hall along with Koch.

243

'He's in a *very* odd mood today,' I muttered.

'It's age, sir,' the sergeant replied gruffly. 'Senility plays the strangest tricks. Even men of genius succumb to it eventually.'

I turned to the servant. 'Do not let him out of your sight, Johannes,' I warned. 'Call the soldiers if danger threatens.'

'I will not hesitate,' Johannes replied, and touched his hand to his heart.

I felt reassured by the solemnity of his promise. Then, calling to the waiting gendarme to follow us, I stepped outside with Koch to find that a howling Arctic gale had taken raging possession of the day. We hurried down the garden path to the coach, where the young soldier had to pit all his strength against the might of the wind to hold the carriage door open for Koch and myself.

I had just set my foot on the step, when something happened to prevent me from boarding the vehicle. At the time, I attached no importance to the incident. A tiny woman came trotting out of the villa next door, hurrying down the garden path, a black woollen shawl covering her head. This shawl whipped wildly about her shoulders, but provided little protection from the cold. She seemed to have grabbed the first thing that came to hand in rushing out of the house.

'Are you a friend of Professor Kant's?' she asked, stopping by the carriage door. Through the folds of the black shawl I could see that this woman was about the same age as her illustrious neighbour.

'I enjoy that privilege,' I replied.

'Is he well?' she asked bluntly.

'For his age, remarkably well,' I replied. 'May I ask the reason for your concern, Frau . . .?'

'Mendelssohn. I live next door,' she said, pointing to a large square villa which was almost identical to Kant's. 'I always exchange a word or two with Professor Kant when he passes on his daily walks in spring and autumn. He never refuses a sprig of fresh parsley from my kitchen garden.'

And I suppose you set your living-room clock by his comings and goings, I added silently. She gave me the impression of being one of those infernal busybodies who pay more careful attention to other people's business than they do to their own.

'I was worried about him,' she continued. 'I haven't seen him much of late. So, when I saw Herr Lampe, the gendarmes, and persons such as yourself, going in and out of the house at all hours of the day and night, well, I feared that some ill might have befallen him.'

'Herr Lampe?'

'His valet,' she explained. 'The man who tends to his needs.'

She has confused the new servant with the old one, I thought, and I made no attempt to correct her. 'Professor Kant has a slight cold,' I added. 'The inclement weather does not permit him to go out as often as he might like.'

The woman nodded her head. 'That's probably why he comes so often. He always did have a winning way with his master.'

The wind had risen to a fury, and it began to snow again in a flurry. I had no time for useless conversation with an old chatterbox.

'Frau Mendelssohn, I thank you on Professor Kant's behalf for your good intentions and wish you a good day.' I did not wait for a reply, but skipped up the steps and into the carriage, thinking to myself that Martin Lampe seemed to be a persistent ghost in the existence of Immanuel Kant.

Safe on board, shivering with the cold despite the weight of the borrowed cloak, I put that conversation out of my mind and let myself be hurried away in pursuit of Anna Rostova and the Truth.

'Has the prisoner been taken to the Fortess?' I asked the gendarme who was sitting stiffly opposite me in the coach. He was very young. His straggling blond moustache still bore traces of the scrambled eggs he had eaten for his breakfast.

'No, sir. She's still out by the Haaf, where she was found.'

'No one has laid a hand on the woman, I hope?'

'Oh no, sir,' the soldier replied. 'Your orders have been followed to the letter. Officer Stadtschen warned us very strictly not to touch her.'

'Very good,' I said with a genuine sense of relief. One glance at the soles of her shoes would be enough to condemn or redeem her.

Having spoken with Kant, I was mightily swayed to believe that Anna was guilty, though I still preferred to hope that she was not. As for motives – whether driven by witchcraft or some other mania – I would have the time and opportunity to discover everything. For the moment, I needed only to prepare myself for what lay ahead. I had already felt the power of the woman's attractions. Her mesmerising eyes and seductive mannerisms had entranced me then, and I would need to fortify myself against her charms. This time, I silently pledged, I would be more precise and insistent in my interrogation. Helena's face would not be so easily displaced in my mind and heart by that woman's white skin, piercing eyes and silver curls.

It took us almost thirty minutes to reach the Haaf, a sandy promontory not far from Anna Rostova's dwelling. But as we struggled across the windswept beach towards a group of soldiers huddling by the water's edge, I realised that there would be no questions, no interrogation, no temptation. Not unless I decided to avail myself of the services of Doctor Vigilantius. Anna Rostova was floating face down in the cold, grey waters of the Pregel estuary, her arms spread wide as if attempting to scoop up whatever the tide might bring within her reach. The driving sleet and the rippling waves bumped her corpse rhythmically against the whispering shingle. That distinctive red gown had ballooned above her white legs and ridden up her thighs. Her feet were caught up in a dense tangle of black seawort. Strands of tangled white hair were spread out on the water around her head like the rays of the moon. Five soldiers sat on the pebbles smoking pipes and swearing at one other and at the louring sky above, as they grumbled about who should fish the body out of the estuary.

Sergeant Koch spoke up sharply, and two of the men waded reluctantly into the icy flood and began to drag the body towards the shore, while I stood apart on the strand, watching in silence. Anna looked like one of those mythical creatures that Baltic fishermen sometimes report finding tangled in their nets, half human, half fish. Distracted thoughts rushed round wildly inside my head like a flight of disorientated swifts. Without the albino woman's testimony, would I be able to prove that she had killed those people? And if she were innocent, if she had been murdered like all the others, then the murderer was still free. In either case, I would be obliged to start my investigation from the beginning again.

At my back, Koch shouted angrily at the gendarme who had brought us out to the Haaf in the coach. 'Why was Herr Procurator not told that the woman was dead?' he thundered. 'You'll be punished! That thin white stripe of yours will be torn off, Lance-Corporal!'

I turned and laid a hand on his arm. 'It doesn't matter, Koch. Just tell them, at all costs, not to lose her shoes.'

Koch gave instructions to the soldiers.

'D'you think the killer got to her, sir?' he asked, standing by my side again, his eyes never shifting from the work-party.

I shook my head. 'I really don't know what to think,' I said.

'Suicide, perhaps?'

Anna Rostova's face flashed before me, and I had to force the image from my mind. 'Anything could have happened,' I replied. 'And yet, she did not strike me as the sort of woman who would take her own life.'

I followed the progress of the soldiers as they hauled the body onto the shore and laid her out on the cold shingle. 'God forgive me!' I murmured to Koch. 'She may be as useful to us dead as alive. One look at the base of her skull will clinch it. And her footwear will speak the truth more plainly than she ever did.'

I closed my eyes, gathering my strength for the physical examination I would soon have to undertake.

'Excuse me, sir.'

Looking up, I found a lean young soldier standing before me. His angular face might have been shaped with a blunt hatchet, his eyes pinched and raw. He was white with cold, his pointed nose red and runny. 'Officer Glinka, sir.'

'What is it?' I snapped.

'I spotted that woman's body while we were patrolling the shore, sir,' he said. 'Rolling in the shallows, I though it was a dead seal at first.'

'Did you see anyone else on the beach?'

'In winter, sir? The whalermen use this place in summer and autumn. Maybe smugglers land by night, but otherwise . . .' He stopped abruptly, staring out across the water to an isolated building on the far bank.

'Well?' I asked impatiently.

Glinka took off his forage-cap and flattened his lank hair. 'There's a sort of . . . well, there's a . . . a place over yonder, sir,' he said. 'On the other bank. A drinking den where tramps and suchlike seek shelter for the night. Oh, and felons are taken aboard there for the transportations.'

'Transportations?' I asked.

'To Siberia, sir. She might have been over there carousing, last night. A body could easily have floated across on the tide. Especially with this wind, sir.'

'Thank you for your suggestion, Glinka,' I said, dismissing him.

I walked down to the water's edge, looking across the estuary at the place that Glinka had mentioned. There was little to be seen at such a distance, just a breakwater, a small jetty, a building or two. The mountainous sky seemed to crush and flatten the scene like an immense lead weight.

'Sir!' Koch called.

I turned and found him standing beside the body. The seaweed had been removed from her corpse, and I was able to see Anna Rostova's feet at last. They were slender, fine-boned, as white as marble. And they were naked . . . Two of the gendarmes were busily throwing grappling irons into the turgid waters, hauling great swathes of black seawort onto the pebbly shore, while another group were sorting through the filthy mess then discarding the wrack further up the shelving beach, where it lay in stinking piles. If they were working with method it was only because Koch stood over them, barking orders from time to time, reminding them to look for the woman's shoes.

'Have the body taken to that hut over there, Koch,' I ordered, pointing up the beach a hundred yards. 'It looks deserted. Let's hope that no one thinks of going fishing.'

'Not today, sir,' he said, glancing around. 'Not with all these uniforms on the beach. Not in this weather.'

'So much the better,' I grunted, looking across the estuary again while Sergeant Koch gave the order for the body to be taken up.

Cold and wet as the gendarmes were, neither their shoulders nor their hearts were in the work. What did they care for Anna Rostova? She was dead, and she was heavy. That was more than enough for them. I walked behind the stumbling funeral procession as the soldiers staggered up the steeply shelving beach with the dripping corpse, the pebbles shifting and sliding beneath their boots, shuffling on towards the abandoned shack. Then the body had to be laid down, the door broken open, before Anna could be accommodated on the floor. It was dark in there, the atmosphere cloying, suffocating, impregnated with the smell of ancient, dead fish. Without waiting to be dismissed, muttering bitter complaints about the stench, the men began to drift outside.

'Bring a lamp,' I called after them.

Sergeant Koch went outside to repeat my order. No one had a lamp, of course. No one knew where to find one either.

'Run up to the carriage,' Koch shouted sharply. 'Tell the coachman to light his carriage-lamp for you, then bring it back here.'

I went outside to join him, and we waited in silence for the lantern to appear.

'I'll wait out here, Herr Stiffeniis, sir, if you don't mind. A corpse last night, another one this morning, it's more than enough for me. I'll make sure that no one disturbs you,' he said. 'And I'll need to keep an eye on this lot, sir. There's still work to be done on the shore, and . . .'

'Very good, Sergeant,' I said, cutting him short. I had forgotten all too quickly that he was an office worker, not a policeman or a soldier used to the rough-and-tumble of life of the streets. 'Sights such as this are good for no man.'

Glinka returned at a run, panting as he held the carriage-lamp out to me.

'Thank you,' I said, turning away and stepping into the hut.

I placed the glimmering light on the carpet of pebbles, and knelt down beside the body. It was, I reflected, the first time that I had ever been alone with Anna Rostova. Closing my eyes, I instantly recalled her house in The Pillau. The darkness in that hut was heavy with nauseous unfamiliar smells, the space full of strange objects cast up on the shore, like those that she had draped upon the walls of her house. It was the sort of out-of-the-way place, I guessed, that she had often visited in pursuance of her trade.

I opened my eyes and looked down. A shudder of sadness and regret shook my body. Had it not been for Anna's silvery hair, I doubt that I would ever have recognised her. Her once-beautiful face was puffed and bloated. Jagged cuts and a thousand scratches scarred her fine features. The abrasive motion of the waves against the rocky, pebbled shore had removed the skin from her chin, nose and forehead. The whiteness of the skull-bone was a fraction paler than the natural pallor of her complexion. The crabs of the Pregel had done their scavenging well. Her eyes were gone, leaving two raw, black holes in their place. Those piercing lights would frighten Officer Lublinsky no more. Nor tempt myself, or any other vulnerable man, with their unspoken promises of lust and luxury. Seaweed draped her throat and her breasts, and other strands of the same rubbery stuff still clung to her legs and naked feet. I brushed away a sea-slug, then carefully unwound the straggling weeds that were matted around her bare throat. Dull, brown bruises stained the sides of her neck. I studied those marks for quite some time, aware only of the steady pounding of my heart as I turned my attention to her breasts and legs, and took her hands in mine to examine the nails, which were ragged, torn and ripped. Now that she could not reproach me, I held those cold hands for longer than I ought . . .

'She's been strangled, sir.'

Koch was at my shoulder. I had not heard him enter. Nor had I expected him to do so.

'So it would seem,' I said, gently setting down the dead woman's hand and standing up. I flexed my stiff knees, and gazed down at her. 'Turn her body over, Koch, would you?'

I was reluctant to touch her again in front of him. And yet, I had no other choice if I wished to examine the base of her skull. That important detail could not be avoided. The woman's body squelched, flopped, then lolled and settled, as Koch made himself useful.

'There you are, sir,' he said, shaking water from his hands.

Dropping down again on one knee, I removed the heavy wet hair from her alabaster neck, and felt the clammy coldness of her lifeless flesh. I ran my finger up along the knobbly vertebrae of her spine from the shoulder-blades to the start of the hairline. There was no sign of the Devil's claw. 'Whoever killed her,' I said, 'it is not the person we are looking for. We'll never know if she was the intruder in Professor Kant's garden unless her shoes . . .'

'Sir,' a voice called from the door.

Glinka entered, and in his outstretched hand he held a shoe.

A glass of iced water offered to a man who had just crossed a desert on foot would not have been more welcome. I sprang forward eagerly, and took hold of it with both hands.

'It was further down the shoreline,' he added. 'The other one must be somewhere near as well.'

'This is more than enough,' I replied, turning it over quickly, examining the shoe, the left one of a pair. My heart, which had soared not a moment before, now sank like a stone. The sole was as smooth and as worn as a pebble that had been washed and wearied by the tireless sea for a million years. There was no sign of the distinctive cross-cut that Officer Lublinsky had drawn at the scene of the first murder.

'It wasn't her,' I said, my feeling of disappointment and confusion growing.

'Do you think she may have had another pair, sir?' Koch suggested.

'I doubt it, Sergeant.'

We remained in silence, looking first at the shoe in my hand, then at the lifeless body on the ground, finally at one another.

'What now, Herr Procurator?' he asked, his voice subdued, distant, respectful. My investigation had come unstuck, and Koch knew it.

I thought for some moments before replying.

'I wish to go across to that tiny port on the far bank,' I said. 'She may have been seen over there last night.'

'But, sir!' Koch protested. 'This woman's death is not relevant to the case. It's a matter for the civil police . . .'

'Can you find a rowing boat to take us?' I insisted.

Koch's eyes widened at this suggestion.

'There's a footbridge down the way, sir. We can walk there and back in less than half an hour!'

I had to smile, despite the seriousness of our business. Suddenly, I realised just how much Koch's salt-of-the-earth common sense comforted me. I needed his presence, the dullness of his blinkered point-of-view provided a vital counterbalance to my own excitable nature. He never dared to ask me why, he only asked me how. For the same reason, I did not tell him truly why I wished to travel to the other side of the estuary. The fact was that I hoped to collar the person who had murdered her, and see him hang.

I stepped to the door and called in the gendarmes.

'Cover her up,' I said, though nothing better could be found after a great deal of raising dust than some dirty, stinking sacks and a tattered roll of netting.

I turned my head away as they carried her out, though I did not withdraw my hand when her damp curls brushed against my fingers. Koch and I followed them out, watching while the soldiers lifted her body onto a ramshackle cart they had found behind the hut.

Would Anna Rostova find peace beneath the earth? Or would she become one of those ghouls that country folk believe in, hovering between life and death, feeding on the blood of the living by the light of the Moon?

I dismissed these childish whimsies from my mind.

'Are you ready, Koch?'

Without another word, the sergeant clasped his hat more tightly to his head to keep it from blowing away in the roaring wind and the driving sprays of sleet, then he turned in the direction of a chain bridge which spanned the estuary, and marched away.

I had to run to catch up with him.

Chapter 24

'We're taking a bit of a risk going in here, sir,' Sergeant Koch warned, his hand on the door. The rough-hewn timber glistened black, stained here and there with salt, as if some miscreant had attempted to burn the place down, and someone else had put out the flames with sea-water. 'Do you want me to call up some of the squaddies?'

Hardly the Gates of Hell, I thought, as we stood before the low entrance.

'That won't be necessary, Sergeant,' I said boldly, but I began to catch his drift as soon as we entered the place. I had to halt for some moments while my eyes adjusted to the smoke and gloom, my lungs contracting at the rancid stench of unwashed humanity that fouled the air. Koch had ennobled the place when he called it a tavern. We were in an abandoned warehouse where some enterprising soul was plying small ale and strong spirits to lost souls with no better refuge.

The lingering sweetness of malt suggested that the edifice had once been a grain store. Rough stone walls had been raised directly on the quay, the cobbled floor within impregnated with mud and mulch. An open fire in the centre of the room softened the bitter cold, the wood-smoke drifting up to a ragged hole in the raftered ceiling, where it fought a losing battle to get out, then settled in a suffocating cloud upon the occupants. Despite the bonfire, everything was slick with damp, which ran down the walls in rivulets. A solitary hanging lantern gave light enough to enter, hardly enough to leave, though no one gave the impression of wishing to go anywhere. There were forty men at a guess, lost to drink, sprawling on the floor or huddled together along the walls. A circle of them had gathered around the blazing bonfire. So many people, so close together, yet barely a word was said. The silence was sullen, oppressive, resentful. Eyes flashed nervously in our direction, as if they were expecting somebody. One quick glance supplied the answer to a question that no one had voiced aloud. They looked away, sank their faces in their ale, or turned back to their mute vigil beside the dancing flames. In a moment, we were forgotten.

'Over there, sir,' Koch murmured by my ear, nodding towards the wall on the left. Eight men were crowded shoulder to shoulder on a bench, like sparrows perching on a garden fence. I could not see the chain that tied them ankle to ankle, but a rattle and a clink as we moved in their direction gave the game away. Each prisoner wore a grey blanket around his shoulders. One man nursed a bandaged stump, his right hand had been amputated, probably for repeated thieving. Their heads were scraped bare to the scalp, with the exception of one felon, who wore a strange fur coat and cap of the same material that he appeared to have fashioned for himself, a mass of uncured pelts sewn roughly together. At either end of the bench sat a guard in a soiled white uniform and cap with a red-and-blue cockade, a musket erect between his knees. One of the soldiers appeared to be sleeping, his head low on his chest.

'They've been hanging about since yesterday, sir,' Koch murmured. 'The ship for Narva hasn't landed yet. There's some concern about its fate.'

The night before, in Rhunken's office, I had carelessly signed the order for this batch of deportees. The most dangerous men in Prussia were being herded together in Narva on the Baltic coast of Finland. A forced march across the frozen continent to the Mongolia–Manchuria border, six thousand miles distant, was planned to commence at the first sign of a thaw. Alexander Romanov had reduced the price of the grain he exported to Prussia in exchange for the men. 'Sold into Slavery', one Berlin paper had controversially reported the agreement, adding that their new owner was keen to make the most of his bargain. 'There is infinite labour for idle hands in the silver mines of Nerchinsk,' the new Tsar was reputed to have said with a smile, having inherited the agreement from the father he had murdered.

'We must find the landlord,' I said.

'I doubt there is one,' Koch replied. 'That's contraband they're selling. Strong liquor is the only cure for cold in The Pillau. God knows what those devils will do when they reach Siberia!'

'Indeed,' I said, calculating whether I might be able to purchase the confidence of one of the condemned men, or their guards. I had money enough in my purse to buy a barrel of gin to stave off the most violent ague.

But I had barely taken two steps towards the bench, when the soldier at the far end jumped up and swung his musket in my direction, clicking the flintlock into place. His companion followed suit, one eye wide with surprise, the other closed in a permanent palsied wink. His musket came to rest an inch from my heart.

'Hold fast!' he cried, his eyelid tremoring. 'One step, you're dead!'

I raised my hands in surrender.

'I am an Investigating Magistrate of the Crown,' I said loftily, attempting to maintain some semblance of dignity by means of my voice alone, for my posture was ridiculous. 'A woman has been found dead in the river. I wish to know if you or your prisoners saw her last night.'

The lazy-eyed soldier moved his musket down a trifle, no longer menacing my heart, now threatening to blow a large hole in my stomach. He was an ugly brute, his jaw a curving, monstrous thing, such as I had seen around in the woods around Magdeburg, where the peasants are allowed to marry their cousins. The other one, a tall, thin man with a corporal's tab on his sleeve, raised his musket level with his shoulder and sighted along the muzzle into Koch's face.

'An' you?' he said with a snarl.

'The Procurator's assistant,' the sergeant replied. He slowly raised his forefinger like a pistol and pointed it at the guard. 'You are obstructing Herr Stiffeniis in the pursuance of his duties!'

Warily, they shifted the direction of their muskets.

'Did you see any women here last night?' Koch insisted.

'There were lots of folk,' the Magdeburger began uncertainly.

'The cold was bone-shaking . . .'

'Were there any *women*?' I snapped.

'This ain't no chapel, sir,' the man replied, resting the stock of his musket on the ground and stroking his jaw thoughtfully. 'We do what we can to keep the prisoners apart, but the night is long. The sooner they get on board the transport, the better. There'll be trouble if we have to hang around much longer . . .'

'I am interested in an albino woman,' I said, pointedly ignoring his laments. 'White hair, white skin, eyes as clear as . . .'

A startled look flashed between them.

'Was the woman alone?' I asked.

'It . . . well, a few hours after we got here, sir, that woman came in. Made her way to the fire. Shivering fit to crumble, she were. No coat, just a dress . . .'

Another glance passed between the guards. They were evidently gauging what to admit, what to deny.

'I am not interested in how you go about your duties,' I said energetically. 'I want to know who that woman was with, nothing more.'

'General Katowice will have your names within the hour,' Koch threatened. 'Speak out!'

'That'll serve ya!' one of the prisoners snarled at the guards.

'Well?' I said to the corporal.

'She were alone, sir,' he admitted. 'Stuck out like a parakeet, the colour of her. Soon as this lot saw her, the cat-calling started.'

'Did they know her?' I asked, my hopes rising.

The soldier shook his head. 'I doubt it. That red dress made them sit up smartish, though. They ain't seen a wench in months. Jailbirds all of 'em, sir. An' she weren't one to look the other way, know what I mean?'

It was not difficult to visualise the scene. Anna Rostova had been the only bright thing in the gloomy darkness of that den. The sight of her must have warmed the hearts and wakened the hopes of every man in the place, including the two guards.

'Did you speak with her?'

Both men shook their heads in violent denial.

'What about the prisoners?'

Furtively, they looked again from one to the other.

'You'll find yourself in irons aboard the ship carrying this lot to their fate,' I menaced, taking a step closer.

'She wanted to go a-ship herself,' the Magdeburger muttered. 'When no one was looking. To stow away, she said.'

He dropped his eyes to the ground.

'Did she offer to pay?' I asked. I had no need to guess what Anna Rostova would offer in exchange for help in getting away from Königsberg.

'I . . . I told you, sir. An' I told *her* too. There *was* no ship. We'd no idea how long we'd have to hang around. I couldn't, well, like, *promise* anything . . .'

'You used her, didn't you?' I tried to quell my mounting anger.

'No one forced her,' the Magdeburger objected. 'She was up for it, sir. Been a-ship before, she had. Worked her *passage*, was what she said. Passage. There was no mistaking what she . . .'

Wild shouts and bloodcurdling screams erupted behind us. Instinctively, the soldiers raised their firearms and pointed them into the ruck of people who had fallen to their knees in a tight circle gathered around two large grey rats, the bonfire forgotten at their backs. The rodents were light grey in colour, as large as cats, with curving front teeth, not unlike the massive *pantegane* I had seen creeping in their thousands along the alleys and the water's edge in the foul-smelling sewer that was Venice. These rats were battling for their lives, ripping and tearing at each other, raising wilder and louder cries from the spectators with each successful attack. No sooner had the fight begun than it was over. One man raised the loser by its tail, showing it off to the crowd. He whizzed it round and round his head in a wide circle splattering the crowd with blood, which brought more angry cries and protests, then suddenly he let the rodent go. It flew across the room, crashing against the stone wall with a sickening slap and a spray of blood.

The noise grew louder, with ear-splitting shouts of triumph as money changed hands; a brief scuffle broke out, then one man came hurrying over to the bench where the prisoners sat chained, and handed some coins to the felon I had noticed previously, the one who wore the strange fur garments.

'Who is that man?' I asked.

'Helmut Schuppe, sir,' the corporal ventured with a smirk. 'Bound for Siberia. If not for that, he'd be a lucky beggar. Been betting half the night, an' winning too. He spoke to her, though *spoke* is hardly the word I'd use for what 'e done . . .'

His voice trailed away.

'His crime?' I asked, studying the prisoner as he pulled out a fur pouch from inside his shirt, and put away his winnings. Though short in height, Helmut Schuppe was as heavy as a bear, and looked well able to defend himself if any man should think to rob him.

The corporal pulled a soiled sheet of paper from his pocket. 'Here we are,' he said, reading off what followed with great difficulty. 'Murdered his brother. In cold blood. Then ate his liver. Raw.'

So, I thought, this is the monster I had read about the night before.

'Free him of his chains,' I ordered, as the commotion started up again. More rats had been found, and another fierce argument was going on regarding their fighting qualities. I turned my back, unwilling to watch, though my ears were not deaf to the squealing and whistling of the rodents as their patrons held them up and taunted their opponents.

'Free him, sir?' the corporal answered insolently.

'You heard me,' I said.

He slouched to the bench, dropped on one knee, pulled a key from his pocket, and began to unlock the man's shackles. In a minute, Helmut Schuppe was free, but by no means liberated. The Magdeburger stood close behind him, his musket pushing into the prisoner's back, urging him in my direction.

Schuppe was not so tall as I, but his fur coat made him seem fatter than he was. With high cheekbones, narrow slits for eyes, a large nose and thin, sensual mouth, I took him to be a Laplander, despite his name. The leaping flames of the fire illuminated the livid brands he bore on his cheeks. A large letter 'M'.

'You've won a fair bit on those creatures,' I began in a friendly fashion. Koch stood close beside me, and though the soldiers had retreated a pace or two, they held their muskets ready.

'Want to know which one to bet on, do you?' the man replied with a lazy nasal hiss. There was no Arctic inflection in his voice, his German precise enough. 'I know them critters,' he said with a rumbling laugh which shook the loose skins of his furs.

'Indeed,' I agreed. 'Now, tell me about the woman.'

Schuppe narrowed his eyes and studied my face. 'What woman?'

'Anna Rostova,' I replied.

'Ah, *that* woman,' he smiled, and that laugh rumbled out of him again. 'When a man's condemned, he takes his pleasure where he can. He can't take nothing with him. Only money, sir. Money buys a dram, a warm blanket. There's not much else. A bite to eat. Women . . . I spent mine well enough last night. Grog, a bet, a warm body rubbing up to mine.'

'Tell me more about the warm body,' I said, as casually as I could, though it cost me a great deal. The image of Anna Rostova copulating like a beast in the darkest corner of that dark pit with a fiend who not only killed his brother, but ate him too, took my breath away.

'What did she tell you?' I insisted.

The rough laugh which erupted from his throat made all eyes turn in our direction. 'Between their thighs, they got warm lips that don't say much!'

'Before you part for the North, I may decide to have you whipped within an inch of your life, Helmut Schuppe,' I said coldly. 'Or worse, if I discover that you played any part in her death.'

The threat had had no effect on him, as I was soon to realise, but what he had heard from my tongue had worked its own small miracle. I had pitched a rock into a pool, and the ripples told me what I would never otherwise have believed. Helmut Schuppe, fratricide and cannibal, was moved by the news of the death of Anna Rostova.

'Dead, sir?' he whispered, his voice as tender as a child's.

'Strangled,' I replied.

'I saw her killer, sir,' he whispered, staring me in the eyes.

I caught my breath. 'Can you describe him?'

Schuppe shook his head and looked away. 'A shadow, sir. A shadow carried her off. I know evil when I see it. The rats went quiet when he entered here.'

'Beware!' I hissed angrily. 'Speak plainly, if you please.'

He stared at me intently for some moments. 'That man was hunting her like a hungry wolf. She knew where we were bound, sir. Wanted to come along, she did, so she tried it on with them two.'

He looked at the soldiers, his eyes flicking from one to the other.

'Over there,' Schuppe indicated the corner furthest from the fire and the lanterns, then he spat at the soldiers, staring hard at them. 'I'd give an arm an' a leg to get my teeth in those pigs' livers! But they got guns, and I must live. You can't get rid of *me* in Russia, bastards!' he shouted at them with hatred. 'I'll be back to feast on your warm guts!'

Six thousand miles on foot through a hostile country. The felons would be lucky to arrive, I thought, let alone come back.

'So, then she turned to the prisoners,' I said, my voice hoarse, low.

'One or two fancied their chance,' he said proudly, 'but I got money, I have. I gave her *Geld* to keep her close beside me. Promised this lot I'd make coats for 'em afore we got to Narva. Keep 'em quiet, like. There's rats a-ship. Fur's more warmin' in the ice and snow than the memory of a whore.'

I felt a wave of confused gratitude towards that rough man. Unlike the soldiers, his heart was not immune to the bewitching charm of beauty.

'You said that she was afraid. Of what? Of whom?'

Schuppe shook his head. 'People are dying in Königsberg, that was all she said.' He looked at me intently. 'What did she mean, sir? Is there a pestilence in the city?'

I ignored the question.' What passed between you?'

Schuppe blew out his cheeks and scratched his nose. 'Siberia, I told her. Forget it, women can't survive out there!'

He was right about that. The deportation agreement had been signed with Paulus Romanov in 1801, and two women had been shipped out with the first consignment. One was a prostitute, the other wretch had killed her husband and her children. I remembered the reports that had appeared in all the newspapers, the scandal that had emerged. The women had been raped repeatedly by the other prisoners, and the cold had killed them before they reached their destination. State Minister von Arnim had issued a Circular correcting the first, prohibiting any magistrate or prison commander from deporting a woman. Arnim insisted that only strong, healthy men should be sent, as the Tsar would not accept malingerers in his labour colonies. Ironically, the inflexibility of the Romanovs had worked more wonders on our penal system than any Enlightened discussion of the nature of crime and punishment would ever do.

'She'd been there,' he added. 'Siberia and back!'

'Deported?' I quizzed.

Schuppe nodded. '"Look at my hair, my skin," she said. "Where d'you think I turned to ice?"'

He was silent for a moment. 'I live by hunting animals, sir. I sells their skins and I chews their meat. Moles in the summer, rats in the winter. God knows how many towns in Prussia I've rid o'vermin! I'll make warm socks to see me through the snow. I'll be back!' he shouted, turning to the soldiers. 'White as ice like her, but I'll come back for you bastards!'

Come back from Nerchinsk? Only a ghost could return. A ghost or a tern, able to fly across the ice and the snow, flying high above the ravaging wolves of the tundra forest, the hungry polar bears, the frozen desert of the Steppe. No one would be coming back from Nerchinsk. A man who was deported there was dead before he set a foot outside Prussia. Again, that newspaper report flashed through my mind:

. . . the temperature of minus 55 degrees, 5250 miles from St Petersburg, 480 miles north of the Great Wall of China, 100 miles west of the Pacific Ocean, remote not only from Western Europe, but from the trade routes between Russia and China. Desolate steppe and bare mountain stretching for vast distances, inhabited only by a wandering horde of Tartar savages.

There was something gleefully punitive in the official gazette from Berlin.

Was this the final act of Anna Rostova? She had told a brazen lie and brought hope to this man. I prayed for her soul. For that falsehood, if for nothing else.

'She left you, Schuppe,' I said, flatly. 'Why was that?'

'I fell asleep after the ratting stopped. I'd had a skinful. Then I woke with a start, and I saw her near the door. Chained to this lot, I couldn't do nowt but yell at him. She glanced back, then they was gone. He dragged her out by the hair . . .'

'A man, you say?'

'In a big black coat, a hat pulled down low. They was gone in a flash.'

'Thank you, Schuppe,' I began to say, nodding to the guard to return him to the bench and his chains.

'You know what I done, don't you, sir?' he interrupted in an urgent whisper, moving his head close to mine.

I nodded in silence, drawing back from his person.

'I killed my brother,' he said, looking deep into my eyes.

'Why?'

He shrugged. 'I needed shelter, soldiers were searching for me. He told me to get lost, threatened me with an axe. I took it off him, an' I gave it back to him by the blade.'

He told this tale with stark simplicity. As if the sequence were inevitable. The brother. The need for sanctuary. The axe. As if there was nothing else to be done.

Could I have done the same? Could I have given a similar uncomplicated account of what had happened between Stefan and myself? This man was fated to die in Siberia, while I was hunting a killer in the company of Immanuel Kant . . .

'I have eaten human flesh,' he said, breaking in upon my thoughts. 'I'll do the same again, given the circumstances.'

'Which circumstances are you talking of?' I asked, curiously.

'War. Famine. A long march. Wait 'til Bonaparte gets here, sir, then see how many souls end up in the cooking-pot. When a man is desperate . . .'

I recalled the scene I had witnessed on my way to Königsberg with Koch, the gang of robbers at the bridge who had butchered the farmer's horse for meat.

'I'll eat my way across the Arctic waste unless you help me . . .'

'Help you, Schuppe?' I asked. 'How, in the name of Heaven, can I help you?'

He stepped so close that one of the soldiers shouted and dug his musket fiercely into the prisoner's spine.

'A man in furs can die of hunger,' he hissed, clacking his teeth together noisily, working his jaws as if he were chewing something tough but tasty. 'Save these poor creatures from my sharp fangs, sir.'

We stared at each other for a moment, then his hand rose up before my face clasping a stub of graphite.

'Extra rations,' he said with a disarming smile.

'Shackle this prisoner,' I ordered the soldiers, taking the pencil, turning towards the meagre light from the fire. 'And let me see your list.'

At my back I heard the clink of chains as Helmut Schuppe was returned to his place. Then I made a note next to the name of the last man who had shown any tenderness to Anna Rostova, a man who been condemned for murdering his brother and eating his liver, the man with 'Murderer' branded on his cheeks in large capital letters: 'Merits extra food'.

I turned to Koch. 'Take the names of the guards, Sergeant. I'll have them punished for negligence in the exercise of their duties. For taking advantage of the woman with false promises of a passage to Siberia.'

'They might end up in chains themselves, sir,' Koch advised. 'With a long, cold march in front of them.'

I turned away and strode towards the exit. I had no sympathy for animals who had slaked their lust on a vulnerable wench, then failed to protect her from the man who had murdered her. Outside, the smell of the estuary at low water was foul and damp.

'What now, Herr Procurator?' Koch asked, his voice subdued.

'Did you get their names?' I replied.

'Yes, sir.'

'Very well. Let's make our way back to town. To the Infirmary,' I said. 'Lublinsky had a motive to kill her. But did he have the opportunity?'

Koch was silent, and I thought that he might be sulking, that he dared to question my decision, though I could not have been more mistaken. He was a professional. Having closed the door on that hellhole, his mind was already moving forward.

'With your permission, sir,' he said, 'I'll not come with you.'

'Not come? What are you plotting, Koch?' I asked.

'I was thinking of my wife, Herr Stiffeniis,' he replied, and there was such abject melancholy in his voice that I was unable to meet his glittering eyes.

'Your wife?' I echoed, astounded. 'You told me that you lived alone.'

'Merete was taken during the last typhoid epidemic,' he continued in a low voice. The loss still caused him evident pain. 'She was an embroidress, sir. I was thinking of the needles that she used. I always knew what to buy on her nameday, or for the Saint Nicolaus feast. Last night, when you discovered the murder weapon, sir, I could not help but think of Merete. If I could find the man who sold those needles, I thought, perhaps he'd recall the people who had bought them in the past. It might provide a lead, don't you agree?'

'If such things are so commonly used by housewives, there may be a multitude of users in Königsberg,' I objected, but Sergeant Koch did not back down.

'Merete mentioned a man in the trade,' he went on with conviction. 'A gentleman who could supply anything that a person might need. If I could trace him, sir, he might be able to tell us something about the type of needle, and the people who buy them. It's not the common sort my wife used.'

The proverbial search in the haystack came to mind, but I had no wish to dampen Koch's enthusiasm.

'You don't need me at the Infirmary, sir,' he continued. 'Perhaps I can locate the man. There aren't many shops in Königsberg selling haberdashery.'

'That's a good idea,' I encouraged, though I had little hope of success.

Thus, it was decided. Koch would accompany me back to town, then our ways would part. As we stood there talking in the salty, windblown air, rivulets of damp formed on the waterproof surface of the cape Professor Kant had given me. I shook them off as we boarded the coach. At the same time, I could not help but notice that the sergeant's pea-jacket was soaking wet.

'You look like a drowned rat,' I said lightly. 'Take this cape. You'll be obliged to walk in town, while I will have the coach.'

'There's no need, really, sir,' he protested weakly.

I slipped the cape from my shoulders and handed it to him.

'Precisely, Koch. My lack of need is greater than yours,' I said, unfolding my woollen cloak once more and wrapping myself up in it.

Having crossed any number of wooden bridges to the centre of town, the carriage stopped; Sergeant Koch climbed down and strode off purposefully into the gathering gloom. Dressed in Kant's glistening waterproof cloak, I seemed to see myself in hot pursuit of the murderer. I had to smile, though it would be many a day before I managed to smile again.

Chapter 25

'Anton Theodor Lublinsky,' Colonel-Surgeon Franzich nodded vigorously. 'Lost his left eye, of course. No help for that, Herr Procurator. Putrefaction had set in. He'd have lost the other one, too. Do take a seat.'

As soon as I introduced myself, he had led me up three steps to his room, one wall of which appeared to have been recently constructed. Unlike any other room that I had observed inside the Fortress of Königsberg, this wall was entirely made of panes of glass.

'Far easier to keep a watch on the inmates,' Colonel Franzich said by way of explanation, waving his hand in the direction of the ward. 'All you have to do is stand up. Like a skipper on the bridge.'

'Ingenious,' I replied with an appreciative smile.

'They, of course, are forbidden to stand. We have "condemned" them to bed!' he joked with a tired smile. 'They cannot see us. All they can see is this wall at my back.'

'Indeed,' I replied.

'The Wailing Wall, I call it. Biblical reference, you know?' he replied with the same fixed, tired smile.

From where I sat, my back to the glass partition, I was obliged to look at the very wall he was talking of. And more than once, I asked myself whether the array of objects so carefully positioned on that Wailing Wall would convince any sick man to place his trust in Colonel-Surgeon Franzich. That wall was guaranteed to frighten all remaining hope out of any man at risk of dying, or losing a limb from the injuries he had suffered.

'Are those figures made of wax?' I asked.

'Most certainly,' he replied. 'Most of the victims are still alive and . . . relatively well, I suppose. Military surgery has come on by leaps and bounds in the past decade. Before these patients were allowed to leave the Infirmary, I had a wax cast made of their injuries. To an expert eye, the possibilities of reconstruction are . . . well, they are evident.'

His smile was meant to be reassuring, but it reminded me, disconcertingly, of Gerta Totz's. The exhibits arrayed on the wall were macabre in the extreme. Wax castings of hands, arms and legs which had been severed and torn by grapeshot, or lost forever to the chop and slash of bayonets and sabres. But worst of all were the faces. They hung in a row at the top like ghostly death masks. The faces of men unlucky enough to suffer the cruel and crushing deformation of cannonballs and the heavy machinery of war.

Surgeon Franzich sat calmly in his chair before these monstrous mementoes of his carving-block like the proud owner of a wax museum selling tickets to his tent of human horrors. The flame from the lighted oil lamp on his desk flickered and fluttered in the gloom, and I was reminded suddenly of a summer evening I had spent in a splendid hunting lodge with my father and his elder brother, Edgard Stiffeniis, in the hills near Spandau over a decade before. As moths and insects threw themselves wildly at the dancing candlelight, dying in an unending sequence of flashes of light and sharp crackles, Uncle Edgard recounted the hunting adventures which had resulted in the collection of stuffed, mounted heads of bears and boars which decorated the walls of his lodge. This was far, far worse. Those faces immortalised on the wailing wall of Surgeon Franzich seemed to live and breathe an agony of tortured nerves and stretched skin. The impression that the effigies made on my mind was not softened by the unmistakable stains of blood which had dried on the Company Surgeon's workmanlike grey apron.

One face in particular attracted my unwilling attention. It was hard to look away, more painful still to look. The man had lost his lower jaw. His upper teeth hung jagged, exposed and broken above the unthinkable gap, his tongue a naked, bulging purple snake with no place to hide, nowhere to rest, slopping forward where his lips had once been. The exposed parts of the poor man's throat and neck had been carefully painted in the colours of life, a brutal kaleidoscope of indigo, red and adipose yellow. As the light from the candle shifted and stirred, the tendons, muscles and membranes appeared to pulse with all the vitality of everlasting pain.

'You signed the death warrant for Rudolph Aleph Kopka, I believe?'

'Kopka?' the colonel replied guardedly, as if he had never heard the man's name before.

'A deserter. Six months ago, he died of a fractured larynx.'

Colonel Franzich drummed his fingers on the edge of the table for some moments. 'I'll need to check the files,' he said.

'You won't find much there,' I replied. 'I have already looked.'

'Well, then?' he shrugged. 'What more can I tell you?'

A great deal, I thought, but I did not say so.

'Let's speak about Lublinsky,' I said instead.

'What a face!' exclaimed the Surgeon with bounding enthusiasm. 'Once that eye of his has dried out, I'll have a cast made. Such wicked devastation! Smallpox, that lip, now the eye. My students at the University . . .'

'Is his life in danger?' I asked.

'Not in the least!' he replied energetically. 'No, no, that man's as strong as a lion. Refused to let me tie him down! Can you imagine? Refused to let me draw the pus from the socket with hiruda worms! "Get on with it," he said. "Just tell me when you've finished." You'd have thought he had some more important business in hand than saving his own life! Can you believe that?'

'May I see him?' I asked. I had a good idea what Lublinsky's more important business might have been.

'Certainly, sir,' Colonel Franzich returned. 'But let me warn you, that man has suffered a terrible injury, yet he seems to shrug it off. So far as I can gather, he doesn't care a damned fig about the loss of his eye. No, no,' he continued as he tapped his forefinger to his head, 'his problems are up here. He may turn on you. Shall we go?'

The Colonel-Surgeon led me down to the ward.

'There he is,' he said, pointing to the far end of the aisle.

There were fifty or sixty single beds lined up on either side of the room, but only one other patient shared the large hospital ward with Lublinsky. This patient had been allocated a bed next to the door, while Anton Lublinsky was placed on the opposite side, and at the farthest end, as if Colonel Franzich had decided that they were two very different species of wild animal and better kept apart.

'Is there any way a man can leave this room?' I asked.

Colonel Franzich looked at me in puzzlement. 'Not before he is fully recovered and fit for duty,' he replied.

'That's not what I meant,' I interrupted. 'Are they allowed free passage in and out of this ward while being treated?'

'This is not a prison, Herr Procurator. Just look at them! Do you believe that either man could have walked out of here without assistance? This man's leg has been amputated below the knee, while the fellow you wish to see has not eaten, or shifted from his chair since they brought him in last night.'

I nodded, though I was not convinced.

'Be careful how you speak to him,' Surgeon Franzich urged. 'I have rarely seen a man in such a dismal state of depression.'

'A few words, no more,' I murmured quickly, walking away towards the far end of the room.

Lublinsky sat facing a large window, though he did not seem to be gazing out at the world. He might have been looking at himself in a mirror. Wrapped up tightly in a large black great-cloak, his shaved head tucked into the high collar of his uniform, there was an air of such abject melancholy and shrunken manhood about him that I hesitated for a moment before addressing him.

'So, we meet again, Lublinsky,' I said.

He did not move. Nor did he turn or shy away, though he must surely have recognised my voice.

'I hardly thought to meet you,' he muttered after some moments. There was something flat and inexpressive in his manner that I took at first to be a doomed acceptance of his fate. 'I hardly thought to meet anyone ever again.'

269

I sat down on the bed and looked at him. A large padded dressing had been draped over the left side of his face. It was held in place with bandages. He shifted on his chair and fixed his good eye on me. He made a better impression than he had the first time we had met, the deformity of his face hidden by the medical dressings.

'I'm glad to find you better, Lublinsky.'

'Better than the last time, you mean?' His attempt at a smile appeared like a horrible distortion on his lips. 'You're right, though. I feel at home here. In a soldiers' hospice they've seen worse faces than mine. They don't baulk away from such revolting things, if you catch my drift.'

'We must talk, Lublinsky.'

He shifted in his seat again, showing only the bandaged side of his face. Clearly, he was not going to let me forget what he had been subjected to. Even so, I did not mean to harm him further. My only wish was to extract the truth and so conclude my investigation.

'I've told you all I know,' he said.

'Not all, Lublinsky,' I replied. 'Not everything. Anna Rostova is dead. But you know that for a fact already.'

He sat up stiffly. 'Do you believe that loss of sight has given me greater powers of vision? I have not learnt *that* trick yet.'

I noted this change of attitude. There was a sarcastic bitterness about him. A desperate vein of dark humour had ousted the timidity which marked him out at our first meeting. And yet, fear of what I could do to him was there. Resentment too. It seemed to charge his being, as if he lacked strength of character to master it. Well, I thought, I have played on his fear of my office once before, and I mean to do so again.

'You've told me but half the truth,' I began. 'I want to hear the rest. How did you manage to escape from this place last night?'

'I don't know what you're talking about,' he protested in that mewling nasal voice, raising the back of his hand to wipe the spittle from his lips.

'You know nothing of the murder of Anna Rostova?'

'Must I answer such a question?'

'I think you must, Lublinsky.'

'You know the answer, then.'

'Yesternight you swore to murder her,' I insisted.

Lublinsky turned full-face, and brought his good eye to bear on mine like a man-of-war coming around broadside and lining up its heavy cannons. There was something majestic in his manner of doing so which surprised me. I realised then that his life had changed. He had altered since our meeting the night before. I had expected a mutation, but I was not prepared for the nature of it. There was, as I have mentioned, majesty and dignity, but they were the majesty and the dignity of malevolence. Lucifer after the Fall. There was no evidence of self-disgust, no sign of repentance, nothing to denote the agony of a tortured Christian conscience. Had I been able to remove the bandages from his face, I doubt I would have found the features I had come to know. There was evil in him, and he made no attempt to suppress it. He appeared capable of any act, any offence, any degradation, and I felt myself defenceless before him.

As he stared at me in silence, his eye seemed to gleam and swell with evil pride. I could not tell what was going through his mind. I only knew that I would not like it. He did not flinch or look down as he had done the first time that Koch had called him into my presence.

'You killed her,' I said quietly. 'What have you to lose by admitting it?'

He held his silence for some moments.

'I was here in the Infirmary, Herr Procurator,' he said with a bitter-sweet smile. 'Anna saw to that.'

'She was seen with a man last night in a tavern out at Pillau,' I pressed on. 'They were coupling, Lublinsky. Rutting like wild animals. Is that her power of attraction over you, too?'

'Over *me*, Herr Procurator? Me? Over *you*, I would have thought!' he rattled off angrily. 'I've seen the way you ogled her. Me? With half a chance, you'd have given her a length! In spite of what she is. For that reason, maybe.'

I swallowed hard before I spoke.

'Do not accuse me of your own sins. I am a happily married man!'

'That's what they all say,' he replied with a dismissive shake of the head. 'Then they hand over the coin and unbutton their pants. A wife is only a wife. Anna was something really special.'

'It does not change the fact that you murdered her last night.'

Lublinsky did not reply immediately.

'Let's say, for just one moment, that you are right, Herr Procurator,' he said at last, and he was taunting me. 'What bloody difference does it make? Whoever killed her, God will forgive the deed. That man did the world a favour.'

'I am not interested in your opinions of Divine Justice,' I snapped. 'Nor am I interested particularly in the murder of Anna Rostova last night. The only thing I want from you is an admission of the truth.'

The pupil of his eye dilated, and I was faced with a dark, imponderable hole. 'What are you talking about, sir?' he said with a flash of exasperation. 'The truth about *what*?'

'I want to know what you really saw and did when you went to examine those murdered corpses in the streets with Kopka.'

Lublinsky swivelled towards the window and studied himself in the glass. A dense fog had swept in from the sea with the turn of the tide. It had suffocated the wind and banished the sleet, transforming the world into a silent milky void.

'I've told you *that* before,' he snarled. 'I saw what I drew.'

'I've seen your sketches, Lublinsky,' I said. 'They are incomplete.'

'What do you want from a soldier? I'm not an artist. I said that to the odd old gentleman, but he didn't seem to mind. He had money to throw away. I just did as he asked.'

'You didn't draw the footprints that the killer left on the ground beside the bodies,' I accused.

'Which footprints?'

'In the case of the first murder, you sketched in what you found around the body, including footprints bearing a knife-cut in the shape of a cross. But you did not trace out those marks in all the other cases.'

'Satan leaves no prints,' Lublinsky said with a bitter laugh. 'His cloven feet don't touch the ground.'

'Do not joke with me,' I flared with anger. Had he really omitted the footprints from his later drawings, or were there none to be seen? 'You believed that Anna Rostova was the culprit. And when the killings continued, you convinced yourself that she had committed them all. She was a witch sacrificing human lives to her demons. You chose to consort with her to cure your face. So, you covered the tracks that she had left behind her. That is why you drew no more prints. You thought that they would lead to her.'

A noise like shifting gravel rattled from Lublinsky's throat. He was laughing. 'That needle must have entered my brain,' he said. 'I don't follow you, sir. How could I have done such diabolical things? Kopka was with me.'

'Kopka is dead, and the dead cannot speak. You killed him, didn't you?' I hissed. 'He must have guessed what you were up to, that you were covering up for a criminal. Rather than denounce you, he tried to desert from the regiment. But you chased him, and you brought him back. *You* were the capturing officer the report talks about, Lublinsky, were you not? Kopka was made to run the gauntlet, while every man in the regiment, yourself included, tried to crack his skull open with a stick.'

'Deserters know the score,' he growled. 'It's no easy thing to leave the Prussian army. That bastard got what was coming to him.'

'How very convenient for you, Lublinsky.'

'You cannot frighten me, Herr Procurator,' he replied boldly. 'I've nothing left to lose. If you wish to believe that Anna Rostova was the murderer and that I was her accomplice, you're free to do so. If you think that I connived at Kopka's death, dream on. But you'll not put those words into my mouth. You won't get me to confess . . .'

I played my final card. God help me, I had no alternative.

'You are proud to be a soldier, are you not?'

'It was my life,' he grunted. 'I'll be cast off now, I suppose.'

'A dishonourable discharge,' I added, 'a barebacked whipping out of the regiment. Then civil charges to face. Complicity to murder, obstruction of Justice, theft from a corpse. You are going to pay in full for Anna Rostova's crimes, as well as for your own. You won't find much in the way of sympathy in any prison. An officer who's betrayed his trust? The lowest of the low. Sentence? Life. With forced labour and reduced rations. With a bit of luck, you may survive a year or two. I want you to suffer, Lublinsky. And to make quite sure of it, I will condemn you to serve out your time in a . . . military prison!'

'You can't do that!' he roared, the enormity of the threat opening up before him. He would be hated and brutalised by his guards, reviled and tormented by his fellow prisoners. Each moment of every day he would be hounded and harried by a heartless pack of wild dogs.

'Can I not, Lublinsky? You know the legal code by heart, I suppose? I can condemn any man to the sentence I think most fit. Article 137 of the Penal Code. You go where I decide to send you.'

There is no such article, but Lublinsky was not to know. I pronounced this threat like a pagan god who knows no pity for the creatures under his jurisdiction. And like a deity devoid of all Christian compassion, I obtained what I insisted on having. He blubbered for a moment, but then he found his voice. His mutilated tongue began to squawk in fractured measures.

'The first time, that morning, I went to see the corpse she'd found. I guessed she was hiding something. Some *secret* . . .' His voice was strained, low, and I had to struggle to understand. 'Then, Kopka went for gin. For her, for Anna. She put her spell on me while he was gone. "I'll cure your face," she said.'

'There is nothing new or interesting in this, Lublinsky,' I cut in. 'I want to hear the rest. I want to know about those footprints.'

'Kopka saw them . . .'

'And you assumed that the woman had left them?'

Lublinsky shook his head. 'Not the first time, sir.'

'You drew them on that occasion, did you not?'

'I drew what I could recall. It was months afterwards. I was no good at it, but Professor Kant was happy. There were footprints all around that body. On the ground. In the snow,' Lublinsky went on.

'There was a cross on the sole. When I told Anna, she said that cross was the sign of the Devil mocking the crucifixion. It was a sacrilege, she said. So when I saw that cross again, I did not draw it. Nor did I report everything that I found there . . .'

He paused, and peered into my face, looking for approval. He was offering me something, working to save his miserable hide, just as he had done when he surrendered Anna Rostova into my hands the day before.

'What did you find?' I asked, trying to sound detached.

'A chain,' he said. 'In the hand of Jan Konnen. A watch-chain with a broken link.'

'What did you do with it?'

'When Kopka wasn't looking, I slipped it in my pocket. It was silver.'

'That's theft,' I sneered.

He hesitated for a moment. 'I gave it to Anna. A gift from Satan, she said, and I'd be rewarded 'cause I'd done the right thing. She told me then what she had done. She'd pulled the Devil's claw from the dead man's neck before we arrived. Afterwards, she made me bring her any trifle that I found at the murder scenes. Those things were charged with the power of life and death . . .'

'If she was the murderer, why didn't she take them herself?' I objected.

'She wanted to tie me to her, sir,' Lublinsky mumbled. 'To make me her accomplice. She promised she'd heal me with the Devil's claw. I had to swear an oath. Tell anyone this secret, she said, and the spell won't work.'

'The second time, you found the same footprints by the body?'

Lublinsky nodded. 'There was that cross-cut again. It was hers, I'd swear, though I didn't see her that time. Her power was growing with each murder, she said. I thought she'd put a spell on Professor Kant 'cause he insisted that I should be sent out. Whenever there was another murder, I had to go and draw it. An' while I was there, I collected the Devil's gifts for Anna.'

I frowned. 'What are you talking about?'

'They all had something hidden in their hands, sir. All of them.

Those corpses . . . I took the objects and I gave them to Anna Rostova like an obedient dog.'

My heart beat fast. A new light shone on what I knew.

'What did you find?'

'A key in the fist of the dead lady.'

Professor Kant had surely been referring to something of the sort
when he spoke of the murderer having used some stratagem to induce
the victims to fall down on their knees. The list that Lublinsky gave
me contained nothing of any import or value. The victims had died
clasping banal objects of everyday use, sinister and mysterious by
their association only with murder and witchcraft. The chain of Konnen, the key in Frau Brunner's hand, a brass button stamped with an
anchor in the hand of the third, a groat from the fingers of Lawyer
Tifferch.

'I cleaned the bones of the dead for her. I sorted through the
muck for Anna Rostova,' Lublinsky went on. 'Like a carrion crow.'

'Did you take the weapon for her, too?'

'No, sir. She must have spirited it away. I never saw her there
again. Not once after the first time.'

He stared at me in disbelief, as if awaking from a dream.

'She killed them, but I didn't give a damn. Not me. If people
dying meant her power was growing, I was glad of it. God help me!
I wanted her to kill again.'

He let out a strange cry, a strangled whimper, and I realised he
was laughing.

'I carried a mirror in my pocket,' he said, his shoulders heaving, 'to see my face. Waiting for it to change after each murder.
She promised much, but nothing changed. Still the same. Ugly
brute . . .'

He was mad, lost in a world of vain hopes of his own creating.

'It's funny, is it not?' he said with sudden vehemence, his head
jerking round at me. 'That woman terrified the city and commanded the King. No one would have given her a second glance if
Nature hadn't marked her out. We're two of a kind, we are. Me,
with a face disfigured by smallpox. That wild silver hair she had.
Those blazing eyes. I wanted her. Even as she plunged that dart in

my eye . . .' He fixed me with that mocking eye of his. 'Did you think to find the answer to your mystery in two such monsters, Herr Stiffeniis?'

There was a claim to omnipotence in his tone, I suddenly realised. He was proud of what he had done. He seemed to think that he and Anna Rostova had held Königsberg in their hands. And he was right. They had toyed with the authorities, with the police, the King. Professor Kant had been taken in by them. And so had I. Anger burst from me like hot water gushing from a Greenland geyser. All pity gone, I felt the urge to harm him, to repay him for his arrogance.

'You murdered Anna Rostova last night. You convinced yourself that she was the killer.' I struggled to control my voice, caught my breath, checked my anger before I continued. 'You were wrong, Lublinsky. *Wrong!* Now, how did you leave this room?'

He did not trouble himself to answer. Instead, like some hideous parody of Narcissus, he turned his head towards the winter scene outside the window and studied himself once more in the glass.

'By means of that window? Is that how you escaped? You're practically alone,' I nodded over my shoulder at the amputee. 'That fellow down there has pain enough. They give him something to help him sleep, I bet. But vengeance is the most powerful painkiller, and your legs are not hampered, soldier.'

'She'll be happy with the Devil she worshipped,' Lublinsky said with bitter intensity.

'She was *not* the killer,' I insisted coldly. 'Do you hear me? She did not *kill* those people.'

'I know what I know,' he growled angrily.

I shook my head. 'Those footprints that you saw beside the corpses were not left by Anna Rostova. She played with you, tricked you time and time again. She made you believe what she wanted. She took your money. You were her dupe . . .'

'Hang me, sir,' he moaned suddenly. 'Kill me. I was a good soldier before black wolves began to howl in my soul. Snap my neck in two. 'Twill all be over in a second.'

I looked at him in disgust. His face was deformed by anguish and

277

fear, as well as ruined by uncaring Nature. Even so, I realised, the surgeon had been right. Lublinsky's soul was blacker still. I rose, grabbed for my hat, and strode from the room without a word or a backward glance.

I saw Anton Lublinsky no more. I had lied to him on that count. In the report I wrote that evening, unable once again to prove what I knew, I glossed over his part in the death of Anna Rostova, concluding that the midwife had been killed by a person, or by persons, unknown. I heard no immediate news of Lublinsky's fate, though when news did eventually come, it was not good. Demoted to assist in the regimental kitchen after losing his eye, he was subsequently condemned to a military prison for murdering a soldier who had mocked him once too often. There, Lublinsky swallowed broken glass and slowly haemorrhaged to death.

Outside the Infirmary, I stopped to try and collect my thoughts. I felt depressed, sick at heart, thoroughly dispirited. Perhaps desperate was the most apposite word to describe my state of mind. Where should I turn? What should I do now? If only I could find the courage to resign this thankless task and return to the monotony of my life in Lotingen with my wife and children, I would be taking a step in the right direction. I ought to write to the King, explain my incapacity, and ask to be released immediately from my burdensome duties.

But then, as always in times of doubt, my thoughts turned to Immanuel Kant. How would I justify the renunciation in his eyes? Would he dismiss me as a faint-hearted coward incapable of putting his suggestions to good use? If not for me, I could almost hear him say, Morik, the Totzes and Anna Rostova might still be alive, and Lublinsky might not have lost his eye and his soul.

'Herr Stiffeniis?' a voice sliced through my thoughts. A gendarme had appeared at my side. 'I've been looking all over the place for you, sir,' he said, rummaging in his shoulder-bag. 'I've got a dispatch here from Herr Sergeant Koch. And there's someone . . .'

'From Koch?' I interrupted.

I tore the letter open, and began to read.

Herr Stiffeniis,

I have found the man! His name is Arnold Lutbatz and he supplies various shops in Königsberg with wool, cotton, knitting implements, etc., for domestic use. Herr Lutbatz recognised the needle instantly from my description. The Devil's claw is used for carding tapestry wool!

I told him that I needed to know the names of persons here in town who use such instruments, and he informed me that he keeps a list of clients. He supplies private persons, as well as shops. I asked to see the list on your behalf and authority.

I am directed this instant to his lodging, and will inform you immediately of the outcome, sir, not wishing to delay the search a moment longer.

Obsequiously,

Amadeus Koch.

I had the sensation of joy one feels after a long, hard winter, opening a window one morning and finding the first frail butterfly of Spring quivering on the glass. All hope lost a minute before, my strength and determination returned with every word that I read. Each sentence sounded to my ears like a military fanfare calling me to battle once again.

'Herr Procurator?'

I had forgotten the presence of the soldier.

'An old gentleman is waiting for you downstairs, sir. He says his name's Professor Immanuel Kant.'

Chapter 26

If Immanuel Kant had come to the Fortress, I reasoned, something serious had happened, an event of such urgency that it had obliged him to break with his usual routine. Something so simple for other men, any unforeseen change of plan constituted a sort of cataclysm for Professor Kant. Add to this the thick fog that day, a phenomenon for which he declared an unmitigated hatred, and the enormity of Kant's decision can be imagined. I ran down the stairs without delay, and out into the courtyard, where a single solid figure was barely discernible in the swirling fog. It was not the person I had been expecting.

'I'm so sorry, sir!' Johannes Odum exclaimed at the sound of my footstep. 'I *had* to bring him. I was left no choice.'

'Is he well?' I asked, recalling his master's agitated state of mind earlier that morning, hoping that his indisposition had not deteriorated further.

The valet looked perplexed. 'He's not been right since you left the house,' he said, his voice tense with concern. 'Then, he insisted on speaking to you again, sir. At once, he said. He . . . he needs that cloak he gave you.'

If I had been puzzled by the Professor's generosity that morning, I was even more surprised by this sudden *volte face*. If that heavy garment were so essential to his physical well-being, why had he left the warmth of his fire for the freezing cold and the rheumatic damp without waiting for me to bring it back?

'Whatever for?' I asked.

There seemed to be nothing logical or even rational in such behaviour.

'I've no idea, sir,' Johannes replied. 'He has no clear idea what he wants himself. You saw the way he was this morning. So keen to give you that garment, insistent almost . . . Well, he wants it back! He was so overwrought that I hitched the horse to the landau, and drove him here to calm him down. I didn't know what else to do.'

'Where is he now?' I interrupted.

'In the guard-room. But let me tell you what happened this morning . . .'

I felt the hand of fright clasp at my heart.

'After you left the house with Sergeant Koch,' Johannes continued, 'he sat himself down in the front parlour for the best part of an hour and stared fretfully out of the window.'

'Was he expecting visitors?'

'Oh, no, sir,' Johannes said emphatically. 'No one comes to the house these days. You are the first visitor he's had in a month or more. I took him his morning coffee at eleven o'clock, as usual, but he didn't touch it. He jumped up suddenly, saying that he urgently needed a book from Herr Flaccovius, his editor, in town. It was for his treatise, he said. He could not go on without it.'

'That mysterious treatise again,' I said, hoping that Johannes might have discovered something in the mean time.

He did not rise to the bait. 'Professor Kant ordered me to run all the way to the bookshop,' he reported instead. 'He was a bundle of nerves until I had put on my overcoat and hat, and was preparing to leave the house.'

'You left him alone?' I burst out angrily. 'Unprotected again? Is that what you are trying to tell me?'

'What else could I do, sir?' Johannes whined. 'He was safe in his own home, it was daytime, and you had sent those soldiers to watch the house. There was no danger at all. How could I refuse to go?'

'The fog is so thick, I doubt that the gendarmes can see their own noses,' I seethed, truly vexed and frustrated by the news.

'I took my own precautions, Herr Procurator,' Johannes replied in an attempt to soothe me. 'I stopped at Frau Mendelssohn's and asked her to go across and sit with him while I was out. Frau Mendelssohn lives . . .'

'I know who the woman is,' I broke in, recalling my chance meeting with the inquisitive old lady as I left the house that very morning.

'She's a devoted admirer of Professor Kant's,' Johannes continued. 'I told her that I was obliged to run to town on an errand, and warned her not to let my master out of her sight. I made no mention of the real motive for doing so, saying that he wasn't feeling as well as he should. Then, I rushed off to the bookshop. But when I got there, Herr Flaccovius had no idea what I was talking about. He checked his ledger and found that my master had, indeed, ordered that particular book. But Herr Flaccovius himself had delivered it into Professor Kant's hands four months ago. I returned home rapidly, thinking I had made a mistake with the title of the volume. I expected Professor Kant to be angry, but when I told him of the mix-up, he didn't seem put out in the least.'

'We have witnessed many unpredictable and disconcerting changes of mood in him. He has a great deal on his mind with this investigation,' I said to mask my own perplexity, which was great enough. Could Herr Professor Kant be so wholly confused?

'The oddest thing comes last,' Johannes went on quickly, as if I had spoken my puzzlement aloud. 'When I saw her to the door, Frau Mendelssohn told me that my master had been in the most excellent high spirits. Not sick at all, she said. He had entertained her to a disquisition on the cause of her migraine headaches, which he attributes to an excess of magnetism in the damp air of the town. He had been so concerned about her health, he went to get some anatomical prints from his study to show her the nerves which react to humidity. Frau Mendelssohn offered to look for the illustrations, but he insisted on searching them out for himself.'

'So, he *was* left alone,' I concluded, angry with myself, above all. No matter how carefully I tried to guarantee his safety, Professor Kant still managed to slip outside my net.

'Could she prevent him from retiring to his private study?' Johannes protested with a show of helplessness. 'But then . . . then . . .'

'Then, *what*?' I prodded.

The valet ran his hand across his brow, as if to wipe away the troubled frown that etched itself there. 'She says that she heard voices.'

'Perhaps he was murmuring as he sorted through the prints? Old people often talk to themselves without being aware of it.'

My reassuring words did not sound convincing, not even to myself.

'It wasn't that, sir,' Johannes added with a sigh. 'She actually *saw* the visitor leaving by the garden path. The path where you and I examined those footprints in the snow last night, sir.'

I felt cold sweat break out on my brow.

Had the murderer somehow managed to set foot in the house despite the presence of the soldiers on guard? But no, Frau Mendelssohn reported that she had heard them speaking together. Would the killer have entered the house merely to speak with Kant? And even more to the point, what would Immanuel Kant have had to say to *him*?

'Was your master upset?'

'Not at all, sir,' Johannes replied promptly. 'As Frau Mendelssohn said herself, what possible harm could there be in Martin Lampe?'

'Martin Lampe?' I asked, recalling my brief conversation with Frau Mendelssohn that morning. 'What in heaven's name was he doing there?'

'I've no idea, sir. I could hardly ask Herr Professor.'

'Do you know Martin Lampe?' I asked.

'No, sir. I've never met him. Herr Jachmann forbade him ever to return to the house.'

'Where does he live, Johannes?'

Johannes shrugged his shoulders. 'Herr Jachmann might know, though I'd rather you didn't ask him, sir. Professor Kant certainly knows, but I have no idea myself.'

The cold was even sharper than before as night came on. The air nipped at my cold hands and at the surface of my face like an angry puppy, and I regretted my act of generosity to Sergeant Koch.

'Take me to your master,' I said. 'I have a confession to make, regarding the cloak that he so desperately wants.'

Professor Kant was seated comfortably before a huge, black,

cast-iron monster of a stove in the guard-room, staring fixedly at the little blue flames that darted playfully from its open maw, a brown felt hat resting on his bony knees. In the far corner, off-duty soldiers played pinochle and smoked their long clay pipes, blissfully ignorant of the hallowed company they were keeping. Seeing him there, so old and physically frail, I felt an overwhelming urge to protect him. Such bleak surroundings seemed so unnatural for a man of his immense talents.

'Procurator Stiffeniis has come, sir,' Johannes announced.

Professor Kant jumped to his feet, spilling his hat onto the floor. He was clearly surprised to see me. 'You are well, then?' he asked, as if I had just that minute returned from a long and dangerous journey. 'But where is my cloak?' he added with that sudden shift of focus that had become so characteristic of late, and so disconcerting.

I hesitated by the door, unable to reply. Such attention to inconsequential detail robbed me of the capability to form a thought. Was Kant offended by my appearing in his presence without the gift? Or had a more general concern for the state of my health provoked the first of his two questions?

'I loaned your cloak to Sergeant Koch, sir,' I said, not quite certain if it were the correct thing to say. It was, anyhow, the truth, and the confession was made. 'The poor man was soaked to the skin,' I added by way of explanation.

Kant looked at me in silence as if my words had enchanted him. He seemed put out by the news. I had done something unforgivable, it appeared. But what wrong had I done? Such an uncompromising reaction to a simple act of kindness amazed me. It was inexplicable in the light of his own selfless generosity to me. Desperately I searched for something to say that would placate his anger, but before I could speak, he turned and smiled at me. The brainstorm had passed. He was himself once more.

'Isn't it odd, Stiffeniis?' he said calmly.

'Sir?' I asked with circumspection.

'How circumstances alter cases. Unleash Chaos on the world and it has a boundless energy all its own.' His eyes looked straight ahead. He seemed to be staring at some solid figure, which he alone could see.

'What do you mean, sir?' I murmured, now doubly afraid of disturbing him in this perplexing state of distraction, wherever it might be leading him.

'I mean to say that the further I progress in this experiment, the more I understand that Reason operates on the surface alone. What happens *beneath* the surface shapes events. The Imponderable overrules us all. For the first time in my life, I can feel the invincible strength of blind Destiny.'

He turned to look at me. 'Don't you feel it, Hanno?'

He was deathly pale, and seemed more fragile than ever, his voice trailing away to a hollow whisper.

'Go home, Professor Kant,' I urged, my heart sinking within me. In that instant, I lost all hope of making my way forward. Immanuel Kant, my anchor, my compass in the storm, had gone adrift. He had left me alone on the angry, empty sea.

'I'll give you back your cloak,' I said soothingly, as if it were the answer to all his problems. 'The instant Koch returns . . . .'

'I do not want it,' he replied gruffly, turning to his valet. 'Leave us alone, Johannes. Be gone!'

Johannes darted a worried glance at me.

'Wait next door,' I said with a nod. 'I'll call you when it is time to leave.'

As the door closed, Immanuel Kant placed his hand lightly on my arm. Leaning forward, he peered straight into my eyes. 'That woman is *innocent*, Stiffeniis,' he whispered.

I was amazed. 'How did you reach this conclusion, sir?' I asked. These swings of the pendulum between confusion and lucidity were disconcerting. I could do no more than follow his lead.

'Am I not correct?'

I nodded slowly. 'You are, indeed, sir. But how did you discover it?'

Kant ignored my question. 'Never mind that now. What leads you to revise *your* opinion of the woman, Stiffeniis? You seemed so convinced of her guilt this morning when you spoke of witchcraft.'

'She is dead,' I replied. 'Murdered before I had the chance to question her.'

Kant hunched forward in his seat. 'The Devil's claw?'

'Strangled.'

'Go on,' he said.

'Those drawings that you instructed Lublinsky to make have been invaluable, sir,' I began. 'There were footprints left at the scene of the first murder, but Anna Rostova did not leave them. I have examined her shoes. The drawings rule her out. Your method of enquiry deserves to be publicised, sir,' I continued with enthusiasm. 'As soon as this affair is successfully concluded, I plan to write a memorandum which will, I hope, explain your methods to a wider public . . .'

'Your opinion is most gratifying,' Kant cut in with cold sarcasm. 'Perhaps I will find some new admirers now that the old ones have deserted me. Is that what you intend?'

I thought I knew what troubled his mind. 'Without your ground-breaking work in metaphysical speculation, sir,' I said with justified vehemence, 'there would be *no* new generation of philosophers.'

But he would not be halted. His temper exploded, his eyes flashed, his hands waved wildly about him. 'Nutcracker Kant, the scoundrels call me, claiming that I have imprisoned the mind and the soul in a world of rigid schemes and immutable laws. My last days at the University were unbearable. So humiliating. I have never been treated in such a way before. The *agony* I have suffered!'

Kant's eyes gleamed with passion. His voice was hoarse with malice. There was no suggestion of humour in the rancorous laughter which now escaped from his lips. 'They are such fools! Romantic dreamers . . . they cannot *imagine* what I alone have been able to conceive and carry out. They will never know the beauty of . . . of . . .'

He did not finish the sentence. His eyes slid away from mine and came to rest on an imprecise point on the barrack-room wall. He was silent for quite some time, and I knelt beside his chair, afraid to speak, uncertain how to quell the high tide of bitter resentment in his breast. Suddenly, his right hand falling to rest on my sleeve, he began to speak again, his voice all but inaudible above the hissing flames of the stove.

'Can't you see the answer? Can you not, Hanno? I expected you to strike to the heart of the mystery. You're all I have left now that everyone else has deserted me. I cannot finish my work without your help . . .'

Clearly, I had let him down once again. But how exactly had I deluded him? What did he expect me to see that I still failed to see? Was it no more than an old man's dream of unattainable greatness? There is no quiet journey to the grave, I thought. What need had he of the good opinion of the new breed of philosophers? His genius was beyond the judgement of his peers.

'What made you decide that Anna Rostova was not the killer?' I asked, hoping to divert him from his morbid thoughts.

Kant seemed to shake himself from his torpor.

'A simple intuition, nothing more,' he said quietly. 'Would the murderer have chosen a weapon so decidedly feminine if she truly were a woman? This was a double bluff. You overlooked one important detail.' He raised his forefinger, bowed his head, and tapped the nape of his neck. 'A precise point of attack was chosen. This is the work of someone with a history of service in the Prussian army. A soldier, Stiffeniis. Such a mortal blow is used, so far as I can ascertain, only in two specific cases: for the immediate disabling of an enemy from behind, a sentry or guard who might give the alarm, or to dispatch a wounded comrade who is bound to suffer agony before dying on the battlefield.'

'A soldier, sir?' I was astonished by his perspicacity, and thought again of Lublinsky. Had I failed to see what was obvious to Kant? I let out a sigh, then all of my self-doubt came rushing out. 'Perhaps I am not the man for this task, Herr Professor. I have stumbled from one blind alley to the next. To be honest, sir, I am tempted to admit defeat and return to Lotingen.'

He stared at me as if trying to penetrate to the deepest recesses of my soul.

'You wish to resign?'

'I am not up to the challenge, sir,' I said, my voice breaking as I made the admission. 'I am lost in a maze. Every turn leads to another dead end. Something, or someone, confounds my every step. My blundering has produced more victims than the killer has claimed. I . . .'

I halted, unable to continue.

Kant's grip tightened on my sleeve. 'You ask yourself where you have failed. Is that it? You wonder what is the obvious fact that you have overlooked.'

'I do, sir. You have provided all the instruments necessary to comprehend what is happening here in Königsberg. Yet I have failed miserably. Can you still believe that I am capable of solving these murders?'

Kant did not reply immediately. He laid his hand on mine. His dry flesh settled gently on my own like dust. It was meant to be a comforting gesture, and I could not fail to respond to it. Then, he leaned closer, whispering into my ear.

'When you came to me this morning,' he said, 'with the murder weapon and a new theory about a witch, I admit it, I doubted whether I had done the right thing in naming you to run this investigation. I thought that it might be better to . . . free you from the tiresome burden I had placed upon you.'

'You did, sir?' I asked, the breath escaping from my body like the last wheeze of a punctured bellows. This judgement was the final blow to what was left of my pride and my faith in myself.

He sighed aloud. 'But I have changed my mind. That's why I came,' he said. 'My time on earth is short. In spite of your mistakes, you must continue what you have begun.'

'But I have failed you, sir! Ever since . . .'

He did not let me finish.

'You know something that the likes of Rhunken could never imagine,' he said with relish. 'I prepared the evidence in my laboratory for a rational man who would understand the logic of cause and effect. A leads to B, B to C, and nowhere else, of course. But this is only one side of the coin. There is another vital aspect to consider in these murders. The most important of all.'

'What is it, sir?' I asked, clasping my hands in a gesture of impotence. 'What can there be that you have not already indicated to me?'

'*The bent wood of the human soul*, Hanno. Logic has no place in human affairs. Have you forgotten what you came to tell me the first day that we met?' He did not wait for me to respond. 'I have never forgotten your words for one instant. I referred back to that first colloquy of ours when we were standing together over the body of that boy on the banks of the River Pregel the other day. Sergeant Koch – that perceptive man – expressed his surprise when I proposed the idea. He must have thought me quite a monster. But you ignored the suggestion, and now you persist in your obstinacy. You have known the answer for longer than you care to admit. "There is one human experience equal to the unbridled power of Nature," you said. "The most diabolical of them all. Cold-blooded murder. Murder without a motive." You remember saying that, don't you?'

His eyes searched mine. Then, he patted my arm again.

'You should take account of it, strange and horrible as it may sound. You are closer to the truth than you think,' he encouraged with a blinding smile. 'And this morning you told me about the mud stains on the victims' clothes.'

I frowned uncomfortably, while Kant sat back, his eyes narrowed. 'The killer induces his victims to kneel before he strikes them. We agreed on that, did we not?'

'And I assumed that a woman might be responsible.'

'But the killer was *not* a woman,' he said with a spurt of energy. 'This stratagem tells us much about the kind of person that the killer is.'

'You have formed an idea, Professor?' I asked eagerly, but Kant held up a finger to silence me, then laid it on his forehead as if to indicate the notion that was taking shape in his head.

'This person's desire to kill is greater than his ability to carry out the deed. He chose that weapon for its precision and the minimal effort its use required. Do you recall what I said when I showed you the severed heads and the incision at the base of the victim's skull?'

'"It went in like a hot knife cutting lard,"' I quoted.

'Precisely! But how did the killer induce the victims to stay still?'

'Lublinsky,' I murmured to myself.

Kant stared at me as if he thought I were mad. 'What about him?'

'I spoke with him an hour ago, sir. He told me something which would seem to support your argument. He said that each of the victims was holding an object clasped in their hand when they died. He did not mention the fact in his reports to his superiors. Nor to you, I imagine.'

'You see?' Kant exclaimed vigorously, his eyes shining brightly with excitement. 'Such purposeful cunning! Lublinsky is "bent wood" of the first order. But let us put the pieces of this mosaic together. First, the victims do not shy away from the person who approaches them. Second, they kneel down voluntarily before him. Third, they hold an object in their hands. Then they die. You prefer the path of Logic, Hanno,' he said with an ironic smile. 'Tell me, what do you deduce from these elements?'

Before I could reply, he continued in the same didactic tone: 'The killer asked for help. He appealed to human kindness, inviting the chosen one to pick up some small object that he had dropped on purpose as a bait. Of course, they all complied. That is human nature. And as they knelt, each one exposed the nape of his neck to the fatal dart. There, I've told you what I came to say. Now, I'll leave you to your task.'

In attempting to stand up, he succeeded only in scraping the bench on the stone floor as I jumped up to assist him.

'You must promise me one thing, sir,' I said.

'I never make promises,' he replied with a bewitching smile, 'until I know precisely what they involve.'

'Very well,' I laughed, my care and confusion set aside by his show of fresh confidence in me. 'In the future, if you have anything to tell me, send for me, and I will come to you.'

I did not finish the sentence. In that instant, the door flew open and a cold draught swept through the room as a soldier came bursting in. Johannes trailed behind, a worried look written on his pale round face.

'I hope you have good reason to enter in this rude manner?' I snapped.

The guardsman stepped forward and removed his black leather kepi.

'News, sir,' he said with a brisk salute, and my thoughts turned to Koch immediately. Had he sent another message?

'Body found in Sturtenstrasse fifteen minutes ago,' the soldier announced. He glanced hesitantly at Professor Kant, then back to me. 'I left the rest of the squad behind, and ran down here. Herr Stadtschen told me to run across an' tell you direct, Herr Procurator.'

'You were patrolling the area?'

'Marketplace to the town hall, sir. Up an' down. Every thirty minutes, sir, reg'lar as clockwork. Cathedral bell struck three. Daylight fading . . .'

Immanuel Kant's voice fractured the soldier's report.

'Behold, Darkness will cover the Earth!' he intoned with solemnity.

I turned to look at him in the half-light, and a smile seemed to flash across his face as he completed the citation like a clever child displaying his knowledge of the Holy Scriptures: 'Isaiah, Chapter 60, Verses 2 and 3'.

Chapter 27

Before my arrival in the city, the gendarmes had been instructed to report every instance of violent death to Procurator Rhunken. Having stepped into Herr Rhunken's shoes, so to speak, I was now directly responsible for the action to be taken in any such case. The fact that there was a cold-blooded murderer abroad in Königsberg did not simultaneously put an end to domestic squabbling or other crimes which might end in loss of life. I did not automatically attribute every new death to the chain of killings that I was investigating, therefore. Indeed, from what the messenger had told me, there were many reasons to induce me to think otherwise.

The timing of the murder was an important factor in my chain of reasoning. With the single exception of Paula-Anne Brunner, whose time of death had never been precisely ascertained, all the other victims had been killed at night, and I had no reason to expect such a dramatic change of modus operandi in my quarry. This latest corpse had been discovered as the clock was striking three, which suggested that the person had died during the hours of daylight. Next, there was the question of where the body had been found. Even I, who knew so little of the urban geography of Königsberg, realised that Sturtenstrasse was a busy street leading down to the fish market. The other murders had been committed in out-of-the-way places – again, with the exception of Paula-Anne Brunner, who had been killed in the deserted Public Gardens. Would the murderer I was chasing have taken the unwarranted risk of being seen and identified in Sturtenstrasse?

'Have you any idea who the victim is?' I asked, turning to the soldier. 'Or what may have caused the death?'

He shook his head. 'It's a man, sir, but we didn't go near the body. Our orders are to touch nothing if we chance upon a corpse.'

I turned away, satisfied.

'You pass near Sturtenstrasse on your way home, do you not, Johannes?'

'Indeed, sir,' he replied.

'With your permission,' I said to Professor Kant, 'I'll ride along with you in the coach. Johannes may set me down near my destination.'

Kant did not reply, though he did accept my supporting arm as we left the room. But outside in the courtyard, something very odd happened. As I was helping him into the coach, he grasped my sleeve and pulled me so close that the point of his hat struck me square in the centre of my forehead.

'Don't you understand?' he hissed in a sibilant whisper. 'I . . . I am losing control.'

'Control, sir?' I asked, disconcerted by his words. 'What do you mean?'

But he had lapsed into a graveyard silence. Johannes jumped aboard with a heavy woollen travelling-rug to cover his master's knees, while Kant seemed lost in deepest distraction, staring at me like a man who had seen a ghost. The fact that I had failed to understand yet again what, according to him, I ought to have understood seemed to have pitched him into a pit of depression.

'Something has frightened him, sir,' Johannes whispered.

'Let's take him home quickly, Johannes,' I said, as the valet prepared to leave the coach and take charge of the horse. 'I will walk back to Sturtenstrasse.'

I sat on the bench across from Professor Kant as the vehicle pulled away, uncertain whether to speak in an attempt to comfort him, or to remain silent. I might have been alone in the embalming room with the body of a dead Egyptian who was about to be mummified. His state was catatonic. He did not speak, or make a sound, as we drove the rest of the way to his house. Johannes jumped down at the gate, hitched the horse, and together we helped Kant to the ground, supporting him up the garden path as far as the front door.

'He has taken a fever,' Johannes whispered over his master's drooping head. Kant seemed to have lost the use of his legs, which trailed behind him, the toes of his boots dragging pigeon-toed on the paving-stones.

'Let's get him to bed,' I said.

Kant was ill. His face was pale, his breathing troubled; he seemed bereft of strength, his life force quite dissolved away.

We helped him across the hall, taking his arms on our shoulders, then we literally carried him up the stairs to his chamber. Johannes was a true tower of strength, somehow managing to do far more than I, and all the while carrying a lantern. In better circumstances, the fact that I was privileged to enter the *sancta sanctorum* of Professor Kant, by which I mean his private study and bedchamber, would have been a cause for elation. None of his friends or biographers had ever been allowed in there. Despite the fact that all my attention and concern were so concentrated on his well-being, I could not help but cast a quick glance around. The room was far smaller than I could have imagined. 'Monastic' was the word I would have chosen to describe it. A narrow cot stood hard up against one wall, a little chest of drawers by another, a tiny writing desk and a chair pressed close to the third wall. The fourth wall was taken up by a narrow slit of a window looking onto the rear garden of the house. Everything appeared to be sober, neat, functional, and I was moved by the thought that Immanuel Kant had written out sections of his monumental works at that very desk, including his latest, unseen treatise.

At the same time, my awe was stifled by the peculiar odour in that room. It simply could not be ignored. The narrow window I had noted to my left, looking onto the garden, had apparently never been opened. The air in the room was stale and mouldy, I would have said, as if the ceiling, floor and furniture were infected with woodworm, or dry rot. The atmosphere was impregnated with the smell of age and overused bedclothes which had never been adequately or frequently aired. I could not ignore the dry acridity of it. Without a doubt, Johannes took good care of his master, but I silently made a wish that he would attend more carefully to the laundry and house cleaning. What made it even more odd was the fact that all the other rooms in the house were immaculately clean and dusted. I jotted down a mental note to remind him of my critical observations before I left the house. But first, we had to get Kant into bed. As the light of the lantern fell on the pillowcase, a pale grey cloud seemed to shift and dissolve.

'What's that on the bed?' I whispered, breathing heavily after the effort of struggling up the narrow staircase with the inert body.

'Fleas, sir,' Johannes replied calmly.

My anger flared. 'The mattress needs disinfesting!'

'Oh, he won't have that, sir,' the servant responded blandly. 'Professor Kant has a method of his own to keep them off. It doesn't work, but he won't be moved.'

We had had similar problems at home two summers before. The fleas had invaded all the bedrooms and made our lives a misery until Lotte came up with a solution. She left a sheepskin out on the landing for two days and nights, then she rolled it up and burnt it out in the garden, far from the house. She and the children watched with glee as the poor fleas leapt up and down in the flames, crackling and popping, unable to escape their immolation.

'It's the only thing we've ever argued about,' Johannes continued. 'He says that lack of air and light will kill them off, and ordered me to stop up the window. Martin Lampe was a firm believer in the notion. That man's a constant presence here. Sometimes it seems as if he never left the house! Professor Kant has called me by his name on more occasions than I can count.'

Abruptly, he turned his attention to his master, preparing him for bed with a practised mixture of coaxing and firmness. 'Come, come, Herr Professor!' he called.

Sitting stiffly to attention on the edge of the bed while Johannes undressed him and put him into his nightgown, Professor Kant might have been a helpless infant waiting for his nurse to step up, turn the sheets, and hurry him to the Land of Nod. But unlike any child that I have ever known, he was struck dumb. He did not acknowledge my own presence by so much as a look. Johannes pulled back the covers and puffed up the pillows, ready to receive him.

Kant seemed lost in a deep trance as he settled back on the mattress and the eiderdown was pulled up to his chin. Though I felt better for seeing him safely to his own house, the fact that he was so completely passive did not augur well. The troubled frown on the face of Johannes reflected my own concern.

'My work . . . It must be finished . . .'

The low murmur came from the bed. Johannes was standing over Kant, staring down at his master. 'Herr Professor?' he called, his voice too loud in the muffled silence of the room.

'Professor Kant,' I urged, stepping up to the flea-ridden bed myself. 'Is all well with you, sir?'

Kant's left eye flashed open and he stared at me for a moment.

'A cold-blooded murderer,' he muttered. 'He bows to no one . . .'

He repeated the last two words over and over again.

'What is he saying, Herr Procurator?' Johannes whispered across the bed.

I shook my head, wanting silence, wanting Kant to stop this raving. My mind was in a whirl. Did he view my failure to catch the murderer as the defeat of Rationality and Analytical Science? Had the killer overstepped some mark that only Kant could see? Could this threat to the world as he conceived it account for his altered state of mind?

Suddenly, Professor Kant let out a shrill whimper.

'Oh, Lord!' Johannes exclaimed. 'He needs help, sir. Call a doctor!'

'Who takes care of him?' I asked.

'He treats himself, as a rule. His knowledge of physic is beyond the skills of most of the physicians in Königsberg . . .'

'In this state,' I insisted, 'he cannot help himself. He needs to be bled and poulticed. We need a professional.'

'There is a doctor living close by. He sometimes takes tea with my master. Perhaps he would be . . .' Johannes seemed to waver, as if crushed beneath the new responsibility that had been unexpectedly thrust upon him. 'But then again . . .'

A single glance at Professor Kant was enough to tell me that the time for hesitation was past. His eyes were closed, his face pale and expressionless, his respiration shallow and laboured.

'Where does this doctor live?' I asked.

'At the end of the street, sir. The first house on the left.'

I turned without another word and ran, the voice of Johannes following me down the stairs.

'But the man is *Italian*, sir, and he's very *young*!'

Five minutes later, short of breath, I reached the door of 'Dott. Danilo Gioacchini, Medico-Chirurgo', as the brass plaque described him. Beyond the door, I thought I heard the muffled sound of crying, and almost feared to break in on some domestic crisis. The house was made of weathered clapperboard that had once been painted blue, but now was a sadly faded grey. Crushed in between more substantial brick buildings on either side, I wondered whether its air of genteel poverty mirrored the cramped situation of the people living there. Was that the cause of the tears? It could not be easy for an Italian to make his way in Königsberg, despite the friendship of Immanuel Kant. Foreigners were held in low regard, Papists even more so, not only by the likes of Agneta Süsterich and Johannes Odum, but by every devout Pietist.

But what else could I do? I raised the iron knocker which was shaped like a closed fist, and let it drop. A moment later, the door opened a crack to reveal the face of a pretty, dark-haired woman. Standing by her knee, holding tightly to the young woman's skirts, a little girl of two or three years of age stared solemnly up at me.

'I am looking for the doctor,' I said, choosing my words with care for fear of not being understood. If this was the doctor's wife, she had probably come with him from Italy. 'It concerns Professor Kant . . .'

The name of Kant brought a fleeting smile to the housewife's lips.

'Danilo!' she called, turning towards the interior of the house, opening the door wide for me, and waving me to enter.

A moment later, the doctor himself appeared in the hall. He was, indeed, young, thirty-five at the most, though his long blond hair was thinning. Tall, slim, stylishly dressed in a high-collared jacket of black velvet, he welcomed me with a warm smile and sparkling brown eyes. Cradled one in each arm, he held up two identical infants which might have been born within the week. Both babies were screaming with all the strength in their tiny lungs.

'Twins!' he said. From the sudden creasing of his brow I could not have guessed whether he was proud of the fact, or apologising for the disturbance.

'I am sorry to bother you,' I said. 'Professor Kant needs help.'

He did not let me finish.

'I'll get my bag,' he said in flawless German. Then he spoke rapidly in Italian to his wife, who stepped forward immediately and took the wailing babies from him. A minute later, we left the house behind us.

Five minutes more, and we came to a stop in front of Professor Kant's. As we ran side by side along the snow-covered street, I had told him as well as I was able all that had happened, and tried to describe the patient's condition.

'Shall I come in with you?' I asked.

'It would serve no purpose,' the doctor replied, his foreign accent barely noticeable. 'His servant is with him, I presume?'

'Johannes is waiting for you. I am obliged to go to Sturten-strasse,' I apologised, recalling my neglected duty. 'But I'll return the instant I can.'

I heard the front door open, then close, as I walked away quickly through the darkening, empty streets in the direction of the fish market, arriving out of breath and ruffled about ten minutes later. The fog was thicker near the harbour and the estuary. A solitary soldier was standing guard at the corner of the street. He might have been carved from ice, his leather cap and black waterproof cape glistening in the orange light of the flaming torch that he held in his hand. Until that instant, I had not given a thought to the identity of the person who was lying dead in that place. Kant's sudden collapse had been the only thing on my mind.

The guard stepped forward, his musket crooked beneath his arm, preventing me from advancing further.

'I am Hanno Stiffeniis,' I announced. 'The investigating magistrate. Where is the body?'

'Down that way, sir,' the man replied, glancing back over his shoulder. 'There's another squaddie standing over the corpse.'

'Nothing has been removed, I hope?'

'No, sir. We were told to wait for you.'

This phrase was uttered between gritted teeth, as if the harshness of the cold and the length of time he had been required to wait had turned to harsh resentment against my person.

'Let no one pass,' I said sharply. 'Except for Sergeant Koch, my assistant. He should be here soon.'

I had no idea where Koch's hunt for Herr Lutbatz, the haberdasher, might have taken him, but I was certain that he would appear at the scene once he learnt what had happened. And I wished to have him there at my side. His experience, company and sound good sense would help me in the examination that I was about to undertake. My heart skipped a beat as I caught my first glimpse of the dark form huddled on the ground, and noticed at the same time the imprint of a man's shoe frozen in the ice. It bore a distinctive cross-cut . . .

Since that day, I have oftentimes asked myself whether Emanuel Swedenborg somehow touched upon a truth when he described the secret language of the dead. Now, I know for a fact that it exists. But then, I was incapable of translating the cold, silent mouthings into words. That night, I clearly heard the murmurings of the mysterious energy that Swedenborg tells us every departed soul transmits to the living.

Moving closer to the corpse, half-stumbling in a state of mounting anxiety which suddenly seized upon me, I was unable to swallow.

The young gendarme saluted and took a step backwards.

'Herr Procurator? I am glad you've come, sir,' he said with evident relief. The lantern in his left hand cast a sparkling aureola of dancing light on the packed blue ice of the pavement.

'Hold up your light,' I said. 'I wish to see the body.'

He closed the shutter with a sharp, metallic click, directing the narrow beam of yellow light against the high, brick wall which ran the length of the street. The dead man was kneeling on the ground, head bent forward on his chest, his right shoulder resting hard up against the wall. I stopped short, that question thudding in my head like a hammer beating heavily on an anvil.

'Draw close!' I cried sharply.

The soldier's teeth were chattering loudly. Little more than a lad, he was frightened. How long had he been standing there alone, waiting for me to come, not daring to look at the dark shape pressed against the wall in case the murderer emerged from the shadows and struck again?

As I drew near, a traveller's tale I had read flashed into my mind. It concerned the members of a mystic Asiatic sect, who believed that the souls of the dead lingered near the corpse until the moment of burial. I seemed to hover above the body kneeling there in the street wrapped in a glittering mantle, just like the one that . . .

Falling down on my knees on the frozen stones, I found myself staring hopelessly into the lifeless face of Amadeus Koch. His mouth gaped, as if he had attempted to shout for help, his eyes wide open in a startled flash of realisation. I knew there would be a tiny pinprick at the base of his skull. My thoughts began to rush in a maelstrom of guilt and regret, blood swooshing loudly in my ears and throbbing painfully at my temples.

Kant's cloak. My cloak. The cloak I had loaned to Koch . . .

Whom had the killer intended to strike: Professor Immanuel Kant? Me? Or had he chanced upon Koch by accident? I had to lean against the wall for fear of fainting, paralysed with horror, the muscles in my arms and legs as stiff and rigid as they were bereft of strength. Had the murderer mistaken his man?

As the cold penetrated my knees, the words Professor Kant had spoken earlier returned to plague me: 'Where is that cloak I gave you?' Had he somehow foreseen what would come to pass? Had he abandoned the high ground of Logic for the murky paths of Divination? Had Science led Kant to a conclusion that I myself could never have imagined? Was this the cause of his indisposition?

I remained some time in this bewildered state, kneeling beside the lifeless corpse of my assistant. Koch's eyes were twisted upwards and to the left, as if he had had an intuition an instant before the blow was struck. A film of ice had solidified the liquid surface of those sightless orbs. The lamplight flashed in a bewitching illusion of Life.

'Are you all right, sir?' a voice behind me asked.

The young soldier leaned forward with his torch, the light and shadows playing mercilessly across Koch's face. The sergeant seemed to live and breathe again.

'Herr Procurator,' he said. 'This man is holding something in his fist.'

With as much gentle care as I could summon, I introduced my forefinger inside Koch's clenched palm and prised his frozen fingers back. A bronze ring dropped to the ground with a clink and rolled away. The bait. Koch had exposed his neck to the murderer in Sturtenstrasse while picking up a bauble. Muttering a prayer, I asked his forgiveness as I rifled through his pockets and extracted all the objects that a cautious man carries around with him. A fine linen handkerchief, a house key, a couple of thaler notes, and a piece of paper that had been carefully folded and folded upon itself until it formed a square no larger than a snuff-box. Equally carefully, for fear of tearing it, I unfolded the sheet of paper and held it close to the lamp.

In all that I have written so far, I have endeavoured to lay bare the facts alone, to avoid weighing one detail more heavily than any other. It seemed to be the most objective method of describing the slow progress that my investigation made, and it provides the true sequence of events by which the affair in Königsberg clarified itself to the point at which I can give a true account of the matter. But now, I must allow my heart to speak for once. I must, for my head had no part in it.

As I read what was written on that paper, something died inside me. For an infinity of frozen time, I held my breath, my heart battering and flailing painfully within the confines of my breast while I examined that note and saw the asterisk that only Sergeant Koch could have made, the rest written out in a hand not his.

The note reported the complete list of shops and private persons who had purchased fabrics and needles for knitting and embroidery. It must have been supplied by the man from whom Koch's deceased wife had purchased such things. I write it out word for word as I read it there in the Sturtenstrasse:

6 reels of silk, colour ochre – Frau Jagger
10 skeins of undyed wool – ditto
6 pairs of knitting needles – Emporium Reutlingen
10 balls of wool, light blue – ditto
15 balls ditto, white – ditto
Four yards, Burano, embroidered – Fraulein Eggars

The list went on, but I had stopped at a large asterisk imprinted halfway down the page like a royal seal. The item reported was the following: '6 whalebone needles, size 8, for the beading of oiled tapestry wool'. Next to it was written the name of the purchaser. It was the only male name on the list.

I read the item again and again, spelling out the letters one by one like a child learning the alphabet on his first unhappy day at dame school. Like the puzzled boy, I had to conclude that the letter 'K' was truly a K, that the letter 'A' followed it, an 'N' came next, and that the 'T' which ended the name was the vilest letter in the whole alphabet. I chained the letters together to form the name of the person who had purchased those lethal ivory needles from Herr Roland Lutbatz.

Chapter 28

A biting easterly wind whistled up the hill from the nearby port and fish market, sweeping away the fog in rolling waves. High above my head, windowpanes rattled and shutters shook. Somewhere close by, a heavy metal gate groaned on its hinges, clanging shut, then opening again, with every fresh gust that came charging in from the Baltic Sea.

Alone in Sturtenstrasse with the lifeless body of Amadeus Koch, I started nervously at every sound. Frost formed crackling in my hair, my body seemed to be turning into stone, but only one thought possessed my mind: I would not desert him again. I had let Koch go his own way that afternoon, and his life had been stolen away. As I stared down with awe and nervous fright at the lifelorn body kneeling against the wall on the frozen pavement, I could only ask myself whether Sergeant Koch had understood what was happening as the needle bit home. Had he recognised the face of his killer?

'Herr Stiffeniis?'

I spun around. In the wailing wind I had heard no one approach.

A man in uniform towered above me. Another soldier even taller than the first, a dark scarf wrapped around his face, came slithering up the hill, dragging a long, wooden box over the ice and snow as if it were a sled. I recognised those men in a flash. I stretched to my full height, but I was still dwarfed by Corporal Mullen and his Magyar companion, Walter.

'What do you want?' I asked.

'That body's for the cellar, sir. Orders of Doctor Vigilantius . . .'

I did not wait to hear the rest. A tidal wave of resentment swept over me.

'He will not touch *this* body!' My voice bounded back off the stone wall and echoed down the empty street. My stiff limbs quivered with violent emotion. A sort of desperate hysteria, a cocktail of hopelessness and guilt, possessed me. 'There'll be no more dismembering here. Vigilantius has gone from Königsberg. He'll not be coming back! Koch must be buried whole. In Christian fashion. I want him taken to a church.'

The two giants exchanged glances.

'There's a chapel in the Fortress, sir,' Corporal Mullen suggested. 'Being as it's the only dry room in the place, they use it . . .'

'I don't care what they use it for,' I countered sharply. 'If it's been consecrated, I intend to see Koch's body laid out there. I'll pay for your trouble.'

Mullen's dark eyes glistened. His companion grunted.

'We'll see what we can do,' the Corporal replied. His tone suggested that my whim would cost God knew what effort to satisfy. 'Now, let's be getting the poor, unfortunate gentleman into the box, shall we, Walter?'

Rigor mortis and the freezing wind had fixed Koch's body in the kneeling position in which he had been found. Ice had formed on that waterproof cloak, and the soldiers struggled without success to find a hand-hold on the glistening material, their clumsy fingers slipping and fumbling.

'Strip that cloak from his back,' I ordered.

I must have sounded wild and heartless, for Mullen let out an excited hoot.

'Strip his cloak off? What for, sir? He's stiff as a board already. It won't come off that easy.'

The waxen fabric of Professor Kant's cape – the cause of Koch's murder, as I believed – encased the corpse like a gleaming winding-sheet. 'I'll not have Koch buried in that garment,' I insisted peevishly. 'Get – it – *off* – him!'

Mullen stared at me for a moment.

'Here, give us your knife, Walter,' he said with a groan. 'We'll

304

need to lay him on his flank, sir. There's no other way to go about the business.'

'Do it!' I snapped, watching as they obeyed my instructions.

The blade was short but sharp, and Mullen made a slicing laceration from the collar down to the hem. Then, having freed one side, they rolled the body over onto the other flank, and exerted themselves to release the sergeant's arms from the sleeves. Kicking the ruined remnants of the cloak aside, the soldiers lifted up the heavy corpse with some difficulty by the stiff arms and bent legs.

'Go gently,' I urged, as they set him down on his back inside the box.

'We'll have to straighten him out,' Mullen stated flatly, 'or that lid won't go on.'

'What are you waiting for?'

They pressed down hard on his knees, first the left, then the right, and the joints gave way with a sharp crack. It was a heartrending sound, yet my spirits lifted a trifle, seeing Koch laid at rest, and in his own clothes. For one instant, I allowed myself to believe that life might return, that my faithful assistant would sit up, breathe and talk to me once more.

'Can I close it, sir?' Mullen asked.

I took one long last look, then nodded.

Walter put the lid on, covering Amadeus Koch for ever. Then Mullen slammed home half a dozen nails, and we prepared to march away through the dark, empty streets. News of the murder would keep the townspeople behind their doors more surely than any curfew. Mullen and Walter went first, pulling their heavy sled with vigour, swishing and bumping through the ice and the slush. I followed close behind them, the gendarmes who had discovered the body bringing up the rear.

Along the way, we were obliged to pass the entrance to the lane which ran alongside the rear of Professor Kant's house. A feeble light glimmered behind the curtains of the window of his bedchamber on the first floor.

'Go faster, Mullen,' I urged, looking dead ahead, wishing to be far away from the sight of that window and that house as quickly as possible. The paper that I had found in the sergeant's pocket weighed on my conscience like a ton of lead: '6 whalebone needles, size 8, for the beading of oiled tapestry wool – Herr Kant'.

A show of bustle was made, but the procession advanced no faster than it had gone before, and we reached our destination no sooner. As we came in sight of the Fortress, I strode on ahead and ordered the gate to be swung open to receive the party.

'Corpse for Procurator Stiffeniis,' Mullen snarled at the watch as he and Walter passed inside. The sentinels crossed themselves and looked shyly away. One man half-turned and touched his crotch superstitiously, the way soldiers do when they see a coffin.

'Has he got a wife, sir?' Mullen asked, drawing up with the box in front of a low building on the far side of the courtyard. 'She'll surely want to watch over him this night.'

'I'll keep the wake,' I said. 'There's no one else.'

Mullen nodded to Walter, who muttered something back in that strange language of his, then they pushed open the chapel door, and began to haul the coffin inside. I followed them in. Then, a lamp was brought, and others hanging from the walls were lit from it. Inside the church, everything glistened. Pyramids of large silvery cannon-balls and chain-shot had been built in orderly piles as tall as a man down the central aisle. Along one wall, artillery pieces were stacked one on top of another like glossy black cheroots in a tobacco shop. The far wall was blocked by gun carriages stacked end to end. An odour of rats, of rat poison and decaying vermin stifled the air. Large canvas maps covered the vast walls. A plain wooden crucifix hung by a long chain from the roof. There was no other religious symbol in the place.

'This is the regimental chapel,' Mullen confided in a whisper. 'I tried to tell you before, sir. They keep the arms and explosives stored in here. The rest of the Fortress is as damp as a washer-woman's mop. We can set the coffin in that space over there, sir. They shifted the altar out to make more room, but the place is holy. Will it do you, Herr Procurator?'

I did not trouble to answer. Searching in my pouch, I found a ten-thaler note and handed it over. 'Drink something strong tonight in memory of the man who lies here, Mullen. Bring a pastor at dawn. We'll bury him then. Send Stadtschen to me on your way out.'

Corporal Mullen saluted, Walter clicked his heels, the door closed behind them, and I listened to the sound of their voices laughing and joking as they faded away in the distance. Alone in the chapel, I moved past the stacks of cannon and the heaps of munitions, and knelt down beside the coffin. I placed my hand on the cold wood, closed my eyes, and began to pray to God, imploring Him to welcome the soul of Amadeus Koch with open arms. Even more earnestly, I begged the Sergeant to forgive me. I had failed to understand the immediacy of the danger in which I had placed him. I have never forgiven myself for giving him that cloak. When my little ones kneel down beside their cots each night, join their tiny hands and say their simple prayers, they invoke the name of Amadeus Koch, as I have taught them to do in memory of the man who lost his life while innocently trying to help their father.

Behind me, the door-latch scraped and footsteps sounded sharply on the stone flags. I turned and composed myself as Stadtschen marched into the chapel. He glanced at the coffin for a moment, then looked at me, a puzzled expression on his broad red face.

'Herr Procurator?'

'It's Koch,' I said, and his name died on my tongue.

Stadtschen took off his cap and bowed his head towards the coffin.

'I want you to find a person for me,' I said, breaking in on his respectful silence. 'The man's name is Lutbatz. Roland Lutbatz. His testimony may be vital for the investigation.'

'Where do you want me to start, sir?'

'He must be staying somewhere. He's not a local man. A cheap hotel, or a lodging-house, perhaps.'

'I'll send the watch out.'

'Jump to it,' I said. 'He could leave town at any moment. Herr Lutbatz deals in haberdashery, supplying shops and emporia here in Königsberg.'

Stadtschen frowned. 'Haber-*what* did you say, sir?'

'Dashery, Stadtschen. Cotton, needles, thread, that sort of thing. People selling such items might know where he sleeps.'

'I've got an idea where to start,' the officer replied, to my surprise.
'Your wife?' I asked.

A light twinkled in Stadtschen's eyes. I took it to be a sign of amusement, though I would soon be obliged to revise my opinion. 'Not likely, sir! There's an old biddy that lives here inside the Fortress. She does . . . well, she offers various services for the soldiers of the regiment.'

'Services?' I returned, unable to suppress the note of sarcasm in my voice.

'Not what you are thinking, sir,' Stadtschen replied. 'She's long past that! She washes, mends and sews for bachelors who need a helping hand. She might well know the man you're looking for.'

'Inside the Fortress, you say? There can't be many women living here.'

'None at all, just her, sir,' Stadtschen confirmed.

I glanced towards the coffin. I had not intended to abandon my vigil so soon. But my most immediate duty was to the living. Who, better than Koch, could understand my motives? He would not feel abandoned in the Fortress chapel, surrounded by munitions, maps and firearms. He would hear the trumpet sounding as the guard was changed that night, the measured crash of heavy boots on the cobbled square-ground, the reassuring shout of orders, the rush to obey. His life had been lived among such things. I had brought him home, for he had no other home to go to.

Five minutes later, Stadtschen and I were walking quickly through a dingy honeycomb of towering stone walls and cluttered paved courtyards. We were in the medieval core of the Fortress, which seemed to accommodate all the trades and the services that make a barracks function. Each separate courtyard seemed to proclaim its trade by the odour it gave off: horses here, kitchens there, stinking of boiling meat; leather shops and bootmakers; bakers' furnaces; the foundry full of smoke and steam and coal-dust where shot and cannonballs were forged. It was a world within itself, it seemed to grow darker and become more odoriferous the further in we went, stinking of open latrines, vile excrement, and finally, total abandonment. In the darkest shadows, grey rats skipped squeaking from beneath our feet.

'Good work, Stadtschen,' I commented, as we stopped before a rotting door which had not seen paint since the coronation day of King Frederick the Great, or perhaps even before.

'This is the place, sir,' he confided, pounding at the flimsy wooden panels with force enough to smash them to matchwood.

A wizened old woman appeared almost immediately, peeping out, eyeing the white double-sash and the chevron stripes on Stadtschen's uniform. She might have been ninety years of age, or a hundred years older. There was so little light, it was impossible to tell, her complexion black with ingrained dirt, wrinkles engraved in her dewlapped cheeks and forehead like those of a stone gargoyle. Her ragged clothing seemed to cling to her like a skin. Ancient brown sacking for a dress, her bonnet of the same rough material, all stiff with grime. No doubt, she stank to high heaven, but the stench that issued from her dwelling was strong enough to overmatch the filthiest of ancient sluts.

'I was expecting His Excellency,' she said, peering up at Stadtschen.

'We've other business on our hands, mother,' he replied. The tone of his voice surprised me greatly. This giant had been entrusted with the watch, he was responsible for Section D of the prison with murderers, cannibals, thieves and forgers under his command. He ruled them all with an iron fist, yet his voice was soft, even deferential, when he addressed himself to this old hag.

'Three times I done it. Three! Allus comes out the same,' she muttered, her voice fading away to nothing. She looked up suddenly and said fiercely to no one: 'It will not be Königsberg, I'll tell ye that again. He'll not strike here, soldier, ye can rest assured of that!'

I glanced at the ancient, then back at Officer Stadtschen. Neither said a word, their eyes locked in silent communion, as if they understood each other perfectly well.

'What *is* she talking of, Stadtschen?' I asked.

I repeated the question more loudly when neither answered, and a terrific noise exploded in the farthest, deepest, darkest corner of the room. The flurried beating of wings, the cries of birds, many birds, a whole flock of them, chattering away excitedly like hungry starlings gathering in a wood as the winter comes on, before migrating in a swirling black mass. But what were these birds doing in the Fortress?

The woman pointed a gnarled and twisted finger into Stadtschen's face.

'Tell that booby not to scare my babes!' she screeched. 'His Excellency won't stand for it!'

Suddenly, she waddled away into the room, moving through the darkness like a fish through water, the door swinging open on its hinges.

'Come in,' she called over her shoulder. 'See for yourself, soldier. You can tell the General from me.'

Stadtschen stepped forward eagerly, like a hunting-dog that had spotted a falling grouse.

'What's going on?' I said, catching at him, holding him back by the sleeve. 'Let's waste no time. I intend to trace Roland Lutbatz tonight.'

Stadtschen snapped to attention, as if he had awakened from a trance.

'Her name is Margreta Lungrenek, sir,' he confided. 'She knows the man you're after, sir. I'd swear it . . .'

'Tell him what I do!' the woman shouted from the darkness of the room. Old she might have been, but her hearing was not impaired. 'I'll not invite ye in again!'

'Five minutes, no more,' I snapped, stepping into the room, holding up my lantern. 'Lutbatz, or we leave. I hold you responsible.'

In the receding gloom, I could just make out a pile of wicker cages stacked one above the other against the far wall. There were dozens of these cages, each one stuffed full of birds of all colours, shapes and sizes. I recognised sparrows, blue tits, pigeons, ravens, starlings, blackbirds, but there were more, far more, a hooded barn owl among them.

'Herr General loves 'em,' the woman clucked, waving her hand in a sweeping gesture towards the cages. 'He knows plain truth when it's laid out before his eyes.'

'She'd fallen on hard times, sir,' Stadtschen whispered. 'Her eyesight's failing. Can't hardly hold a needle no more. Then, the General heard about her talents. He gave her shelter in the Fort . . .'

'General Katowice?' I asked, astounded. What had he to do with this old woman and her winged menagerie? I had taken Mistress Lungrenek's references to the garrison commander as nothing more than the ragings of folly.

'She sees the future,' Stadtschen continued. 'His Excellency won't make a single move these days without consulting her. He's obsessed with the thought of Napoleon invading the city. Since these killings started, he's convinced himself that it's the work of French infiltrators. The General is a great admirer of Julius Caesar, sir. He swears them Romans never went to war without consulting people like her.'

'*Aruspices*,' I murmured. 'That was the name for them.'

Stadtschen stared at me wide-eyed. 'It's true, then?' he murmured.

The notion of Katowice trusting in omens and believing oracles was disconcerting in the extreme. If the commander of the Fortress and defender of the city placed his undivided trust in divination, all was lost. I recalled the energetic figure, the determination of speech, the directness of manner, which had seemed so reassuring on my own arrival at the Fortress. Was his ebullient state of mind induced by knowing that his forces were strong, his strategy secure? Or was it all bluster, based on the visions of a mad old woman?

'Look here!' she snapped, moving away from the cages, stooping over a small, round table in the darkest corner. A large, black bird, a dead carrion crow, had been laid out on the wooden surface. Its curving sabre of a beak hung loose, its plumage glistened red with blood, and the table had been strewn with its guts. The carcass had been arranged inside a circle of letters chalked apparently at random on the wooden surface. The innards had been ripped from the bird's breast, and arranged all around the body. The beak pointed one way, the rigid wings stretched out on either side. For all the world, it looked as if the bird had been crucified.

'Note the beak,' the ancient whispered, placing her hands on the table, leaning close and breathing in the stench. 'It points to this letter here. The wings indicate these two vowels. An' see the claws! That's the place, there, sirs! Jena! It's far from Königsberg. That's where General Katowice should be. Not here, messin' about!'

She peered short-sightedly at Stadtschen, a thin knowing smile on her lips.

I realised that I ought to have been chasing hot on the heels of Herr Lutbatz and the killer of Koch, but that woman's claim to read the future in the entrails of birds pricked my new-gained curiosity. If I had learnt anything from Immanuel Kant regarding my experience with Vigilantius, it was to pursue the light, even if it were nothing more than a pinpoint glimmer at the end of a long, dark tunnel.

'I'll tell him, mother,' Stadtschen said, his voice quick, nervous. 'I promise you, I'll tell him straight. But Procurator Stiffeniis has a question for you. Just answer him, then we'll be on our way.'

'Do you know a man named Roland Lutbatz?' I asked.

'Aye, sir, I do,' she replied quickly. 'I'd be lost without him. I know him like I know my birds. I saw him yesterday.'

'And where was that?'

'The Blue Unicorn, sir. That's where he stays when he's in Königsberg.'

'That tavern's near the Ferkel bridge,' Stadtschen explained. 'On foot, it's five minutes from here, sir.'

'I know far cheaper, if you want their names,' Margreta Lungrenek offered, as I thrust a thaler into her hand and made to leave.

'God curse you, sir!' the woman screeched, throwing the coin to the ground and rubbing her hand as if she had just been scorched. 'There's a presence hovering over you!'

'Now, mother,' Stadtschen warned her, his courage coming back as we prepared to leave. 'Watch that tongue of yours!'

'The Devil knows his own,' she hissed back, gathering her clenched fists close to her breasts, as if to fight the malignant presence off. 'I knows a troubled soul when I sees one. Don't I just!'

'A troubled soul?' I echoed, despite my wiser instincts.

My heart thrashed in my chest and rose up into my throat in a choaking, suffocating ball as the ageless one fixed me with her bright unseeing eyes.

'Your father's dead,' she said slowly. 'Dead and buried, but not at rest. He rises from the tomb by light o' moon, but he'll rest soon,' she chanted in a strange singsong voice.

I turned to Stadtschen quickly.

'This wise dame has told us all we need to know. Let's go.'

Outside in the courtyard, the cold, damp air was almost fresh enough to be invigorating after the suffocating pestilence inside that fetid hovel. We turned away and began to retrace our steps through the dark alleys of the Fortress in the general direction of the main gate.

'May I ask you something, sir?' Stadtschen enquired after he had walked in silence for some minutes at my side. 'General Katowice uses that old crone to see into the future, sir. And he believes her, too. One time, I asked her to read my own future life. She killed and gutted a bird, and told me lots of things that I would rather not believe, sir.'

'Such as?' I asked, glancing up at him. His face was dark, perplexed and puzzled.

'She strewed those guts on the table, like the one we just saw . . .'

He halted suddenly, and I was forced to stop.

'What did she see?' I asked him.

'She spoke just now of your father, sir. Is it true? Did she see the truth?'

Fear shone brightly in the soldier's eyes. He seemed to be affected by the sort of innocent fright that I had seen often enough in the eyes of my children when Lotte told them ghoulish bedtime tales of goblins and fairies, wolves and captured princesses lost in the woods. Lotte was a storyteller of awesome power, enough to frighten a child out of its wits if she chose. I had often taken her to task for the wildness of her imagination and the freeness of her tongue.

'What did you ask her, Stadtschen?'

'Oh, you know, sir!' he said, smiling with embarrassment. 'The things all soldiers want to know. I asked her what would be my fate if Napoleon ever came to Prussia . . .'

'My father is not dead,' I cut in, carefully measuring my words. 'Nor will he be for a long time yet, I hope most sincerely. Margreta Lungrenek was wrong about my father. Totally wrong. She has no idea at all what she's talking of. Curse her ignorance! I wonder that Herr General Katowice should take such nonsense seriously.'

His face lit up like the sun bursting forth from a dark cloud, though that same cloud still hung menacingly over me.

Shortly afterwards, we left the Fortress, turned left and dived into the town. And Stadtschen was correct in his estimates. Minutes later, we emerged from the maze of alleyways near an ancient stone bridge, one of the many that crossed the River Pregel as it wound back and forth upon itself within the confines of the city. We stopped by a quay lined with heavy barges, watching the sailors smoking their pipes and chatting quietly, taking a moment to catch our breaths, then we turned towards an inn sign fanning in the wind. A blue-painted mythical creature galloped across a field of silver clouds with golden sparks flying from its hooves.

'The Blue Unicorn, sir,' he announced.

Chapter 29

As Officer Stadtschen hauled on a bell-rope, all the church bells in the city of Königsberg seemed to clang and chime together. Before they fell silent again, a window creaked open high above the Unicorn sign, and a pale round face peered down at us in the street.

'D'you know what time o' night it is?'

'Police,' Stadtschen yelled. 'Open up, and quick about it!'

The same fat, frightened man unbolted his door some moments later and waved us into the bar. He seemed unduly concerned to be discovered in his nightgown and bedcap. All was dark in the low-ceilinged room except for a pale glow in the chimney-place from the dying embers in the grate.

'I was asleep, sir,' the innkeeper whined, wringing his hands and looking as thoroughly guilty as I have ever seen a man who might reasonably be supposed to have done nothing criminal.

Then, Stadtschen alarmed him all the more.

'Bring the register for Herr Procurator Stiffeniis to see,' he barked.

A large leather-bound ledger was quickly laid flat on the table in front of me. I sat down and began to turn the pages, all of which were blank.

'Is this some sort of joke?' I asked, looking up. 'Is no one staying here?'

Stadtschen leaned threateningly over the shoulder of the man and hissed into his ear. 'Withholding names from the police, land-lord?'

The fat man's fears became ever more visible. 'I would not

dare, sir! The beadles search the town so frequently in the present situation.' He bent over the book, saying, 'With your permission, sir?'

He licked the tip of his finger and fumbled his way through the pages. 'We've had so few guests, sir. Especially in the last month. Who'd come to town to be murdered? But here we are, sir.'

He pulled back and showed me what he had found. One name was written on the page, together with a date.

'Herr Lutbatz, sir. A merchant,' he murmured. 'There's no one else staying here tonight. He's a travelling gentleman, highly respected in his trade, I'm told. A touch eccentric in his way of er . . . doing, and . . . er, dressing, but I ain't got nothing against that, sir, 'ave I?'

There was something decidedly shifty about the landlord. He seemed to be dropping hints of some sort, and I believed I had a good idea of what he might be hinting at. 'Does anyone visit him?' I asked, leaning closer.

'Well, sir,' he began nervously, 'you know how it is, sir. When a man is travelling all alone, like he is, he . . . well, how can I put it? He sometimes falls into *company*, sir. That's what I would call it. Company . . . There's not a great deal I can do about it. His visitors come, then they go. We have so few guests to stay these days, I tends to close a blind eye. He is alone tonight, I do know that. Said he was feeling like junk for the knacker's yard when I gave him his dinner . . .'

He stuttered to a halt, looking at me with a sort of pleading grimace of helplessness.

I leaned back in my chair. Women! I thought. I had been hoping that the landlord might have something to say about the customers who had recently been to visit Lutbatz.

'Do any of his customers call on him here?'

'Not this trip, sir. Times is hard in Königsberg. For all of us.'

'I wish to have a word with this man,' I said.

'Shall I tell him to come down here, sir?'

'No,' I replied. 'I'd prefer to speak to him in the privacy of his chamber. Would you step up and tell him that I am here?'

The innkeeper wiped his damp brow with the back of his hand

and let out a sigh of evident relief. Another man's trouble was no trouble at all, so long as he himself was not involved in it, it appeared. He scuttled away up the stairs, returning a minute later to say that Herr Lutbatz was waiting for me in his room.

'Shall I come up with you, Herr Procurator?' Stadtschen asked.

'I do not need a nursemaid,' I replied sharply. The truth was that I did not intend to risk making public the name that Roland Lutbatz had inscribed on his list for Sergeant Koch. 'Return to the Fortress, if you will, Stadtschen. And remind Mullen to find a priest for the funeral.'

He saluted and left, while I began to climb the stairs to the second floor, where Roland Lutbatz was hovering by his bedroom door. I saw immediately what the innkeeper had meant when he used the word 'eccentric' to describe the man. Had I stumbled by accident into a house of ill repute, the whores would not have been half so extravagantly dressed for bed as Herr Lutbatz was. He emerged coyly into the corridor, and smiled anxiously in welcome. His peccadillo had little to do with women, I realised. The lemon-coloured turban on his head might have been bobbing on the surface of a tropical sea. His nightgown was a rich emerald-green damask with chevron patterns in a darker weave, the silky material shimmering and undulating in the candlelight.

'Herr Procurator?' he asked, stepping nimbly to one side and bowing me into his boudoir, the air of which was richly perfumed.

'What a fright I got when the landlord knocked!' he exclaimed, pushing a chair close to the fire for me. He threw a log onto the embers, which flared up in a bright explosion of sparks, and adjusted the lemon-coloured turban on his head. 'Now, what can I do for you, sir?'

'I need to ask you some questions, Herr Lutbatz.'

The man sat down on the opposite side of the fireplace, pursed his red lips in a most exaggerated and feminine expression of alarm and began to pat himself lightly on the chest, as if to calm the rapid palpitations of his troubled heart.

'Oh, do! Please *do*, sir,' he replied, spreading his hands on his knees as if to brace himself. His nails were carefully cut and buffed, except for those of the little finger on each hand which curled like an eagle's talons.

'There has been a spate of murders in Königsberg. You know that, don't you, Herr Lutbatz?'

He nodded gravely. Then, his dainty features grimaced into a mask of alarm. His eyes blazed. 'You do not think that *I* am involved, sir?'

I smiled to reassure him.

'I need some information connected with your trade, sir. Nothing more.'

His mouth formed a gaping 'O' of surprise.

'But I deal in fabrics,' he said. 'Are you sure that I'm the man for you?'

Without waiting for my answer, he leapt up from his seat with unexpected agility and ran to the far side of the room. 'Here, you see? This is my business, sir. Material of the finest quality.'

He threw open one of the boxes which covered a good part of the floor and drew out a sample weft of dark red velvet. 'I travel all over the continent, France and the Low Countries for the most part, to buy my wares, and I sell them here in Prussia. All the shops in Königsberg buy from me, and private customers too, of course. All the very best people . . .'

'Like Frau Koch?' I asked.

'Frau Koch, sir?' he repeated, his eyes wide with surprise. 'Frau Koch has been dead these past five years. The poor lady . . .'

He fell silent, evidently unsure where I was leading him.

'Sit down, Herr Lutbatz,' I said. 'I am not here to see your goods.'

He sank unhappily onto his chair and stared at me.

'Frau Koch was the wife of my assistant. Sergeant Koch came to see you today, did he not?'

He let out another sigh of relief. 'He did, sir. His wife was a seamstress. She traded with me for many years. I gave her material in exchange for samples of her best work. Frau Merete was a delightful woman.'

'I want to know what Herr Koch asked of you, and what you told him in reply.'

Lutbatz looked at me with a puzzled expression. 'I thought you said that he was your assistant, sir? Did he not tell you himself?'

'I wish to hear from you what the outcome of the meeting was,' I said drily.

'Well, he came to ask about some needles, sir,' Herr Lutbatz replied in a nervous flurry. 'The sort we use in tapestry work. I let him see my samples, and Herr Sergeant asked if I had sold any to persons living here in Königsberg.'

'And what was your reply?'

'I checked my books and found the information he was seeking, sir. I've sold no needles of that type so far this trip. But Sergeant Koch was interested in others I had sold in the past and I gave him the records.'

I took out the paper I had found on Koch's corpse and handed it to him.

'Do you recognise this as the list that you gave him earlier today?'

'I believe it is,' he said, jumping up and running to the other side of the room. He clipped a silver pince-nez on the bridge of his nose and peered intently at the note. 'Yes, yes, this is my handwriting. These are customers of mine. I had one or two more to see tomorrow, then I meant to leave for Potsdam.'

'Do you mean to say that you have not yet completed your business in town, Herr Lutbatz?'

'That is correct,' he replied.

'Have you spoken to Herr Kant yet?'

'Now, isn't that a coincidence!' he exclaimed. 'Sergeant Koch asked me the very same question. I can show you the needles Herr Kant ordered. Sergeant Koch was most interested in those.'

He stood up and crossed the room. 'Does Herr Kant come here, or do you attend on him at his home?' I asked.

'He comes to me, sir,' he answered, dropping to his knees, throwing open a large brown trunk. 'Here they are!' he cried, taking out a wooden box and showing it to me.

'Does Herr Kant buy only these?' I asked, as Lutbatz extracted a rolled bundle and placed it into my hands.

'Oh no, sir,' the merchant prattled on. 'He purchases other things as well, cotton, wool, sometimes a little strip of Flemish linen, or a bit of French silk. But these big needles! I don't know what he does with them all.'

'Have you ever asked him?'

'Oh no. No, sir. I supposed they were for his wife. It hardly seems delicate to ask, if he doesn't say for himself. I've often wondered what her work is like,' the merchant chattered on nervously. 'I'm on excellent terms with all my clients, they often show me the things they make. If their work is of a reasonably good standard, I sometimes buy it to add to my stock. In the case of poor Frau Koch, I would exchange finished work for fresh materials. There's an excellent trade hereabouts in local craft for a person such as myself that travels around, but . . .'

'But Herr Kant never offered to trade his wife's needlework for stock,' I concluded. 'And I don't suppose you've ever been invited to their house either?'

He arched his eyebrows in surprise. 'How did you guess, sir? She must be an invalid, I thought. If she sends her husband shopping for her, she can hardly be in the best of health, can she?'

I did not reply. As I unrolled the bundle, I was trying to imagine Koch's thoughts when he read the name of Kant on the list and saw the articles that the philosopher had purchased. I held the cloth in the palm of my hand, folded it back, and stared at the needles. There were six of them.

'Whalebone ivory,' Herr Lutbatz said proudly. 'Such a lovely colour! Creamy white with an undertone of yellow.'

They were a fraction longer than the one that Anna Rostova had hidden, a fraction brighter, as if whoever had made them had polished them lovingly. There was a large eye-hole at one end, a sharp point at the other. My head was spinning and I offered no resistance as Herr Lutbatz picked up one of the needles, and weighed it in his hand.

'These are perfect. Light, well-balanced,' he said. 'They need careful handling, but they're far more robust than they look. A skilled worker can do an excellent job with one of these. Can I give them to Herr Kant if he calls before I leave?'

'I doubt he'll have much use for them after today,' I replied.

'He won't find better anywhere else,' Herr Lutbatz insisted with an impatient shrug of his shoulders. 'That's what Sergeant Koch said. He'd never seen such fine tools before. His wife would have loved them.'

'I am sure she would, Herr Lutbatz. You can put them away now,' I said, and watched as he rolled the needles up, placed them in their box, and returned them to the trunk from which he had taken them. 'Thank you, sir. You have been a great help.'

'Think nothing of it, Herr Procurator. I've done my duty, I hope. But may I ask you something?' He looked at me for a moment. 'Why are you so interested in Herr Kant?'

'Do you know who he is?' I countered.

Roland Lutbatz did not hesitate. 'I told you, sir. He's one of my customers. Not the most regular, but in my business you must count the pennies as well as the pounds.'

'Herr Professor Immanuel Kant is a famous man,' I added. 'He used to teach philosophy at the university here in Königsberg.'

'Oh, that!' the haberdasher returned with a flutter of his eyebrows. 'He told me all about himself the first time he came to see me. It must be a year ago now. He was full of himself. A real peacock, I'd say! He was a famous *philosopher*, he taught at the *university*, he'd published any number of important *books*. I didn't take him seriously, I must admit.'

'Whyever not?' I asked.

He hesitated, searching for a word. 'He told me that he was on . . . intimate terms with the *King*. Well, I played along, of course, but I didn't believe the half of it.'

'Did Herr Kant tell you the sort of work his wife did?' I asked.

'What a question, sir!' Lutbatz cried, clapping his hands together excitedly. 'Naturally, when he returned to me the second time, I asked him if his wife had found the needles to her liking.'

'And how did he reply?'

'I found him most evasive. She was little more than an amateur, he told me, but she enjoyed herself, which was good enough for him.'

I glanced out of the window. Dawn comes early in the North and the sky was a rippled pearly pink.

'Forgive me, Herr Lutbatz,' I said. 'I have robbed you of your sleep. Thank you for all that you have told me. It will be most useful.'

I was still speaking when Roland Lutbatz went scurrying across to that table on the other side of the room again. 'Before you go, Herr Procurator, I hope that you will leave an inscription in my autograph album,' he said, carrying a volume across to me. 'I ask every visitor to sign his name and write a phrase to remember him by. It's a great comfort when you travel the world without a constant friend. I do hope you won't disappoint me? Sergeant Koch ran off without signing. But I won't be disappointed twice in one day!'

I took the book in my hands – it was a small thing to do by way of thanks – and examined the neat leather-bound volume. A large red velvet heart and the word 'Memories' had been embroidered diagonally across the cover in elegant white letters.

'I stitched it myself,' Herr Lutbatz said proudly. 'All my own work!'

'It's quite remarkable,' I admitted. Indeed, any housewife would have been proud of such handiwork.

'Now, here's a pen, sir,' he said, bringing over a pot of ink and a quill, while I wondered what on earth to write. 'If you turn back a way, you'll see the phrase that Herr Kant inscribed with his own hand.'

My hands trembled as I turned the pages and saw what the visitor had written the night that he came to Roland Lutbatz to collect the instruments with which he would inflict sudden death on so many unsuspecting souls:

Two things fill my mind with wonder – the starry sky above my head, the obscurity deep within my soul.

The epigram was signed 'Immanuel Kant'.

'Go on, sir,' Herr Lutbatz urged with a shrill laugh of excitement, 'let's see if you can do better!'

I took the quill and in a few seconds I had composed and written the following phrase of my own: 'Reason has vanquished the clouds of Obscurity, bringing Light.' Then, as Immanuel Kant had done before me, I signed my name beneath the inscription.

The first rays of the rising sun caressed the dark horizon in a golden fan as I left The Blue Unicorn and walked out into the new morning with a lighter step, and an even lighter heart.

Chapter 30

Did I truly believe that Immanuel Kant was the murderer? Even for a single instant? Had I been able to conjure up a mental picture of Roland Lutbatz chatting amiably away, while Professor Kant purchased six ivory needles for the purpose of massacring the innocent citizens of Königsberg in cold blood? At his age? In his frail physical condition?

If the idea had ever flitted across the ruffled surface of my troubled mind for the tiniest fraction of a second, that phrase written out so boldly in the merchant's autograph book saved me from taking a further plunge into unthinkable error. What I had read was a godless parody of the Immanuel Kant that all the world knew and respected. As I studied those ungainly letters written out so awkwardly, in such an immature and childlike hand, I suddenly realised that a familiar ghost had brushed my sleeve many times in the past few days, and that he had gained ground each time that I failed to recognise him.

The very first time I had *not* seen this ghostly presence was the day that I came to Königsberg seven years before and found myself so unexpectedly invited to lunch at Professor Kant's home. His ancient valet was absent that day, attending the funeral of his sister. In thirty years of constant domestic service, it was the only day when he had *not* been present at Professor Kant's table. And just a short while after I returned home to Lotingen, the sixty-year-old servant had been summarily dismissed from the house, forbidden ever to return. Yet, Frau Mendelssohn had seen him repeatedly entering and leaving at all hours of the day and the night. She had told me so. She had seen Martin Lampe!

Lampe had managed to worm his way in and out of Professor Kant's drawing room soon after I had left it, or shortly before I entered. Martin Lampe and I had been like twin satellites in parallel orbits around the same mighty planet, always circling, never meeting. But why had Kant allowed Martin Lampe to return from banishment?

I could only guess. Maybe the servant had played on the generosity of his former master. Perhaps he had answered some need, given comfort in the form of the regularity and continuity of his visits, or provided that sense of order and fixity which seemed to be so essential to the ageing philosopher's well-being. What must have sounded to Kant like harmless chatter with an old, familiar confidant was the key to Martin Lampe's power. Like an alien cuckoo in the nest, one by one, he had thrown out all the other chicks. Kant's dearest friends had thought to unsaddle the valet, but he had pitched them headlong from the intimacy of his master. Martin Lampe had never distanced himself from Immanuel Kant. Not for one single moment. He had known my every move. As I began to displace him in his master's confidence, he had sought to eliminate me. He had killed Sergeant Koch in the belief that he was murdering me. That waterproof cloak had been the signal. Kant must have mentioned in passing that he had given it to me; Martin Lampe could not have known that I had handed on the cloak to Sergeant Koch.

But why had Lampe killed the others? Had each one of them had some tenuous connection with Professor Kant that I had not yet been able to discover? That Professor Kant might consult a notary was certainly possible, but what about the others? Jan Konnen was a blacksmith, Paula-Anne Brunner sold eggs, Johann Gottfried Haase was a social derelict. And why had Kant himself said nothing about them if he knew these people?

I had identified the killer, but I could not fathom what had made him do it. I had to find him, and make him talk. But where should I start to look? Where did he live, where could he hide? I took out my fob-watch. It was half past five in the morning. Nevertheless, I walked away quickly down Königstrasse in the opposite direction from the Fortress, a nervous litany running through my head.

'Dear God, forgive the Totzes, husband and wife. Pardon Anna Rostova for her sins and her crimes. Excuse the weakness of Lublinsky,' I intoned. They had all been savaged by my blundering incapacity.

'And help me stop Martin Lampe!' He had found a modus operandi and a weapon ideally suited to his physical condition and his age. Like a watchful spider, he had woven a web of cunning to immobilise his prey. When the fly was caught and helpless, he had struck with all the venom at his disposal.

'O Lord,' I spoke out loud, 'preserve the soul of Amadeus Koch.' Koch would never know how close he had come to the truth. I prayed most fervently for his honest soul as I pulled my cloak more tightly against the freezing cold of dawn.

'And Heaven help me!' I thought finally, though there was more irony than piety in the notion. I had been deceived, but I had not been forced to pay for the error with my life.

I reached my destination, pushed open the creaking garden gate once again, and knocked more furiously on the door than I had intended. The servant came at last. While straightening his wig, he announced brusquely that it was too early for his master to receive a social call. 'It's barely six o'clock!' he added. 'And in any case, my master has a head cold. He'll be seeing no one today.'

'He will make an exception,' I insisted stubbornly. 'Tell him that Procurator Stiffeniis must speak to him on a matter of the greatest urgency.'

The fellow closed the door in my face, only to open it again a few minutes later. Without a word of apology for his rudeness, he stepped back, waved me into the hall, and pointed to the top of the stairs.

Herr Jachmann was propped up in bed on a mountain of pillows, his head covered by a grey woollen cap which was pulled low on his brow. The air in the room hung heavy with the fumes of camphor.

'You again?' he greeted me without warmth. 'The last nightmare of a long night.'

I sat down on a chair near the bed without apologising or waiting for an invitation. 'I have come about Martin Lampe,' I said.

Jachmann sat up quickly.

'I want you to tell me all that you know about him.'

Falling back against the pillows with a loud sigh, he closed his red-ringed eyes. 'I thought your task was to find a murderer, Stiffeniis, not gossip about the servants.'

'I need your help if I am to protect Professor Kant,' I said stiffly, and waited for him to open his eyes and look at me, though he remained silent and still. 'Do you know Frau Mendelssohn?' I ploughed on.

He nodded without speaking.

'She told me that she thought she had seen Martin Lampe entering Professor Kant's house on more than one occasion.'

Had I told Jachmann that an Arctic tiger was roaming unchained on the streets of Königsberg, the effect could not have been more pronounced. His eyes flashed open, and he glared at me angrily. 'Keep that man away from Kant,' he cried with such force that he was afflicted by a fit of coughing. The violence of his disavowal of Lampe disconcerted me.

'Have you told me everything I should know about him, Herr Jachmann?'

The old man did not answer, but fussed instead with the woollen cap on his head, pulling his shawl more tightly about his shoulders, as if I had brought the winter cold into the room with me.

'Lampe was not simply a servant,' Jachmann replied slowly. 'He was more, much more. Without him, Professor Kant was lost. Like a child without a mother. Kant's intellectual accomplishments are due in very large part to the contribution of Martin Lampe.'

The incredulity on my face must have been clear.

'Do you think I am exaggerating?' Jachmann smiled a wan smile. 'Martin Lampe was discharged from the army, Kant was in need of a personal servant. At the time, it was a happy coincidence. Kant is incapable of the simplest household task; Lampe was taken on to remedy the omission. Why, he couldn't even put his own *stockings* on! Kant's daily life was arranged by this rough-and-ready soldier.

When the Professor gave instructions to be called at five o'clock each morning, Corporal Lampe obeyed that order to the letter. If the master attempted to snooze after the hour had struck, the servant pitched him mercilessly from his bed like a lazy child. And Kant thanked him for it. He needs the sort of inflexible discipline which only a mother, or a man like Martin Lampe, can provide.'

He stopped to wipe his nose.

'Why drive him off after a life of dedicated service?' I insisted.

'He represented the greatest danger to his master,' Herr Jachmann snuffled into his handkerchief. 'Martin Lampe had become . . . irreplaceable.'

I studied Jachmann's pale face. His lips trembled, his eyes were feverish. He seemed to be terrified of Martin Lampe himself. 'But *how* was he a danger, sir? I do not comprehend you.'

'Do you know Gottlieb Fichte?' he asked abruptly. He did not wait for me to answer. 'Fichte was one of Kant's most promising students. When his doctoral thesis was published, many people believed that Kant had written it. They thought he had used the name of Fichte as a convenient pseudonym, but there was no truth in the rumour. Fichte often went to visit him, and the professor had always greeted him with friendly warmth. But after that thesis was published, a degree of coldness and animosity crept into their intimacy. Philosophical thought had shifted direction. Sentiment, Irrationality and Pathos were the new keywords. Reason had had its day; Logic was long out of fashion, and Immanuel Kant was set aside. Then, Fichte published a stinging attack on Kant for no apparent motive, accusing him of intellectual idleness. And a short while after, as bold as brass, he appeared at the door, saying that he desired to speak to his former mentor.'

'Did Kant receive him?'

'Of course he did. You know what he's like. He declared himself keener than ever to talk to someone capable of formulating new concepts. But Martin Lampe saw the affair in a different light.'

I considered this for a moment. 'Lampe was only a servant. What could he do about it?'

Jachmann ignored my objection. 'Fichte wrote to tell me what had happened that day,' he went on. 'He'd been frightened for his life, he said.'

He sank back on the pillow as if he had no energy left.

'What did he tell you?' I pressed without allowing him a second's pause.

Jachmann placed a flannel to his mouth, breathed in deeply, and the cloying smell of camphor wafted through the room. 'Leaving Kant's house that evening, Fichte found himself alone in the lane. It was dark and foggy, and he thought that someone might be following him. He quickened his pace, but still those footsteps dogged his own. There was no one to whom he could turn for help. And so, at last, he turned to face the stalker.'

'Did he recognise the person?' I asked.

Jachmann nodded. 'He did. It was Immanuel Kant.'

For a moment I thought the fever had possessed his reason.

'Not the amiable Kant that Fichte had left at the house,' Jachmann went on. 'This was a demon, a terrifying parody who looked like Kant, dressed like Kant. He ran at Fichte with a kitchen knife, and would have slit his throat if the younger man had not been so nimble. Fichte recognised him then. He saw that it was *not* Professor Kant, but the aged domestic who had poured tea for them both in subservient silence half an hour before in Kant's own sitting room.'

'God help us!' I exclaimed, wondering whether Martin Lampe's madness had begun that night.

'Fichte described him as the evil personification of his master.'

'Why did you not tell me this before?' I asked.

Herr Jachmann stared at me in silence for some moments. 'What good would the knowledge have done you?' he replied coldly.

'Did Kant ever learn of the incident?' I corrected myself.

Jachmann jerked beneath the sheets as if an adder had nipped him. 'Do you take me for a complete fool, Stiffeniis? There was a catastrophic overlapping of personalities in that house. The servant had become the master.'

'So you dismissed him,' I concluded.

'I fobbed Kant off with the notion that he needed a younger

329

man. Then, I wrote to you, Stiffeniis, asking you to stay away from him. I wanted Kant to live out his mature years in peace. Professor Kant needs to be guarded from the world. He must avoid unsettling influences like yourself and Martin Lampe. Age has taken its toll on the stability and lucidity of his mind.'

The connection that Herr Jachmann had made between Lampe and myself distressed me. He still resented my short-lived intimacy with his former friend, and made no secret of his opinion. He viewed us both as a danger to Immanuel Kant.

'Soon after I dismissed him,' he went on, 'I made another discovery. It was most distressing. Lampe had a wife! He'd been married for six-and-twenty years, and no one knew of it.'

'But he'd been living in Kant's house . . .'

'Night and day. For all those years.' Jachmann shook his head. 'Marriage was strictly forbidden in the terms of Lampe's employment.'

He relapsed into a moody silence.

'Does Lampe know anything of philosophy?' I asked.

Jachmann shrugged. 'What does a footsoldier know of such things? He could read and write, I suppose, but a fixation had taken hold of his mind. Kant's work cannot proceed without my help, he told me one day. And on more than one occasion I found him sitting in the kitchen, leafing through his master's published works. God knows what he made of them! As he left the house for the last time, he warned me that Kant would never write another word without his assistance. The prophecy was all too true, I'm afraid.'

'Did you hear anything more of him afterwards?' I asked.

Jachmann seemed to swell with rage.

'I have little or no contact with Kant these days. Even so, I did everything in my power to make sure that Lampe was kept away from the house. I shudder to think that he has disobeyed my prohibition.' He looked at me with feverish eyes, rheumy tears trickling down his cheeks. 'Is Frau Mendelssohn quite certain of her facts?'

'She saw him leaving the house. Just yesterday. She told me so.'

'Find him, Stiffeniis,' Jachmann cried. 'Find that man before he does any more harm.'

'Do you have any idea where he is, sir?'

Jachmann stared at me like a hawk. 'The wife will know. She lives . . . *they* are living,' he corrected himself, 'somewhere near Königsberg. I do not know exactly where. I never felt the wish to learn anything more about him. And now, Stiffeniis' – he leaned forward stiffly and offered his cold, damp hand to me – 'you must excuse me. I am grateful for all that you have done to help Professor Kant.'

I noted the stinging sarcasm in his voice as he pronounced the last phrase.

'I will do everything that I can to prevent Martin Lampe . . .'

I halted, afraid that I might have said too much, but Jachmann was not listening. He had taken up his towel again from a small porcelain basin and had placed his head beneath the tent to inhale the fumes. Clearly, my visit was at an end.

I left the house, caught a two-wheeled cab at the end of the street, and told the sleepy driver to take me to the Fortress. I had not slept all the night, but that was the last thing on my mind as I rushed up to my bedroom. Where was Lampe? Where was his wife? I could not use the gendarmes to locate them. No one must ever know the connection between Lampe, those murders and Professor Kant. I closed the door behind me and felt like a house-fly trapped in a bottle. I buzzed up and down, hopelessly butting my nose against the glass, although the opening was there, if I cared to look for it. If I *dared* . . . The solution was all too obvious. There was one person I could ask about Martin Lampe: Professor Kant himself. He must know where the man was to be found. But could I ask him without revealing my reasons for seeking Lampe out?

A sharp double rap at my door sent this thought scuttling for the darkest corner like a fugitive sewer rat.

A bleary-eyed soldier stood before me when I opened up, his fist raised to knock again. 'An urgent message, sir.'

'What is it?'

'Downstairs, sir. A woman's asking for you.'

I was expecting no one. Had Helena, for some reason, taken it into her head to come to Königsberg? Just as she had gone on impulse to visit Ruisling and my brother's grave the week before?

'Says her name's Frau Lampe, sir,' the soldier added.

I hurried down the stairs, greatly relieved and thanking Providence. God works in mysterious ways, they say. And how truly impenetrable they are! Hope surged in my breast in that moment. But that noble sentiment was no more than the final step on my long slide to perdition and delusion. The messenger had brought me the key to a closed vault that I had been trying in vain to enter. I could never have foreseen the horror awaiting me once the key had turned.

Chapter 31

Frau Lampe was younger than I had expected. She could hardly have been forty-five years of age. Standing in the corridor outside the guard-room, her face was finely sculpted by the dark shadows. The flickering lamplight cast a waxen gloss on her pale skin. A thin shawl of grey worsted material covered her head and shoulders in meagre defiance of the rigours of the weather. Although she looked worn and tired, there was something timeless and beautiful about her appearance. She might have been a gypsy girl begging on a street corner for coins. Glancing up at me with a look of the most intense concern, her large black eyes glinted with unexpected directness into mine.

'Procurator Stiffeniis?'

'You must be Frau Lampe,' I said.

She bowed her head in reply.

'You'd better come out of the cold,' I said, and led her into a little room that was used as a rule by the officer of the night-watch.

'Thank you, sir,' she said with an eagerness which took me by surprise as I struck a flint to the wick of a candle. I imagined there could be only one reason for her coming: she had decided to confess all that she knew about her husband and his crimes.

'I should have come before, sir,' she began. 'It concerns my husband.'

I waved her to a chair and sat myself behind the desk.

'I know who your husband is,' I said.

Her eyes opened wide with surprise. 'Do you, sir?'

'I have heard his name mentioned many a time in connection with the affairs of Herr Professor Kant.'

Frau Lampe looked down, as if to hide her face. Her dignified bearing seemed to diminish like a sail when the wind suddenly drops. It was the work of an instant. At the mention of Kant's name, a change came over her.

'You know Professor Kant, then?' she murmured.

'Indeed,' I said, 'I have that pleasure . . .'

'Pleasure?' she interrupted sharply. 'I know him too, sir. Like a cripple knows his withered limb.'

Her words were like a blasphemy spoken aloud in a church. 'You had better tell me what you've come to say, Frau Lampe,' I said gruffly, managing with an effort to control my temper.

'You think me rude, I suppose?' she replied, looking me squarely in the face. 'Professor Kant may well be a friend to you, sir, but me and my husband know the darker side of his character. It's no lack of respect, but the fruit of bitter experience.'

Suddenly, I felt uncomfortable in the presence of that woman. There was a calm determination in her manner which I did not know how to handle or direct.

'I doubt that you've come merely to express your rancour towards Professor Kant,' I continued hastily. 'Very well, then. What brings you here?'

'Professor Kant is the cause of all my husband's troubles, sir,' she replied. 'That's why I've come.'

'If you have something to say to me as a magistrate,' I urged her, 'then say it at once. The fact is that I need to speak to your husband, Frau Lampe. Do you know where I might find him?'

She raised her coal-black eyes, a pitiful, tragic expression like a stain on her handsome face. 'That's just it, sir,' she said, and her voice broke into a sob. 'I've no idea where Martin is. He disappeared the night before last. I came to report him missing, and they told me to ask for you. But you are investigating murders, sir,' she said, mopping at her tears with her shawl. 'Why did they tell me to speak to you? Has something happened to him?'

Was there some further aspect of the case that escaped me? Sergeant Koch had been murdered the previous afternoon, so the killer was still at large. What the woman had just told me cast doubt on my suspicions regarding her husband's involvement in Koch's death. She had placed his disappearance almost twenty-four hours before the murder of my assistant. Might something tragic have happened to Lampe as well? Or had he come out of hiding solely to commit another crime? There was still a chance that Lampe was innocent. But then a more cynical idea took hold, and I studied the woman's face attentively. Did she possess the skill to act the role that she appeared to be playing? Might she be trying to provide an alibi for her husband?

I stood up with decision.

'I need to search your home, Frau Lampe.'

If he was hiding there with her connivance, I would catch him off his guard. If he were not, I would have the opportunity to scour the house for evidence that might be used against him.

To my surprise, Frau Lampe stood up and prepared to leave without a moment's hesitation. 'I'll do anything if it helps you to find Martin, sir,' she said, forcing a weak smile, following me in silence out of the gate to where a police coach was parked. I woke the driver with a shake, and we climbed aboard.

'Tell him where to go, Frau Lampe,' I ordered, and she gave the coachman an address in the Belefest village area.

'Will seeing the house help you to discover where he is?' she asked uncertainly as the vehicle gathered speed. 'I've searched it myself from top to bottom. He left no note, and nothing at all's been carried away, sir.'

'It is normal police procedure, Frau Lampe,' I replied in the vaguest terms. 'There may be some clue that you have missed.'

She nodded eagerly and seemed relieved to hand the business over to me.

A church bell tolled eight of the clock. At this hour, I reflected, looking out of the window of the coach, any other town in Prussia would be wide awake, the workrooms, shops and offices open for trade. But under the arches of the low porticos on either side of the narrow street, all was closed and tightly shuttered. There was not a soul to be seen in Königsberg, with the exception of the armed soldiers guarding every crossroads. Truly, the city was under siege.

And it was all the doing of Martin Lampe. Bonaparte's marauding army posed less of a threat than the enemy already within the city walls. I had to find him. Perhaps then, the city would begin to live again.

After two or three kilometres, the carriage began to slow down, then came to rest at last beside a sad row of dingy little country cottages with sagging roofs of ancient thatch the colour of ash. We were in the village of Belefest, the lady told me as I helped her to climb down into an unpaved muddy lane. There were tall leafless trees on either flank. In the spring and summer, when brilliant green and the brighter tints of hedgerow flowers salvage the world, the hamlet might have made a first impression which was less dreary, grey and depressing.

'You won't find much sign of Martin's presence in the house, sir. My husband and I have lived together so little. Professor Kant could not, *would* not, get along without him,' she said harshly. There was no mistaking her tone, or her meaning. She did not like Immanuel Kant. His name seemed to burn on her tongue like acid.

The house was tiny, standing at the lower end of the row. A small garden stood before the front door. Poor, I judged, but not destitute. Then, Frau Lampe explained that she and her husband occupied only two rooms of the place: they had been obliged to let the whole upper floor to lodgers. She opened the door with her key and an overwhelming odour of stale boiled cabbage drifted out. A lamp was brought, the tinder struck – in that room, it was never day – and soon the humble dwelling was crudely illuminated for me to see.

'May I look around?' I asked, glancing quickly about me, taking in the meagre furnishings. Frau Lampe watched me as I searched the place, opening cupboards and drawers, feeling under every cushion and coverlet, excusing myself as I stripped away the bed and examined the straw mattress for anything that might be hidden inside or underneath it. I found nothing more exceptional in the dwelling than a few cracked mugs and mismatched plates, the dirty old clothes they had used to work in the garden, odd remnants of Martin Lampe's past glories in the army, which consisted of a pair of corporal's epaulettes and a faded, moth-eaten uniform jacket.

Inside a chest, washed-out household linen, nondescript rags of clothing, an ancient horse-blanket Lampe had brought back from Belorussia, together with a pair of yellow spare sheets and some faded fineries Frau Lampe had worn when she was younger and had known better days.

'We had much, much more,' she murmured, 'but the pawnbroker got it all. My first husband, Albrecht Kolber, was the beadle. We were well-to-do, but he died of choleric dysentery.' The widow Kolber had married Martin Lampe nine years after his honourable discharge from the Prussian army, where he had served in Poland and in Western Russia under King Frederick the Great. Without any other trade to his name, Martin Lampe had entered into service as the valet to Immanuel Kant.

'Martin wanted to marry me, and I needed a husband,' she explained flatly. 'We had to wed in secret, of course. Professor Kant wanted only bachelors in his employ.'

I wiped the dust from my hands and turned to face her. My search had told me nothing more than Frau Lampe herself had told me while I was sifting through the material wreckage of her life. First, of her short but happy marriage to Beadle Kolber, then, her impoverished widowhood, and, finally, the new lease of married life she had found with Martin Lampe.

She watched as I turned away from what I had been doing and looked around helplessly. Had some detail escaped my notice? Were Martin Lampe's secrets locked up in his brain and nowhere else?

'I told you before, Herr Procurator,' she said gently. 'You won't find any sign of his presence here. There's nothing worth a brass half-farthing. Nothing worth a memory.'

'Do you have a hiding-place for money, papers, valuables?'

She shook her head ruefully. 'Everything I own, I wear on my back, sir. You're looking in the wrong place. If you want to know what Martin had on his mind, there's only one place to turn for help.'

'And where is that?'

An air of concern clouded the woman's face, but in an instant the look was gone. 'You say you are a particular friend of Professor

Kant's, sir. Why not ask him where Martin is? I'd ask him myself, but I cannot . . .'

I stiffened. 'What makes you think that Kant would know?'

'Martin often goes to his house,' she replied without hesitation. 'He's been helping Kant to write a book.'

'He's been doing . . . *what?*' I spluttered.

'Not that he makes a penny out of it,' she went on resentfully. 'I've no idea what he does precisely. He comes home so tired out, he's not fit for work in the garden.'

'After your husband was dismissed from service,' I interposed, 'he was prohibited from ever visiting the house again. Professor Kant's friends keep a close watch to make sure there's no communication between them.'

Frau Lampe laughed shrilly. 'Even his dearest friends have to sleep, sir. Martin goes there after dark. I warned him, but he would not listen to me. The forest is a dangerous place at night.' She frowned and her voice was suddenly tense. 'You've no idea what my Martin's life was like in that house, have you? For thirty years he waited hand and foot on the most famous man in Prussia. If you knew the truth, sir, you wouldn't envy him.'

'Your husband has been most fortunate,' I said stiffly, 'in having served the noblest mind that ever lived in Prussia.'

A veil seemed to fall over her face. 'I could tell you things that Kant's best friends don't know,' she replied in a low voice.

'Go on,' I said, steeling myself to hear the gossip that cast-off servants and their irate wives reserve for their former employers.

'Everyone in Königsberg – and elsewhere for all I know – has heard of Professor Kant. His precise way of thinking, the regularity of his habits, the stern morality of his temperament, the impeccable elegance of his dress. Not a hair out of place, not a word out of turn, not a spot on his reputation. A living clock, they call him in this town. A clockwork man, says I. Nothing happens in his life by chance. No accidents befall him. Have you ever stopped to think how that affects the people in his service? Martin had no freedom, no life. Every single instant of every day, from the moment Martin woke him in the morning to the second when he tucked the Professor up in bed and blew out his candle, my husband was at his side, and never a single thought in his head but what his master put there. Waiting hand and foot on that man like a slave.'

She halted, her facial expression changed. Some rebellious thought seemed to pass through her mind and ripple the furrows on her brow like wind over still water.

'My husband was obsessed with the need to assist Professor Kant. When Herr Jachmann dismissed him, I realised that something was wrong. He blamed Martin . . .'

'It was not a question of blame,' I interrupted. 'Herr Jachmann decided that a younger man was needed.'

'Perhaps,' she replied, shrugging her shoulders. A nervous motion of her hands and the glinting brightness of her eyes suggested a fear of something that I could not name. 'Martin had a special task in that house. Something only *he* could do,' she added, her voice sinking to a barely audible whisper.

'A special task?' I echoed. Distressed by her husband's disappearance, I wondered whether she had begun to imagine plots.

'"I am the water in Kant's well," Martin told me once.'

'And what do you think he meant by that?'

Frau Lampe's eyes flashed up at me.

'Why, the book Professor Kant was writing!' she exclaimed. 'Martin told me he was helping his master to put the finishing touches to his final work. Kant's hand was not so steady as it used to be, his sight was poor, he needed a secretary to write it out for him.'

'Kant was dictating the text to your husband?' I burst out incredulously. 'Is that what you are suggesting, ma'am?'

Frau Lampe closed her eyes and nodded. 'Night after night after night. Often dawn was breaking before he got home. Martin isn't young any more, but he always was so diligent. He was so proud of what they were doing together. Helping Professor Kant rewrite his philosophy. That was what he said.'

'When did all of this begin?'

Frau Lampe grimaced with the effort of recall. A chasm split her brow. 'More than a year ago, sir. Martin was torn from my bed once more by that ogre. He came home when he could, but some nights he didn't come at all. And when he did come, he was not the same man. He'd sit by that window there, looking out like a haunted soul. He didn't say a word to me.'

I gazed at the murky window and tried to imagine what Martin Lampe had been thinking about. Had the murdering demon in his soul risen to the surface while his wife looked helplessly on?

'Did he tell you what this work involved?' I asked.

'He said I wouldn't understand. He and his master were exploring a new dimension. That's what he said, sir. A new dimension.'

Martin and Professor Kant, I noted. *Not* Professor Kant and Martin. Was that how she had interpreted Lampe's words, or had the husband presented the case to his wife in that light?

'Has your husband ever studied philosophy?' I asked.

'Oh no, sir. But he learnt a great deal from his master. Martin was always going on about the new philosophers who'd been attacking Kant. He said they'd be obliged to eat their words when the book came out.'

There it was again. The final testament of Immanuel Kant. The book that no one had ever seen. Nobody, apart from Martin Lampe . . .

'That book turned Martin into a different man,' she continued. 'He frightened the life out of me sometimes, sir. He was obsessed, driven, and it was all Kant's doing.'

'Your husband was only executing his duty,' I suggested vaguely, 'unpleasant as it might have been.'

'Unpleasant?' she hissed. 'It was worse than that. Kant brought Martin to the verge of murder.'

'Indeed?' I said coldly, as if what she had just told me was a reasonable argument and not an obscene calumny.

'Martin told me so. One day a young gentleman came to visit Kant. When Martin served them tea, he said that they were pleasantly engaged in a discussion of philosophy . . .'

The relationship Jachmann had mentioned earlier flashed through my mind. 'Was the name of the visitor Gottlieb Fichte?'

Frau Lampe shook her head. 'I've no idea, sir. After they'd finished talking, Professor Kant accompanied his visitor to the door and saw him out.' She stared at me, a smile frozen on her face.

'What happened?' I asked.

'Kant told my husband to run after that young man and kill him with a knife.'

Here was the other side of Herr Jachmann's coin. Not a mad Martin Lampe, but a mad and murderous Immanuel Kant.

'Did your husband obey?'

'Of course, he did, sir. It was his duty. But that young philosopher ran away before Martin could catch up with him.'

'Would your husband have obeyed Kant up to that final point?'

She joined her hands as if she to pray. 'I begged him not to listen,' she whispered with a moan. 'Kant is senile, I said. He's demented. To tell you the truth, sir, I was glad when Herr Jachmann dismissed my husband. I thought he'd be out of harm's way. But nothing really changed. Professor Kant sent a secret message, calling him to the house under cover of night.'

'Frau Lampe,' I said, turning the argument aside, pointing to a piece of embroidered linen draped over the back of a chair. 'Are you interested in needlework?'

She glanced up in perplexity, then nodded.

'Where do you purchase your materials?'

She looked at me as if I were deranged.

'From a shop? A travelling draper, perhaps?' I suggested.

'There are two shops that I go to,' she said hesitantly.

'Do you know a man named Roland Lutbatz?'

'Yes, sir.'

'Have you bought anything from him recently?'

'I do not know him personally, sir,' she replied. 'He supplies goods to shopkeeper Reutlingen. I've seen him there on one or two occasions.' She stopped and frowned. 'What has Herr Lutbatz to do with my husband's disappearance?'

'He says that he spoke to your husband recently,' I answered. 'Martin was interested in buying needles for carding tapestry wool.'

'Carding wool?' she repeated, as if she did not understand.

'Did you instruct your husband to buy them for you?'

341

She did not reply. She was too frightened to answer, I could see that, calculating whether her husband would gain or lose by what she might have to say. I knew how I wished her to answer. I desired it with all the impelling force that Doctor Mesmer mentions when he speaks of the transference of thought. I wanted her to tell me that her husband had, indeed, bought those needles for her, and for no other purpose than that for which they were intended. I prayed with all my heart that the certainty I had felt in identifying the murderer would be dashed to smithereens. I wanted Lampe to be innocent. If Kant's unwitting influence had driven him to murder, there would be no end to the scandal.

'I did not ask my husband to purchase anything from Herr Lutbatz,' she said at last. 'He may have wished to surprise me with a gift. He sometimes does.' She studied my face carefully. 'Will this help you to understand what has happened to him, sir?'

'You have been a great help to me, Frau Lampe,' I said, standing up and preparing to leave, ever more convinced of the guilt of her husband. 'Please contact me if anything else occurs to you. With your assistance the police will find him soon, I'm certain.'

'There's something else, sir,' she said, stopping me on the doorstep. 'I should have mentioned it before, but I hoped it would not be necessary.'

'Of what are you speaking, Frau Lampe?'

'I'll show you, sir.'

She led the way quickly into the back garden, tramping through the deep, packed snow to the farthest corner of the enclosed land. It was a small plot in which Frau Lampe and her husband had managed to cultivate an apple tree and some rows of vegetables, the plants now frozen, black and withered with the frost. A dense, dark, untended wood stretched away up the hill behind the house. There was a vague, menacing quality about the place. Wisps of fog clung to the naked branches and the stark damp trunks. Dripping icicles hung from the trees like the stalactites in the gloomy caves of Bad Merrenheim.

'Can you see these marks?' she said, bending to the ground and indicating footprints in the frozen snow.

I knelt to examine them. They were little more than scuffs left by someone in a hurry wearing shoes unsuited to the weather and the terrain.

'It was snowing the night that Martin disappeared. I saw these tracks the morning after, when I went to the shed over there to get some dried herbs. It has not snowed since.'

'Why should he come this way?' I asked.

'It's a short cut to Professor . . . to the town,' she corrected herself.

Leaving her at the garden's edge, I ventured further into the wood, following the tracks until I reached a wild plum tree. Enshrined in the frozen snow was the first clearly delineated footprint. I stared at it for what seemed an eternity of time.

'Are you certain these traces were left by your husband?' I called back.

'I cut the soles of Martin's shoes myself. The leather was worn. I did not want him to fall and injure himself.'

I had seen the distinctive cross-cut that Frau Lampe had made three times before. In the drawing made by Officer Lublinsky at the scene of the first murder. The previous afternoon in Professor Kant's garden. And the night before, beside the lifeless body of Amadeus Koch in Sturtenstrasse.

Chapter 32

After leaving Belefest, I returned to my office in a troubled mood.

I knew exactly what I ought to do. The killer had a name. Martin Lampe should be hunted down and prevented from striking again. Yet, there was something else that I had to do, something no magistrate should *ever* do. I determined to hide the identity of the killer. Professor Kant must never learn who he was, or know how close he had been. If the murderer could be stopped, if I could cover his tracks, I would lead the investigation away from him until it fizzled out. If any man spoke the name of Martin Lampe again, it must only be to remember him as Professor Kant's valet. Anything else was a blasphemy.

I planted my elbows on the desk, pressed my head between my hands. I felt as though my brain might erupt from my throbbing skull. The first thing to do was to draw him into my net. He had murdered Sergeant Koch, but *I* had been the real target. Lampe had set his heart on slaughtering me, and he would not rest until he had eliminated the danger. Could I offer myself as a bait to entice him out of his hiding hole?

Suddenly, another course of action opened up before me, one which would set me for ever beyond the pale of the law.

Lampe had disappeared. His wife presumed that he was dead. She had come to the Fortress to report him missing. Could I turn the situation to my advantage? All I had to do was call Stadtschen, inform him that the man was nowhere to be found, provide a detailed description, and suggest that Lampe might have been murdered. A search would be set in motion. If he were found alive, he would be brought to me for questioning. Then, I

344

would have him where I wanted him.

I poured myself a glass of wine, and drank it off in a single draught. As the liquid traced its acid path to my stomach, I realised with a shudder what would follow on once I had him in my custody. A terrible energy began to surge through my veins. My thoughts were swept up, invaded, conquered by the recollection of a cold grey morning ten years before. The intoxicating smell of blood as the blade scythed effortlessly through the neck of the French king. I clutched my fists to my eyes, trying to cancel that image from my memory.

I would kill Martin Lampe.

I sat still for quite some time, seeking to reclaim possession of myself, struggling to remember who I was, to understand what I had become – what I was *about* to become. I could not risk a public trial. The manipulation of justice is no simple matter. If Lampe were forced to stand before me in the dock, I would have to prove his guilt in full. A magistrate is charged not only to condemn guilt, he must also demonstrate what led the felon to his error. Too much might be said in a courtroom debate of Professor Kant's influence over his valet. But if I gave orders to take the man up for his own safety, who would question my motives? If something happened while he was in my care, would any man dare to accuse me?

A short time later, a knock came at the door, and a soldier entered carrying despatches. 'Begging your pardon, sir,' he apologised, setting them down on my desk. 'Officer Stadtschen sent these.'

I glanced at the two letters, waiting for the door to close. The larger one, a white envelope with an imposing red seal, brought a lump to my throat as I slit it open. It was one of those missives all Prussians in the civil administration dread to receive, an anonymous secretary informing me that I was to give a full account of myself. A report of my investigation to date was required for submission to His Majesty, King Frederick Wilhelm, the following morning.

I let the paper fall on the table.

What was I to do? Could I avoid the Royal Imperative? Postpone the task until I was in a better position to reveal to the King what I wished him to know of the situation in Königsberg? I picked the letter up, read it once more, let it drop back onto the table, turning my attention to the second despatch, which seemed less intimidating. This message bore no Hohenzollern seal. It was a single sheet of grey paper, folded in four, and closed with a loop of string. But as I read what Stadtschen had written, my heart began to race.

> . . . *a heap of bones. Tatters of clothing suggest the victim may have been a man. He had been chased through the woods, as streaks and stains of blood in the snow reveal, and was torn to pieces as he tried to escape. Pawprints indicate at least a dozen animals in the pack. The beasts were famished . . .*

Another body had been found. Why had I not been informed at once?

My conception of the murders that Martin Lampe had committed was well-defined, precise in every detail. Whoever he was, the victim had not been killed by Lampe. But that did not diminish my impatience with Stadtschen's interfering ways. With Koch dead, he had spotted an opportunity for his own advancement. He had taken upon himself the responsibility to have the soldiers collect the bones in a sack, and bring them to the Fortress. 'The remains will be held for a day in case someone comes to claim the body,' he noted officiously. 'If no one does, burial in a pauper's grave will follow on.'

A groan of angered exasperation escaped me.

Did he think I would tell General Katowice what a clever fellow he was? Did he hope that I would mention him by name in my report to the King? I read on, my annoyance flaring into white-hot anger as I neared the end.

'Though not within the city walls, the place where the body was found still falls within the jurisdiction of Herr Procurator,' Stadtschen continued, 'being the abandoned hunting ground of the ancient feudal manor of . . .'

I jumped up from my chair, threw open the door, and called out the name of Stadtschen with all the force of rage in my lungs.

The empty corridor boomed with the sound. Footsteps clattered further off, and the echo of my cry was taken up by other voices, all of them calling the name of Stadtschen.

The man arrived at a gallop a minute later, his wig set lopsidedly on his head, the top button of his uniform loose, as if my summons to duty had caught him unprepared. His sweaty face might have been wiped with a knob of lard, and I took some pleasure in his discomfiture.

'Sir?' he said, breathing heavily after the exertion.

'Where is it, Stadtschen? Where's the body?'

He stared at me, his face a theatre of alternating expressions: surprise, shock, fear, anxious submission to my authority.

'Body, sir?'

'The man in the woods near Belefest,' I snapped, waving his despatch in his face. 'Who gave you permission to tamper with it? Are you blind to what is going on in Königsberg, Stadtschen? Someone is killing people. The only way to catch him is to search each murder scene for clues. But *you* decided to move the corpse! I suppose your men have trampled all over the place like a herd of cows.'

'Procurator Stiffeniis,' he interrupted, his voice trembling, 'there was no reason to think that he had been killed by any man.' He pointed his finger at the despatch in my hand. 'I reported the fact there, sir. Near the end. "Ravaged by wild animals." Wolves, most probably. They'd torn . . .'

'What makes you think the wolves *killed* him?' I shouted. 'The murderer could have chased this man through the woods. The victim may have been dead before the animals got to him.'

The possibility had never entered the numbskull's mind.

'But, sir!' he protested again. 'The murderer always strikes *inside* the city walls. That's why I thought . . .'

'You *thought*?'

I mimicked him sarcastically, but his desperate reasoning struck a spark of hope in my heart. He was right. Martin Lampe had never killed outside the town. Yet Belefest was where he lived. Was he hiding somewhere near his house, or in the woods behind it? I had seen his footprints in the snow on the path that led from the village to Königsberg less than an hour before. His wife had verified them for me. Had Lampe killed someone else on his way home from town? Or had he himself been torn to pieces after murdering Sergeant Koch?

'Is the body still in the Fortress?'

'Indeed it is, sir.' Officer Stadtschen seemed to grow before my eyes as he replied. Unlike the ones that had gone before, this question had not been prompted by anger, nor tainted by accusation. His massive chest swelled out, his back straightened, his puffy face relaxed once more, taking on its usual air of arrogant self-righteousness. 'We can go there now, sir. If you wish, that is, Herr Stiffeniis,' he added more cautiously.

'Lead on,' I said.

On the ground floor, not far from the main gate, Stadtschen lifted a flaming torch from the wall and handed it to me. He took another one for himself, opened a narrow arched door, and we went spiralling down the staircase that led to the dungeons and maze of passages lying beneath the Fortress. I had been there in the company of Sergeant Koch on the night of my arrival in Königsberg. On that occasion, we had met a necromancer, and heard his animated conversation with the lifeless shell of a murdered man.

This time, I intended the inspection of the body to be strictly factual.

At the bottom, we turned right and entered a narrow tunnel which had been hacked out of the solid rock at some time in the distant past. The rough walls were slick with damp, dark green with moss. Piles of broken chairs, tables, beds and stinking mattresses had been abandoned there to mould and decay. Stacks of ancient breastplates stamped with a double-headed eagle lay rusting and forgotten in a heap. Old-fashioned powder-muskets with blunderbuss barrels were ranged along the walls like fossilised flowers. Each object seemed malignly intent on tripping us up, blocking the way, or falling down and burying us alive. The flickering torchlight saved us from the dangers, but there was little the flames could do against the cold.

As Stadtschen said in utter seriousness: 'We are in the impenetrable bowels of the Earth, sir. Long before Königsberg existed, before men made houses, this is where they used to dwell.'

It was hard to imagine any human being surviving there for very long. The cold was penetrating, it seemed to filter through my skin and take possession of my bones. The heavy woollen garments that had kept me warm – despite the freezing fog and icy winds that had lashed Königsberg since my arrival – were useless in that dismal cave. I might have been naked for all the good they did me. I am not averse to cold weather. A crisp winter's morning, frost fresh on the grass, sparkling sun, clean air, is one of Nature's delights, but the desolate chill of the cold earth has an unpleasant effect on my spirits. I was terrified by the odour of damp and organic decay while still a child. Every year on the anniversary of my grandfather's death, Father would unlock the door and lead the family and servants down to the crypt to pray for the souls of our ancestors. I knew the smell of the tomb from a tender age. Indeed, I often asked myself in gaping terror whether the dead souls of my forebears would be condemned to breathe that musty stench for Eternity.

With a swoosh of his torch, Officer Stadtschen spun round to face me.

'Here we are, sir,' he said, indicating a heavy iron door. He seemed to have regained his mettle. Perhaps he hoped the visual evidence of his good work would convince me to revise my opinion of him. 'Cold it may be, Herr Procurator, but a corpse will not last long down here. It's the damp that does it. Rot sets in, then there's the rats . . .'

'I can imagine!' I cut in sharply. I did not need a catalogue of horrors to compound my discomfort.

'I only meant to say, sir, that bodies are kept in the charnel house as short a time as possible. Most of them have been exposed above ground to all sorts of horrible mis–'

'How long has *this* corpse been here?' I asked more forcefully, drowning out his evident delight in the mechanics of human decomposition.

'I'd hardly call it a corpse . . .'

'How long?' I insisted.

'Four hours, sir,' he said. 'Bills are being posted up around the

349

town. I gave the word myself.' He stopped, uncertain of my reaction. 'Do you want me to stop them from being put up, sir?'

'Let them be,' I replied. 'Someone may come forward with news of the man.'

'I tried to tell you what I was about, sir,' he went on. 'But when I knocked at your door, you did not answer. They told me in the guard-room that you'd left the Fortress in the company of a lady. I wrote that note before I went to bed, and told them to deliver it the minute you came back. I'd been on duty all night, sir.'

I heard him, but I was not listening. I was doing my sums. If the body had been deposited in the charnel house four hours before, then it had probably been found two, three, or even four hours earlier. That is, the man had died at the very least eight, ten, or even more hours before. I glanced at my watch, and noted that it was twenty past nine. Midnight, then, was the likely hour of his demise, though it was possible he had died some hours before. Physical examination would give me a better idea of the state of preservation and the rigidity of the corpse, but the timing did suggest that this *might* be the body of Martin Lampe. If so, I calculated, some hours after killing Sergeant Koch, he had been ravaged by wolves while returning home along the forest path. Of course, he could have died at any time after three o'clock the day before (the hour at which Koch's body had been discovered in Sturtenstrasse), but if, as I believed, midnight proved to be the more likely hour, where had he been hiding? What had he been doing in the interval?

Then again, I reasoned, if the corpse were not Lampe's, but that of another of his victims – that is, having killed Sergeant Koch, he had chosen to attack someone else as he made his way to Belefest – then I was seriously in trouble. Had Lampe abandoned his chosen modus operandi and favourite weapon, and given himself up to casual slaughter? Two murders in one day. Was his homicidal fury growing? Was his lust for blood urging him to kill with greater frequency?

As Stadtschen pulled back the rusty bolt to the charnel house, the iron door grated noisily on the rough stone floor, covering the words of invocation that escaped from my lips. I prayed to God that the corpse of Martin Lampe would be waiting for me. Certain knowledge that he was dead would end the terror that had taken possession of Königsberg, and cancel the murderous obsession that had taken root in my own mind.

'Cover your mouth, sir,' Stadtschen advised, blocking the way, and holding me in check.

'One of our lads was carried off this morning with choleric fever. Spewing his guts up when he wasn't busy on the latrine. Day and night for almost a week. What a way to go!'

Stadtschen raised his hand to his mouth and nose, while I turned my head to the side and used my jacket collar for the same purpose. The stink as we entered the room was hideous and sweet. The walls had been washed with lime, and the flickering light from our torches rebounded off the walls in a blinding flash. The space was empty and bare, except for a large tin bath placed against the far wall. I stepped across, glanced into it, then looked away. The naked corpse of a man had been laid flat on its back, eyes popping, broad chest sunken, skin wrinkled and yellow, the stomach swollen almost to bursting. Though I struggled not to think of it, I realised it would not be long before the nauseous gases exploded out of him.

I struggled to concentrate my mind on the task at hand. I did not have Professor Kant to help or direct me, as he had done when he took me to visit his *Wunderkammer* for the first time, proudly showing me the severed heads of the victims suspended in distilled wine.

'Over there, sir,' Stadtschen replied, waving his torch towards the far corner.

The man found in the wood had been laid on a mat of rough hessian. Stadtschen was right, I admitted. 'Corpse' was not the correct word. I fought the rising tide of revulsion in my gullet, and heard Stadtschen clear his throat and spit behind my back.

'I hope he was dead when they stripped him clean,' he murmured, as I fixed my torch in a ring on the wall.

Resolving to do as Professor Kant had taught me, I knelt down to examine attentively what was left of the body. I noted ribs and bones, sections of vertebrae which had been broken in at least three places, skeletal remains of the arms and the legs, everything tinged pale orange or dark brown where the muscles and flesh had been torn away. Shreds of transparent tendon, scraps of gristle and elastic cartilage still clung to the joints, though hardly a trace of soft tissue remained. It was impossible to determine the state of rigor mortis. So, there was no way of guessing how long ago the man might have been dead.

'Jesus, they were hungry, sir!'

Stadtschen's words were blunt and crude, but I admitted to myself that his observation was apt enough. Searching through my pockets, I drew out the long key that opened the door to my office. With some difficulty, I used it to turn the glistening skull towards me. In that instant, the true significance of the *memento mori* with which we love to decorate our Prussian churches struck me with a force that I had never felt before. Indeed, it took me a moment to pluck up the courage to look more carefully at the skeletal face, and the detached lower jaw. The skin was gone entirely, the ears and flesh of the cheeks and chin having been devoured. On the crown of the head, a tuft of hair had escaped being pulled away from the scalp in the frenzy of feeding. Though the strands were soaked in blood, the tips were clean. And they were white. A man of a certain age, I decided, or one who had aged prematurely. Might his hair have blanched as the attack took place? I dismissed this fanciful notion, my thoughts turning instinctively to Martin Lampe, Kant's valet, the secretary who had transcribed his master's work at dead of night, the servant I had never ever seen. Lampe was almost seventy years old. His hair could well have been white.

'They started with the juicier bits, sir. Cheeks and lips, muscles and fat, the flesh on his arms and legs and whatever was attached to that *thing* there.'

Stadtschen was standing close behind me, leaning forward, peering eagerly over my shoulder. I would have preferred him to stand further off and let me get on with my work in peace, but his finger stretched forward and touched the skull, which lolled and rolled onto its side, then came to rest like a soup bowl, giving an extra twist to the gristly tubes of the trachea and oesophagus, which had somehow survived the onslaught.

'They ripped his head off, sir. It's plain to me, this case bears no relation to the corpse of that man of yours that was stabbed to death yesterday afternoon.'

I paused for a moment, remembering Amadeus Koch, whose body was safely housed in the Fortress chapel. At least, I reflected morosely, his death had been more sudden, and I had preserved him from the horror of the charnel house.

'Begging your pardon, sir. You an' him was close, I know.'

Once more, I tried to ignore this gushing babble as I sifted through the corporeal wreckage looking for some clue to the identity of the unknown man. The ribcage, pelvis, hips, and a mass of tangled bones lay in the centre of a horrid, bloody mash, which was all that remained of the internal organs. The larger bones bore marks of deep indentations made by pointed teeth, or fangs, as I suppose they ought more correctly to be called. Having caught up with their prey, the beasts had evidently dragged him to the ground by his arms and legs. Then, they had set to work. Blood-soaked scraps of clothing were tied up inextricably in the mess, and I made no effort to shift them. What purpose would it serve? Any colour they might have had was irremediably fouled and stained by the blood and the gore.

'No clothes to help us,' I said. 'No shoes.'

'I bet they ate 'em, sir,' Stadtschen answered, blandly unaware of the importance the discovery of those shoes with the distinctive cross-cut on the soles might have made. 'A hungry wolf'll dine on anything, sir. Got a digestion like a French grenadier. They eat their young, I've heard tell. The wolves, I mean.'

I bent even lower, as much to escape Stadtschen as to gain a better view of the skull. The upper teeth were unevenly ranged with broken points and tips, badly consumed with age and use, as if the dead man had chewed long and hard before he swallowed his meat. I peered more closely at the oral cavity, telling Stadtschen to lower his light. The tongue had been ripped out during the assault, blood had caked the gums and everything else, with the exception of a white strip of bone or naked cartilage which stood out like a jagged slit on the roof of his mouth. A fang had evidently penetrated the palate as the beasts tussled with the head of the man.

Could any death be more terrible?

I let out a sigh of helplessness, looking into the blood-rimmed cavities of the skull, the dark empty spaces where the eyes had once nestled. What did you see in the final instant of your life? I wondered. Who were you? Some drunken wretch wandering alone at night through the forest? Another hapless victim of the killer? The murderer himself?

There was nothing in that hideous mess of mute humanity to tell me what I wanted so desperately to know. If this were truly Martin Lampe, his identity had disappeared for ever.

'The medical officer will be coming to inspect them later this morning,' Stadtschen rambled on at my back. 'The innards of this one have begun to putrefy already. That other fellow doesn't look too good, either. The quicker they're in the ground, the better, sir, in my opinion. I should report this to the doctor.'

I could have ordered snow and ice to be carried down there, as Professor Kant had done in his effort to preserve Lawyer Tifferch for Doctor Vigilantius and myself to see, but the corpse was too far gone for physical recognition.

'Before you speak to the doctor,' I said, 'you can do yourself a favour.'

'Sir?'

'You acted out of order, you know that, don't you, Stadtschen?'

He held his breath, waiting for me to continue.

'I ought to mention your impulsive decision to move the remains in my report to the King,' I said, watching him. 'But I may yet be persuaded to change my mind. Find Frau Lampe quickly, and bring her here. The woman lives in Belefest village. She came to see me this morning, saying that her husband had disappeared. I doubt she'll be able to tell us anything, but duty requires it before these men are finally laid to rest. Make sure . . .'

Make sure she recognises him.

That is what I would have liked to say, but I didn't.

'You can count on me,' Stadschen replied with an ingratiating smile and a smart salute.

354

My torch had nearly burnt itself out. The prospect of remaining there without a light prompted me to remove myself quickly. With Stadtschen following hard on my heels, we soon arrived at the main gate. I dismissed him, and was gratified to see him running off in the direction of Belefest.

But the identity of the bones in the charnel house was not my only concern. Nor was the question of finding Martin Lampe, if he were still alive. The King and his report would have to wait until I returned.

'Take me to Magisterstrasse,' I shouted to the driver as I jumped aboard the waiting coach. 'As fast as you can go.'

Chapter 33

I had been so busily engaged the previous afternoon and night that I had hardly given a further thought to Professor Kant. Indeed, I did not realise just how long it had been since I had seen him, nor how tired I was, until I leaned my head back against the comfortable bench of the coach and gave myself up to the swaying rhythm of the vehicle, soon drifting into what must have been a sound sleep.

I sat up with a start as the vehicle drew up before the house in Magisterstrasse. And another alarm bell began to ring in my head when I glanced out of the window. The young Italian doctor that I had met the previous day was running up the garden path towards the door, and he was clutching a large brown medicine bottle in his hands.

I leapt down from the carriage, and hurried to reach the porch before Johannes Odum could close the door.

'What's the matter?' I panted.

'It's my master, sir,' the servant cried, the tears starting from his red-rimmed eyes. 'He's barely conscious. Doctor's been to fetch a cordial.'

I pushed past him, and flew up the stairs to Kant's bedchamber.

As soon as I entered the room, I saw that I had come too late. The tiny, shrivelled creature lying on the bed had already set one foot in the next world. Immanuel Kant's once-delicate face seemed to have turned in upon itself, his cheeks were two great, gaunt hollows, his closed and sunken eyes resting inside deep dark pits. His narrow shoulders protruded through the cotton sheet, like wings flanking his ears. His breathing was loud and regular, but he did not look like a man who was taking his rest. It was the beginning of a sleep from which he would never wake.

Herr Jachmann stood with bowed head on the far side of the room, while Doctor Gioacchini ministered to Professor Kant, gently prising his lips apart and spooning a dark green liquid into his mouth. I took a step closer to the foot of the narow bed. The doctor glanced over his shoulder and nodded quickly to me, then he turned back, concentrating all his attention once again on his patient.

Some minutes passed in silence, then a cry escaped from the physician's lips.

'Herr Professor!'

Kant had opened his eyes. He was staring fixedly at me.

The doctor dropped his head to the philosopher's breast, and listened to the feeble beating of the patient's heart. Moving his ear closer to Kant's gaping mouth, he suddenly looked up at me with a bewildered expression on his face.

'Professor Kant wishes to speak to you,' he whispered, raising his watch, counting off the seconds as he measured the dying man's pulse. 'Be quick, sir,' he urged. 'His strength is ebbing fast.'

I drew near and bent over the bed. Fright swept through me in an awful spasm. I had to struggle to control my emotions as the philosopher's eyes closed once again like shutters. He seemed to me to be drifting beyond the realm of physical communication.

'It is I, sir, Hanno Stiffeniis,' I breathed into his ear.

Kant's eyelids did not so much as flicker, his face was a mask of deathly anticipation, a film of perspiration glistening on his broad forehead.

'How long has he been in this state?' I whispered.

'Too long,' the doctor answered.

I turned to the bed once more. Kant's respiration was more regular, though his pale pinched face seemed to have retreated even more deeply into the hollow cavity between his shoulders.

'Professor Kant,' I called, more loudly than before.

Kant's blue eyes opened suddenly wide, and swivelled to look at me. The closeness of death made the orbs appear more pale and transparent than ever. His lips gaped open, then closed again.

357

'Call him back,' Doctor Gioacchini urged at my shoulder.

'Professor Kant, speak to me,' I implored, lowering my ear so close to his pursed lips that my being was filled with the sweet, rotting odour of approaching death. I did not draw back from it. I breathed it in as if it were the purest mountain air. A wild, mystical ecstasy stirred within my craving soul. Immanuel Kant was in his death throes, and his last desire on Earth was to confide in *me*.

My ear grazed his lips. I felt them quiver at my touch.

'Too late . . .' he said in a hushed, strangled expulsion of breath.

'Sir?' I whispered, swallowing hard, my mouth parched and dry.

He sank back on the pillow, the merest trace of a smile on his lips, like a wisp of cloud in a blue summer sky.

'The killer has not been caught yet,' I began to say, then instantly regretted it.

With a display of strength I could hardly believe possible in that weak state, Kant shook his head slowly from side to side, his eyes staring fixedly into my own.

'But he *will* be stopped,' I added.

The ghost of that body down in the charnel house rose up before me, as if I had called to it. I wanted to reassure Professor Kant that all was well, inform him that the murderer had been defeated, announce that the avenging hand of God had found the killer out, and struck him down as he deserved. But I did not. I could not. Perhaps I never would be allowed to tell him. Time was pressing hard, the sands were running out. Immanuel Kant was, I believed, beyond hearing, beyond hope, beyond pain or any sentient feeling.

'You were right,' he wheezed suddenly.

I held my breath as he continued.

'You saw the truth in Paris. Then, your brother . . .'

I was robbed of the power of sensible speech. I wanted to run away from that room, to escape from that dying man and the implications of what he was saying. But I was caught, unhinged, helpless.

'You watched him die,' he continued, each word a conquest, each pause a march to a mountain top. 'That's why I sent for you, Hanno . . . You have been inside the mind of a murde–'

He sank back exhausted. The air rushed out of his lungs in a long, whistling diminuendo, like a grace-note fading in an organ pipe.

'His mind is drifting,' Doctor Gioacchini murmured, placing his hand on my shoulder and squeezing it hard as an enigmatic smile began slowly to form itself on Kant's bloodless lips.

With a sudden yawning gasp, Immanuel Kant pronounced with crystal clarity the final phrase of his earthly existence. Everyone present heard the declaration. Herr Jachmann faithfully recorded it in his written memorial of the event which was published some months later.

'*Es . . . ist . . . gut.*'

He repeated the phrase again and again, his lips moving soundlessly now, as a heavy burden seemed to fall away from his body in a gentle ripple. Then, he moved no more.

I stood transfixed.

Immanuel Kant was dead.

Beyond the window, grey day surrendered slowly to the onset of dusk, heralding the coming of the night. There was something portentous and fitting in the rotation. My mind was a blank. Some moments later, when I came to myself, I was wailing aloud, clasping my spiritual master's ice-cold hand in mine. In that instant, the horrid nightmare of those frantic days dissolved away. It might all have been nothing worse than a bleak and terrifying dream. I had no thoughts for Martin Lampe, nor for any other creature on the face of the Earth. No space survived for anything, except the tiny corpse stretched out lifeless on the bed before me and the mystery of the words that Professor Kant had murmured as he died.

Es ist gut.

What was good?

What good had Kant discovered in the failure of my investigation?

You were right. You saw the truth . . .

In the name of God, what had I ever been right about?

What *truth* had I ever seen?

The image of Immanuel Kant on his deathbed ought to have swept away all other thoughts and considerations, and for a while it did so. I was consumed with sorrow as I drove away from the house, having taken my leave of Johannes Odum, Doctor Gioacchini and Herr Jachmann. But as I sat alone in the darkness of the coach, and the wheels turned, and the Fortress drew ever closer and closer, that perplexing, enigmatic smile on the dead man's lips began to trouble me. Indeed, it seemed to overlap and blend and meld with the characterless blank of that *other* enigmatic mask of death, the unknown face of the man whose skull and bones lay rotting in the charnel house.

Could any two deaths be more starkly different?

Professor Kant had died peacefully at home in his bed, surrounded by the love and respect that had accompanied him throughout the course of his long life; the man in the morgue had been torn to shreds by snapping fangs, alone and at night in a deserted wilderness. Infinite pain, infinite terror. No hope of salvation for him. It was as if a legion of demons had been released from Hell by a pitiless Creator for an hour, and on one condition: that they wiped out every single trace of that man's existence. I could imagine no more fitting punishment for a heartless killer.

But was he the killer? Was that man truly Martin Lampe?

I would never rest until I could put a name to that corpse. Resolution of that mystery would signal one of two things – that the desperate hunt for Martin Lampe must continue, or that peace had been restored to Königsberg. In the latter case, the troubled souls of those who had been annihilated by the fury of the killer would be laid to rest, along with their bones.

Then, and only then, I would find peace.

I entered the main gate of the Fortress briskly, intent on going down to the charnel house to take a second look. This time, I determined to go alone, without Stadtschen breathing down my neck. I crossed the courtyard and entered the North Tower without meeting anyone, and soon reached the ogive arch and narrow door which led down to the dungeons. Arming myself with a torch from the wall, I opened the door.

Before passing through, I hesitated on the threshold.

The smell of decay seemed to reach out from below like an effluvial tide to greet and drown me. It was a distillation of human and vegetal decomposition, and a million other age-old odours compounded together beneath the ancient mound of the Fortress. For an instant, I almost turned away. Only the desire to know led me onward, the desperate hope that some vital clue might still be found.

I entered, pulling the door closed behind me, and began to descend the dark staircase by torchlight. But as I went down, and down again, I became aware that another torch was coming up the stairwell towards me. Peering into the depths for some moments, I was at last able to discern two shadowy figures down there in the gloom. I recognised Officer Stadtschen at once. But who was the other person? My heart leapt into my throat. Had I come too late? Had the doctor already given the order for those putrid human remains to be taken out of the charnel house and buried?

I halted, anger and frustration mounting, waiting for Stadtschen to draw near, anxious to hear by his own admission what further damage had been inflicted on my investigation in my absence. But then, as they came within ten steps or so, my heart took a leap and a bound. Dressed in a trailing black shawl, which covered her head and her shoulders, was Frau Lampe, and she seemed to be leaning heavily on the arm of the soldier. For that, if for nothing else, I uttered a word of thanks to the Lord. She had seen the paltry remains, then.

They took a few more steps, then Stadtschen looked up, caught sight of me and stopped in his tracks. The woman raised her tear-filled eyes to mine a second later. Her skin was pale: it seemed to be as transparent as melted wax, paler even than the face of Professor Kant. Her cheeks and mouth were puffy and swollen. Her mournful appearance seemed to confirm what I desired to know above all other things. I almost rejoiced in her sorrow.

She had identified Martin Lampe!

'Frau Lampe?' I called, a chirping note in my voice that I hoped she would not perceive or understand.

The woman sobbed loudly, and looked away, shaking off the supporting arm of Officer Stadtschen, as if I had caught her in an unguarded moment of weakness that she did not wish me to see.

'The body was found on the woodland path that your husband

took,' I said as solemnly as I was able. 'Not much remains, I'm afraid. You must be upset, I am truly sorry . . .'

'Upset, sir?' Despite the expression of distress on her face, her voice was firm. Indeed, there was a stinging, acrimonious tone to it. 'Any soul would be *upset*, Herr Stiffeniis. I pray no other woman will be forced to see what I have had to see.'

I studied her face uncertainly.

'Nothing in that loathsome *thing*,' she hissed at me with barely controlled anger, 'can ever make me think it's Martin. Nothing! I hope the search for him is going on?'

I must have held my breath, for it exploded from me in an audible gasp.

It was not finished, then. Martin Lampe was still free to prey upon the innocent and the unsuspecting, like the beasts that had ripped the unknown man to pieces. Hungry for human life, he was hiding out there somewhere, poised to strike again at any moment.

'Frau Lampe was taken ill, sir,' Stadtschen explained quickly.

I heard the sound of his words, but did not absorb the substance of them. My thoughts were already racing wildly through the dark streets and dank alleyways of Königsberg in pursuit of the killer.

'Those bodies ought to be removed, Herr Procurator,' he added. 'Once I have seen the lady safe upstairs, I'll get the doctor to do something. They are no fit sight for any woman. No man, either. They ought to be interred at once, sir, or we'll have an epidemic on our hands.'

'Very well,' I said sharply. 'Inform the doctor. Take Frau Lampe home. But within the hour, Stadtschen, I want a signed affidavit on my desk to the effect that visual recognition was not possible, given the state of . . . alteration of the body. I will be in my office, waiting. I have a report to write, regarding my investigation. For the King.'

I stared at Stadtschen as I rapped out these final words. I had spared him once, I would not do so again. He had failed me, and I fully intended to tell His Majesty of the stupidity of the officer's actions. By removing that unknown corpse from the woods, he had struck a mortal blow against my investigation, leaving me no possibility of drawing any definite conclusion about the death or the identity of the man who would soon be laid to rest in an unmarked grave.

A look of alarm appeared on Stadtschen's face as he bowed his head, clicked his heels, and told me that he would do exactly as I had told him. Clearly, he had understood the meaning of my threat.

'Please accept my apologies,' I said, turning to the woman, 'for the ordeal which you have been subjected to. Had the bones been *left* where they were found, it might have made identification possible.' I glanced at Stadtschen, adding: 'Whoever is to *blame* will be punished.'

I studied the woman's face.

'I wonder if you know, Frau Lampe . . .'

I stopped. For an instant I had been tempted to inform her of the death of Professor Kant. But only for an instant. I contented myself, instead, by witholding the news. It was a small, meaningless act of spite, but she had just dashed my hopes of identifying Martin Lampe.

'What do you wonder, Herr Stiffeniis?' the woman asked.

'Oh, nothing very important,' I said, turning away and clattering up the stairs.

Given her opinion of the philosopher, she would hear the news and rejoice soon enough.

Chapter 34

I went upstairs to my office, calling for the sentry to come and light the candles as I set foot inside the dark room. The day was drawing on, it was high time for me to begin composing my report for the King. I had already put off the task far longer than I ought to have done, and I still had no real idea how much to tell. Nor how much to conceal. With Professor Kant dead, and the possibility that Martin Lampe was still loose on the streets of Königsberg, exactly *how* should I begin and end?

With deliberation, I picked up the feather quill, primed it full of ink, set the point to the smooth surface of the paper, then remained seated in that position like a statue carved from solid granite for fifteen minutes, or more. I felt the ire and the frustration of a shepherd building up inside me, a shepherd vainly trying to round up his unruly flock without the assistance of a trained dog, or a handy wicket gate in which to corner the skittish animals. Whenever I began to think that I had at last marshalled all my thoughts, some glaring inconsistency would jump up suddenly and slip out of the fold, preventing me from making a start.

The easiest way, I convinced myself at last, would be to report only those facts or events for which I had some corroborating written statement.

'On this, the 12th day in the month of February, 1804,' I began,

I, Hanno Stiffeniis of Lotingen, Assistant Procurator to the Second Circuit of the Judicial Magistrature of the High Court of Prussia, called to investigate the murders of four citizens in the Royal city of Königsberg, do solemnly swear and avow, having almost completed my enquiries, that the declaration which follows is true and incontestable. There is good reason to believe . . .

I paused, dipped my pen in the inkwell again, then let out a loud sigh. No good reason to believe *anything* came to my mind. Indeed, all the tiny pieces of the mosaic that I had managed to assemble led me to believe the very worst. I threw down my pen, pushed back my chair, walked across the room, and stared dismally out of the window. The sky was dark, low clouds driving in from the sea, bringing rain, sleet and probably more snow. I threw open the window for a breath of air, though it was already cold enough inside the room. Down below in the courtyard, soldiers were coming and going noisily. It was six o'clock, time for the changing of the guard. Men who had just come off duty ambled aimlessly up and down, laughing and joking, smoking their long clay pipes, exchanging insults and pleasantries, cat-calling and taunting their unfortunate fellows who were destined to pass the night marching round and round the icy ramparts.

Suddenly, I wished that I were one of them. I wanted to be free of this task, free of the responsibility and the care it had placed on my shoulders. More to the point, I wished that I could be at home in Lotingen, in the company of my wife and my children, idly roasting jacket potatoes before a roaring kitchen fire. Until the report was finished, I reminded myself sharply, there was little hope that I would be going anywhere. Unless I could produce a convincing account of every single thing that had happened in Königsberg, I would be left to rot there in the Fortress. With the unresolved question of Martin Lampe still hanging around my neck, I realised, I might be imprisoned there for a long, long . . .

The noise seemed to come from far away.

I had been so deeply lost in melancholy musing that a pitched battle might have been fought and lost for possession of the Fortress, and I would have known nothing of it.

Someone had been knocking at my door.

The sound was repeated a moment later, followed by a deep

voice that I recognised. 'Herr Stiffeniis, may I enter, sir?'

Officer Stadtschen was at my door. No doubt, he had come to plead for leniency. He could have few illusions about my intentions, little doubt of what I might write in his regard.

'Come back later,' I called out sharply. 'The King must have his report!'

But Stadtschen did not go away. He knocked again, louder this time.

'Herr Procurator, I beg you, sir. This cannot wait.'

I closed the window, strode to the door, my temper flaring into a blazing fire. What alternative did he leave me? I would tell Stadtschen *exactly* what I thought of him. By moving that corpse from the woods, he had ruined my investigation. If I had my way, he would be demoted. I would have liked to see him whipped into the bargain.

I threw the door open, saying: 'Well? What is it?'

He was standing to attention, stiff and straight as a flagpole. He glanced nervously into my face, then raised his hand and held out a sheet of paper.

'The affidavit, sir,' he announced. 'Recognition of the corpse by Frau Lampe, sir. That mark's the sign of the widow.'

'*Widow*?' I blurted out, snatching the paper, reading it greedily.

I hereby swear and affirm that the remains of the body found in the woods near Belefest, which I examined in the Fortress of Königsberg in the presence of an officer, belong to my legal husband, Martin Lampe.

The woman's name had been written out in the same bold letters as the text and the signature of Stadtschen. Frau Lampe had witnessed the contents of the affidavit by making a peculiar slanting cross at the bottom of the page.

'The woman cannot write,' Stadtschen clarified.

I studied his face. 'What holy miracle is this?' I quizzed. 'Frau Lampe was most adamant that it was *not* her husband's body.'

'Darn my breeches, sir!' he exclaimed, quickly begging my pardon for his language before he continued. 'It all came about while I was taking her home. The fact is, when I led her down to the charnel house, the smell was . . . well, sir, you know yourself, it was indescribable. Frau Lampe complained at once of feeling ill, and she asked to be taken out of there, insisting that those dreadful remains could not possibly be her husband's. I could hardly force her to examine the bones, could I, sir? When I met you, Herr Procurator, I was taking her up to the courtyard for a breath of fresh air. I'd have taken her down again immediately, but you ordered me to take the woman home instead, sir.'

'Go on,' I said, beginning to suspect that Stadtschen might have forced the woman to sign the affidavit in the hope of salvaging his own position. 'If she didn't even look at the corpse, what made her change her mind?'

'It happened while we were walking out to Belefest, sir,' he explained. 'I didn't speak again about that body. But I did ask her what distinguishing features to look for if we happened to come across him. Officially, he was missing. He might have lost his memory, been wounded, or even killed. I was wondering whether he had a birthmark, or some other sign on his body to identify him by.'

Stadtschen paused, and a shadow of a smile appeared on his face.

'And he *did*, sir! She told me so herself.'

'What was this sign?' I asked. I might have been a man with a terrible illness who had just been told by an eminent physician that it was easily curable.

'We *saw* it, sir, but we took no notice at the time,' Stadtschen replied. A broader smile broke out on his face, as if he found the situation amusing. 'D'you recall that white strip of bone inside his mouth, Herr Stiffeniis? Remember when I turned the skull over? While serving in the Prussian army forty-odd years ago, Herr Lampe was lightly nicked by an enemy bayonet. It sliced through his bottom lip and ended up slitting the roof of his mouth!'

I remembered only too well. I had taken that jagged scar to be the exposed bone of the palate. I had even induced myself to believe that it had been caused by the fang of one of the wolves that had torn him apart. If Martin Lampe's blood-caked mouth had caused me to quake with revulsion then, it now began to seem like one of the most stupendous sights I had seen in my life.

'I hurried her back with me to town, and we arrived just in time. I searched for you, of course, sir,' he added quickly, scrutinising my face to gauge my reaction, 'but you had gone out. The medical officer had issued death certificates, the pastor had been called to adminster the last rites, the graves for him and the other man had already been dug. Another five minutes would have complicated matters. I explained the necessity to the doctor, and he made certain that she examined the skull and saw the scar, though wrapped up in a cloth. It was painless enough, and she identified him. I took her to the office, wrote out the affidavit, read it through to her, and she made her cross. As I said before, sir, Frau Lampe is now a widow.'

I looked away and closed my eyes for a moment.

Königsberg is safe, I marvelled. *My task is over.*

'This is excellent work, Officer Stadtschen,' I said warmly. 'I can now discount this corpse in writing my report. The part that you have played will appear in a more positive light.'

Though his face was stern and composed, I thought I saw a twinkle in his eyes. 'God bless you, sir,' he murmured.

God had already been extremely good to me that day, I realised. Better by far than I deserved. The killer not only had a name, but his corpse had been identified beyond a shadow of a doubt. I closed the door quietly, and sat down to work again. This time, I was brimming with confidence. Divine Providence was pushing me forward with both hands.

'The King shall have his report!' I announced to the empty room.

A triumphant proclamation of success was what I had always hoped to write. A triumphant proclamation of success was what the King would have. Picking up the quill again, I continued with all the artistry of an inspired poet.

There is good reason to believe that the authors of the crimes have been identified as Ulrich Totz, innkeeper of this city, and his wife, Gertrude Totz (née Sonner). By their own frank admission, the miscreants declared that their tavern and

*lodging-house, named 'The Baltic Whaler', was a notorious
meeting-place for Bonapartist sympathisers and for sundry
other rebels. Their intention was to foment chaos in the city
and prepare the way for a military invasion by the French
armies under the command of Napoleon Bonaparte. These
heinous crimes of murder and terrorisation of the population
began, as Your Highness well knows, in January, 1803 . . .*

I stroked my chin for some moments with the feathered quill,
then added more in the same colourful vein:

*. . . and they were perpetrated with the assistance and the
material connivance of a woman of their acquaintance, Anna
Rostova, a known prostitute, dabbler in black magic, and
practitioner of illegal abortions, by her own admission under
unforced questioning. It was not possible fully to ascertain the
precise ideological scope of their rebellious intentions – there
may, indeed, be no formal connection with any foreign state,
nor any invasion planned as a direct consequence of their
actions.*

    *Both Totz and his wife, having admitted their Jacobin
sentiments and their complicity in the murders, including the
slaughter of their own nephew, Morik Lüthe, committed suicide
despite strict surveillance while in prison. The lifeless body of
Anna Rostova was found three days afterwards in the River
Pregel. It remains unclear whether a suicide pact had been
agreed within the group, whether Anna Rostova had threatened
to betray her fellow conspirators and then been punished for
her treachery, or whether some other unknown person, possibly
unconnected with the group, was responsible for her drowning.
No arrest has been made with regard to this incident, though
enquiries are being made to clarify the question. Circumstances
suggest that the remaining members of the terrorist group, three
foreign infiltrators who were lodging at 'The Baltic Whaler', are
in flight. They are no longer to be found in Königsberg, but
warrants have been issued for their arrest. The names of the
three wanted persons, together with all pertinent documents,*

including transcripts of the interrogations, reports of the searches, case notes, etc., etc., are contained in the official case file, number 7–8/1804. With the diaspora of the terrorist cell, we may safely conclude that the spate of murders in Königsberg, together with the consequent risk of internal disorders, has been brought to a definitive conclusion.

I beg leave to take this opportunity to testify to the courage and selfless devotion to his duty of the public official and clerk of police, Amadeus Koch, my chosen assistant, who was the final victim of these desperate conspirators. Without Sergeant Koch's constant and devoted attendance on my person, and his most valuable insights into the workings of the criminal underworld in the city (and the deviancy of the criminal mind in general), the onerous task of identifying the perpetrators would have been one thousand times harder. The murderer of Herr Koch is, in all probability, another member of the Jacobin crew who frequented the inn run by Herr and Frau Totz. The place was a hotbed of treason and conspiracy, as material evidence found there suggests. I contend that following the deaths of the major protagonists, the Totzes and Anna Rostova, Koch was struck down by an unknown hand with the precise intention of confusing the police enquiry into the earlier deaths and lending weight to the misguided conviction expressed by my esteemed predecessor, Procurator Rhunken, that the string of murders was the work of one man alone, a man self-evidently possessed of insane and murderous instincts.

I also wish to express my gratitude to the late Herr Professor Immanuel Kant. The city of Königsberg owes him a debt beyond estimate in terms of his absolute dedication to the resolution of these crimes and the restitution of peace to the city which he loved above all others on earth. The sagacity of Your Royal Highness is known to one and all; I am certain that You, Sire, will appreciate the importance of work undertaken without any financial assistance or material encouragement from the local authorities by this most noble Professor of Philosophy in proposing and actuating a system of logical and analytical police investigation which will be inscribed in the annals of criminal history, not in this particular instance alone, but in every future attempt to counteract the social consequences of a violent crime and bring the culprits to fitting Retribution and Justice. I swear to advocate and disseminate the methods I have learned from Herr Professor Kant in my future career as a magistrate, certain of the fact that the inventor would have granted me permission to do so. I humbly suggest that Herr Professor Kant's revolutionary method be adopted immediately by the competent police authorities throughout Prussia and published at State expense for the benefit of Mankind. It would be a fitting memorial to a great Prussian.

Thus, swearing my allegiance to the Crown of Hohenzollern, and to Your Most Royal Person, I beg leave to return to Lotingen and my family, and take up once again the magisterial position that I was so suddenly called upon to vacate.

Your most humble and obedient servant,

Hanno Stiffeniis, Procurator

PS: Valuable assistance was provided by Officer Stadtschen of the Königsberg garrison. I recommend him for advancement.

I read through what I had written more than once, then made a copy of the document for the benefit of General Katowice without changing a single comma. By the time I set down my pen and sat back in my chair to ease the aching muscles in my spine and neck, the fiction had acquired the high polish of Truth. Indeed, it *was* the Truth. The Truth as I would tell it to my wife, my children, and my grandchildren after them. It was *The Truth* as all the World would know it.

I folded the report and the duplicate, sealing them with a lighted candle, red wax and my ring of office. As I did so, I told myself that I had been guided by the Lord, our God. *He* had brought me to Königsberg, *He* had led me to Immanuel Kant. *He* had induced me to insist that Sergeant Koch take my cloak. In His infinite wisdom, it seemed to me, *He* had declared that Koch should die for one cause, and that I should survive for another. The Lord had brought me to the conclusion of the affair, and *He* had suggested the epilogue that I should write. As I pressed my seal-ring into the hot red wax, I felt *His* heavy hand pressing down upon it. My own hand was the instrument, nothing more.

I set the seal down on the table-top to cool, blew out the flickering candle, and called for a gendarme. Having entrusted my despatches to his charge, I glanced at my watch, then retired to my bedroom. I just had time to wash and change my shirt, then I went down to attend to the burial of Amadeus Koch, which was scheduled to take place in the military cemetery at the rear of the chapel at nine o'clock.

No other mourner but myself was present as the plain wooden casket containing the body was lowered into the cold ground by four squaddies. I offered a silent prayer for the generous soul of Sergeant Koch. His sacrifice had led me directly to the killer. No other words were spoken. None was needed, except for those solemnly pronounced in prayer by the military chaplain.

As I replaced my hat and turned away, the sound of earth crashing down upon the bare wooden coffin, I halted for a moment. Had I done the right thing? After all, Merete Koch was buried somewhere in the city. Perhaps I should have made more careful enquiries before ordering Sergeant Koch's interment inside the walls of the Fortress? They had been partners in Life, they should comfort each other in Death.

But for that single detail, the affair in Königsberg was truly over.

Within two hours, I had packed my travelling-bag and boarded the same state coach that had brought me to the city in the company of Amadeus Koch. There was no 'starry sky' above my head to induce awe and wonder, as Immanuel Kant's most famous epigram declares. There had been a brief snowfall as Sergeant Koch was buried, but the louring sky overhead was now a leaden, pitch-black sheet. It weighed down mercilessly on the city of Königsberg and the irrefutable Truth that I had left behind me, as I thought, for ever.

Chapter 35

The weather went from bad to worse, and Immanuel Kant remained unburied for sixteen days. The earth had frozen so solid, no grave could be dug for him. Day after day, exposed to public view in the University Cathedral in Königsberg, the body withered and shrank. It had begun to look so fearfully like a skeleton, the local newspaper hinted, the city fathers were praying desperately for a break in the weather.

Back home in Lotingen, I threw myself into work. Hard labour should have been the best medicine for my ills, but I made little progress on those cases that had accumulated in my absence. I sat for hour after hour, staring at the repetitive flowery patterns on the walls of my office, or shuffling idly through the papers on my desk at home. The only solace that I could find was in my family. Helena revealed her loving care in a thousand looks and kind gestures. And her gentlest stratagem to ease my pain simply could not be ignored: I mean my beloved little ones. My wife saw to it that we were much together, far more than I had ever permitted before I went away. She was quick to curb the excitement the children showed after my absence, firm in tempering the unexpected freedom they now enjoyed before it got out of hand.

One morning, Helena came bustling into my study with a fresh copy of the *Königsbergische Monatsschrift* in her hand. 'It was as if the Earth refused to take him,' she said, as she lay the news-sheet down on the desk. There had been a heavy rainfall and a sudden thaw, the headlines announced: the burial service for Professor Kant would take place the following day at one o'clock. I read the article carefully, and turned to make some comment to my wife.

'Go to Königsberg, Hanno. See his soul laid to rest,' she said, her voice soft, yet so determined that I was left with little choice in the matter. She might have been comforting one of the children after a painful fall.

Though I had decided in my own mind never again to set foot in Königsberg, at dawn the following morning, dressed in a black suit and overcoat, a new black silk band pinned to the rim of my day-hat, I boarded the mail-coach. There were no other passengers, and I was glad that I would not be obliged to engage in conversation that I felt disinclined to sustain. I sat in splendid isolation, recalling with a heavy heart the last time that I had made the journey, in the company of Amadeus Koch.

The coach arrived at midday, and I made my way directly to the house in Magisterstrasse, where Professor Kant's mortal remains had been removed the previous day. The mass of common people jostling for a vantage point out in the narrow street, and the constant arrival of other persons more closely associated with the philosopher, made the lane seem more like a bustling cattle market than the haven of peace it had been in Kant's lifetime.

Passing in through the garden gate, I was swept up in a rushing sea of mourners, propelled along on the crest of a tidal wave by a large group of students in the academic robes of the Collegium Fridericianum who had come to pay their last respects. In the dining room a lavish oak coffin had been set up on a catafalque surrounded by ivy wreaths, and decorated with elaborate floral arrangements. The coffin lid stood propped against the wall, and I removed my hat in silent tribute to the remains of the philosopher lying there in state. A stark death's head stared up at me, the same enigmatic smile that I remembered written on the rose-painted lips. Neither Death nor the embalmer had been able to wipe it away.

'All is just as he would have wished,' a voice murmured close by my ear, and Herr Jachmann offered me his black-gloved hand. 'You left the town in such a fret, Stiffeniis,' he said. 'I was not certain that I would find you here today.'

'I had to come,' I said, the expression catching in my throat as the wooden lid was taken up, and the carpenter began to bolt it into place.

We watched in silence as six students hoisted the coffin aloft and carried it from the room to the street. Jachmann led me towards the front row of the endless column of mourners lining up behind a black carriage pulled by four black horses. The coffin was fixed securely in its place, the floral tributes and wreaths arranged all around it, then the cortège began to move slowly forward. The procession wound its way through the streets of Königsberg, which were lined on either side with silent crowds.

The University Cathedral was brightly lit by thousands of candles. A muted organ played solemn passages from Buxtehude while the invited mourners and city authorities took their places in the pews reserved for them. Johannes Odum was among them, Frau Mendelssohn and Doctor Gioacchini also. I sat myself down a few rows further back and sorrow swept over me in shuddering waves. I cannot say how long I remained in this distraught state, when my attention was distracted by a woman sitting in the pew in front of mine. As she removed her black scarf to settle it more comfortably on her head, I recognised her. She looked back over her shoulder and held my gaze for an instant.

It was Frau Lampe.

I had not thought for one instant to meet the widow at the funeral of the man she held responsible for all the woes of her husband. What was she doing there? I mulled the question over for some time without finding any answer, then turned my attention back to the memorial service, which was destined to last for another two hours. Herr Jachmann was one of many speakers sounding platitudes, which are as inevitable at a funeral as Death itself. When, at last, no more remained to be said, and no one remained to say it, the coffin-bearers came forward, the casket was taken up again on their young shoulders, and it was carried slowly from the church.

I stepped into the aisle to follow, but Frau Lampe stood blocking my exit, her dark eyes fixed in mine.

'I hoped to find you here, sir,' she said. 'I'd not have come otherwise. Would you have me pay my respects to the creature in that box?'

I made to move around her, but she refused to shift or give ground.

'I have something that you will want to see,' she whispered fiercely, drawing a slim leather document-case from under her cloak.

'Whatever it is,' I said coldly, 'give it to the local police. My jurisdiction here is ended.'

She turned her head, glanced towards the altar, then back to me.

'You were a friend of his,' she said and pursed her lips. 'I think that you should have it, sir.'

I looked down at what she was handing to me.

'I found it some days ago. The book they were working on.'

I studied the woman's face for a moment. She was not stupid by any means. Did she truly not know what her husband had done? Had she never suspected?

'I've taken up too much of your time,' she said quickly.

Thrusting the package into my hand, she turned and ran from the church.

I grasped the unexpected gift to my chest with the same surge of burning excitement that I experienced when the wet-nurse handed me my first-born child. Immanuel Kant's philosophical testament . . . He himself had hinted that it would change the entire course of Moral Philosophy. Falling down on my knees, I uttered my thanks to Almighty God for His immense generosity. I had been chosen as His instrument to exalt the incomparable greatness of the late Immanuel Kant.

I rushed from the cathedral and pushed through the milling throng in the churchyard, not caring about the people I elbowed roughly out of my way. The air was cold, but I was hot with agitation. Herr Jachmann's voice called out my name, but I looked the other way and fought against the high tide of people flooding into the burial ground from the street. And all the while I clutched that precious packet to my heart like Moses carrying the sacred tablets down from the Heights of Sinai.

In the relative quiet of the avenue, I stopped to catch my breath. Where could I read without fear of being disturbed? For a single, guilty moment, my blood froze at the immensity of the greed which consumed me. My only desire was to be alone with Kant's papers.

Why, in the name of all that was sacred, did I not go directly to Herr Jachmann and the other intimates of Professor Kant and tell them the wondrous news? Why did I avoid them all as if they threatened to carry off the priceless treasure that Frau Lampe had placed in my hands? The truth was that I had no intention of sharing the philosopher's last unpublished thoughts with any other living person. Somehow, I felt that Kant intended the words he had dictated to Martin Lampe for me, and no one else. The valet and I were blood brothers in our arrogance.

Further down the street there was a coffee house. It was crowded with university students as a rule, but they would all be at the funeral. Glancing in at the window, I saw that the place was deserted. I went in, sat down at a table in the far corner, and asked for a glass of hot chocolate to justify my presence there. As soon as the beverage arrived and the waiter turned away, I pulled that manuscript from under my cloak like a thief bent on examining his booty.

The leaves were held together with a soiled red ribbon. Sifting through, I noticed that the ink in places was caked with sand which should have dried it. There was no title. No author's name appeared on the cover. Opening the text at the first page, I recognised the writing immediately. The words were strung out in wavering, uneven lines, the letters ugly, childlike both in size and shape. I had seen that script in the autograph book of Roland Lutbatz. The same perplexing thought returned to my mind: what dire necessity had driven Professor Kant to entrust his final thoughts to such an unlikely amanuensis?

As I began to read the opening paragraphs, I began to realise just how jealous I was of Martin Lampe. Kant reiterated his fundamental thesis that the moral nature of duty makes human behaviour subject to universal laws which are based on the precepts of Rationality. All action should strive, he averred, towards a Common Good which represents true Freedom. Despite the valet's

377

dreadful handwriting, I could not fail to recognise the inimitable voice of Immanuel Kant, the purposeful exposition of the rigorous concepts of moral philosophy that he had first expressed in the *Foundations of the Metaphysics of Behaviour*, before expanding them into the monolithic moral code of the *Critique of Practical Reason*.

I cannot say at which point uneasiness began to creep up on me. The fact was that I began to feel increasingly uncomfortable as I read on. The author seemed, somehow, to have veered off the old, familiar path. Suddenly, I found myself lost in a terrain which I did not recognise. Scanning the lines ahead, looking for solid ground on which to rest, I searched for an idea or a concept that I could safely identify as Kant's. Had Frau Lampe made a mistake? Was the document not what she had presumed it to be? There was something so rough and ready about the writing, far removed from the refinement of thought and elegance of expression that one habitually associated with Immanuel Kant. Even so, what I was reading was, somehow, very familiar . . .

I sat back and sipped hot chocolate, trying to gather my thoughts and concentrate my attention. Naturally, I had been upset by the funeral. I glanced around the coffee house and noticed that the empty tables were beginning to fill up. People were coming in from the cold, the service must have ended. Fortunately, I recognised no one, and no one appeared to know me. I drank the remains of my beverage, and called for another cup. The landlord brought a long-necked pot of piping hot chocolate across to my table, and we exchanged a few words about the weather and the magnificent funeral. No other topics were worthy of interest in Königsberg that day. But then, as soon as I decently could, I returned to my reading, struggling with difficulty through another page. And another, until I reached page four. Halfway down.

Oh, God!

My heart throbbed painfully.

I closed my eyes, hoping that everything would be different when I opened them again. Was this the true substance of Hell? Not burning flames, the eternal agony of unbearable pain, but a shadow world where holy angels suddenly threw off their cherubic masks and glistening diaphanous wings to reveal the hideous reality hidden beneath? Heavenly choirs chanting blasphemous rhymes in unified harmony, and making obscene gestures while they sang?

The philosophical testament of Professor Immanuel Kant, written out in the clumsy hand of Martin Lampe, expressed my own words.

The words that I had spoken in private to Kant, seven years before . . .

Chapter 36

The memory of that day seven years before came flooding back, tormenting in its clarity.

'Walk me around the Fortress, Stiffeniis,' Immanuel Kant suggested, as soon as the plates were cleared away after lunch.

'In such dreadful weather?' Herr Jachmann objected, a worried expression plainly written on his face.

Professor Kant chose pointedly to ignore the warning of his friend as we donned our coats and scarves. Out in the lane, the fog was as thick and heavy as a damp towel, and Kant caught hold of my arm immediately.

'You lead, Stiffeniis. I will follow,' he said.

He seemed to suggest that something more than youth and strength were expected of me. As I closed the gate, I spotted Herr Jachmann peeping anxiously from behind the curtains, but the fog was like a living thing. Kant and I walked straight into its gaping maw, and were swallowed up in one gulp.

As we pressed forward, I began to prattle nervously about the previous summer which I had spent in Italy. I told him of the relentless sun, the welcome cool as the autumn came on, the cold dampness of winter as I began my journey homeward through France, my preference for the dry cold of our own mountains.

Kant suddenly halted.

'Enough of the weather!' he snapped. I could barely see him in the faltering light. His deathly pale face seemed to blur in and out of focus, like an ectoplasm struggling to materialise. 'One human experience is equal to the power of Nature, you said during lunch. The most diabolical of them all. Murder without a motive. *Cold-*

blooded murder. What did you mean, Stiffeniis?'

I hesitated before replying. But I had come to Königsberg for that purpose, and for no other. I told him quickly what I had witnessed on a cold, grey morning not two months before. Intoxicated by Enlightened ideals, curious to see how the revolutionaries would deal with the monarch that they now disowned, I broke off my homeward journey in Paris. On 2 January 1793, I was standing in Place de la Revolution when Louis XVI mounted the steps to the guillotine. I had never seen a person put to death before, and I watched in thrall as the King knelt down before that fatal instrument. As the gleaming metal triangle was drawn up, drums rolled thunderously. Their thumping matched the clamour of my heart.

'I stared into the Devil's eyes,' I told Kant, melodramatically, perhaps, 'and the Devil stared back. The blade fell with a loud screech, stopped with a sickening crunch, and the whole of my being was invaded by the smell of blood.

'I inhaled the salty tang as if it were frankincense. I drank in each spasm of that body as the severed head bounced into a waiting basket. The simplicity of the action: a lever shifted, a life was gone. It was the essence of Cause and Effect. So quick, so devastating, so final. I wanted to see it happen again, and again . . .'

A monster had risen up from the depths of the rational person that I had always thought myself to be. This *Doppelgänger* had a taste for death and the wild euphoria it brought. I tried to evoke the sensation for Kant in a word I thought that he would relish. 'The experience was *Sublime*,' I confided. 'I was ravished by it, sir. My mind was petrified, my soul was thrilled.'

There! Finally, I had said it.

Professor Kant was silent for some moments.

'There's more, isn't there?' he said suddenly. 'Why speak of murder *without* a motive? The people of Paris had reason enough to kill the King. You have something more to tell me.'

He seemed to be looking through me.

'Indeed, there is,' I admitted. 'I brought the madness home with me. A month ago my brother died . . .'

What Kant said next was pronounced in the same polite tone

with which, not an hour before, he had asked me whether I preferred my bread with butter, or without.

'Did you murder him?'

Even in my shocked state, I was aware of the lack of emotion in his voice. He had made the connection that I had feared to make for myself, yet he showed no horror, no revulsion at the thought. It was simply a question that needed to be asked.

'Stefan was discharged from the army a year ago,' I hastened to explain. 'He was voted the best cadet at the Academy, the son my father craved. The very opposite of my own moody character. But Stefan was sick. He had begun to fall down in a death-faint for no apparent reason. The sweetness of his urine was the cause. Only honey could revive him. If naught were done to help, the doctors warned, his life was in danger. Everyone in the house knew of it. The servants had all been instructed what to do if a fit came on. A pot of honey and a spoon had been positioned in every room. If Stefan were pale, sweating, confused in speech or behaviour, we must give him honey. He was prohibited from leaving the house unless he took a corked vial in his pocket.'

I paused, expecting some reaction from Professor Kant, but he remained silent, watchful, a pale shadow in the swirling fog.

'When I returned,' I went on, 'the turbulence I had felt in Paris was still inside me, like a poisonous, invisible dart. I dared tell no one. Only Stefan, my brother. He listened to me in silence. He did not judge or criticise, but stared unflinching into my eyes. Then, some days later, out of the blue, he challenged me to do what Father had warned us never to do again.'

'And what was that?' asked Kant, tiring, perhaps, of my narration.

'There is a rocky outcrop near the house called the Richtergade. When we were little children, sir, a race to the top was our favourite sport. I ought, nay, I *should* have refused the dare, but I did not. He egged me on, he provoked me. Stefan had proposed a distraction, a *divertissement*, a game, which I enthusiastically embraced. Physical, exhausting activity would take my mind off the problems which bore down on me. I did not think of him, except to remind him to take a glass of honey in his pocket. He answered with a quick nod, then off we went. It was cold, a good day for a climb, and I was the first to stand on the summit of the rocky mound. I had never ever won the race before. Standing on the brink, facing into the wind, the rush of elements subdued the storm within me. I yearned to tell Stefan of my exhilaration. I wished to thank him. But then I heard him panting as he struggled to grasp the rocky ledge below me. Looking down, I . . . I froze once more in the face of Death. Froth bubbled from his lips, his eyes rolled back, his muscles quivered as he tried to speak. His tongue was a balled fist. His nails scraped and slithered on the damp stone. A battle was being fought before my eyes, but it might have been a . . . a scientific experiment. Stefan slipped, fell back into the void. And what did *I* do? I did nothing. Nothing at all. I watched him fall to his death. Stumbling down from the heights at last, my mind in a turmoil, I found his lifeless body stretched out on the grass. A sharp rock, like an angry beast, had bitten a chunk out of his head as he fell. Blood and tissue spattered that mossy bank.

'That evening, my father stormed into my room. In his hand he held a golden vial of honey. "I found this in *your* pocket," he accused. The expression on his face is engraved in my memory. "Why did you not save your brother?" it seemed to say. Perhaps he had found the honey in a different jacket from the one I wore that day. I cannot say. I swear to you, I had taken no honey along with me. At least, I do not remember doing so.

'He did not call me a murderer. That was the last word my mother spoke before she died. She lay in bed like a statue for weeks after Stefan's death, her glassy eyes staring at nothing. She turned to me at the instant of her death and made an accusation that no faithful son should have to bear. I was allowed to attend her burial, then Father ordered me to leave the house, never to return.'

I paused to catch my breath.

'At the funeral, a friend of my father's spoke of you, Professor Kant. He told me that the moral dictates of Reason are far stronger than the sentimental impulses of Man. I *had* to speak with you, sir. I felt that you might understand. I hoped that Philosophy would rescue me. That's why I came today,' I explained. 'And so, at the end of the lesson, I made my way to your desk, saying . . .'

'"I have been bewitched by Death."' Kant finished the sentence for me. He leaned close and peered into my face, a craving curiosity burning in his eyes.

'Am I a murderer, sir?' I asked.

I might have been standing before God, waiting for supreme judgement, but Kant was silent for some time.

'It was your brother who issued the challenge,' he said quietly at last. 'He knew the risks better than you. Let us say that you picked up the honey mechanically, without thinking. In that case, you really did not know it was in your pocket. Your brother, on the other hand, took for granted that he had done as he always did, whenever he left the house. But he had not done so. The mind plays strange tricks,' he observed with a smile, tapping his forehead with his finger. 'Have you never noticed? Sometimes there is a forgetful blank where habits are concerned. We forget to do the most obvious things, vital as those things may be.'

'A blank, sir? But I stood watching. Why didn't I try to save him?'

'I would guess, Stiffeniis, that you were so unnerved by what was happening that you failed to react. Immobilised by fright, there was no one else to help. You take the burden of his death upon yourself, but this is only half the picture. The same thing might have happened, there or in some other place, whether you were present or not. He was ill, as you said.'

'I was *there*,' I repeated obstinately.

'Unfortunately, yes,' Kant replied soothingly. 'And in a very odd state of mind after what you had seen in Paris, I imagine. You were still haunted by the decapitation of the King when your brother's death occurred. Death commands us all. Horror does possess us. Sublime terror calls forth,' he hesitated, searching for an expression, 'a most *peculiar* state of mind, a mental condition for which I can find no better term . . .'

He paused and stared distractedly at the ground, as if he were searching for a word or concept that stubbornly refused to unbend and make itself known even to his penetrating mind.

'What must I do?' I pleaded, waiting for his verdict.

What Professor Kant said was destined to change my life.

'You've been inside the mind of a murderer, Hanno. You have harboured thoughts that few men would dare to admit. You are *not* alone! And the knowledge makes you special. Now, you must turn it to good account,' he replied warmly.

'But how, sir? How?'

As he spoke, his words settled on my troubled spirit like a healing balm.

'Bring order where crime brings chaos. Right wrongs. Study the law.'

Two weeks later, I enrolled at the University of Halle as a student of Jurisprudence. Five years afterwards, my bachelor's degree confirmed, I began my working career as a magistrate. Accompanied by Helena Jordaenssen, my wife of seven months, I started out in the country town of Lotingen. It was a quiet, regular sort of life, but I enjoyed the drab anonymity of it. I was not called upon to judge and punish, so much as to officiate. But I had only partly followed Kant's advice. Violent crimes being unknown in the town, I had never been truly called upon to test myself.

Until the day that Sergeant Koch entered my office.

I looked down at the page and read what Kant had dictated to Lampe.

The laws of Nature are turned upside down in the exercise of God-like power over another human being. Cold-blooded murder opens the doorway to the Sublime. It is an apotheosis without equal . . .

The question presented itself to my mind with the force of a hammer blow. Had Professor Kant been infected by the insanity that he had meant to cure in me? Had I opened a barred path and handed him the Golden Apple of forbidden knowledge which lay at the end? Kant's philosophy had been foundering on a reef, and I had unwittingly thrown him a lifeline. Had he found, in his declining years, the pathway to Absolute Freedom which the exercise of rational discipline and logical disputation had denied him? Just before the body of Sergeant Koch was found, Kant had been feverish, his voice hoarse with passion.

'They cannot imagine what *I* have been able to conceive,' he had raged. He had been talking of his detractors, the Romantic philosophers, the high priests of *Sturm und Drang*. 'They cannot begin to know what *I* . . .'

I completed the sentence for him.

They cannot begin to know what I have done with your help, Stiffeniis.

This thought erupted in my mind like red-hot magma exploding from an uncapped volcano. Had Immanuel Kant sown the evil seed in the mind of his valet with that book, dictating night after night, knowing that Lampe would take him at his word? Had Kant knowingly created a murderous Golem in his valet, then set him loose on Königsberg?

If Kant knew . . .

Jan Konnen, Paula-Anne Brunner, Johann Gottfried Haase, and Jeronimus Tifferch were his victims. He had provoked the humiliation that led to the death of Procurator Rhunken, he had precipitated the murder of the serving-boy, Morik, driven the Totzes to suicide, pushed Anna Rostova beyond the pale, and made Lublinsky's soul as monstrous as his face. The lives of Frau Tifferch and her embittered maid would be forever blighted by his meddling. Like those of everyone who had known or loved the murdered ones. The city and the people of Königsberg had been entangled in the web of terror that Kant had woven so artfully.

And he had killed Koch. My faithful, stolid adjutant. Humble servant of the State and of myself. Sergeant Koch had found nothing safe in Kantian philosophy, nothing reassuring in Professor Kant himself. Koch had sensed the sinister nature of Kant's involvement in the case, detected evil in that laboratory, while I had been overwhelmed with admiration.

If Kant knew . . .

He had chosen me for one reason alone. I had been inside the mind of a murderer. He had said it himself. He had chosen *me* – not Herr Procurator Rhunken, or any more expert magistrate – to admire the infernal beauty of his final philosophical thesis. The sublime expression of will, the act that went beyond Logic or Reason, Good or Evil:

murder without a motive. The moment when a man is free, unchained from the claims of morality. Like Nature. Or like God. When I insisted on the need for logical proof, credible explanation, when I *failed* to understand what he intended me to see, Kant had opened the door and sent me out to be murdered with his own cloak on my shoulders. But Koch had stepped in the way. He had taken the fatal blow that was meant for me.

If Kant knew . . .

He had not been interested in the man I had become, a diligent magistrate with a wife and two babes from tranquil Lotingen, when he summoned me to him. He had appealed, instead, to a confused and troubled creature he had met only once before, spattered with blood as a king was butchered before his eyes in Paris, a morose individual who had watched his own brother die, a fool who had unwittingly revealed to him the darkest secret of the human soul as they walked together through the fog one cold afternoon beneath the Fortress of Königsberg. By entrusting that case into my hands, Professor Kant had intended to exhume the demon that he had met seven years before.

And during those days in Königsberg, I thought with a violent shudder, had he not almost succeeded in calling up that ghost?

Those heads in jars had thrilled me more than I had dared to admit. Was it science alone that fascinated me? Had I felt no shiver of excitement as I examined the frozen corpse of Lawyer Tifferch? The split skull of Morik? As I smashed my fist into the bloated face of Gerta Totz and gazed on the bloody mask of her husband's self-destruction? I had embraced the idea of torture too warmly when the occasion presented itself, despite Koch's warning. Augustus Vigilantius had poked a gaping hole in my shallow veneer of normality at our first meeting. Then Anna Rostova had bowed before my dark *animus*, recognising a fellow traveller, a nature perverse and damned like her own. I cannot deny that I had been aroused by her murderous carnality . . .

I closed my eyes in shame.

But a protest bubbled up from the depths of my heart.

No! I had done it all to catch a murderer. I had used Kant's laboratory in the interests of science and methodology. *That* was what I admired, not the macabre exhibits for themselves alone. Tifferch's rigid body had told me how the victims had been killed. I had lifted my hand against Gerta Totz to spare her a far greater punishment. I could not have foreseen the desperate determination that had tied the husband and the wife together. Then, Anna Rostova had appeared. She was different from Helena, the woman that I had chosen as my companion. There had been moments when I hoped to protect the albino from the consequences of her crimes. Not to possess her body, but to save that beautiful flesh from the violence of the troopers.

In Kant's eyes, I had failed to appreciate the beauty of those murders. But I was no longer the creature he had thought me to be. That ghost had fled for ever. My heart had been warmed, redeemed, *saved*, by love. Love of my wife. Love of my little ones. Love of the Law. Love of Moral Truth. Nothing that Immanuel Kant had thrown in my way had brought out that dark and secret side of myself again. Seven years before, walking around the Fortress in the freezing fog with Professor Kant, I had been truly cured. I had been reborn. And it was all *his* doing . . .

Sweeping up the papers, I dropped a coin on the table and rushed from the cafe. Outside, the cold night air was a benediction of sorts. It cleared my mind of doubt about what I was going to do. For what I knew I *must* do. As Professor Kant himself would have said, it was a Categorical Imperative. The irony was not lost on me. I had no choice. Reason obliged me. In the circumstances, there was no other way to achieve the Supreme Good.

I dashed along the cobbled lane in the gathering gloom. Rushing out across the stone bridge at the end of the street, I stopped at the middle span. The swollen grey-brown waters of the River Pregel bubbled below me like hot treacle. Leaning out over the flood, I began to shred the leaves of the document that Frau Lampe had entrusted to my care. The white scraps fell like a flurry of fresh snow and were gobbled up by the hungry waters.

Thus, the final work of Immanuel Kant, Professor of Logic at the University of Königsberg, was launched upon an unsuspecting world.

Chapter 37

Back home in Lotingen, I returned to work more convinced than ever that the daily round of a country magistrate was sufficient for my happiness. Disputes about common land and small legacies occupied my days, controversies between rival shopkeepers, farmers stealing fodder from their neighbours' barns by the light of the moon, occasional bad manners, frequent drunkenness, minor breaches of the peace. These were my daily concerns. Nothing more violent troubled my days or disturbed my rest than the accidental crushing of a mature rooster as a horse-drawn cart went trundling home in the dwindling light of dusk.

The events in Königsberg did not fade from my mind, but the experience seemed to retract and diminish with time and distance. That memory was like a raw scar that aches on a cold day, reminding us that the danger and pain are over, that the worst is past, that we are getting better day by day. Indeed, life was all but back to normal when early in April, I received a letter from Olmuth Hanfstaengel, who had been the family lawyer for as long as I could remember. Without any preamble, the writer informed me that my father had expired ten days before of a sudden fit, that he had been buried, according to his last wish, beside my mother and brother in the family plot in Ruisling cemetery, and that Hanfstaengel himself had been appointed to execute my father's will. In this terse communication, the lawyer noted that the estate, the land, the house, and all that it contained had been sold off, with one exception, as my father had specified, and that the proceeds had been donated after death duties to the Junior Military Academy in Druzbha where Stefan had served his country for a few brief months. In a short codicil, Lawyer Hanfstaengel informed me that I had been directly mentioned once in my father's will, and that I would have news from him again within a very short while. And with that scant announcement, the communication ended.

Helena stood mute at my side as I was reading. Hands clasped tightly across her breasts, she seemed to be struggling to quell the mounting anxiety which the arrival of that letter had provoked. Without a word, I handed it her. Her eyes raced over the page, and when she lifted her gaze to mine some moments later, there was a sort of mirthful glee, a welling up of joy in her expression which, try as she might, she could not suppress.

'I do believe that Stefan prayed for us, as I begged him to do when I went to Ruisling to lay fresh flowers on his grave,' she said with a vehemence that I did not expect.

Evidently, she was still inclined to believe that her chance meeting with my father that day in the cemetery had worked a miracle. She seemed to think that a reconciliation had been brought about, a change of heart which had led my father to remember me in his will, posthumously embracing me as his only surviving son. For an instant, I persuaded myself that she was right. But there was something perplexing in that letter, some unspoken impediment which would not permit my own optimism to flourish as hers had done. Whenever he mentioned my brother, my father spoke of 'Stefan, my beloved son,' but when he referred to me, it was by my name alone.

Still, in a state of heightened expectation – if that is the correct word – we waited for further news from Lawyer Hanfstaengel. It arrived two weeks later. A few words, no more: 'Herein lies your inheritance, as prescribed in the last Will and Testament of the late Wilhelm Ignatius Stiffeniis.'

We watched in a state of nervous agitation as the baggage was taken down from the wagon by the carrier and his boy and manhandled into the entrance hall. I recognised that trunk immediately. It was of steel-bound oak. The largest trunk in the house in Ruisling, it had always been kept in my mother's dressing room. I did not need to open it to know what it contained. A creeping paralysis seemed to overpower my limbs. My heart froze within my chest, thudding painfully as it struggled to fight against the horror that consumed my mind.

I knelt down on the cold stone floor and raised the lid.

All the worldly possessions that had belonged to Stefan were stuffed haphazardly into the trunk: the clothes he most loved to wear, the trinkets he had kept in memory of happy days, the favourite books that he had read, and read again. And on the top of the pile, five glass vials of golden honey. For the latter, tormented part of his life, those tubes of sugary sweetness had guaranteed his well-being. A sixth vial had shattered during the journey. Fragments of broken glass and syrupy stickiness lay everywhere.

That was my inheritance.

My father did not intend to let me forget. He would not bequeath me peace of mind. The curse that he had laid on my head while living would not be laid to rest with his mortal remains. The relics of my brother's shattered life had been transported into my own home.

Turning to Helena, I saw that the joy and hope had faded from her eyes. She stared at me accusingly, wonderingly, and in her prolonged silence, I thought I heard again the questions that I had never answered. The questions in that letter she had written to me in Königsberg after her one and only meeting with my father. *What can cause such hatred in a parent, Hanno? What does he think you have done?*

The trunk was consigned without another word to the attic, where it lay collecting dust for some months. An unusually wet summer had passed and a cold and gloomy autumn was upon us when I was obliged one evening to repair to the attic in search of candles. Having found what I was looking for, I was just about to return downstairs when a sudden impulse took hold of me. Morbid curiosity, set aflame by a spark of resentment for my father, prompted me to open the trunk and examine the contents with more care than my first state of shock had allowed. As the lid fell back on its rusty hinges, a dusty cloud of pain and sorrow seemed to rise into the air. The shambles of my brother's brief existence on this earth had been tumbled into that box with violent energy and total disregard. Honey had congealed like amber on a bundle of love letters tied up with a faded pink ribbon, and stained the covers of Stefan's favourite book, *The Sorrows of Young Werther*.

I sat down on the wooden floor, that book as heavy as lead in my hands, recalling how much he had loved the tale. He must have read it a hundred times with a passion which seemed never to diminish, but, rather, to increase with every reading. How often had he recited passages aloud in the study that we shared? And how frequently had I dozed with Goethe's noble phrases ringing unheard in my ears? In a moment of distraction, as I relived this lost Arcadia of youth, the volume slipped from my hands and fell on the floor. Looking down, I saw that the novel had fallen open at the pages that describe the untimely death of the young protagonist. Stefan had scribbled critical notes in the margin with a pencil, as he was wont to do. But then, I espied my own name written there. 'Dearest Hanno,' I read,

You may have asked yourself why I was silent when you spoke of Paris, and the murder of King Louis. All my life I had plagued you with my questions. But I said nothing. You could not know the emotion that your words provoked in my soul. And how was I to tell you? If there is no life after death, no place where we may meet again, I thank you now for sharing your secrets with me. I thank you for showing me the path to follow. Can suicide be defined as cold-blooded murder? It is the most momentous decision that any man can make. Is any freedom more absolute?

If we must wait to be annihilated, to 'suffer the slings and arrows of outrageous fortune', as the English Poet tells us, why defer the crisis another day? To die is the sublimation of every life that was ever lived.

I have decided to end my suffering.

And with your help, dear Hanno, though you will never know it. I doubt that you will ever read this book of mine! Tomorrow we will climb the Richtergade. You will not fail me.

*Our minds and our hearts are troubled, dearest friend. You
have your reasons, I have mine. A race to the top will do us
both the world of good. But I will ne'er return, for I am sick of
honey! Perhaps you will discover the trick . . .*

He had slipped his own life-saving vial of nectar into my empty
pocket as we left the house that morning. Tears came to my eyes as
I read the final line of what he had written:

*As you have given me a glimpse of Freedom, I bequeath you
the vision of my death.*
  Ruisling,17 March 1793.

Thus I came into my true inheritance.

Could I have received a more bountiful legacy? In his unloving
wish to damn me beyond his death, to taunt me with a crime that I
had never committed, my unforgiving father had restored to me the
peace of mind that I had all but lost seven years before.

The following morning, strolling in the countryside around the
house, enjoying the first bright day in weeks and the uncertain trials that little Immanuel made to get about on his own two legs, I
finally answered Helena's questions: I spoke out plainly about Stefan's death, and told her what my father thought I had done. She
listened in silence. Her eyes gazed calmly into mine. Like my
brother when I had told him what I had seen in Paris. Like Kant
when I confessed to him the fear of the obscure creature that had
taken possession of my mind. I told her of the troubled youth that
I had been before we met, and of the man that I had since become.
At that point, she laid her hand tenderly upon mine and raised a
finger to her lips, directing my attention towards our infant son
with a curious gesture of her head. Immanuel had broken free
from her guiding hand and was stumping solemnly but steadily
ahead of us on his own two chubby little legs.

'He is a good, brave lad, Hanno. A trifle independent, perhaps.
Exactly like his father,' Helena observed. 'I do believe the time has
come for us to pay a visit to Ruisling. Don't you?'

That evening, I overheard Lotte and Helena chatting in the kitchen. Our maid sounded both puzzled and concerned, saying that she was glad to find me so serene after the news of my father's death and the financial disappointment it had brought upon us.

'I've never known him so carefree as he was today,' Lotte exclaimed. 'The master seems to have recovered from a long and terrible illness.'

The answer my wife returned was coined in that animated, joyful tone of voice she normally employed with the children.

'He has, Lotte. He most certainly has.'

Two days after, we made our pilgrimage to the family plot in Ruisling. The thanks I addressed to Stefan, the prayers I uttered for the souls of my mother and father rang all the louder for the profound silence of the place, which seemed to wrap itself around me like a warm and comforting cloak.

In the month of May, a bright and sunny morning after a dismal week of lingering, dreamlike fog and early morning frosts which had set the untilled fields a-shimmering, Lotte Havaars entered the kitchen with a theatrical air of secrecy about her.

She held out her clasped hands to the children, then opened her fingers with a sudden gesture, revealing two bright orange ladybirds nestling together in her palm.

'The whole of the country is infested with them, sir,' she announced with a happy smile. 'This summer will be a good 'un. Ladybirds this early in the season! It's an omen of plenty. Napoleon will ne'er prevail against a nation that's so rich an' good an' strong.'

Mindful of how we had laughed at her sour predictions the previous year, and of all that had come to pass in the mean time, Helena and I exchanged a wan smile. We were more than well disposed to believe that Lotte was right.

And so she was.

The summer of 1805 was a season of great bounty and fruitfulness. Peace reigned in Eastern Prussia. Like Königsberg and all the other towns great and small in the kingdom, Lotingen returned to the steady industriousness of former times. Napoleon Bonaparte turned his armies south to face the combined forces of the Austrians and the Russians at the Battle of Austerlitz. To all effects, the French Emperor appeared to have turned his back on us. But how long would the undeclared truce persist? He had marched into Hanover and occupied the city in 1802, and everyone knew that he could do exactly the same again, whenever he chose. Margreta Lungrenek, the *aruspice* to General Katowice, had foreseen the possibility, cunningly divining the name of the nation's graveyard in the tangled, bloody entrails of the dead crow that lay crucified on her table.

History was to prove her right.

The Prussian seed had been planted in Napoleon Bonaparte's indomitable mind, and it would flower within a year, carried south, perhaps, on the innocent wings of a migrant ladybird from a cornfield on the outskirts of Jena . . .

Acknowledgements

Many wonderful books have influenced the development of this novel, but one of the most enlightening explorations of life and thought in Prussia in the early nineteenth century must be *Tales from the German Underworld* by Richard J. Evans (New Haven and London: Yale University Press, 1998). Regarding the life and opinions of Immanuel Kant, the recent *Kant – A Biography* by Manfred Kuehn (Cambridge: Cambridge University Press, 2001) debunks a thousand myths, and adds enormously to our knowledge of the philosopher. Both books are both highly recommended.

Special thanks to agent, Leslie Gardner, for her critical insights and endless encouragement, and to everybody at Faber and Faber in the UK and Thomas Dunne Books / St. Martin's Minotaur in the United States, particularly our editors, Walter Donohue and Peter Joseph.